ISBN 978-1-7341122-8-3

Cover and interior design by Rich Carnahan, Publish Pros

CHARLESTON'S ELEGANT SINNERS

TERRY WARD TUCKER

A dance begins. A tradition repeats.
Shimmering mirrors multiply a hundred flaming tapers
into ten thousand reflections of light.
Couples whirl in a vision lovely, weightless, without blemish.
Who are these ghosts who haunt Southern lore?
Ladies and gentlemen? Gods and goddesses?
Or are they and their progeny nothing more than
elegant sinners?

Prologue

(Arlena)

I have not seen the skyline of Charleston for a year less two days, nor crossed her bridges, nor swum her bays, nor witnessed her red sunsets. Twelve months. You would think I could have put the memories behind me by now. Yet in an eyeblink, a heartbeat, they all come rushing back – incidents, people, places. I have given up trying to stop them. They never slow or fade or change…and they never, ever release a prisoner.

My story has no discernible beginning. You must jump on board in the middle…of a life, a marriage, a dizzying rush of events that lead to the destruction of several human bodies and more human spirits. I have told these secrets to my innermost soul dozens upon dozens of times. I will tell them to you only once.

⌘ ⌘ ⌘

The autumn we signed the lease on the Sullivan's Island beach cottage near Charleston was the seventh autumn Stuart and I had been together. And over the course of those dispiriting years, I had watched him go through a metamorphosis. Oblivious to his own indoctrination, unaware he was being trained in the art of satisfying a neurotic, he had joined me in the worst of my habits. He assumed, erroneously, he was expanding as an individual, moving in a broad arc as an enlightened man toward a richer interpretation of life.

He believed this fiction as a direct result of his relationship with me, for I was an expert liar. Notions of leaving his work at Boston University and starting a consulting business of his own, of living on a barrier island near Charleston, South Carolina and not working a regular job...Stuart thought he had come to these brave decisions alone. He never made the connection between the subtlety of suggestion on my part with the blossoming of an unorthodox idea in his own head. He always had to talk me into the latest outrageous scheme, be it selling the houseful of antiques his grandmother had left him to fund quitting our jobs and moving south, or giving up his tenured position as a professor to try something less dull and predictable, or borrowing money indiscriminately to support a failing business effort. I had to say no to each of his proposals a good long while before giving in. Stuart was required to fight to get his way. This was necessary so that blame could be affixed upon him, not me, should an idea turn sour later.

Unlike my first husband, who told me after eight months he could no longer deal with my need to live on the edge, Stuart made a splendid foil. He was the product of a mother whose most daring deed was to bake a chocolate soufflé from a recipe she had concocted herself, and a father who had devoted his entire career to the hometown savings and loan. All stable and safe. It was I who presented Stuart with a kaleidoscope on life, I who interfered with his predestination of becoming the youngest dean of the English department at Boston University by inflaming his mind with stories of my own free-spirited parents and their lifelong war with the commonplace. But my stories were not altogether true. They concealed the real character of those two irresponsible fools who left me as a helpless child to live out my life hampered by emotional wounds inflicted by them.

When I was six, they left me in the care of a maiden aunt and began a voyage around the world in a sailing vessel they had built themselves with money that should have been spent on me. The morning they departed Boston Harbor, my aunt took me to the municipal dock to watch these two romantic fools christen their boat *Beautiful Ghost Dream.* Sometimes I still want to believe had it not been for the great storm that arose on the Indian Ocean their second autumn out, they would have come back to get me. It happened off the coast of Australia...a smashing, murderous hurricane that in its first horrifying hour splintered *Ghost Dream*'s main mast and sank her ten miles offshore. The little boat took down with her all my parents' worldly possessions and every hope and dream.

My father had fulfilled his destiny of becoming an abject failure, leaving nothing of value in the world but a small rag of a daughter tucked safely away in the home of her only sane relative. My mother died of exposure two days after the storm, minutes before a fishing boat spotted the bit of wreckage that had kept her and her husband afloat. My father wrote to tell my aunt of the tragedy and that he was not coming home. Memories of my mother were too painful he whined in his scrawled letter. He never wanted to see Boston again.

"But what about me?" I cried to my aunt. "Doesn't he want to see me?"

The rejection in his letter became an indictment against a child's self-worth, the beginning of a private journey of fear that drove her as she grew older to stack up accomplishments, all to prove again and again her life had value. It was the reason for the endless testing she put to her own abilities to determine whether she deserved to keep on living. After years of introspection, I have realized I will always be that child, searching for my ultimate foe, my final destroyer. At last, my father would be proven right – his daughter's life was worth nothing, her efforts of no consequence, her existence barren of meaning.

Even as a child, I forced myself along this path to self-destruction, down and down a terrifying spiral that gained momentum daily. But somehow my journey did not turn desperate until I realized I could not stop. I was unable to deliver myself from the bondage of growing up in the house of an upright spinster aunt who blamed my father one hundred percent for the death of her only sister. With me as a gallery of one, she convicted him daily with words burned raw from hatred, language that assaulted a little girl's heart with repeated executions of her father's spirit.

But after four years of silence, letters began arriving from Australia. My father, it appeared, had experienced a change of heart. I was unfamiliar with his personality and did not know that most of what he wrote was pure fabrication. I believed every word of every letter, all his sugared stories of the life we would share when he had saved enough money working at a shipyard in Sydney to build *Ghost Dream II* and sail home. Those letters, infrequent though they were, sustained me for seven years. They expunged all guilt from the man who owed ten lifetimes of penance to me and to my mother. The spell of his letters turned him into Aladdin and me into Scheherazade, my young heart overflowing with poisoned stories I repeated to no one but myself.

My aunt nearly lost her mind trying to convince me of his treachery, but the dreams he spun were too lovely to be destroyed by simple truth. The magic of what might be, what could be, what was promised to be, gilded the starkness of life's reality. I became the main character in a drama I created myself, the princess in a fairy tale with a hundred happy endings. But on the morning I turned seventeen, my hopes faded to nothing when fate forced me to grow up all in one day. A cablegram arrived from Australia informing me that my father had been killed when a scaffold collapsed in the shipyard. My aunt could not resist gloating. "Stop your crying, Arlena," she said. "You knew he wasn't coming back." And I hated her until the day she died for being right. *Ghost Dream* never returned, nor did my father, and I never healed from the heartbreak.

It was not possible for Stuart to understand these origins of my neuroses, though he believed he could. He spent inordinate amounts of time and energy playing therapist/lover to me. But my problems were too complicated for armchair therapy. Moreover, Stuart did not realize the danger to himself of involvement in my certain down slide. He did not know he was contributing to his own destruction as he joined me in mine. His entanglement in the unfair dynamics of a relationship with a half-sick woman soon became permanent. Only once – I think it had to do with the sale of his grandmother's furniture – did he look into my eyes and say he knew he was being controlled in sly ways, but could not pinpoint how or when.

He declared me a master manipulator, though he did not realize I had been accused of the same thing by everyone I'd ever been close to, including most recently the elderly clients to whom I had sold writing projects when we first moved to Charleston.

I discovered early on that Old Charlestonians compete fiercely in every area of their lives, and on their peninsula of extravagance and wealth, the stakes could be exceedingly high. I used my powers as a psychological seductress to make myself irresistible to these southern innocents so ignorant of neurotic duality. I made myself a bauble they could brag about over cocktails, a new curiosity, a fad, an expensive diversion. After all, few people anywhere were important enough to have need of a professional ghostwriter. But how far my game would go I could not guess. How many players would die I could not predict. For the pawns were ignorant of the rules, and I was careful not to let them learn there was only one requirement to keep the game in motion, the necessity of proving again and again that even a child of a father like mine could accomplish incredible things, of which surviving Charleston was the most incredible of all.

1

"Arly, you're running late," Stuart said the third time. "It's ten after nine. Want me to start the car?"

I could have strangled him. He in his t-shirt and shorts telling me in my suit and high heels I was late. It was too much. He was too much. I decided to ignore him.

"Arlena, sweetheart, if the bridge off the island doesn't stop you, traffic into town will. You know Southerners think hurrying is a crime against nature."

That did it. I clenched my teeth "Will you stop with the two-minute warnings, Stuart? I'm nervous enough with the car on the fritz. And my side hurts and my head hurts and I'm burning up."

No breeze at all came off the ocean that morning. Nothing made up for its absence. Not ceiling fans. Not wide-open windows. Nothing. The September sun had already heated our tiny bedroom, the chamber of sweat, Stuart called it. I stared at my face in the dresser mirror, searching for a small sign of confidence in the dark eyes looking back at me. All I could see was my lipstick starting to melt, oily evidence of the scorching day ahead. I hoped it would be the last of an unseasonably tortuous heat wave. Maybe cooler weather would make me less irritable.

Unable to control himself, Stuart began rushing me more instead of less. His urgency caused my thoughts to jump around. They crashed into each other and broke up into anxiety. It was frightening. It killed off reason. I wondered why my first Valium of the day had not taken effect. Stuart knew I could fall apart at any moment, yet he was helpless in the face of it. The look in his eyes bordered on alarm. He was afraid I might work myself into another crying jag, the kind he had seen so often, the kind that would exhaust me for days. Once more he tried to reassure me.

"We're lucky old lady got-rocks came through again," he said too cheerfully, referring to my phone conversation the day before with Miss Fanny Peregrine, my best client. She had agreed to pay me early. The reminder of a potential check made me feel better. Stuart picked up on my slight change in mood and pushed for momentum. "Maybe we can spread some cash over the bills," he said. "Look at you, Arly. You're sweating. Come on the porch. Cool off."

I allowed him to pull me through the sitting room toward the screened porch, but not without making a detour every other step to grab loose papers and cram them into my briefcase.

"Okay," he said when we stumbled into the glorious sunlight that flooded the porch each morning. "Look at that ocean. Breathe the sea air."

I did neither. I was busy fumbling with my briefcase. It slipped when I tried to force it shut, its contents spilling to the floor. Stuart and I bumped heads trying to catch things as they fell.

"Look what you made me do," I said. "Sand is everywhere. What if it gets into my Dictaphone? Oh, no, my pages are out of order."

We were both on our knees sorting through papers, though my stack seemed to get more mixed up. "Take it easy," Stuart said. "Who cares about a little sand? Not when South Carolina's gorgeous beach is right in our own backyard."

I snatched the pages out of his hands and crammed them back into the case. "What's the matter with you?" I said. "We're in debt, terrible debt. Three notes overdue at the bank, a month behind on our rent, no health insurance, no life insurance, nothing. And the car might not make it through the week. I can't stand much more." My voice trembled with bitterness. I could feel myself getting desperate. "Stuart, you have a PhD. I have a master's. What's wrong with us?"

"Nothing, we're fine. No one is forcing us to live like this. Consulting for me, freelancing for you. That's it. No more canned jobs. No more canned bureaucracies. But we have to give ourselves time. We can't attract blue-chip clients overnight. How many times have I told you to be patient? Two years isn't enough..."

"I don't want to hear that speech again. You got away with moving me to this backward little sandpile, but I quit listening to what a great idea it was a long time ago. We never should have left Boston, and you know it. Now get out of my way. I have to find the keys."

"Guess you've forgotten the good old days," he said, calling up our four vacations on Sullivan's Island before finally deciding to stay. He did not mention I was the one who had pushed hardest for the move. "Falling in love with the island...falling in love with Charleston."

"Give up, Stuart. You can't make me feel guilty for expecting to eat. Stop trying to put snakes in my head and help me find the stinking keys."

The shrillness of my voice startled us both. Stuart did not speak. He stood motionless and stared at me with weary eyes. Where did he get the strength to keep going when there was never enough money? Not even to buy himself a decent dress shirt. He had been wearing the same tie a year. I turned away to avoid his eyes and resumed my search. But Stuart would not be defeated. For the millionth time he deflected my chronic black mood. "Why don't you look in that trash bag you call a purse?" he said when it became obvious I was getting nowhere with my search.

"Leave me alone. I'm going out to look in the car. Maybe I left them in the ignition."

"Arlena, you're not paying attention. I saw you put them in your purse, last night. Here, look for yourself." He jerked the purse from its permanent home, hanging by its leather straps from the back of the Boston rocker, and held it upside down over the couch. The keys tumbled out. He grabbed them and jingled them in my face. "There," he said. "Now tell me you're sorry for every little thing."

I lunged for the keys and missed. "Yeah, yeah, whatever. Now let me go. Miss Peregrine might not pay me if I'm late."

"No one's stopping you, but I'll carry the keys. You'll carry the briefcase. We don't want to risk another search."

I turned on my heel and marched through the house, Stuart right behind me. He continued talking; I continued ignoring him. "It wouldn't matter if you were a month late," he said. "Miss Peregrine would still love you. Yesterday when I dropped off last week's chapter pages at her humble little mansion on the harbor, she wasted half my morning telling me what a precious darling girl you are. Never mind the chapters were a week overdue. It was clear she'd confused you with someone else. But did that matter? No-o-o. All she wanted was to bore me with a ten-minute soliloquy on how you've given her better things to do than contemplate pills and old age."

"What things?" I said, wheeling around.

He bumped into me and stepped on my foot, which helped my mood not at all. "Good grief. Get off me. What was Miss Peregrine talking about?"

"How the devil am I supposed to know? You're the one who works for her. Maybe that elephantine manuscript you helped her put together last spring, the one we've been using as a doorstop. She probably thinks some lunatic might still publish it. What was the title again? *Tarnished... Tarnished...?*"

"*Tarnished Honor*, smart-mouth, as if you didn't know. Now give me the keys. I hate being late."

He widened his eyes and grinned. "No," he whispered.

I hesitated a second, weighing whether it was worth exhausting myself to get my way. Usually, it was. But this morning I felt so tired.

"You win," I said in my most controlled voice. "You may drive me, but only to Mount Pleasant, after which you must drop into a very deep hole."

By the time I got to the car, Stuart was already inside leaning over the steering wheel, a race driver gunning his engine. I fell into the passenger seat, and we roared down Atlantic Avenue, my door half open. It did not close until we veered right to avoid an overweight jogger.

Stuart had turned obnoxious. “I always love it when we're on our way to schmooze Fanny Peregrine,” he shouted. “She's so deliciously rich.”

“Stop yelling. I'm twelve inches away. And stop driving like a maniac. I want to get there in one piece, on time, for once. You're sure she wasn't upset that last week's chapters were late?”

“Nope, too busy raving about your la-de-da writing class at Southern Prep. She's tickled clear through her shriveled little soul you decided to teach there again this year.”

“She'd better be. I would never have agreed to such miserable thing if she hadn't insisted. It wasn't the pay or the kids. They're worse than the Marquis de Sade. Stuart, watch the road. You're weaving.”

“Hey, a couple hours a week at hoity-toity Southern Prep won't hurt if it makes dear Miss Peregrine happy…dear well-heeled Miss Peregrine. There've been plenty of times we needed that extra few bucks at the end of a dry month.”

“I don't care. I wouldn't go back if it weren't for Raven FitzSimons. Last year, she was the only kid in the school who treated me like I was human. The rest acted like creeps. Oh, no. Is that a sailboat in the channel? The bridge is opening. Slow down.”

“So much for being on time, precious darling girl. Now you're going to sit here and sweat your pretty little backside off fifteen minutes while the biggest schooner in Charleston drags her expensive hull, on no wind, through the middle of this rusted out bridge.”

“I swear, Stuart, if you don't stop talking, I'm going to scream. You get on my nerves so bad.”

“Scream all you want. That sailboat doesn't care about some pseudo-sophisticated schoolteacher – excuse me – pseudo-sophisticated private schoolteacher of adolescent snoblets in attendance at the prestigious Southern Preparatory School of Old Charleston. I don't know what you expect from those brats, Arly. They can't help it if their addresses are South of Broad. Parents and grandparents of kids like that wouldn't dare let them soil their flip-flops on the steps of a public school. It's no wonder they're warped.

They've had it drilled into their heads since the day they were born that Southern Prep is God's gift. This is old stuff we're talking about here. Elitist stuff. Snotty traditions that go back before the Civil War. Yankees like us will never understand southern attitudes about that kind of thing."

"I told you, I don't care. Southern Prep is provincial and offensive, and the only reason you're defending it is you're on payroll too. I may quit to make a statement – despite Raven, despite Miss Peregrine, and most of all despite you, if I don't die of heat prostration on this bridge first."

"Stop showing off. You can't afford to quit. It would be suicide for you and homicide for me. Admit it, the last thing you want is for Southern Prep's Board of Directors to start looking for a new fundraising flunky to replace little old me, even if the job is only a half-assed consulting gig. And you can't ignore what Miss Peregrine wants. She's got too much money to ignore."

"I hate the way you talk. Miss Peregrine is a person, not a caricature. And she's not a cash vending machine."

"Aren't we high and mighty, precious darling girl. Forgive me for having to be concerned about something as mundane as cash."

I glowered at him but decided it expedient to let him have the last word. It was too sticky hot to fight. I could feel the humidity in my lungs. Instead of wasting more energy sparring with Stuart, I decided to kill him off in my mind. I pictured him sinking beneath the surface of the Intracoastal Waterway. He sank without a ripple along with the slow-crawling sailboat that seemed to have but one purpose for existing…making me late to Miss Peregrine's.

Stuart studied me. I sighed and paused to let him know I had conceded the moment. With less of a tone, I said, "You know how peculiar Miss Peregrine is. I don't understand her at all."

Skeptical of my rare surrender, he glanced at me again to make sure I wasn't planning an ambush. Though still suspicious, he propped his head back on the car seat and closed his eyes against the heat…while the sailboat bobbled along merrily. Once more I envisioned it sinking, only this time I did not make Stuart go down with it. This time I let him stay beside me in the car.

I spoke again, voice calm. "It's as if she's tough and fragile at the same time. And I feel so sorry for her having to live with that nasty housekeeper. She's the meanest woman I've ever met."

Stuart cracked his eyes and looked at me sideways. He decided against remarking on who was the meanest woman he'd ever met. "Hill?" he said after a pause. "Louisa Hill is a saint."

"How would you know? You've never laid eyes on her."

"True, but anyone who could stand Fanny Peregrine for years on end is more than a saint. I don't know how you've stood her fourteen months."

"You don't mind cashing her checks, though, do you, smart boy?" I was about to let him sink again with the boat. "No one should have to put up with a crank like Louisa Hill. She's repulsive, goes out of her way to make Miss Peregrine look senile. Look, the bridge is closing. Drive."

"Maybe we ought to let the guard rail go up first, and maybe stop worrying about weirdos like Louisa Hill. Miss Peregrine is a tough old bird. She can take care of herself."

"You don't know what you're talking about. She's tired and weak…turned into an old, old woman just in the last few weeks."

"You can't solve everyone's problems. We have enough of our own. Don't think about anything but getting paid and getting out."

Stuart was right, and I knew it, but I also knew he didn't care about Miss Peregrine, not the way I did. He couldn't. He hardly knew her. I was the one who had worked for her over a year, three mornings a week, hour after tedious hour. And all that time I'd watched her grow more and more frail. To Stuart, she was just another client. But to me…she was my Miss Peregrine.

"What time do I have to have the car back?" I said.

Stuart paused before answering. He was busy pulling the Romeo onto a side-street off Mount Pleasant's marsh bank. "I have an appointment today with Bill Martin," he said, squinting against the white glare of a Southern morning shimmering above the marsh. "It's at two, here in Mount Pleasant. You'll make it back in plenty of time. But Bill isn't the problem. It's money again. We have to get Miss Peregrine's check to the bank by one. I've already written a few of our own against it. Hope they haven't bounced yet. Can you finish your meeting with her by twelve thirty or so?"

"I'll try. What will you do while I'm gone?"

He shook his head. "Don't know what to tackle first. Guess I'll hitchhike back to the cottage and write Bill's sales promo for Sea Bird Condos. He might hire me to create his long-range marketing plan if I cut my price again."

"Do it. We need the cash."

"You do it," he said, climbing out of the car and motioning me into the driver's seat. "You're supposed to bring home the big bucks today."

I saluted him through the car window and revved the engine. He watched, curious, as I rummaged through the glove box.

"What now?" he said.

"My side aches. I'm looking for my Darvon in case I get in trouble at Miss Peregrine's."

"Check under the seat. I saw a prescription bottle rolling around on the floorboard yesterday. When are you going back to the doctor? You can't ignore this pain forever. You'll be down with a fever again."

"I'm fine. I'll rest this afternoon. It only hurts when I'm tired."

"I don't like it."

"Me, neither…but I can't do anything about it now. This meeting means dough."

He gave me a last hard look and gripped the door handle as if to hold the little Romeo back. "Stuart, the car is moving."

Scowling, he let go and stepped away. "After Miss Peregrine… you have to lie down," he said.

I held up the Darvon bottle and rattled it. "Yeah, me and my little friends here plan to stay in bed all afternoon. Want to join us?"

Stuart did not look happy. From the way he staring at me, I was glad I hadn't mentioned the Valium. He said no more, but his face showed the same fear that had been gnawing at him for months. He was afraid we had lost perspective...might get permanently hurt if we did not stop taking chances. But therein lay the problem. I had become addicted to the risks, more than to the Darvon and Valium. And worse, I had introduced Stuart to the same rush.

As I drove toward the city and my meeting with Miss Peregrine, yet one more meeting where I would have to make something impossible happen, like collecting an undeserved check, I fought back a case of nerves. My heart pounded. It felt like the unraveling of my soul. Too much, too much, I thought. I'll rest after the meeting. That's all I need, a couple hours of sleep. But even as I talked myself down, I became aware that the drama I had started in Charleston – indeed, the drama of my entire life – was completely out of control.

2

"Come in, come in, child," said Miss Peregrine. "You're letting my air conditioning out. Can't afford to cool High Battery. And don't think I haven't noticed you're late again."

Miss Fanny Peregrine pulled me through the front door of her Old Charleston mansion. Gooseflesh jumped up on my bare arm where her fingers dug in. I shivered. The air in the foyer was freezing compared to the sweltering heat outdoors. I hunched against the cold and swore at myself for leaving my suit jacket in the car. I'd taken it off earlier to keep from soaking it in sweat on the drive over from Mount Pleasant. The Alfa Romeo Stuart and I had coddled along forever was too sporty for anything as common as air conditioning. We had long ago surrendered ourselves to Charleston's killing heat. Many days, dozens of days, I longed for an SUV and the suburban life that would along go with it. Still contemplating the pleasant numbness of suburbia, I followed Miss Peregrine's labored steps from her cold foyer to her colder parlor.

"How's that old cesspool, Sullivan's Island?" she croaked, then cackled at her own irreverence. As always, I swallowed the bait.

"Why do you go on like that about Sullivan's, Miss Peregrine? You know it's beautiful out there. You've told me over and over how you spent your childhood roaming the island beach."

"Beautiful, my backside. Nothing but sandspurs and frogs and lizards and snakes and rats..."

"Stop, please. I have to live there all winter."

"And I don't feel one whit sorry for you. You could have found a reasonable place right here on the peninsula, and for less money. Why anyone would want to live in one of those miserable, broken-down beach houses is beyond me."

"But..."

"Don't but me. I've known Lucretia Middleton since she was a snotnose brat playing up and down Water Street. She was reared to be a lady. Sorry to say it didn't take. Grew up to be a blood-sucking vampire bat. It's a sin for you to pay her a pocketful of rent money every month for that pile of rotten lumber she calls a cottage. She ought to be paying you to stay there and keep the bums out. I'll bet it doesn't have proper heat."

"Yes, it does, an oil furnace...just no air conditioning, but beach breezes make up for that."

Miss Peregrine pretended not to hear and grumbled on. "Lucretia's horse thief of a father left her that island house thirty years ago and more property in town. Trouble is he didn't leave her enough money to keep any of it up. But that's not unusual in Charleston. Pompous people here make me sick. Can't tell a rich man from a poor man so much play-acting is going on."

"Miss Peregrine, I know you think Sullivan's is shabby, but Stuart and I want to live on the water, and the only way we can afford that right now is to rent something during the winter months when things are cheaper."

I felt close to tears for the second time that morning. Miss Peregrine was unrelenting. "I do not think Sullivan's is shabby," she said, irritated by my lack of discernment. "I know paradise when I see it. It's the people I can't stand, all those pretentious socialites from town. Most of them are insensitive fools who wouldn't recognize a natural treasure if they tripped over one on their way to a garden party. Sullivan's is nothing but a dollar mark to those boneheads. They wouldn't hesitate a minute to cut it into quilt squares and build peach-colored high-rises up and down front beach...like in Florida, for heaven's sake. No one of quality owns at Sullivan's anymore."

"Maybe you're right, but a few nice people rent there during the off season. It's like a neighborhood instead of a summer place. That's why Stuart and I love it so much."

The old woman sniffed and put her chin in the air. "You don't fool me," she said, eyes narrowed to accusatory slits. "You like it 'cause there's no diversity. Yankees are no better than tartuffes... rather live in a lowdown shack in a stinking sand pile than associate with people who don't look like them, all the while talking their liberal talk. A hurricane ought to blow you off the island for being so two-faced."

I gave up. I did not feel strong enough to debate a master debater, especially one who had the power to make me examine my own motives.

"Would you like some coffee, Miss Peregrine?" I said in an effort to change the subject. I needed her to be in a better mood before reminding her about my check. But I had to be careful. She did not like to be patronized.

"No, it's time for my medication. I take it with fruit juice. You can help me."

We retraced our steps through the antique-filled parlor to the massive curving staircase in the foyer. But we did not walk up. Miss Peregrine opened a closet door opposite the stairs. Inside the former closet was a six-by-six elevator. We stepped inside. I reached out to steady my feeble companion for the ride. She pressed the button labeled Level Two. We waited in silence as the elevator wheezed its way up to the kitchen.

A year of negotiating the strange floor plan in Peregrine House had made it seem a little less odd for the kitchen and dining room to be on the second floor, but the idea of an elevator in a private residence still struck me as peculiar. There was no question about Miss Peregrine needing it. Four stories and endless stairs were too much for her eighty-six-year-old legs to manage. When the elevator stopped, its automatic door opened onto the kitchen. Miss

Peregrine held the door back with her walking cane and nudged me out. I refused to move without first securing her elbow.

"Tycie, where are you?" my aging employer shouted in her usual unladylike manner. She mumbled something under her breath about servants and loafing. There were times in Miss Peregrine's home I felt as if I'd stepped backward into another century. Had the movement accomplished so little in this place?

"Yes ma'am, Missy Peregrine. I'm coming," Tycie called out. I could hear her gimpy feet shuffling through the pantry on the far side of the kitchen. "Look who the wind blew in," she said when she saw me. I smiled. Tycie was my favorite person in all of downtown Charleston, the only true lady I had met in that neighborhood of mansions South of Broad. A true aristocrat. From what I had observed, every person in every house claimed aristocracy, but not one had Tycie's high cheek bones or narrow hands and feet. I considered her of royal lineage, a descendant of some noble African chieftain.

"Hello, Tycie, how are you?" I said.

"Fine," she answered. "Glad the good Lord gave me another day to praise him." She rolled her eyes toward an invisible heaven beyond the ceiling.

I helped Miss Peregrine into her favorite kitchen chair before walking across the room to hug Tycie. I would have walked the whole distance had she not met me halfway. "It's good to see you, Tycie," I said and patted her skinny shoulder. Bits of white fuzzy hair stuck out around the edge of her blue headcloth. I wondered how old Tycie was. I wondered if she knew.

"Tycie," Miss Peregrine said with no patience. "Get my jar of peach brandy out of the pantry."

Tycie stiffened. I saw the whites of her eyes. "You ought not to make me do that, Missy Peregrine. Your cousin said for you not to drink no more of that brandy."

Miss Peregrine rose from her chair and stood erect. She cracked her walking cane across the kitchen table. Tycie and I jumped. "Do what I say and get my brandy this instant. And don't tell me another word Louisa Hill has uttered. She is my housekeeper, not my cousin, and I'm thinking about firing you both."

"Oh, Missy Peregrine, don't hit the stick no more. I'll get the brandy."

She hobbled toward the pantry in a pitiful attempt to hurry. Her humiliation made me sad. She was old and did not deserve it. I despised seeing her mistreated, though not enough to challenge a stick-wielding tyrant who had promised me an early paycheck. I considered disappearing into the pantry alongside Tycie. For all I knew, Miss Peregrine was planning to fire me as well. I glanced at her, hoping she would not catch me looking. She remained standing, eyes closed, eyelids twitching. Slowly, too slowly for someone in real control, she eased back into her chair. I could bear the silence no longer and began talking in the falsetto voice teachers use with difficult little children. "Maybe we'll all feel better after some good, cold juice."

"Get my pills," Miss Peregrine said.

Thankful for something to do, I scurried to the cabinet. There were thirteen bottles. I knew. I'd helped open them before.

"No, no," Miss Peregrine said when I began collecting them. "The plastic bag up there." She pointed with her cane toward the upper part of the cabinet. I felt around on the top shelf. When the sealed bag tumbled into my hands, the sight of it shocked me. It was transparent and quite large, fully as large as a bread bag, and a quarter full of candy-colored pills and capsules.

"Why did you put all these together?" I said. "It's bad to mix medications."

Miss Peregrine snorted and snatched the bag from me. "Got tired of hurting my arthritic fingers on those curs-ed child-proof caps."

When she had finished picking out her pills and capsules and lining them up on the kitchen table, she handed the bag to me. "Reseal it and put it back on the shelf…next to the bottles," she said. "I might need them later to get my prescriptions refilled."

"But I'm afraid you'll get everything mixed up. What if you took the wrong pills?"

I was accustomed to my private collection of Darvon and Valium tablets, even my lovely Percodans, but the pill bag had a dangerous look. What was Miss Peregrine thinking to mix meds like that? I watched her arrange the tablets and capsules and count them.

"After all these years, I ought to know what medicine to take," she said, poking at the pills with a trembly index finger. "Besides, it's none of your business what I do. Is that thirteen?"

I made a second count while she poured a glass of orange juice from the carton Tycie had left on the table. "Looks like it. Let me check again."

But she did not give me the chance. I stood by helpless as she scooped up the pills and capsules and tossed them into her mouth. She held the juice glass high in the air and mumbled a toast. I watched her tilt the glass and wash down the pills with several long gulps.

"What did you say, Miss Peregrine? I couldn't hear."

"Mud-in-your-eye, what else?"

"Oh, mud-in-your-eye." I nodded and smiled, pretending everything in the south made sense. Deliberately and slowly, I pulled a chair away from the table and sat down to rest. I placed my hands in my lap and breathed evenly, concentrating on staying calm. My side ached in rhythmical cramps. I grimaced and tried to force the pain from my mind. I did not intend to let Miss Peregrine get the best of me, not this morning. There was the check to collect and the client relationship to preserve. I knew my relationship with Miss Peregrine had to remain one-sided. My own anxieties were of no concern to her. She did not care about my feelings any more than she cared about Tycie's. We were hired help. Nothing more. And we both knew our places.

"Arlena," Miss Peregrine said, jerking me out of self-pity mode. "Look in the icebox. See if Tycie sliced any cantaloupe." I waited a moment before rising to follow orders. It was amazing how spoiled she was. "Well?" she said. "Do you intend to fetch my cantaloupe or not?" I stared at her another second, perhaps a bit too defiantly, before sliding back my chair with a disagreeable scrape.

⌘ ⌘ ⌘

"Pour," Miss Peregrine said as I set two brandy snifters on the miniature tea table next to the parlor fireplace. We had moved downstairs for our work session after she'd finished her breakfast. I was hoping the food would improve her disposition, but clearly it did not.

"I shouldn't be drinking. I have to drive back to Sullivan's... across two bridges."

"Pour," she repeated.

I poured.

"How are plans for your writing class coming along?" she said, changing the subject as capriciously as a child.

Oh, no, not that again, I thought. I hated talking about Southern Prep. "The semester doesn't start for another week, but if last year is any indication, I'm sure everything will go fine. I want the kids to participate in competitions again this year. Maybe we'll have another short story place in Charleston Literary Society's student contest. Last year, Raven FitzSimons came in first."

"Dear, dear Raven. Thank goodness she doesn't take after her mother."

I kept quiet. Raven FitzSimons' mother was Miss Peregrine's personal attorney. It would not do to start voicing opinions about fellow employees.

"Still working for that old poser, Grayson Pinckney?" she said after a moment.

"Yes," I answered, though resentful at being quizzed.

"I approve. Grayson is quality. What about Caroline St. Cloud?"

"I delivered her book of reminiscences to the printer last week. Can't believe it's done. Mrs. St. Cloud's illness made it difficult for her to recall things."

"And the dear thing probably wanted to record the truth, unlike Grayson, who I'm certain has lied magnificently through hundreds of pages. I'm glad you didn't give up on dear Caroline. She's my cousin twice-removed, you know. There's a great deal of therapy in writing one's memoirs."

I studied Miss Peregrine's face. Occasionally, she would surprise me. I wondered what other insight she was hiding behind those cloudy blue eyes and pleated wrinkles.

"How many sets of reminiscences have you worked on in Charleston?" she said.

"Fourteen."

"That's a prodigious amount of boredom for one young woman to survive. How did you ever stand it?"

"I was paid to, but I'm hoping to get ahead enough soon to spend more time on my own projects. I don't suppose you'd finance one or two?"

"I'd consider it," she said, but I knew she would not. She was too busy thinking about her own manuscript, *Tarnished Honor.*

"Have you heard from New York?" she asked.

I detected a measure of calm easing into her voice, the brandy, I hoped. "You mean about your manuscript?"

"No, our manuscript. Did you forget I gave you half ownership? I had to, or you'd never have had the fortitude to finish the tome."

"I haven't forgotten. It was a generous thing to do, but the story is yours."

"Don't be saccharine, Arlena. And don't flatter me. You know I'm not generous. I gave you half the copyright to light a fire under your rear end to do a good job. I may be old as Adam, but I'm not stupid. And don't think you can change the subject and make me forget my question. Have you heard from New York?"

"No, but it's only been four weeks. Sometimes, it takes months to get rejected."

"*Tarnished Honor* won't be rejected. Too juicy, too much spice. And you wrote it far better than I expected. You have more spunk than you let on."

Definitely, the brandy. "Thank you, Miss Peregrine, but I've tried to warn you, Charleston gossip may not be of interest to New Yorker editors."

"They'll like what's in *Tarnished Honor.* Half a brain could see the commercial value in the title alone."

I had no intention of telling Miss Peregrine the New-York-facts-of-life. Maybe allowing her to rattle on would hasten her mellowing mood.

"Everyone wants to see rich people laid bare," she said, "especially if they're arrogant arses like Old Charlestonians. It's why tourists parade through here every day in those mule carriages. They think they might get a glimpse of what goes on behind the doors of a mansion. *Tarnished Honor* gives them more than a glimpse."

Miss Peregrine chuckled at the delicious prospect of creating a stir with her manuscript. She held up her snifter for a refill. I poured, again. It was clear she did not want to work. I was relieved. I'd grown tired of the endless dictation. It had not been enough to slog through four hundred pages of quasi fiction. Now she wanted memoirs. Banal, boring, somnambulistic memoirs. But for the desperately needed paychecks, I could not have mustered the self-discipline to keep going.

And yet, after *Tarnished Honor* was done, I found myself proud of it. The story itself was simple, Miss Peregrine's personal account of life in wicked Old Charleston. But she had been fearless in the telling of it, explicit, naming names. So explicit, in fact, that she felt compelled to keep the project under wraps. Supposedly she had been working on her memoirs these past few months. If pressed, I was to say she was moving along slowly due to her advancing age.

I did not think as highly of *Tarnished Honor* as its author did, however. For example, I never had the slightest hope of ever seeing it in print, a fact which nagged at me. It was, I think, the closest I had ever come to guilt. Which changed nothing. I continued to let Miss Peregrine believe it had a chance. She had no way of knowing I had lied about contacting New York – indeed, had not written the first letter. It was my professional opinion that trying to sell *Tarnished Honor* would be a waste of time. But I knew Miss Peregrine would not entertain any opinion of mine. She never had before. Nonetheless, I sometimes questioned my own motives for leading her on. Was I taking advantage of an old woman's vanity, or giving her something enjoyable to do with her diminishing time on the planet? My answer was different on different days, depending on how badly Stuart and I needed money. Though not once did I turn down a paycheck out of guilt. Not once did I tell Miss Peregrine she was wasting her time and money. I did not know or care where she came by her grandiose ideas. All I wanted was to work and get paid. It was necessary. How else could I earn enough money to help Stuart with the grim business of making a living?

"Miss Peregrine," I said brightly to get her mind off *Tarnished Honor*. "I brought you two more chapters of your memoirs. Would you like to take a look?" I was trying to call attention to how hard I had been working to justify asking for an early check.

"I don't want to see any of that pabulum. The museum board only asked me to write it to oil the water for next year. They're hoping I'll give them another stack of money when their fundraising drive rolls around."

"I'll leave the pages here on the tea table. It won't hurt to wait 'til Thursday to go over them." I glanced at my watch. Half past eleven. I had to do something about the check. Miss Peregrine was already showing signs of drowsiness.

"Did you make changes on the pages Stuart dropped off yesterday? If so, I can look them over while you write my check. You told me you didn't mind paying me early this time."

"It's already drawn," she said, "in the secretary drawer over there. You'll have to wait until tomorrow to deposit it. I haven't instructed Jeannette to transfer monies to my checking account yet. But don't worry…I'll tell her this afternoon."

I tried to be unobtrusive about collecting the check. Fifteen hundred dollars. Life or death. Stuart would be ecstatic. He would not like having to delay making a deposit, but he'd be grateful for any reprieve. Beans and wieners would go down easier one more night, knowing we'd have cash tomorrow. Miss Peregrine's voice interrupted my thoughts. "I haven't corrected a page of that memoir rubbish."

I heard her words, but for a moment I could not process them. The trauma of asking for the check had caused a momentary lapse in brain function. I recovered and walked to my usual chair. With much officiousness, I began riffling through papers in my briefcase. "It's best to make corrections together," I said. "That way it won't be a burden on you. And next time Mrs. Heyward calls from the museum and asks about how you're coming along on your memoirs, you can tell her you're making progress."

"If she pesters me about that one more time, I'm going to ask if she's still sleeping with the plumber. Susannah Heyward is an ugly old bat, worse than Lucretia Middleton. I'll bet her husband hasn't kissed her twice in thirty years. Wouldn't surprise me if she were paying the plumber to sleep with her."

I snickered and cleared my throat to cover it. Miss Peregrine's coarseness spared no one. I was afraid she would come after me next. "Mrs. Heyward adores you, and so do the other board members. You're the only living founder of the Charleston Fathers' Museum. That's why they fawn all over you."

"Hypocrites," Miss Peregrine said. "They don't care if I live or die. It's my money they want. And why? To support the precious façade of false southern pride that's eating this city alive." She leaned her head back on the silk-tufted settee and closed her brandied eyes. "I'm weary of deceit."

I looked at my watch and thought of Stuart back at the cottage pacing the porch. I hoped he had hung onto the few dollars left from yesterday's trip to the grocery store. One more bridge crossing to Mt. Pleasant, and the Romeo would be on empty. When I realized Miss Peregrine had fallen asleep, I moved from the chair to the settee. Leaning over, I whispered into her ear. "See you on Thursday. Rest now…and thank you for the check."

She opened her lizard eyes to two slits and smiled almost imperceptibly. I squeezed her bony hand in mine, placed an afghan across her knees, and tiptoed toward the tall French doors that opened off the parlor to the foyer. Once inside the foyer, I set my briefcase down and pulled the glass-paned doors shut as quietly as their squeaking would allow.

"What are you doing?" a voice behind me rasped. It was Louisa Hill. I jerked around and banged my arm against the grandfather clock that dominated the foyer. Its metal works clanged. I touched the wooden cabinet to try to stop the vibrations, which did not help.

"What are you doing?" Hill said louder.

"Louisa," I breathed. "You frightened me. I was just leaving. Miss Peregrine fell asleep."

"Yes, well, I came home early from my church meeting. I hope you didn't exhaust her again."

"No, no," I said, moving closer to the front door. "I'll be back on Thursday at my regular time."

"If she decides to cancel, I'll call you," she said in her northern accent.

I tripped over my own feet backing out the door. "Fine…fine," I said. She ignored my stammering and closed the door in my face. I blinked and tried to focus on the ornate brass doorknocker that had jumped into my line of vision. I shuddered, my back crawling the way it always did on encounters with Louisa Hill. Again she had turned a simple exchange into a hostile confrontation, but this time her offensiveness was more intense than usual. Its presence penetrated the heavy wooden door. I could almost smell it.

I shrugged my shoulders, disbelieving I had allowed her to intimidate me yet again. If she were no more than a paid housekeeper, why didn't Miss Peregrine fire her, or at the least restrain her? The polished brass kick-plate on the lower part of the door caught my eye. It gleamed in hot noonday light, making me aware that my neck was starting to sweat. I leaned toward the door to rest a moment before turning to face the heat. Not a smart move. I bumped my head on the doorknocker. Why not? I thought, as pain in my head mingled with pain in my side. Why not deal myself one more blow? Then I remembered Miss Peregrine, imprisoned in a mansion with no one to buffer her from Louisa Hill except feeble old Tycie. It was a sobering thought, more than enough to curb my own self-pity. I focused again on the closed door and whispered an unheard goodbye.

3

"Did you get the check?" Stuart shouted from the kitchen window. I angled the Romeo along the driveway, but before I could call out a response, Stu burst through the back door like a football player and came running down the outside steps two and three at a time. I watched the ends of his necktie flutter in the midday breeze. It was like him to be in a hurry. Any day, I expected him to charge through that same door and tumble, fanny over teakettle, down the same stairway.

"Whatever happened to hello?" I said.

"No time. I have to get to the bank by one."

"Forget the bank. The check is postdated."

"Postdated? Fanny Peregrine gave Southern Prep a hundred and fifty thousand dollars last month. I know. I was the one who drafted the request letter from the Board. Why would she jerk you around for a measly fifteen hundred?"

Stuart pulled me and my briefcase out of the Romeo and climbed in himself. He leaned into the rearview mirror to adjust his Windsor knot. I sailed the check through the car window and watched with pleasure as he scrambled for it.

"Go," I said. "I have to lie down. My side hurts so much I can't think."

Stuart shouted after me as I climbed the treacherous steps. "Hey, you…you on the stairs. I love your beautiful behind."

I gave him a look before letting the door slam. It was good, very good, he would be gone for a while. I could swallow more Valium in peace.

It was after four when I began the slow agony of waking up from a drugged sleep. I had been dreaming of foghorns, low and sorrowful, that had sounded before dawn. Stuart and I had lain in bed listening to ships in the harbor warning each other of position, speed, and course. Deep in our chests we felt the vibrations of their enormous engines. The cottage also felt them. Sometimes, a glass pane would rattle, or a window box bounce around in its casement.

A cold washcloth helped me shake off dreams. Two mugs of coffee gave me courage to pack a blanket and my transcribing things into a canvas tote and walk up the beach toward the lighthouse. My goal was to find a peaceful place to work. I had been at it two hours when Raven FitzSimons came running toward me from the point. Her long blond hair blew about as she darted back and forth playing dodge with the brazen seagulls who patrolled the beach each day. She did not look like a girl who should be called Raven, not this fair-skinned, aqua-eyed beauty. But her name was not intended to suit her appearance. It was a family name, probably the surname of a grandmother or great-grandmother. To Old Charlestonians, the naming of names was one of many traditions they practiced to sharpen the lines between themselves and ordinary people.

By birth and upbringing, Raven FitzSimons was an aristocrat. The trouble was she had no taste for the life and rejected social graces. It did not matter her mother, Jeannette FitzSimons, had been deserted by her husband and was forced to exhaust herself working as a third-rate attorney for difficult clients like Fanny Peregrine, or the FitzSimons family had limped along five years in reduced financial circumstances caused by the divorce, or Raven was uninterested in high society. None of those things mattered if one lived South of Broad and had a name like FitzSimons. As long as certain appearances could be kept up – the right schools, trips, clothes, parties, and such – Raven would be included in age-old social rituals so exclusive they required guarding by the most viciously territorial beasts in all of South Carolina, the genteel ladies and gentlemen of Old Charleston.

Raven planted herself on the edge of my blanket and dripped salt water onto my legal pads. "Hi, Mrs. Prince," she said. "What were you listening to on your player? You were in another world."

"Cripes, Raven, back off. You're ruining all my things."

"Sorry, didn't mean to. I came out to walk on the beach. Nothing is going on in Charleston. It's deader than a nail."

I switched off my dictaphone. It would be useless to try to work with Raven around. "What's new in the mountains?" I said to her after a hug. "You were in Flat Rock for the summer, right?"

Raven plopped down cross-legged in the sand and put on a melancholy face. I summoned my patience. "Spent three months reading psychic stuff," she said. "Spirit guides are helping me now. They're showing me how to be a better person so I can be reincarnated at a higher level next time."

I stared at Raven. For a second, I wondered if she were serious. Then I remembered her personality. Of course, she was serious.

"That's nice," I said, "and did you hike or play tennis or anything else mundane?"

"Yes, I did all the correct things. Aunt Lucia made me. She's like Mother…except with money. I do wish she had children of her own and would stop inviting me to Flat Rock every summer. Mountains bore me to madness."

"I'm surprised the natural setting didn't free up your psychic awareness." I meant to be facetious. Raven missed it.

"Yes, well, it helped with meditation, but it's hard to keep your mind on spiritual things when you're surrounded by shallow people."

"I'm sure your mother was glad when you got home."

"Are you crazy? All she does is work and complain about the zillions of sacrifices she makes for my brother and me. I hate it. Mills left for Virginia last week. He said he was going to visit his roommate's family in Charlottesville 'til school opens. But I know he skipped out early to get away from Mother. This is his last year at UVA. He'll finish in May and go to law school…if he's accepted anywhere."

"What about you, Rav…after high school?"

"Mother thinks I'm going to Sweet Briar like she did, but I'm not. I'm going to California…study Zen or something."

I laughed. "Not before you graduate, I hope. I don't think your mother is ready for Zen. Look at those black clouds rolling in. Shouldn't you be heading home? I don't like the idea of your driving the bridges after dark, especially if it's raining."

Raven pretended not to hear. I tried again. "Don't you have to be home in time for dinner? Or supper? Or whatever you guys call it down here?"

"No, Mother is working late again, same as last night and the night before and the night before that. Same as always."

"Oh, I get it. We're feeling sorry for ourselves again. Let's collapse and be miserable. Forget sunsets and oceans and music and flowers. Forget everything. Lie down and wallow in manure."

Raven put her hands on her hips and nodded. "Yes, I'm going straight home and do just that, and I know where to find more manure than anyone could ever want. The Tourist Carriage Company has a ton of it over on Market Street. They get it out of those stupid leather diapers the carriage mules wear. Stinks about as bad as my mood."

"Go home and write a smelly poem for class next week. You sound inspired."

"I'm going," she said, brushing sand from her khaki shorts. "But you may as well know, I'm coming back tomorrow. I hate the thought of spending a single minute at home."

"Deal," I said and struggled to stand up. I made a show of gathering my things to try to hurry her. She gave me a quick hug before sprinting toward the public path to the street.

I shivered as I watched her run past the dunes. It was cooler out now than when I had first come on the beach and too dark for safety. Already I could make out the lighthouse beam on the north end of the island. It crawled across sky and ocean, lighting up the double row of rock jetties that formed the ships' lane to the harbor. The beach would be dark tonight, except for the measured circling of the beam. Banks of purple clouds had already obscured the moon. I glanced at their billowing duskiness and hurried along the shoreline to beat the night. I looked back once to check on Raven, to make sure she was progressing through the gloom. Her youthful gait made me remember my own fatigue. It had been a difficult day. I felt old and tired despite my afternoon nap. Old and tired and paranoid. More cruel inroads had eaten their way into my already wormy self-confidence. I suspected everyone around me knew I was caving in.

As I trudged toward the cottage alone, half frightened by the deepening dusk, a familiar voice whispered to me from the recesses of my mind, a cruel visitor from my childhood that still haunted me: I am the voice of self-doubt, Arlena. I have come to devour you. Living on a beach and writing, indeed. Using alcohol and drugs. Five and six drinks a day and too many pain pills to count. Stuart has no idea how bad it is. He does not see.

⌘ ⌘ ⌘

Stuart stepped into the twilight of the porch, a drink in each hand. "A perfect spritzer for the lady," he said, bowing before my chair. "Want to take a moonlight stroll?"

"You're such an optimist, Stu. The moon hasn't been out all week. Please…sit with me and relax. I'm exhausted from this morning, all that worry about the check, not to mention dealing with Miss Peregrine. She started on me the second I walked through the door, called Sullivan's a cesspool."

"More like Charleston is the cesspool," he said. "Have you walked by one of those carriage mules lately? They don't smell like roses."

"Believe me, I know. Miss Peregrine complains about them all the time, but then she complains about everything, even what goes on out here on Sullivan's, always grumbling about her blue-blooded neighbors milking the place for rent money every summer. And she despises the younger people who've inherited island property, says they don't have the foresight to protect the natural environment, would sell loggerhead eggs for the hope of a dollar."

"Don't forget, precious darling girl, the two of us have done far worse than that for the hope of a thin dime."

"Stop trying to be funny," I said. "Miss Peregrine doesn't care about money. She has a ton of it. And she doesn't care about real estate. It's the environment that concerns her, the abiding importance of nature. But all she can see in every direction is greedy adult children and grandchildren of her peers taking advantage of things they didn't earn. She's convinced they're too stupid to realize that someone, sometime, is going to have to take responsibility for preserving South Carolina's coastline, particularly the beach and marsh areas. Miss Peregrine is convinced property owners on Sullivan's don't take care of their own cottages, much less the beach. She gripes about them nonstop."

"What difference does it make?" Stuart said. "Let's say she's right, and for the record I think she is. Too many people play slum landlord out here. But it wouldn't matter if they let every house rot where it stands. The bottom line wouldn't change a peso. These people know what they're doing. It's the land that's valuable, not a bunch of insect-infested cottages. And it'll command even more attention when some loaded developer shows up and starts poking around. We'll have high rise heaven then."

"I wonder about us, Stuart. We talk, but we don't talk. I just spent ten minutes pointing out that Miss Peregrine rejects the idea of money being the only important thing, and you missed the point entirely. That's exactly what she's afraid of, owners selling out and letting developers take over. Don't forget, families who own these cottages have houses in town as well, monsters they've inherited and can barely afford to maintain. Some of them have lived in those mausoleums South of Broad three, four, five generations. And it doesn't matter if they're dead broke. They're intent on keeping up appearances. Miss Peregrine says they'd do anything to protect their interests downtown, including selling Sullivan's to Philistines...New Yorkers even."

"Yeah," Stuart said in a yawn. "I know all about that crowd. It's the same clique I put up with at Southern Prep, the revered academic institution known affectionately as the South-Is-Gonna-Rise-Again

Academy. A bunch of fancy names on the roll, but the board has to hire an inexperienced outsider like me to write their tiddlywink fundraising brochure. Money, or lack thereof, is forevermore the problem with these people. Every year, it's the same old question: Will there be enough dough to keep the school open?"

"Precisely," I said. "Now make me another spritzer. I need to get some sleep tonight. Mr. Pinckney and his memoirs will come early tomorrow morning. He likes me in his office at nine sharp."

"Honored to oblige, my lady," Stuart said in his worst Southern drawl, "but wouldn't y'all rather have a mint julep?"

"I'll save it for tomorrow. Mr. Pinckney will try to make me drink three or four all before noon."

4

"Send her up," Grayson Pinckney bellowed through the intercom when the receptionist announced my arrival. "I've grown faint from the anticipation of seeing her."

"Is he always like that?" I asked when she clicked off her machine. "Always," she said. "Never serious."

"Maybe he's tired of being serious after practicing law half a century."

The receptionist pursed her lipstick lips and looked disgusted. "Must've gotten tired of it a long time ago. I've been here ten years, and he was the same the first day I walked in this building. You'd better hustle. He'll be hollering your name through the P.A. system next."

I hurried toward the stairs and ran up without thinking what it would do to my colicky side. "Come in, beautiful rose," Mr. Pinckney said, his deep bass rolling through his secretary's office and down the narrow hallway. "I've been waiting for you, pining for you. Ask Lillian there if you don't believe me."

I glanced at the bespectacled woman, who looked up from her computer monitor long enough to wink. Without slowing, I walked into Mr. Pinckney's office, around his desk, and gave him a huge hug. He liked that kind of thing, and I made certain he got what he liked. Mr. Pinckney paid me well each month. I was glad he was not the false-fronted, financially strapped type Miss Peregrine complained about, although it was difficult to tell among Old Charlestonians. Miss Peregrine approved of Grayson Pinckney, declared him quality. It was the single non-derisive observation I had ever heard her make about any of her neighbors South of Broad.

In August, Mr. Pinckney tipped me five, new one-hundred-dollar bills, which I concealed from Stuart. It was the only way I could pay for my pills and doctor visits. I could not tell Stu I was seeing three different doctors and collecting pain prescriptions from all three. He had seen me through a terrible infection in my side over the winter. I didn't want him to have to go through that again. Dear, sweet, unsuspecting Stuart. He was a careful, observant man who thought he knew every detail of my life. But I was cunning about my pills. Not even Stuart knew everything.

"Am I still your favorite gentlemen client?" Mr. Pinckney said.

I coughed. He had hugged me too hard. "Yes, sir, but I think you should know, my only other client right now is female…Miss Fanny Peregrine."

Grayson Pinckney laughed and struck his desktop. "Next, you'll be recording the ghoulish memoirs of Louisa Hill, Fanny's ill-bred housekeeper. She's a worse old biddy than Fanny, I'm told. I understand that's what happens to women when they go too long without male attention."

He took out his handkerchief and wiped laughter tears from his eyes as he motioned me toward a chair. "Sit," he said. And I knew that all talk of elderly ladies was dismissed from our conversation.

"Get out your recording machine, girl," he said. "Today I feel like talking about the seashore…boyhood trips and such. I'll tell you a few things about handline fishing and wading through pluff mud. My mother used to take me to Bluffton every summer to visit our poor relations. That's where I learned about females and sex, but we won't put that part in. Wouldn't want to upset Miss Roz."

"I agree. She might abandon you to take care of Pinckney House alone. Then you'd be out of the best wife in Charleston."

"Not such a joke as you might imagine, my pretty, but it wouldn't be just housekeeping she'd leave me to manage alone. That daughter of ours is thirty-nine years old, married eighteen years, and her good-for-nothing husband has never had a job I didn't hand him on a platter. Ignorant chowderhead still takes up space in this law office, not to mention he and Caroline have lived with us at Pinckney House since the day they tied the knot."

It was not the first time Mr. Pinckney had told me about his daughter and son-in-law. He complained about them at every opportunity. Jonathan Prioleau, disappointing son-in-law, and Margaret Honor Pinckney Prioleau, disobedient daughter. She was the sort of adult offspring Miss Peregrine enjoyed lambasting, the not-too-bright variety whose biggest ambition in life was to stay in good graces with moneyed parents. Miss Peregrine raked Honor's type unmercifully in *Tarnished Honor,* exposing several generations of the rotting society that had spawned her.

Mr. Pinckney forgot between meetings he had already told me certain things. Or maybe he did not forget. Maybe he was just grateful to have someone's undivided attention, even if he had to pay for the courtesy. Mr. Pinckney was the best client I'd ever had as far as process was concerned. He was good at dictating and a natural raconteur. Unlike Miss Peregrine, who spouted gore and gall, Mr. Pinckney told lighthearted, whimsical stories about his boyhood days in the gigantic residence on South Battery Street known as Pinckney House. The house still stands on High Battery of Charleston's historic harbor. It presides over White Point Garden and South Battery Street four doors down from the mansion of Fanny Peregrine and midpoint in the long row of magnificent homes fronting South Battery.

Early in our relationship, I offended Mr. Pinckney about Pinckney House. Nine times I called it Pink House in the first two chapters of his reminiscences. He was incensed anyone could be so ignorant. He scratched out all the Pinks and scrawled Pinckney in large letters at the top of every page. I did not have the courage to tell him the problem was his Charleston accent, not my spelling. I would have sworn he'd been saying Pink all along. Miss Peregrine hooted when I told her about it. "Vainglorious old geezer," she said. "Thinks it's his family name that makes him a man of respect, a common affliction among our kind. But rest assured, Grayson Pinckney needn't worry about his good name. In this town, he's known as a man of integrity, which would not change if his name were Rasputin."

"Enough," Mr. Pinckney said at noon. "Shut off your recorder, lassie. Let's have a drink." He turned to the credenza behind his desk, which from other sessions I knew was stocked with expensive liquors. "Hope you're not too much of a sissy to drink your whiskey straight up."

"I shouldn't be drinking at all. Don't you want me to get your dictation transcribed this afternoon?"

"I think you should follow my example and take the rest of the day off. Work can continue without us. Let those young bucks downstairs wrestle with legal matters. As for you, sweet rose, I want you to be our guest for two o'clock dinner at Pinckney House. Miss Roz will be delighted to have you."

I watched Mr. Pinckney pour whiskey into two shot glasses. One he handed to me, the other he tossed down. I took a burning sip and tried to keep from shuddering. Mr. Pinckney poured himself another. From college days through eight years of career life, I had yet to come across a people who knew how to drink with the same style as highborn Charlestonians. It was a study in socially accepted excess.

Two o'clock dinner at Pinckney House. I thought of calling Stuart to let him know my change in schedule, then immediately forgot. "Thank you, Mr. Pinckney, but I have an errand to run before I break for lunch. Would you like me to come back when I'm done, or go straight to South Battery?"

"Come here at half past one. That will give us time to take a turn around White Point. I understand there's a regatta in the harbor today. Maybe we can catch the finish."

I turned up my shot glass for a last try at swallowing fire, an acquired taste, like the entire southern way of life.

"I'd better run if you want me back that early. Don't work too hard while I'm gone."

Mr. Pinckney jumped to his feet and rushed around the desk. I knew his purpose. "See you in an hour," he said and took great advantage of the opportunity to kiss a young woman on the cheek. I submitted with a minimum of resistance. I tried my best, but Grayson Pinckney made it impossible for me to leave in a businesslike manner. Much blocking and handshaking helped. Mr. Pinckney pretended he did not like this, but I knew he did. It was my duty to maintain propriety. He expected it almost as much as he expected to have the pleasure of undermining my efforts. It was an unspoken agreement.

I waited for the elevator door to slide shut before taking a bottle of Valium from my skirt pocket. My plan to spend the afternoon working had been sabotaged. What harm could a few pills do now? I swallowed two tablets, stepped off the elevator at the basement level, and started toward the water fountain at the far end of the hall. My stomach churned as I walked. The bitterness of the Valium had brought on a familiar queasiness. I hurried faster toward the end of the corridor, where the water cooler hummed against the wall. I drank a long moment before realizing Jonathan Prioleau was watching me. I cringed under his gaze. No wonder Mr. Pinckney hated him.

"Hello, Mr. Prioleau," I said, trying to cover my jitters. "Thought I'd get a drink before going out in the heat."

"Call me Jonathan…and why bother leaving just yet? The building is pleasant on these lower levels, cool as vanilla ice cream. Why don't you join me in my office?"

He pointed toward his door, but made no move to step aside. I did not have to wonder why his office was on the farthest back hall. Mr. Pinckney despised him. "I'm sorry, Mr. Prioleau. I'd like to, but I'm in a hurry. Maybe another time."

"Maybe," he said. "Or maybe not. I want you now."

I stepped back, making contact with the wall. My breath caught in my throat. "Mr. Prioleau…I have to go."

"Jonathan," he whispered. "Say it. I want to hear you say my name."

"Jonathan," I said without moving a muscle.

"Say it again."

"Jon-athan." My voice cracked.

He placed both palms flat on the wall, one on each side of my head, and nuzzled my cheek and ear. His breath reeked of bourbon. The odor invaded my stomach, making my nausea worse. "Please, I work here," I said. "Mr. Pinckney is my boss."

"Don't worry," Prioleau mumbled in his sickening southern accent. I smelled his breath again. "It's always done in Charleston. The Holy City isn't nearly as holy as everyone pretends. And for all you know, a well-placed word from me to Miss Roz might do you more harm than if you spent a little time in my office. If you don't be nice to me, I might tell her how fond the old man is of his solicitous little ghostwriter. She'd make him get rid of you in a second."

"I can't. I'm sick."

"Don't fret. I'm a patient man. We'll work this out eventually." He kissed me hard on the mouth, grinding my shoulder blades into the wall. Then he stepped aside and swept out his right arm in a false gesture of courtesy. At that moment, if I'd had a gun in my pocket, Jonathan Prioleau would have been a dead man.

5

A blast of hot air burned my face. It invaded my lungs as it rushed into Grayson Pinckney's office building through the polished walnut door off Broad Street. The door had been stuck when I first tried to escape, like a tightly vacuumed refrigerator door on a hot day. But my anger at Jonathan Prioleau gave me strength. I pushed against the unforgiving wood until the door sprang open with a loud sucking sound. Gauzy heat flooded the reception area, reminding me I was still in sultry Charleston.

A short walk to the corner of Meeting and Queen brought me to the Mills House Hotel, shelter from the burning sidewalks and unbreathable midday air of a Southern city laboring through early autumn. The Mills House and its grandeur made me glad Stuart and I had moved to Charleston. Within the sanctuary of its lobby, I forgot the city's cruelty to outsiders and remembered her exquisite beauty, the satisfying loveliness of symmetry and color, order and light, line and grace. Each time I passed through the Meeting Street entryway, I felt a surge of Lowcountry ambiance. For me, the feeling was almost erotic, though I knew the Southern fullness of it could never be wholly experienced by a woman whose maiden name was Giello.

I planned my agenda as I approached the antique double doors - call Stuart and tell him I would ride the bus home later, grab a few minutes of rest in the lounge area off the ladies' room, cool my face and hands with wet paper towels. It was a good plan that would give the Valium I had just taken a chance to calm the anxiety brought on by Jonathan Prioleau.

As my heels clicked on the sidewalk, I shielded my eyes from the morning glare. Even with sunglasses, my retinas ached. On clear days, brilliant beams of light poured down on Charleston. Light bounced back and forth between high buff walls of historically correct buildings. With burning intensity its unfiltered radiance baptized common chimney pots on rooftops and sharpened spires of great churches like St. Philip's and St. Michael's. No spare beauty, this. It was generous and profuse, far too extravagant for the needs of one small city.

On entering the spacious lobby, it took only ten strides across the black and white marble tiles to reach the portrait-lined east hallway. At one end was the Grand Bar, at the other a series of carved doors to alcoves and salons. I was moving toward my favorite secluded spot when an unfamiliar voice hailed me.

"Ms. Prince," a man called out.

I whirled around in a huff, not bothering to cover my irritation at being discovered in my one secure hiding place in downtown Charleston. "Ms. Prince," Dr. Croomer Legare said again. He stepped into the hall through the golden bar's narrow archway. I could see the luxurious space shining at his back, all brass and crystal and mirrors. It looked inviting. For a moment, the tanned and handsome Dr. Croomer Legare looked inviting, like a gentleman of privilege and breeding. But despite his charm, I could not warm to him the way I could to Grayson Pinckney.

I knew at this time of day, Legare should be drinking martinis at the Carolina Yacht Club on East Bay Street or wearing tennis whites on the courts of the Charleston Country Club. My confusion disappeared when a leggy girl occupying one of the banquettes in the distant bar waved and smiled a knowing little smile. Ah, now we know what Dr. Legare does with his Wednesday afternoons, and the lady in question is too intoxicated to care about discovery. I had the feeling I should have already been aware of Legare's indiscretions. He did not seem concerned about my seeing him in a compromising position with a woman a third his age. With him, philandering appeared to be nothing new. Perhaps his wife no longer cared. Perhaps she gave tacit approval as long as he kept his women away from people who mattered socially.

"Excuse me, Ms. Prince," Legare said, his words echoing in the uncarpeted hallway. "I've been wanting to speak to you about Miss Peregrine. Matter of fact, I was going to call you this very evening, but here you are in the flesh and looking as lovely as ever. You're stunning in white."

"It's Mrs. Prince," I said, ice on my words, "but you may call me Arlena if you like." I looked him straight in his patrician blue eyes, enjoying it when he faltered at my offer to shake his hand. He was more accustomed to kissing women, but he would not be kissing me.

There was a difference in how I had to deal with Croomer Legare and Jonathan Prioleau. Both disgusted me equally, but I had to treat Prioleau with restraint. His position in the Pinckney family gave him power. I could not insult him outright, nor expose him to Mr. Pinckney, not if I valued my job. But of Legare, I had no fear. There was nothing he could do to hurt me. I was certain weeks went by without his even thinking of me. And when he did, I suspected I flitted in and out of his consciousness like some irritating insect with no purpose in life but to stir up venomous creatures like Louisa Hill and Jeannette FitzSimons, the two flighty females who hounded him about every concern of Miss Peregrine's. Dr. Legare's role as her physician made him their perfect target. Out of respect for Miss Peregrine's age and social standing, he ministered to her by way of house calls. She was the only patient ever to receive such personal attention in all his thirty years of practice. He also visited her informally at fitting intervals.

Dr. Croomer Legare, Louisa Hill, and Jeannette FitzSimons, the three bad actors who surrounded Fanny Peregrine...her houseful of scalene personalities, one male swimming alone against a tidal wave of unpredictable emotion from two frustrated females who fluttered around the old woman like a pair of harpies. If Legare wanted to continue attending Miss Peregrine and collecting fat payments for his services, he had to fend off Louisa and Jeannette. He understood this. What he could not fathom was why a new harpy had to appear out of nowhere, one in the disturbing form of an insolent northern female who demanded he shake her hand, a lowborn woman who knew he had no power over her, a woman whose foreign name made him think lustfully of prostitutes and princesses, but whose eyes froze his blood with icy stares and whose body language threatened to emasculate him if he took one step too close, a woman called Arlena Prince.

Miss Peregrine valued the members of her entourage. She said they were like her children, no matter how unattractive. Soon after I began working at Peregrine House, her children sent out small and large signals to remind me I was unwelcome. I was made to feel like an interloper with impure motives. As weeks passed, I recognized the elements of a campaign – open snubs from Louisa Hill, snide phone calls from Dr. Legare, and difficulties with my paychecks perpetrated by Jeannette FitzSimons. But Miss Peregrine protected me. I did not deceive myself into believing she was noble enough to look after me out of generosity. I knew she did so to maintain her independence. But the queen had to be judicious with her favors if she did not want to estrange the members of her court, particularly the self-proclaimed prince of infidelity now standing before me in the entrance to the Mills House Grand Bar. He was, after all, the most respected physician in Old Charleston, Dr. Croomer Legare.

"It's about Miss Peregrine," he said again, his tone as smooth as oil. I braced for a confrontation. He continued. "I want to know why you keep pushing her to continue her reminiscences? Have you no mercy? Don't you think the poor woman is too old to be exhausting herself?"

I started to answer, but Legare bared his teeth in a false smile and stopped me. Said he, "I'm sure the board members of Charleston Fathers Museum had no idea how draining this project was going to be, or they'd never have asked Fanny to embark upon it, not at her age. Jeannette and Louisa are beside themselves, worried sick she's working too hard, and that you don't understand her situation. I have to agree, you appear to be ignoring the seriousness of her physical condition."

"Is that so?" I said. "And what else do you think?"

"Don't be offended, dear. Surely you realize how much we all love Fanny. And now that she's old and feeble, we cannot allow anyone to take advantage. I'm afraid she's been showing signs of Alzheimer's these last months, which appear to be getting worse. Every time I visit Peregrine House, Louisa and Jeannette have a different tale about her forgetfulness. Do you believe, considering her health, it's wise to keep after her to go on with this memoir work?"

Croomer Legare made me sick with his veiled questions that were actually demands. Who does he think he is? I thought. He's not talking to some southern belle trained to obey men. A well-dressed dandy with lace on his underwear will never get away with ordering me about, not with two Valium tablets and an ounce of whiskey in my gut.

"I don't mean to be rude, Dr. Legare," I said, "but I find it distasteful to discuss Miss Peregrine's condition behind her back. Besides, she is my employer, not Jeannette FitzSimons, not Louisa Hill, and certainly not you. And until she tells me she no longer needs me, I will continue working for her. And by the way, I take direction from Miss Peregrine alone, no one else, so you can fold your suggestions ten different ways and stick them where the moon don't shine."

I wished I had not said it. Oh, how I wished I had not. But it was too late. Croomer Legare's aristocratic jaw dropped. I flashed my eyes at him one more time before turning and marching away. He did not move, just stood blinking in the hallway of the elegant Mills House Hotel.

6

"Come into my inner sanctum, you sweet summer rose," Grayson Pinckney thundered when I appeared in the doorway of his private office. I had returned to go to two o'clock dinner at his home. "If I may but gaze on your blushing cheeks and florid lips one trembling moment, I'll gladly spend the rest of my life a thorn upon your slender stem."

"Kind sir," I said with a simper, "I cannot be a summer rose, for summer has fled. And the stain upon my cheek is not eternal youth, but a burn from the Carolina sun. I am but mortal woman, you see – weak and susceptible – and I beg you not to tease me unless you wish to break my heart."

"Break your heart? No, no, sweet lady. I'd fall on my own sword first." He administered the ritual kiss, this time upon my hand.

"But Mr. Pinckney, it's been rumored you've made a career of breaking hearts. Some claim hordes of weeping women are scattered over every state in the Union and several foreign countries."

"It isn't true. You're the only woman I've ever loved, except for my good wife, Miss Roz. I would give my right arm for the privilege of running away with you."

"May we go to two o'clock dinner first? I understand they put out quite a spread over at Pinckney House."

"Splendid idea. Lillian, tell Caesar to bring the car around. We've decided to go tooling."

Mr. Pinckney lifted his walking cane from the umbrella rack and hooked it over his left arm. He guided me toward the hallway, his right hand at my elbow. I felt I was in the presence of an endangered species when I spent time with Grayson Pinckney. He was a good man, warm and kind to his core. Sometimes, I longed to fall weeping on his shoulder and tell him all my problems. But instead, I walked with him through Lillian's office and played the role of lady. We stepped into the corridor, startling several young attorneys who fell into two straight lines on either side of the hallway, a double row of tin soldiers. Mr. Pinckney nodded and called each by name. They responded, in turn, smiling tense smiles. I walked ahead and did not acknowledge the young men. Being escorted by Grayson Pinckney had its advantages.

Mr. Pinckney's patter may make one think he would be a problem for a woman in a close place like an elevator. Not true. He said nothing; I said nothing. The elevator became a neutral space that could not be violated by a gentleman of Mr. Pinckney's code of honor. I had been learning about that code for several months now, and the more I learned, the more I admired the man who lived it.

As we rode to the ground floor, I studied Mr. Pinckney's profile. The chiseled definition of his features showed not the faintest hint of jowl so common among older men, and his white wavy hair made age a friend instead of an enemy. I thought Mr. Pinckney's hair beautiful in contrast to the deep tan of his face and neck. He wore a navy-blue blazer, gray trousers, and a starched white Oxford shirt. The brightness of the shirt made his skin a warm bronze repeated subtlety in the burnished gold of his Citadel class ring. But best of all was his posture. He stood tall and erect, chin tilted upward. As I gazed at him, I stood a little taller myself. There was much to learn about presence and carriage from a man like Grayson Pinckney.

The elevator grumbled to a stop. Mr. Pinckney checked his pocket watch and gave me a wink. Neutral space had been cleared. "Wonderful," he said, "plenty of time for a stroll around the battery. Are you game?"

"Yes, sir," I said, smiling sweetly.

We walked to the back door of the office building where we met Caesar, Mr. Pinckney's chauffeur of the last forty-five years. Caesar pushed open the door to the porte cochère, where his silver Cadillac sat idling. "Good afternoon, my man," Mr. Pinckney said and slapped Caesar on the back.

"Afternoon to you, too, sir," Caesar responded. He helped me into the car and waited as I slid across the cool softness of cream-colored leather seats. The AC was on high, a luxury unheard of in the Romeo.

"To the battery, Julius Caesar," Mr. Pinckney commanded, his words a military bark. The long car traversed the length of Broad Street in less than a minute and stopped perpendicular to East Bay. The Exchange Building stood in front of us.

"Fourteen of my Pinckney relatives were held prisoner in that crusty old building during the American Revolution," Mr. Pinckney intoned as Caesar negotiated the corner of Broad and East Bay. "One was my great-great-great-great-grandfather. The city was occupied by those greedy-assed Redcoats at the time."

"Really? As I recall, my own great-great-great-great grandfather was still picking olives in Sicily." Mr. Pinckney looked at me sideways, but decided against making inquiries into my parentage. He continued his own speech.

"And in the next century, a passel of Yankees came south to stay with us a while. Those weasels threw a different set of my relatives into the clink. Now that I think of it, I must be the only Pinckney in three hundred years not to insult some foreign contingent and be thrown in jail a fortnight."

"You call Yankees foreigners?" A smile twitched at my lips.

"Or worse," he said. Caesar chuckled.

"You're still young," I said. "Maybe you'll find a reason to go to jail for honor yet."

Mr. Pinckney slapped his knee in agreement and leaned forward. He began pointing out landmarks on East Bay. From the pride in his voice, you'd have thought everything belonged solely to him. Rainbow Row, Adger's Wharf, Tradd Street, the Carolina Yacht Club. All reminded him of some anecdote or relative. All reaffirmed his heritage.

From East Bay, we tuned onto South Battery and cruised toward the corner of King where we observed the grandeur of Pinckney House from the angle of tourists. I understood why they flocked to see it. Four mansions down stood Peregrine House, the sight of which triggered a primitive response in my brain. I saw in a frightening vision the people closest to Miss Peregrine: Louisa Hill, Jeannette FitzSimons, Dr. Croomer Legare. I imagined them riding monster horses on a black carrousel that played music out of tune. The skin on my forearms prickled. I jumped when Mr. Pinckney's voice vibrated through the Cadillac, directing Caesar where to park. I already knew that every act in Charleston had a proper execution, and I was about to be instructed in the correct way to stroll High Battery.

It was familiar walk to Grayson Pinckney. A daily walk. His lungs thrived on the rich sea air, his eyes and heart on the ever-changing view. White sailboats dotted the harbor lining up to race. Mr. Pinckney steered me to the corner railing of the sea wall to secure a better vantage point. I put a hand up to shade my eyes from the early afternoon sun. Thousands of glittering points and needles reflected off every wave. The effect was dazzling, like Charleston herself, and every bit as severe and unyielding.

I glanced at Mr. Pinckney and wondered how he withstood the glare. He stared straight ahead without blinking. Small beads of perspiration gathered on his forehead. It was a blistering time of day in the city. I was glad for the breeze that whipped our hair and clothing. It tempered the heat and fishy odors of the harbor. Compared to the broiling streets of the small business district, High Battery was the most pleasant place on the Charleston peninsula.

"Can you see Sullivan's?" Mr. Pinckney said. I strained my eyes, but could see nothing. He pointed. "Look for the lighthouse...beyond Morris Island and Fort Sumter."

"Yes, yes," I said, happy to have spotted something, anything.

"I've spent many a summer day on that old isle," Mr. Pinckney said. "When I was a boy, my family used to take the ferry, *The Commodious and Pleasant Sappho,* to Mount Pleasant and on to Sullivan's Island. We'd get off at the public dock and ride the trolley out to the beach. Not so many bridges and automobiles back then."

I did not interrupt Mr. Pinckney. Sometimes at odd moments like this, he'd give me nuggets to liven up his memoirs that he could not recall in the more constrained setting of his office. I made mental notes.

After a pause, he addressed another subject: "Fanny Peregrine called me yesterday." I detected a note of purpose in his voice. "Wanted to make an appointment…at my office of all things. Can't imagine why. She knows I'd come to see her at Peregrine House any time. I offered to send Caesar around to pick her up and bring her to Pinckney Building, but she said you'd be driving her. Strange… Fanny seldom calls except to twist my arm about contributing to some charity. Wonder what the old eagle has on her mind?"

"I don't know," I said. "She hasn't asked me to drive her anywhere."

Mr. Pinckney's face grew red. For a second, I thought he was angry, before realizing he was embarrassed at having betrayed a confidence. He began stammering. "I thought…naturally, I thought if you'd been engaged to drive her, you would know we had an appointment. Tarnation, I never should have mentioned it."

"I won't say anything, Mr. Pinckney…promise."

The ethically upright Grayson Lockwood Pinckney, IV did not feel better. He winced and moaned as if in physical pain and suggested we might create less trouble for ourselves if we moved along to dinner. And though neither of us ever brought up the conversation again, I thought it a glorious thing to have a man like Grayson Pinckney in my debt.

⌘ ⌘ ⌘

Stepping into Pinckney House was like stepping into an abode of royalty. Peter opened the door. Peter opened the door to everyone who had reason to visit the Pinckneys. He had done so for three generations. On this day, as Peter stood before us in all his shining beauty, Mr. Pinckney gathered himself to his full height, stood at attention, and clicked his heels.

"Mrs. Prince, meet Peter. He is the same Peter who welcomed Miss Roz and me home after our month-long honeymoon in Europe…fifty-one years ago. Today he welcomes you."

"I'm honored," I said.

Peter bowed. I shook hands with him. "Good afternoon, missy…Mr. Pinckney," Peter said with an easy-going grin. I knew from his demeanor he had been introduced the same way a thousand times.

When Miss Roz came floating in, I was surprised by her appearance. "Too tall, too large, too plainly dressed. She should have come off as unattractive, even homely. But she did not. She, like Mr. Pinckney, had a special quality that made itself apparent immediately. She was handsome, if not beautiful, and appeared to be unaware she was two inches taller than her husband.

"You must be Arlena," she cooed. "Grayson has told me so much about you. Come inside…out of that dreadful heat. Peter, take Miss Arlena's jacket and case, please. Grayson, darling, will you join us in the parlor? We ladies do so enjoy a bit of masculine conversation."

"Of course, dearest, but let's not bore the girl. She came to be refreshed, not bored. And for pity's sake, don't ask who her people are. They don't go into that kind of thing where she hails. She'll think we've never been out of the state."

"Oh, Grayson, everyone knows Charlestonians still travel. It's those hillbillies from the upcountry who never leave their farms. They're so backward. Ellen Ruth Gervais told me some of them north of Columbia still put on those dreadful gatherings called pig-pickings. I was mortified. Pig-pickings, indeed, still going on in our fair state. Sometimes, I think those of us who live in Charleston are the only souls left in South Carolina holding up the banner of culture."

"There, there, Roz," Mr. Pinckney said. "Let's not dwell on unpleasant things. Mrs. Prince didn't come for that, either."

"Let's hope she came to have a drink," interjected a voice from the hallway. "May I pour you something, Mrs. Prince?" I flinched. The voice belonged to Jonathan Prioleau.

"Perrier would be nice, if it isn't too much trouble." Tensions of the day began closing in at this inopportune moment. Relax, I thought. Mr. and Mrs. Pinckney are trying to be kind. Ignore Prioleau…breathe.

"Hell, no, don't give her that bottled branch water," Mr. Pinckney said. "Make her a gin and tonic. She needs to loosen up, enjoy herself. This gal works like a man, Miss Roz. True grit, she has."

"I'm sure, dear…true grit. Let's all slip out to the piazza. The harbor breeze is delightful, Arlena, even in the heat of the day. I want you to see the garden. It's on the museum tour of historic homes. We're so very proud of it. Old Mrs. Pinckney, Grayson's mother, designed it forever ago when Grayson was still a yard child in nappies."

Miss Roz took my arm and walked me to a white wicker paradise on the harbor side of the house. Fluted columns a foot in diameter stood at intervals along the three open sides of the piazza. The columns were whiter than the fleecy clouds floating in the sky above. Gigantic hanging baskets of pink and white impatiens swung gently near each column. There was no railing. The porch was bordered instead by pots and pots of geraniums and forest ferns. They were arranged on a low terrace of graduated shelves. More pots sat in corners, beside chairs, and on either side of the beveled glass doors that opened off the parlor. They marched up and down porch steps and lined brick walkways throughout the garden. They hung prettily from low limbs of trees in the side yard. Never had I seen so many uncut blossoms in September.

"Too bad the garden isn't at its best" Miss Roz said. "That's why I keep all these potted ladies around this time of year. You'll have to come back in spring to see the azaleas."

I nodded, mouth open, eyes wide, trying to look in every direction at once. The flowers, harbor, garden, colonnades, furniture.

Miss Roz smiled, pleased by my reaction to this fantasy world, though to her it was not a fantasy. It was home.

My drink arrived via Jonathan Prioleau. Miss Roz suggested we sit and chat. As we were arranging ourselves in cushioned wicker, Margaret Honor Prioleau fluttered onto the piazza like a lovely brainless butterfly. Miss Roz introduced us, whereupon I spent several hopeless moments trying to express how much I had enjoyed having her son, Jon Prioleau, Jr., in my writing class the previous year. She did not know what I was talking about, and the explanation got so confused, Mr. Pinckney lost patience and began swearing.

"Honor," Mrs. Pinckney said to her daughter in an effort to smooth things over. "Arlena is the young lady who is helping your father with his memoirs. You remember...I told you about her weeks ago."

"Oh, yes," she said. Her tone smacked of condescension. "I can't believe you have time to teach school too. And let me guess, you have a husband and no household help at all. Women like you make me feel absolutely incompetent. I can barely keep my own closet straight, much less manage a career. I admire you so, Mrs. Prince."

Her voice went up and down like an upper register scale on a piano. I did not realize until later she had insulted me. The deprecating language of cloistered Charlestonians is a subtle thing. They can rip out your insides with exquisite politeness.

"Dinner is served, Mrs. Pinckney," said a hump-shouldered woman who had shuffled out to the piazza

"Thank you, Wilhemina. We'll be right there."

Everyone filed into the house behind the diminutive major-domo. The dining room was a picture, enchanting in every detail. Matching French chandeliers hung above a long mahogany table surrounded by ten heavy chairs. Miss Roz told the servants to draw back the brocade draperies and let in the afternoon light. The result was stunning. Sunbeams set the crystal chandeliers aflame. Refracted colors trembled within dozens of teardrop prisms as light slid over the room. It shimmered and glowed in a golden wash just outside the human plane of vision. The air seemed almost liquid.

Mr. Pinckney helped Miss Roz and me with our chairs. Jonathan attended his wife. We bowed our heads for a blessing asked by Mr. Pinckney, not a word of which I understood through his heavy accent. Wilhemina and a younger servant in identical dress served at table. They brought bowls and tureens of food from the sideboard in courses. Never had I tasted anything more delicious. She-crab soup, cucumber salad drizzled with raspberry vinegar, squash pie, tomato aspic, scalloped shrimp, spoon bread, and three kinds of pickles. Mr. Pinckney sat at the head of the table with me at his left near the corner. He guided me through the meal like a father might guide an inexperienced child through a first visit to a fine restaurant. I loved Grayson Pinckney that day. I loved him for his sensitivity and manners. I loved him for taking care of me. Everything went swimmingly...until Jon Prioleau opened his vindictive mouth.

"I understand you do an extraordinary amount of memoir work, Mrs. Prince. Didn't someone tell me Fanny Peregrine is your client?"

"Miss Fanny Peregrine to you, Jonathan," Mr. Pinckney said.

"Sorry, sir. It certainly is Miss. Well, Mrs. Prince, is it true? Is the grand dame of Old Charleston your employer?"

"Yes," I said and for the first time thought I might be able to converse about something.

Prioleau continued, "Must be fascinating, compiling the old biddy's life story, what with her checkered past."

My ears pricked. His words were out of line. I looked at Mr. Pinckney for help.

"Fanny's past will not be discussed at the table, Jonathan," Mr. Pinckney said, "and you will refrain from referring to her as a biddy." Miss Roz and Honor stopped their side conversation. An uncomfortable silence ensued.

"Oh, Daddy, don't be tedious," Honor said. "The skeletons in Miss Peregrine's closet are common knowledge in Charleston."

"That's right, sir," said Jonathan. "Anyway, it was her father who behaved like an ass, not Miss Peregrine. I'd say he ruined the poor woman's life." Then in an aside to me, "She had a baby in her younger days. Isn't that a shocker? Gossips say it was sired by a Yankee. Frankly, I've always thought it the reason her father made her give the little thing away. Heartless bastard, he must have been."

My throat constricted. What Prioleau was saying could not be true. I looked back and forth between him and Mr. Pinckney.

"I...didn't know," I said, "that Miss Peregrine had ever been married."

"Married?" Prioleau said. "If she had, I'm guessing he wouldn't have made her do such a thing."

"Enough," Mr. Pinckney bellowed and hit the table with his fist. Every dish clattered. Prioleau held up his wine glass in retreat, though it was too late. I was already undone. A single tear fell as I leaned over my plate. I saw it make a tiny splash on my sterling silver fork. Wilhemina, oblivious to everything but service, was taking away my dinner plate when the first sob escaped my throat. She jumped back in fright. Honor Prioleau shouted at her husband.

"You beast," she said. "Now you've made her cry with your vicious talk."

Miss Roz flew around the table and helped me out of my chair. She walked me to the south parlor and seated me in a wingback so that I might weep in comfort.

"Oh dear, oh dear," she said and thrust a napkin into my hands. Mr. Pinckney's voice boomed from the dining room threatening Jonathan Prioleau with a throttling.

And I cried...deep loud racking sobs that antidepressants and fatigue had set free. Honor Prioleau rushed into the room carrying a stack of handkerchiefs. I took them and buried my face in lavender. And still I wept. Mrs. Pinckney became distraught. She hovered, apologized, offered me water, declared her son-in-law an uncivilized boor, begged me to sip some brandy. Honor proclaimed herself mortally embarrassed and said she might cry herself if I did not soon stop.

"Dear God in heaven," she said. "Here it is my female time of the month, and the world has gone mad. Every hair on my head is standing out on end."

I found myself laughing and crying at the same time. Mrs. Pinckney and Honor laughed with me, and we knew the worst was over. I was humiliated at having created such a scene in the home of Grayson Pinckney. Every time I thought of it, I had to fight breaking down again. Over and over, I told Miss Roz how sorry I was to have ruined her beautiful meal. Honor declared it Jonathan's fault entirely and offered to drive me anywhere I wanted to go. I asked to be taken to the Mills House. I lied and said Stuart was going to meet me there.

As we rode toward the hotel in her black Jaguar, Honor assured me Jonathan was not as bad as he seemed. He had been bullied so long by her father, she confided, that every so often he popped out in warts and disgraced the whole family. After she dropped me off, I staggered along Queen Street and made my way to the bus stop. The skin on my face felt swollen and dry as if stretched across my cheekbones. When I entered the safety of the Sullivan's Island Transit, I sank onto the front seat and closed my stinging eyes. Who knew, I thought, as I was falling asleep in the stinky old bus, that socializing in Charleston was such hard work.

7

"Missy, wake up." I heard the voice from far away, too far to bother heeding. "This is Sullivan's. You always get off here."

"What?" I said to the disembodied voice. I struggled to drag myself up from the deep sleep known only to those who use antidepressants. Focusing on the voice, I realized it had a wrinkled face, one I had seen many times before on the Island Transit. Its owner was looking at me as if he thought I might be dead.

"Oh, thank you," I said. "I didn't realize." I picked up my briefcase and stumbled off the bus, fighting the disorientation of sleep. As the driver pulled away, and I began the short trek to the beach cottage, Raven FitzSimons called to me from across the street.

"Mrs. Prince, Mrs. Prince, wait," she piped in her flute-like soprano. She ran toward me, hair flying, eyes shining.

"Hi, Rav," I said. "Don't you ever stay home?"

"I hate home, and I hate Charleston. Come on. Walk with me before it gets dark. You can put your things in my car. Croom and

Jon Jr. are running on the beach, training for cross-country. I'm waiting for them. You remember Jon. He was in our writing class last year."

I frowned, thinking of the conversation I'd had with his mother a few hours earlier. Though Jon Prioleau was a nice enough boy, his name grated on my nerves. So did that of Croom Legare Jr., Dr. Croomer Legare's son.

"A walk sounds great," I said. "Have you seen Stuart?"

"He was jogging toward the cottage when we first got here. Said he was on his way home to make crab salad for you. How do you get him to do stuff like that? Croom won't do a thing for me."

I pushed on toward the dunes without answering. It felt wonderful to be back on the island. I breathed in the ebb tide muskiness of mud flats and decomposing marsh grass. Fecund marsh smells mingled with the sweeter fragrances of oleander and newly cut grass. Every odor was tinged with ocean salt. I inhaled again and remembered a remark Stuart had made the day before. He was right. Air on Sullivan's did have rejuvenating properties.

"You look tired, Mrs. Prince," Raven said as we tromped through the shifting sand of the dunes.

"Long day, but don't worry. I'll turn back into my frisky old self when we get closer to the water. This soft sand slows me down."

Raven took my arm and helped me along like an adult daughter would help an aging mother.

"And how is dear old Croom?" I said. "Horny as ever?"

"That's Croom all right."

I clucked my tongue. "Raven, I've told you. Croom will only go as far as you let him. Don't you want to finish high school and go to college?"

"You can't give me advice," she said. "You weren't even twenty the first time you got married. You told me last year, remember?"

"And I also remember telling you what a mistake it was, an eight-month-long mistake. Wouldn't it be wonderful if I could convince you not to fall into the same pit?"

Raven patted my arm with mock reassurance. "You can stop worrying," she said. "The last thing Croom Jr. wants is to get married. His father would kill him. The man is intent on Croom going to medical school, the same one he went to, of course…right across town. Nope, Croom Legare can't get married any time soon, not if he plans to live out his natural life."

"Marriage isn't the only thing, Rav. You and Croom could hurt yourselves in other ways."

"I can't believe you think I might get pregnant. No way. Croom and I know everything about sex. We'd never scandalize two upper-crust families like the FitzSimons and Legares, not that it would be anything new in Charleston. Happens every generation. I'd bet my life five or six unwed mothers-to-be were on the first ship that sailed into Charleston Harbor, packed off to the New World to keep from embarrassing their families back home."

I sniggered, though my heart ached for Miss Peregrine. Indeed, it had been happening for generations. "Maybe so, Rav, but I'm not concerned about your families. I'm concerned about you. I don't want to see you get hurt. You could injure your body, your emotions."

"My body and emotions belong to me. I'll do with them whatever I please."

"All right, case closed. If you want to let Croom make a mess of your life, go ahead."

"Croom isn't the problem, Mrs. Prince. It's my mother who drives me up the wall. I'm supposed to be coming out this year. Can you imagine? Me, a ditsy debutante. Mother is going crazier by the day. The closer the winter social season, the weirder she acts. All she talks about is Cotillion and tea dances and the St. Cecilia Society. I don't know if I can live through it. Maybe it would be easier if my father were around. I was barely twelve when he left, and now I'm seventeen and haven't seen or heard from him since the day he walked out."

"You can make it without him. Both my parents took off when I was a lot younger than twelve."

Raven shrugged. "We don't know where he is. Mother stopped talking about him years ago, about the time I started wearing bras and shaving my legs. I think she looked at me one day and saw herself. Now she's trying to re-live her life through me. That's why I have to go through the debutante thing, and Southern Prep, and summers at Flat Rock."

"I have trouble feeling sorry for you, young lady. Other girls would kill for your opportunities."

"You sound like Mother, reciting guilt lecture ninety-nine. It would be great if all those things were for me. But they aren't. They're for her. Last night I caught her looking at an old photo of herself and my grandfather at the St. Cecilia dance thirty years ago, studying the stupid dress. After she passed out from her nightly booze, I took a close look at that picture…to find out what kind of gown she's going to try to make me wear."

"You're exaggerating. She only wants what's best for you. That's what all mothers want."

"No…my mother wants tradition. She popped out of a two-hundred-year-old cookie cutter, the same one I popped out of. Our lives were all sewn up before we were ever born. But those things don't bother me like they used to. I concentrate on higher things now. Our true selves aren't bound up in this physical world, you know. The earthly plane is only a fraction of our existence. Mother can't get to my inner being no matter what torture she dreams up. My soul is thousands of years old. Knows everything in the universe. You ought to try meditating, Mrs. Prince. It's cosmic. Might help you keep from getting so tired all the time."

"Wise old Raven," I said, "And what does Croom think about cosmic things?"

"Are you kidding? Croom never thinks at all. Too shallow."

"He doesn't look shallow now," I said. "Looks like a model."

Croom and Jon Jr. were running toward us on the beach, sweat glistening on their chests. They were perfect specimens of well-formed young men, statues of Greek athletes come to life. Raven was unimpressed. She proclaimed them foul smelling and tossed them the towels she was carrying. She would have handed them over from the end of a long stick if one had been handy. The boys said hello to me with formal courtesy. Croom began sending messages to Raven with his eyes that he wanted to leave…fast. He knew I didn't like him, nor his attitude toward Raven. But a boy like Croom Legare did not have to pay attention to the disapproval of outsiders.

"Ready to go?" he said to Raven after the barest of conversational niceties.

"Sure," she said. "Let me rinse the sand off my feet."

The boys and I waited in silence while Raven ran to the ocean's edge. They did not know what to say to me. I'm sure they considered me a boring, oldish female with nothing but English grammar in my head. I forgave them because they were still boys and had no way of knowing they would not think themselves old at thirty. We said our goodbyes when Raven returned, and I watched as the three beautiful young people trotted toward the dunes. It occurred to me that in thirteen short years, they'd all know what it felt like to be thirty. That alone would temper the arrogance of Croom Legare, Jr..

⌘ ⌘ ⌘

"What took you so long?" Stuart called from the porch. "I got worried." He had spied me walking up the beach path toward the cottage.

"I'm not late," I said. "Been gone eleven hours and seventeen-and-a-half-minutes. Isn't that a normal workday around here?"

"Pretty normal, I guess. Raven dropped your stuff off ten minutes ago...said you were on your way."

"Oh, no. I forgot everything. Left it all in her car. Did she bring my briefcase?"

"Yeah, shoes, too. Hurry up. It's past dinner time."

Stuart had turned on every lamp in the cottage. The windows glowed with storybook light. I thought I might cry when I saw how warm and cheerful they looked. I remembered Stuart's crab salad and realized I was ravenous. My crying spell at Pinckney House had used up my two o'clock dinner calories. Stuart always made okra soup and yeast rolls to go with crab salad. He found his recipes in Lowcountry cookbooks. My stomach rolled with hunger.

"You have time for a quick shower," he said. "I'm putting the finishing touches on dinner...found some half-burned candles for the table. We're having your favorite tonight."

"You're my favorite," I said and hugged him with surprising strength from someone so exhausted. I thought dreamily of a warm shower, good food, and relaxing on the porch swing with a spritzer and my favorite wool blanket. All because of Stuart. All the comfort I had in the world was because of Stuart. The evening passed quietly and peacefully. I felt soothed by the routine of home. Everything would have been perfect...except for a late phone call.

"I'm sorry, she's already in bed," Stuart said on answering. "I'll tell her to get back with you in the morning. Yes, thank you, goodbye."

"Trouble?" I said when he came back to the porch.

He paused a second. "Couldn't tell for sure. It was Jeannette FitzSimons, Raven's mom. Sounded like she had a case of the means. What would she want at this hour?"

"Please, Stu, I can't think about it now. Can't it wait 'til tomorrow?"

My plea was so pitiful he put his arms around my shoulders and rocked me to ease my shivering. "That's funny." I said through chattering teeth. "I didn't realize I was cold."

8

I awoke to an insistent Stuart kissing and groping me under the covers. By silent mutual consent, it had been weeks since we had made love. Discontent has a strange way of needing to be nourished. Stuart fed his by brooding. I fed mine by denying myself simple comforts as sex. But biology betrayed me. When awake, I could easily say no to Stuart's half-hearted advances and my own stirrings. Sleep, however, released the truth, the surprise of which flowered in the darkness like some exotic deep-sea plant. Sleep brought dreams filled with sensual temptations that rendered me defenseless. In dreams, I found myself in the arms of pagan gods and dark princes, Jonathan Prioleau one.

Jonathan, who tasted of bourbon and cigarettes and smelled of expensive cologne…I wanted his hands to drag me downward to the floor. In light, I spurned him. In darkness, in dreams, I accepted his every invitation to meet him secretly in the lower level of Pinckney Building and go with him behind closed doors while other partners argued cases in antiseptic court rooms. My dreams had the same sequence of events – Jonathan pulling me into his shadowy office and turning away briefly to lock the door, me murmuring for him to hurry with the lock and take me quickly down and down to a place we both knew too well, where our bodies burned with lust and our consciences knew no guilt. How long since I'd wanted Stuart like that? How long since he'd wanted me? I closed my eyes and let him love me in our marriage bed, hoping he had not heard me call him Jonathan.

On waking alone the next morning, I felt disoriented and panicky. A ringing phone had off alarms in my head. I got out of bed and walked on unsteady legs to the bedroom door. From there I could see Stuart, phone to ear, standing by occasional table on the other side of the sitting room. He signaled me to be quiet.

"I'm fine, Mr. Pinckney," he said. "How are you?" He held the receiver two feet from his ear. Across the room, I could hear Mr. Pinckney's voice echoing through the earpiece.

"Couldn't be better, thank you," the old aristocrat shouted. "I'm calling to ask after your lovely wife. We aren't scheduled to meet this morning, but if by luck she's coming into town, I'd like to see her."

Stuart mouthed words to me desperately. "Do you want to talk?"

I shook my head no.

Mr. Pinckney again. "Are you there, Prince? I'm having trouble hearing you."

"I'm here, but Arlena isn't. She usually checks in for messages around ten. I'll tell her you called."

Stuart stared at me with anxious eyes. He was rattled at having to deal with Grayson Pinckney alone.

"Good," Mr. Pinckney said. "Do what you can."

"Certainly, sir. I'll make sure she gets back with you sometime this morning."

"Splendid. I'll look forward to hearing from her. Thank you and goodbye."

"Goodbye," Stuart said and hung up. He stood for a moment without speaking, combing his fingers through his hair. Still frowning, he said, "Does he always talk that loud?"

"Always. What time is it? Seems late."

"Nine thirty. I decided not to wake you. You were dead on your feet yesterday. And after last night, I thought you could use some extra rest. Frankly, precious darling girl, I thought I was in the wrong bed."

I ignored his smirk. "I hate it when you make decisions for me."

"And I hate it when you get up in a bad mood. What's going on with Pinckney?"

"Probably wants to apologize."

I went to the bathroom to avoid further explanation. Stuart followed. I closed the door in his face, which he did not seem to notice.

"What for?" he said through the door.

"I had a little trouble with his son-in-law. Not important…forget it."

"I want to know what's going on."

I opened the bathroom door to another of his frowns that irritated me worse. "Nothing is going on," I said. "Everything is great. Let's talk about something pleasant for a change. Do we have enough cash to go out for breakfast? I need coffee before I start transcribing."

"A few dollars," he said, dissatisfied I had brushed him off. "But we don't have time. You have to call Jeannette FitzSimons and Mr. Pinckney."

"I'm not calling either one. Today I'm not going to do anything but what I want. Those high-assed aristocrats South of Broad expect me to jump every time they belch, but this is one day it isn't happening. Consider it a revolt."

"Think again, Arly. They're paying customers."

"Jeannette FitzSimons doesn't pay me anything, and Mr. Pinckney doesn't pay me enough." My voice was too loud. A quaver had crept in. Time for my first Valium.

"Maybe not, but Mr. Pinckney is steady, and FitzSimons is connected to Peregrine."

"How much do you think I can stand? Do you want me to let these people eat me alive, like they do their stinking oysters?"

"No, just humor them…return their calls. It isn't too much to ask. I don't know why you're making such an issue."

I took a slow breath. Stuart looked hopeful. I decided to give in. Besides, I had a private errand to run that could only be taken care of downtown. "All right," I said, pretending he had beaten me down. "Did FitzSimons leave her number?"

He sighed with relief, pulled a slip of paper from his shirt pocket, held it up. "Yes, I wrote it down for you. Had to ask her for it twice."

I stomped across the room – the house shook on its pilings – and jerked the paper from his hand. Stuart looked at me with a half-grin. Usually, he teased me about rattling lumber, but this morning he did not have the courage.

"At least I walk with purpose," I said. "Wouldn't want to sneak around like a cat and startle people like you do."

He shrugged and stuffed his hands in his pockets, watching in silence as I keyed in the number.

"This is Arlena Prince," I said to the female voice that answered, "returning a call to Mrs. FitzSimons."

"Please hold," the woman said with a nasal southern inflection. Her two syllables sounded like six. I mimicked her in an ugly whisper. "Ple-e-ese ho-o-old."

Stuart narrowed his eyes in a weak attempt to control me from across the room.

"Mrs. Prince?" a different voice said, also nasal, also with rotten diction.

"Yes," I said.

"Jeannette FitzSimons here. Thank you for calling back. I hate to ask, but could you drop by my office today? I need to speak with you about Miss Peregrine."

"That would be difficult. I'm busy with deadlines."

"Yes, we all have heavy schedules, but I thought you'd be willing to carve out a few minutes for the sake of Miss Fanny."

"Oh, don't misunderstand. I'd do anything to help Miss Peregrine. It's extraneous things I try to avoid, like unnecessary meetings."

"If you happen to change your mind, I'll be in my office all day, through lunch. Feel free to come in unannounced. We're going to have to talk eventually. I thought it would be better to get it out of the way rather than wait for an emergency."

"If it's that important, I'll see what I can arrange."

"How nice of you to work me in. I'll look forward to seeing you around noon. Goodbye."

I slammed the phone down on the tabletop and let loose a cascade of words. "I can't believe she has the gall to summon me like that. It's infuriating. And I'd bet a hundred dollars Miss Peregrine doesn't know a thing about it. Louisa Hill and Croomer Legare will probably call next to demand their own pro rata share of my time."

I paced the room to add drama to my snit. Stuart was a good audience. "Look," he said, "now that you know you're going, let's make it as easy on you as possible. I'll call Mr. Pinckney and tell him you'll stop by around eleven. That'll put you at FitzSimons' office by twelve-thirty or one. Which, if we hustle, gives us time for coffee at Mama Chloe's."

I did not feel like hustling. I felt like staring in dejection at the dirty seagrass rug that had been unsuccessful at keeping sand off our feet for too many long months. "Just once, I'd like to spend a day doing what I'm paid to do," I said. "Why do these people think manuscript pages appear by magic? Mr. Pinckney is expecting a new chapter next week."

"And he'll get it," Stuart said. "We'll write it over the week-end. Perk up. Things aren't that bad. At least, you have clients to raise heck about. Time was, you had none."

"Probably better off then. I'll be taking the car, right?"

"Sure, I'll stay here and write marketing letters. We need a new project pronto. Coffers are empty again."

I nodded, though I was not listening. I was thinking about my errand. I had noticed the night before that my pills were running low. I had to do something about getting more.

⌘ ⌘ ⌘

I stepped into Pinckney Building at two minutes of eleven. The receptionist was on the phone. She covered the receiver and whispered that Mr. Pinckney was expecting me. I rode up on the elevator to find Lillian on the phone also. I waved to her as I tapped on the door of Mr. Pinckney's private office.

"Come in," he shouted.

"Good morning, sir." I was worried about facing him. Maybe he had thought it over and decided he did not want to work with an unstable female who cried her way through dinner. Maybe this was the morning he would fire me.

"Thank goodness, my dear. You look much better than yesterday."

"I'm fine now, Mr. Pinckney. Sorry for what happened. I'll return Mrs. Pinckney's handkerchiefs as soon as I've washed them."

"She'll be glad to hear you're all right. And you owe us no apology. It is we who should apologize to you. I regret anything was said in our home that could bring you to such bitter tears."

"It wasn't your fault. I was tired, maybe a little sick, but it wasn't your..."

I turned to see Jonathan Prioleau in the doorway. My face grew warm. "I hope I didn't frighten you, Mrs. Prince. Why-oh-why has it been my fate to trounce upon your tender feelings? Can you find it in your heart to forgive me? If not, I shall spend the rest of my life a miserable man."

"That will do," Mr. Pinckney said with emphasis. Jonathan's face went redder than my own. Mr. Pinckney turned toward me and spoke more softly. "Arlena, I asked Mr. Prioleau – Jonathan – to apologize to you in person, though I wish he had sounded more sincere. I hope you don't mind my presumption."

"Yes, I mean, no. I mean...it wasn't necessary, but thank you."

"All right, Jonathan. She's letting you off the hook. You may go."

Prioleau tried to milk the moment. "Good day, Mrs. Prince. I hope you'll give us another chance to entertain you at Pinckney House..." He was about to say more, but Mr. Pinckney gave him a scalding look. Prioleau fled the room mid-thought.

"The man is a horse's ass," Mr. Pinckney said when the office door clicked shut. "I begged Honor not to marry him. Offered her a year abroad, designer clothes, fancy car...but it's difficult to bribe someone who already has everything. So she married the idiot, and now she has a son by him. It makes me sick to think of Jonathan Prioleau as father to my only grandson. Looks like it would make me dislike him less. But every day I get out of bed and promise myself I'm not going to let him rile me, and every day I get mad enough to beat the living hell out of him. If only I were ten years younger..."

⌘ ⌘ ⌘

Between morning meetings with Mr. Pinckney and Jeannette FitzSimons, I took care of my secret errand. It did not take long. The people I had to deal with were in a bigger hurry than I. "Thank you," I said when a doctor whose name I did not remember handed over my fourth Valium prescription in six months. I studied the prescription, but could not decipher the handwriting. "Excuse, me," I said. "Is this refillable?"

"Yes," he said and handed me the paperwork for the billing clerk. "Pay on your way out."

"I forgot to mention my headaches. They're unbearable. Do you think Darvon or Percodan might help?"

"Percodan is strong. Have you used it before?"

"Once," I lied.

"No, twice" He was looking at my chart. After a brief study, he wrote something on a prescription pad. "This is Darvon," he said, ripping off the top sheet. He scribbled something else on the next page. "Percodan. Take it only if the pain is bad. It can affect the brain adversely. Be careful."

"Are these refillable too?" I said.

"Yes, same as the Valium. Pay at the counter by the door."

The thought of his hundred-dollar fee increased the churning in my stomach. And the prescriptions would be a hundred more. I felt lightheaded when I thought of Stuart having to juggle rent and utility bills to keep us in groceries. If Mr. Pinckney hadn't tipped me in August, I would not have had the cash for my current medical errand. Taking it out of monthly money was not an option. We were far too pressed for that. And if I had admitted to Stuart why I needed so many pain meds, how much and how badly my side ached, he would have insisted I stop seeing my new doctors and go back to the ones who had treated me over the summer. He might have tried to make me stop working. My new doctors asked no questions. As long as I paid them in cash, they would write any prescription I wanted.

The doctor I was seeing on this particular day ran his clinic out of a rundown building on the north end of King Street two blocks from Hampton's Pharmacy, a conveniently impersonal sundries store where I was able to get my prescriptions filled quickly and anonymously. The ordeal, including doctor visit and prescription purchase, took less than an hour and yielded enough pills to last two full weeks, six counting refills. After that, I'd need more money to pay for a different doctor across town. The three hundred I had left over from today's expenditure would finance refills, but six weeks was a long time away. I could not think about what might happen in six weeks, not when I had to face Jeannette FitzSimons in ten minutes.

⌘ ⌘ ⌘

"Mrs. Prince," FitzSimons said when I walked into her unkempt office. "You decided to come after all, and on such short notice. I'm honored. Your reputation precedes you, I must say. My daughter, Raven, is still rhapsodizing about your English class last year. And Miss Peregrine is charmed by every little word you utter."

Jeannette FitzSimons sat behind the most cluttered desk in the most cluttered office I had ever seen. She looked like an aging Raven, a graying, bulging, nearsighted, frumpy Raven. I took a seat opposite her and prepared for battle.

"It was a writing class," I said. "I'm not certified in secondary English."

"Whatever…you know how teenagers obfuscate. Most of the time I couldn't tell you what Raven is studying. But enough of that. You're here to talk about Miss Peregrine."

"No, I'm here to listen. You're here to talk."

FitzSimons straightened in her chair and dropped the superficial friendliness. I had succeeded in making her angry. "Yes," she said, nostrils flaring. "I want to appeal to your sense of fair play, if you have any, that is. Miss Peregrine isn't well. You know that. And you also know her judgment isn't what it should be, yet you continue to encourage her in a ridiculous writing project. You flatter her, play to her vanity, tell her the work is good when you know very well it's nothing but an expensive indulgence. The fact is that she's been working on her reminiscences over a year with no progress. Her friends and family agree, you are talking criminal advantage, bleeding an old woman of money. Some have suggested you harbor notions Svengali in nature. I'm asking you now in clear and simple terms…leave the employ of Miss Peregrine at once."

I was staggered. Now I knew why Raven hated to go home. "Svengali," I said in a voice hoarse with rage. "You accuse me of your own crime, Jeannette FitzSimons. Yours and Louisa Hill's. I won't be intimidated by either of you, and I won't stop working for Miss Peregrine unless she dismisses me herself. You'll have to find someone else to bully."

The perfect oval of Raven's face sprang into my mind as I spoke those last few words, though I dared not mention her name. I could not tell Jeannette FitzSimons how close I was to her daughter.

"Eloquent, Mrs. Prince, though ineffective, However, there's one small detail you're forgetting. Every member of Southern Prep's Board of Trustees is a personal friend of mine. Aren't you planning to teach there again this year? And isn't your husband a paid consultant for our development program?"

"Is that a threat?"

"Call it whatever you like."

"Coercion is what I call it." I stomped out of her office, slamming the door in my wake. As I fled the building, I thought with relief of my new cache of pills.

9

"Would anyone like to read something you wrote over the summer?" No one in the class stirred. My eyes moved row to row. I felt intimidated by the cold expressions and expensive clothing of Southern Prep students. Why didn't I get a job at Bishop England? How did I end up in this wasp nest?

"I'd like to," a male voice said from the farthest corner. It was Croom, son of Dr. Croomer Legare.

"Great," I said, though Croom's offer seemed odd. He had never volunteered before.

"Do I have to stand?"

"Not if we can hear you still seated."

He fidgeted and coughed before beginning: "Early morning is a time of magic in Charleston. In the gray time after the light has come and before the sun has risen, Charleston seems to hang suspended out of time in the silvery light. The streetlights go out and the weeds are a brilliant green. The corrugated iron of building roofs glow with the pearly lucence of platinum or old pewter. No automobiles are running then. The streets are silent of progress and business. And the rush and drag of waves can be heard as they splash. It is a time of great peace, a deserted time, a little era of rest. Cats drip over fences and slither like syrup over the ground to look for fish heads. Silent early morning dogs parade majestically, picking and choosing judiciously whereupon to pee."

The class snickered. I hesitated before speaking. For the first time since we had known each other, Croom and I looked into each other's eyes. The other students grew uncomfortable with the silence and began shifting in their desks. I glanced at Raven. She lowered her eyes and stared at the gold eagle on her Southern Prep notebook. I looked back at Croom.

"Is this supposed to be a joke, Croom?"

"I don't know what you mean."

"Yes, you do. You know exactly what I mean." He leaned far back in his desk. It creaked. I paused again before continuing. "I'm trying to understand. At first, I thought you wanted us to think you wrote that piece. I thought you were playing a trick on the class. But now I have to think the trick was intended for me."

"I don't know what you're talking about."

"Croom, we both know that passage is from *Cannery Row,* Steinbeck, except for the places you hacked it up. I wasn't going to say anything, didn't want to expose you. But I missed the point. You wanted to expose me. You wanted to make me look foolish if I didn't recognize the passage. And you succeeded. I do feel foolish, but not because of the passage…because I didn't realize you disliked me so much. I'm sorry for that, Croom."

His cheeks flushed redder than mine, which showed age was on my side. It would be difficult for a seventeen-year-old boy to outwit an experienced teacher. Croom was at a disadvantage, yet he came at me again.

"Yesterday at dinner, my dad said you don't know any more about writing than he does." A giggle rippled across the rows of desks. I kept my composure.

"That may or may not be true, Croom. I would never challenge anyone as erudite as your father. I'm flattered, though, to be the subject of your family's dinner table conversation."

"Dad says you're a vanity publisher, and the writing instruction is nothing but a come-on. You've never had anything of your own published, and you're not a real teacher, either…not certified. That's why you have to work in a private school instead of public. You don't have a state credential."

I felt dizzy. I had to fight to stand firm. "He's confused about nomenclature, Croom. Vanity publishers charge writers for the manufacture of their books. They talk them into paying for printing costs by leading them to believe there's a market for their work. But family histories and personal memoirs aren't intended for market. They're private publications done for the purpose of preserving social history to keep threads between generations unbroken." I forced myself to breathe slowly. "Your father is right about my being unpublished personally and uncertified as an educator. But if I were either, do you think I'd be teaching a writing class in a small private school in South Carolina, one with the distinction of paying its faculty less than any other school in the state? Seriously, do you think I'd be doing that?"

He glared at me. The metal feet of his desk clattered as he scrambled out of it. His notebook slid off the slanted surface and fell open on the floor. Croom tried harder to intimidate me with a stare, but I maintained steady eye contact, which, being a boy, he could not return. He scooped up his notebook and blustered out of the room. The sound of the door slamming behind him was enough to let me know he would not be back for the rest of the day and probably no other. I looked at Raven and was saddened to see she had her head on her desktop, weeping.

⌘ ⌘ ⌘

"Mrs. Prince, wait," someone called from among the hoard of young people scurrying up and down George Street. But these were not Southern Prep kids. These were college students rushing to and from the juice bar across the street from the College of Charleston campus. I turned to see Raven in the crowd, waving frantically with one hand, gripping a handlebar of a wayward bicycle with the other. I waved back, but I did not smile. She rolled the bike along the sidewalk, trying with slow progress to catch up with me. I waited until she got closer to start lecturing her.

"What are you doing here, Rav? Did you skip out of school early? I just left you there not an hour ago."

"I'm cutting, okay? And if the headmaster calls Mother and rats on me, it won't matter a dip. She'll tell him I'm sick, like always. Last thing she wants is for him to kick me out. Then her only daughter wouldn't be a student at fabulous Southern Prep."

Raven's disregard for authority did not surprise me. For all her innocent look, she was cunning. "You may be able to skip school, chicky, but I can't skip work. Hope you aren't planning to spend the afternoon tagging after me."

"I'm on my way out to Sullivan's, if I ever make it home with this stupid bike to pick up my car. But I wanted to tell you something first. I'm sorry for what Croom did in class. It was a dirty rotten trick. He can be a creep sometimes."

"Don't worry, Raven. Teachers know things like that can happen with students. It's not as big a deal as Croom thought."

Raven looked around to make sure no familiar face was in the vicinity. She did not want anyone to hear what she had to say next. "You have to watch Croom, Mrs. Prince. He's like me. If he gets mad at you, he won't keep his mouth shut. You made him look stupid in front of his friends. He might try to get back at you."

"How did it get to be my fault he acted like a jerk? Guess that's Southern Prep, huh. Look, I didn't mean to embarrass Croom. Surely, he has better things to do than swear out revenge on a poor teacher. Now turn around and take a good look at that building across the street. It's the College of Charleston Library, the quiet and lovely place I intend to spend the rest of my afternoon. I have work to do. Get it? Work."

I walked past Raven toward the curb of George Street. She followed. "Mrs. Prince," she said between short breaths as she trailed me with her bike. "Don't make Croom mad again. Things could get out of hand. He and his father might talk behind your back and ruin your reputation. Then you'd never get anywhere in Charleston."

"My reputation is safe enough, not that I give a flip one way or the other. What you don't understand, Raven…as intelligent as you are…is that most people don't care what the dignified citizens of Old Charleston think. You grew up here. It's your world, but it's not mine, nor a lot of other people's. Hundreds of kids not much older than you and Croom live and work and go to school in this area – at the medical school, nursing school, The Citadel, and several other colleges and tech schools. They're from all over the country…Iowa, Kansas, California…and I'd bet not ten of them know your vacuous little society South of Broad Street even exits. And if they did, they'd think it ridiculous. Grow up. There's a whole universe out there you've never experienced."

She looked at me with pain in her eyes. This was the girl who wanted to talk about cosmic awareness, but never bothered to venture above Broad Street except for brief excursions to Sullivan's Island or the mountains of Flat Rock. I pressed her further. "Why did you mention Croom's father? Is there something else I should know?"

She blushed and turned away. "I listen in on Mother's phone conversations. The other night I heard her talking to Dr. Legare about you, some trouble you've been causing with Miss Peregrine. Sounded like he was tired of it, didn't want to hear any more. Everyone knows he doesn't like my mother, but he has to put up with her. They work together taking care of Miss Peregrine. Anyway, Mother was mad on the phone, complaining you upset Miss Peregrine."

A flutter of fear made my heart skip a beat, an unexplained caution alerting me to danger. I don't know why I ignored it. Raven interpreted my silence as disapproval of her listening in on her mother.

"I don't care what you think about my eavesdropping," she said. "You'd do it, too, if your mother were like mine. You should be thanking me for trying to help you. I don't want you to get fired from Southern Prep."

I gave the nervous girl a quick hug. "You've helped me enough. And now you must stop worrying. I can take care of myself."

She sighed and hugged me back. "Be careful," she said, blinking her larkspur eyes that were now shining with new tears. She wiped them with her sleeve, climbed on the bike, and pedaled up George Street. I would not let myself watch her go. I shrugged off her small drama and headed toward the college library.

But as I started up the concrete steps, something occurred to me more interesting than Raven-loves-Croom. I paused on the tenth step, thought a moment, walked back down. There was something I wanted to find out, something that had been nagging at me since my two o'clock dinner at Pinckney House, and the only place I could think of that might have the information I wanted was the South Carolina Historical Society Library on the corner of Chalmers and Meeting, one block from the Mills House.

I walked too fast and paid for it with pains in my side. It was a hike from George Street to the Fireproof Building – nickname for the Historical Society Library – but I didn't care. I did not break pace 'til I crossed the cobblestones of Chalmers and climbed a different set of library steps. But this was no ordinary library. This was the library designed by Robert Mills, South Carolina's most famous architect. It had survived earthquake, tornado, hurricane, flood, and fire. Now it would have to survive a search by a determined female Yankee.

Not just anyone could enter those hallowed halls, only recommended, dues-paying members of the South Carolina Historical Society, of which I was one, thanks to Miss Peregrine. I rang the bell beside the bolted front door. A fussy matron peeped out, looked me up and down, checked over my shoulder to make sure no one was with me. Reluctantly, she pushed open the door. I explained my reason for being there, whereupon she helped me fill out the correct form and told me where to sit and wait while she searched the sequestered stacks for my request.

"Here it is," she said triumphantly on returning. In her arms was a huge rectangular package wrapped in brown paper and tied up neatly with string.

"We store all our important Bibles like this," she said, emphasizing the word, important. "This is one of our newer acquisitions."

"Miss Peregrine told me she had allowed you to catalog it."

The librarian looked pleased. "She brought it in herself five years ago. Told us she was getting on in years and thought it time to dispose of such things properly. As far as I know, it hasn't been touched since."

"Thank you," I said.

The woman shifted the enormous weight of the Bible from her arms to mine. "Be careful with it," she said. I could not respond. It took all my strength to heft the book to a table.

The binding strings were tied in bowknots which made them easy to undo. Carefully and quickly, I opened the Bible to its middle the way I had been taught to find Psalms in my childhood. But today I was not looking for Psalms. Today I was looking for the genealogy pages with their handwritten records of births and deaths. There were dozens of names, most with the surname Peregrine, but one stood out like blood on white satin. It was the last name on the list, Constantia Elizabeth Peregrine. Beside it was a brief annotation. I recognized Miss Peregrine's handwriting:

> Constantia Elizabeth Peregrine b.1 May 1926. d.___ Illegitimate child of Fanny Hampton Peregrine (b. 24 June 1910. d. ___). Constantia Elizabeth was born secretly in Schenectady, New York, 1926, and was turned over by her grandfather, Smythe Hampton Peregrine (b. 17 November 1890. d. 7 October 1950), to Our Lady of grace Foundling Home. There she was offered for public adoption. Her father was Grayson Lockwood Pinckney III (b. 2 May 1900. d. 14 August 1943). This entry was set down by Fanny Lockwood Peregrine, Constantia Elizabeth Peregrine's birth mother.

I calculated quickly. If she were still alive, Constantia Elizabeth Peregrine would be over sixty. I had hoped Jonathan Prioleau wrong about Miss Peregrine's past, but he was not, save one important detail. The baby's father was no northerner. He was a Pinckney, father of Grayson Lockwood Pinckney IV. That made Miss Peregrine's child Mr. Pinckney's half-sister. I wondered if he knew. One thing was certain, Jonathan Prioleau did not know, or else he would have said so the day I was a guest at Pinckney House.

I read the entry again and took pleasure in Miss Peregrine's decision not to let her child go nameless and unrecorded. By including her in the Pinckney Bible, she had given Constantia Elizabeth her rightful place in family history.

"You're a tough old bird, Fanny Peregrine," I said to myself. "I wonder what other secrets you're keeping."

10

"You shouldn't be going," Stuart said, his anxiety palpable. I ignored him as he followed me room to room through the cottage. My shoes were on the porch, jacket hanging from the bedroom doorknob, blouse over a towel bar in the bathroom. It was a disorganized effort at dressing.

"I mean it, Arly. I've got a bad feeling about this."

"I don't care. I'm going anyway. Miss Peregrine is expecting me."

"No, she isn't. Why do I get the feeling we aren't communicating? I told you. Louisa Hill called after you fell asleep last night. She said Miss Peregrine asked her to cancel your session this morning. Did you hear me? I said cancel, c-a-n-c-e-l."

"Surely you don't believe a word that woman says. Where's my hairbrush?"

"Haven't seen it. Use mine…in the bedroom on the dresser."

I pushed past him into our room, but stopped short when I caught a glimpse of myself in the dresser mirror. Leaning forward,

I frowned at my reflection. "Sallow," I said under my breath. "What happened to my tan?"

I smeared on lipstick and blush, gathered my hair into a ponytail, and gave it a few extra swipes with Stuart's brush. He sat on the bedside and watched.

"What difference does it make if she's lying?" he said. "No use confronting her. Let old lady Peregrine handle it. She will sooner or later."

"Sure, and in the meantime, Louisa Hill gets her way again. But not this time. I'm keeping my appointment. If Miss Peregrine wants to cancel, she can tell me when I get there."

Stuart went from nervous to exasperated. "You should call before you go, to confirm."

I laughed with no humor. "Terrific idea. I'll call and Louisa will answer and tell me another pack of lies. I'll be right back where I started, only worse. At least this way I can pretend you forgot to give me the message. What are you so worried about? Most of the time you don't mind if I risk life and limb for a buck."

Sarcasm put barbs on my word. Stuart's expression made it obvious I had pricked his conscience. "Look," I said less caustically. "I've been given orders, issued ultimatums, practically threatened with banishment from the state of South Carolina by Miss Peregrine's so-called friends. It's time I defended myself."

"It's a mistake," Stuart said, "I know it is, but I refuse to let it ruin my day. Go, joust with windmills, but don't come home complaining when you get your arm cut off."

He stomped out of the house through the back porch door and caught himself as he stumbled down the concrete steps. Suddenly unsure of myself, I watched him run along the path toward the ocean at a pace too fast for simple exercise. I pretended not to care and turned my attention back to dressing, relegating any remorse over attacking Stuart to a lockbox deep in my soul. It was the secret place I had been stashing all my troublesome emotions of late. I noticed it was getting crowded.

Tasks completed, I left the house and went forward to challenge Louisa Hill, avenge unfairness, unmask evil motives. But when I stood before the grand front door of Peregrine House, my great wave of courage vanished. If Louisa Hill would slam doors in my face, she might do worse. I backed away from the door without touching the knocker. Looking around to make sure no one was watching, I walked to the left of the house and opened the wrought iron gate to the back grounds. Behind the gate was a brick drive that curved around a row of overgrown azaleas. It continued to the door of an old-fashioned carriage house stationed at the back left of the garden. I walked to the ancient structure and peered through a window. Miss Peregrine's black Cadillac sat alone and gleaming near the far wall. Louisa's car was absent. I turned away and looked over the house and lawn. Everything seemed friendly now that I knew Louisa wasn't home. Birds sang in the garden, gray squirrels chased each other up and down Judas trees, and somewhere in the distance, a wind chime tinkled.

My courage returned. I walked to the back entrance of the mansion and rapped on the door. No answer. "Tycie, it's me...Arlena. Let me in." Still nothing. "Tycie," I shouted and reached for the knob. It turned in my hand. Gently, I pushed it and watched, fearful, as it swung open. "Tycie, are you there? I'm coming in."

Just as I stepped inside, a draft caught the door and swung it shut behind me. My heart skipped into double time. As I scanned the area for a place to hide, a buzzer sounded in bursts toward the front of the house. I panicked and clamped my hands over my ears. Squatting to the floor, I waited for something terrible to happen. Nothing did. The buzzer stopped as abruptly as it had started and was replaced by a clanging sound. I tried to stay still despite my aching calf muscles. I shifted on my haunches. A minute passed without disaster. A second minute. By will alone, I subdued my fear and talked myself down from panic.

This is senseless, I thought. I'm a rat cowering in a musty storage room. I shall stand up straight, walk through the house, and find out what is going on. Miss Peregrine would want me to. She'd do it herself if she were able.

I stood, moaning as my legs rebelled. When I found the courage to creep into the hallway, I began a timid walk down several back corridors, in and out of odd-shaped rooms, through the study, the parlor, and finally the archway to the foyer. My footsteps sounded amplified on the hardwood floors. At the bottom of the staircase, I stopped a moment and listened to the clanging. It was coming from the upper levels. Maybe Miss Peregrine had gotten trapped upstairs with no one at home to help her. I ran up the steps. On the fourth floor, I heard her calling from a room near the end of the hallway. It was a section of the house I had never visited. The clanging began again. In a second I was down the hall.

"It's me, Miss Peregrine," I shouted. The clanging stopped.

"Get in here, child," I heard her call from behind a closed door on my left. I reached out and pushed it open. Miss Peregrine's disheveled appearance shocked me. She lay against several pillows in a four-poster bed. The bedclothes were a tumble. Two dented silver trays, the source of the clanging, lay on the floor by the bed.

"Is everyone dead?" she said, staring at me from glazed eyes. "Where is Tycie? I've been buzzing her all morning. Confounded buzzer must be broken."

"I don't know, Miss Peregrine. I don't know where anyone is. Are you ill? Should I call a doctor?"

"No, I want you to call Grayson Pinckney's office. Tell his secretary I can't make my appointment today and will call back later to reschedule."

I remained by the bed, silent. The strangeness of the situation had overwhelmed me. "What's the matter?" she said. "Go downstairs and make the call. I have more things for you to do."

I obeyed and returned for my next orders. Miss Peregrine had a long list. Open the shutters; straighten the bedclothes; bring in wet washcloths from the bathroom; find a hairbrush; fetch orange juice and the medicine bag from the kitchen. A busy hour passed before I was allowed to sit and rest.

"I didn't see Tycie anywhere," I said on catching my breath. "Is she out sick?"

Miss Peregrine did not respond right away. She was sipping juice from a water goblet I had brought up from the kitchen. "That little good-for-nothing has never been sick a day in her life. Lazy maybe, but not sick."

I squirmed at the offensive remark, but did not challenge it. "What about you, Miss Peregrine? Are you feeling better now?"

"No, still groggy from too much medication. I was having leg cramps about four this morning. Louisa heard me groaning and talked me into taking an extra pill to finish out the night. It was stupid to take a sleeping med at that hour. I should never have let her convince me, not when I had an appointment with Grayson. Now I'm too weak to go."

"But you and I were supposed to work today. Did you tell Louisa to call me and cancel? She did, you know."

"I did not. I wanted you to come at your usual time and drive me to Grayson's, but that was before the pill. I didn't want Louisa to know I was going. She pesters me so with questions. If there's anything I hate, it's being interrogated."

"I understand," I said, but Miss Peregrine did not hear me. Her attention had fastened on something across the room. I turned to see Louisa standing in the bedroom doorway. Her lips were set in a thin, tight line, and she was looking directly at me.

"What are you doing here?" she said.

I stood up with the intention of answering, but Miss Peregrine cut me off. "Mrs. Prince came for our regular session," she said. "Your phone call fell on deaf ears. I suppose you called Tycie, too. Did you think I wouldn't figure any of this out?"

"Don't be peevish," Louisa said to her mistress without taking her eyes off me. "You've been so weary lately, I thought you'd benefit from a day of rest."

"And you made sure I'd get it with that evil pill, which worked all too well. I'm rested now and hungry. You'll have to take over Tycie's kitchen duties. Too bad you didn't speak to me before calling and telling her not to come in today. You'll never again take it upon yourself to do such a thing without consulting me first. There now, I'm ready for my breakfast. Do the honors, Louisa. And prepare a tray for Mrs. Prince. I'm sure she's as famished as I."

Red streaks appeared on Louisa's throat. I watched as they crept upward to her cheekbones and forehead, yet she did not look at Miss Peregrine. Her eyes, yellow as saffron and glowing hot with fury, remained fixed on me. My muscles trembled as I looked into those animal eyes. I stared, fascinated, as she curled her fingers into knobby fists. Now I had done it. I had turned Louisa Hill into something far worse than a simple adversary. I had made her a raging enemy.

⌘ ⌘ ⌘

"I've been meaning to talk to you about her," Miss Peregrine said after Louisa had clomped out of the room and I'd collapsed into a bedside chair. "She isn't nearly as bad as she makes out. Her attitude is a strange form of sadness, really. Poor thing had a tragic early life, though of late I must admit her mood swings have become unbearable. Yet I always forgive her. She has nowhere else to go, no family, no friends. I try to be firm without chasing her away. If I turned her out of Peregrine House, she'd go insane, what with all her horrendous emotional ups and downs."

"Miss Peregrine, you don't have to..."

"Hush up. I want you to know why Louisa behaves the way she does. I met her thirty years ago, in Schenectady, New York..." My mind jumped to the entry in the Peregrine family Bible. Miss Peregrine droned on in her gravelly voice. "...when I took a trip there just after Father died. I went to present his bequest to Union College in person. That's where he got his Bachelor of Arts degree when he was young. Probably seems strange to you for southerners to go north to be educated, but in Father's day there was a reason. A year or two after the War of Northern Aggression ended, a guilt-stricken Yankee woman traveled south and was heartbroken by the devastation of the war. I suppose she was discomfited by the atrocities committed by her fellow countrymen from up north. At any rate, the experience moved her deeply. She felt compelled to help us rebuild. Her family set up an ongoing scholarship fund at Union College and reserved it for southern boys. She must have realized our only hope for recovery was through the education of our young people. Father's family was destitute for generations from the losses they sustained at the hands of irascible Yankees. He was more than eligible for a scholarship. Later in life, when he became financially able, he began donating money to Union College. I think he felt beholden, especially after making such a fortune over the course of his career factoring phosphate to the north. He married after he became financially secure, but his wife, my mother, became tubercular while still in her twenties. She died when I was seven. After that, I was expected to take her place representing the family. Father dragged me to all sorts of affairs having to do with Peregrine interests. He was on the board of every non-profit in South Carolina and a fair number of states beyond. We traveled to Schenectady countless times to attend special ceremonies at Union – building dedications, alumni gatherings, every kind of function."

Abruptly, she stopped talking and gave me a look. "Bored?" she said.

"No, Miss Peregrine, but you don't have to go into all this. I understand about Louisa."

"I'll go into whatever I want. That visit to Union after Father died was my last trip to Schenectady. I decided as long as I was there, I ought to call on Our Lady of Grace Foundling Home, another of Father's philanthropic interests. He'd become attached to the little orphanage while a student at Union. His fraternity maintained a tradition of doing for the needy, and the children at Our Lady of Grace were beneficiaries of their social responsibility – Christmas parties, new winter coats, toys, fruit baskets. After college and Father's unexpected financial success, he continued to remember the little orphanage. He was a stern, unfeeling man, my father. No one knows that better than I. Yet he knew how to be generous. The foundling home had a wonderful benefactor in Smythe Hampton Peregrine."

Miss Peregrine stopped to rearrange her coverlet. I wondered, was she preparing to tell me about baby Constantia?

"To continue," she said, "when I went to the foundling home on that last visit to determine any financial needs they might have, Louisa was working there as Assistant Director. We talked. I discovered she had grown up an orphan right there at Our Lady of Grace. The poor stunted thing had spent only one year of her life outside the walls of the orphanage, and that was when she hired out at age thirty as a companion to a wealthy spinster who wished to travel abroad. After a number of tours, the woman tired of Louisa and terminated their relationship. Louisa had nowhere to go, so she packed up and went back to her old job at Our Lady of Grace. She felt she did not have a choice. It was the only home she'd ever known, the only place she had ever lived or worked. When I met her there, she was forty-six years old, bereft of family and friends, bitter and alone. I paid her a bit of kind attention and she stuck to me like pitch on a bateau. Wearied me comatose with sad stories about her past, which became more and more heart-wrenching every time she told them. Louisa had learned early the art of inducing pity. I think she confused it with love. Father having just died, I needed someone to keep me company – I was still traveling a great deal in those days – and I also needed help managing Peregrine House. Louisa leapt at the opportunity, and we've been together ever since. Her darker side didn't emerge until later, though I'm sure she'd say the same about me. We've grown old together, Louisa and I, a couple of timeworn dowdies."

I sighed and shifted in my seat. "I still don't see why she wants to be so ill tempered. If nothing else, she should be grateful to live in this beautiful house. I wouldn't think many orphans end up in mansions."

"True, but you and I mustn't judge her. We don't know what demons torment Louisa. She lived out her childhood without parents to love her. Children who grow up like that often develop emotional problems."

"I know, but what I don't understand is why you feel you have to tell me all these details."

"Because that lovely cinnamon skin of yours turns to ashes every time Louisa makes an appearance. I'm trying to ease your anxiety. Tycie lives in fear of Louisa, which I regret, though there's nothing I can say or do to change it. I love Tycie dearly and have tried many times to explain the situation, but in her mind, Louisa will never be anything but an ogre. With you, I felt there was hope. Educated people have certain advantages when it comes to understanding."

"I'm not sure I agree, Miss Peregrine. Tycie has more common sense than the two of us put together. But thank you for your confidence. I'll try not to react next time Louisa creates a scene."

"Oh, you don't have to take her nonsense. Not at all. I just wanted you to know what the matter was. Sh-h-h, here she comes with our breakfast trays. Pretend we've been talking about something else."

Louisa opened the bedroom door and rolled in a cart bearing two perfectly appointed trays. She wheeled the cart next to the bed and pulled a large folding tray from its bottom shelf. With a deftness that comes from performing a task dozens of times, she unfolded the legs of the bed tray and placed it across Miss Peregrine's middle. My smaller tray remained on the cart. Miss Peregrine examined her breakfast and nodded approval. Louisa poured coffee for her mistress and left the room without speaking.

Miss Peregrine insisted I pull my chair closer to the bed to share the meal. Poached eggs, Tycie's warmed-over butter biscuits, glazed figs, and cups and cups of steaming black coffee. For once, my attitude toward Louisa softened. After breakfast, Miss Peregrine asked me to pour her a glass of the forbidden homemade peach brandy. She said Tycie had hidden it from Louisa, along with a crystal glass, in the bottom of the antique highboy opposite her bed. Tycie had gone to the trouble of transferring the brandy from its kitchen fruit jar to an old Jack Daniels bottle. I smiled at her notion of an innocent container. Miss Peregrine proposed a toast to *Tarnished Honor.* There was only one glass, so I sipped from my coffee cup. After the brandy, my ailing boss told me I should leave to allow her to sleep off the medication. I was to come back at my usual time on Tuesday of the following week. She assured me she would be recovered and ready to work. I helped her to the bathroom and back to bed, then I tiptoed out of her bedroom to the stairs. I made it to the stairwell between the first and second floors before being accosted by Louisa. She materialized like a ghost on the step below. I gripped the banister in my struggle to remain poised.

"Thank you for breakfast, Louisa," I said, my vocal cords trembly. "It was wonderful."

"Don't talk down to me. I'm not stupid. I know when people are talking down. Now listen, I have something important to tell you. I have to warn you." She looked all around to make sure we were alone. "It's Miss Peregrine. She's unstable. She'll turn on you in a second."

I stood still and gaped at her. She blinked and continued, "What she's been telling you isn't true. She's the one who's crazy, not me. I know things about her." Louisa wrung her hands as if the things she knew were too hideous to reveal. She stretched her eyes and looked around again. Satisfied we were still alone, she whispered in a voice grainy with agitation, "You'd better not tell anyone we talked like this. If you do, we'll both be punished. Miss Peregrine likes to punish people, especially outsiders like us."

"She does nothing of the kind," I said, "and you have no business talking behind her back."

I had spoken too loudly, trying to cover my fear. Until that moment, I had not realized how truly disturbed Louisa was. I felt certain Miss Peregrine had underestimated the depth of her madness.

"Miss Peregrine cares about you," I went on. "She doesn't want to punish you."

"Yes, she does. And she'll punish you if you aren't careful. She'll fire you and stop your paychecks. I have to make sure she doesn't do that to me. Every day I have to make sure."

"Miss Peregrine would never fire you, Louisa. She loves you."

"No, she hates me. I don't belong here, but she can't get rid of me now. I know too many things…things you'll never find out unless I decide to tell you. It's how I keep her from getting rid of me. She's afraid I'll tell her secrets."

"Stop talking like that. It's disloyal. Miss Peregrine would be furious."

Fear shone in Louisa's yellow eyes. "You won't tell her, will you?" she said.

"No, it would hurt her feelings. This very morning she was telling me how much she cares about you."

"But she was angry. She threatened me."

"She did not threaten you. She was upset because you called Tycie and me and told us not to come to work today. That would have made anyone angry. Now get hold of yourself. Tycie isn't here. You must carry on alone today. And don't forget, Miss Peregrine is your friend."

"I don't know," she said, her eyelids fluttering. "Maybe I should make a pot of tea."

"Good…tea for yourself and Miss Peregrine. Promise you'll take care of her?"

"Yes," she said, though her eyes were lifeless and face ghostly.

"I'm counting on you, Louisa. You have to stay strong. Are you all right now?"

She nodded. I eased past her down the stairs toward the front door, though still unsure of my control of the situation. She followed me with wooden movements. I opened the door, hesitated, then stepped out onto the piazza before turning to speak a last time.

"Goodbye, Louisa," I said, shocked by the greenish pallor of her cheeks in the unforgiving outdoor light. "Don't fret. It's bad for your nerves."

"I won't," she said and shut the door, this time without slamming it.

11

Next day, everything in my schedule had turned upside down by nine A.M. My original intention had been to spend the morning in the College of Charleston Library writing Chapter Eight of Mr. Pinckney's reminiscences, but Cliffton Stanlock, Headmaster of Southern Prep, and Raven FitzSimons, reluctant student, worked simultaneously to get me off track.

The day began easily enough: coffee on the porch with Stuart, kisses instead of arguments, an ocean view to knock your eyes out. Beyond the beach the iridescent Atlantic gleamed in airy morning light. Sea birds flew in concentric circles around shrimp boats anchored in the distance. I counted six white boats, each with butterfly arms lowered to let heavy nets drag bottom. Gulls dove for chum and bait. Stuart and I watched as they hovered, clipped, soared, and screamed, until the telephone rang in a disconcerting jangle, and Stuart left the porch to answer it.

"For you," he called from the sitting room. "It's Raven FitzSimons, whispering, for Pete's sake."

"Grief," I said in a groan. I stood and moved toward the door. "No one calls at this hour with anything else."

Stuart squinted agreement. "Want me to tell her you aren't up yet?"

"It's okay, probably just wants to waste my time with a visit."

I took the phone and pressed it to my chest, working up the courage to speak. "Hi, Rav," I said after a moment. "What's up?"

"I'm scared. That's what. Croom's father is going to school with him this morning. They have an appointment with the headmaster…to talk about you."

"Cliff Stanlock?"

"Yes, and it's trouble. I'm sure of it. Can you meet me in the gazebo at White Point Garden? I want to tell you what's going on in case Dr. Stanlock calls you in. Can you come? I have to get off the phone before Mother gets out of the shower."

"This is silly, Raven. You're getting yourself all worked up over nothing."

"I'll be at the gazebo in thirty minutes. If you show up, I'll help you. If you don't, too bad."

She clicked off without saying goodbye. I crashed the receiver down in frustration, but before I could take my hand away, the phone rang again. I jerked the receiver back to my ear. "I'm going to wring your neck when I get my hands on you…"

Silence…then a snigger. "Cliffton Stanlock here," a tenor said. "I assume you were expecting someone else. This is Mrs. Prince, right?"

"Oh, no, excuse me. I thought you were…"

"Never mind," he interrupted. "I'm glad I caught you. We have a problem to straighten out. Late yesterday, I got a call from Dr. Croomer Legare. He requested a conference with you. Wants me to sit in on it. I know you don't have classes on Fridays, but I thought you'd like to get whatever this is cleared up before the weekend."

"What?"

"Don't know. I was hoping you could fill me in."

"Can't think of a thing. Is it about my class? His son is in it."

"Possibly…can you be here by eleven? I took the liberty of setting that time with Dr. Legare."

"Yes, maybe a little earlier."

"See you then, goodbye."

I hung up again and looked at Stuart. He put his arms around me and patted my back. "Must be the morning for bad calls," he said. "Anything I can do?"

"Play chauffeur. I have to fight the dragon again." I slipped out of his grasp and moved to the bathroom where Percodan would be more comforting than his arms.

⌘ ⌘ ⌘

"Who are you looking for, Rav? The enemy?" I asked.

The startled girl sprang off the gazebo steps. "You scared me," she spluttered. "What took you so long?"

"Stuart broke every speed limit in Mount Pleasant and Charleston, and you ask what took so long? This better be good."

"Don't be mean, Mrs. Prince. It's too much like Mother."

"I don't have time for niceties today. And I don't like being in a public park at this hour. We're the only ones here except for those runners over there, the fools."

"A bum was sleeping in the gazebo when I first got here," Raven said. "Can you believe that?" She stretched her neck and looked all around again. I decided against mentioning the call from Cliff Stanlock. Raven's imagination needed no more fuel.

"Okay, this is how it is," she said. "The other day when Croom tried to get at you in class, he'd made bets with some of the kids in the hall on whether you'd recognize that passage. And when you did, he lost $47.00. I didn't tell you before. It was such a rotten thing for him to do. I try hard to love Croom, but it isn't easy when he pulls stunts like that."

"And what else?" I said.

She blinked, surprised I would think there might be more. "Nothing else. I thought you needed to know what the story was so you could defend yourself in case Dr. Stanlock tries to fire you."

"That's all?" I said, incredulous. "Stuart and I drove over here at this hour for you to tell me Croom Legare, Jr. lost a bet?"

"You're being mean again," she said, her face primped to cry. "Here I am trying to help you not get fired, and you're hurting my feelings. Dr. Legare and Croom want to get rid of you. I don't know why, but I do know they'll go to any length to get what they want. If you don't believe me, you're crazy…crazier than Mother."

"We're talking about a part-time job, Raven…less than a part-time job. It isn't that much to lose. And really, I hardly think a grown man would try to get me fired over an insignificant incident in one of his son's high school classes."

"He would, he would, I know he would," she wailed.

"All right, I believe you. Now be quiet. That policeman over there is looking this way." She hushed, but continued sniveling. "Listen," I said. "I want you to go to school and forget this. I can handle it from here. You're a dear, sweet friend to warn me. I'm grateful, and I promise not to use your name if anything comes up. Now get going. I'll give you a head start."

She gathered her books and moped toward the King Street boundary of White Point Garden. Morning dew outlined her footprints in the wet grass. They appeared behind her in two black-green rows that stretched the length of the grounds. Raven kept her head down, turning back every other step to wave. The girl could make a blue mood seem fatal.

I watched her disappear around the corner of King and South Battery. Turning my attention to the mansions across the street, I stared at Peregrine House. Pinckney House was farther down, closer to the corner of East Bay. I felt squeamish about the occupants of those dwellings observing me in White Point at such an odd hour. I sat for a long time in the gazebo, feeling miserable and out of place, trying in vain to sort out the morning's events. It was hopeless. My fate lay in the hands of Cliffton Stanlock, a wimp who considered me a smart-mouthed Yankee feminist. He would not help me if he could. He had asked me idly once when I first started teaching at Southern Prep why I didn't consider going back to graduate school and earn a PhD in administration like he had done. I told him I objected to the required frontal lobotomy. He disliked me after that.

The longer I sat thinking, the more depressed I became. After fifteen minutes of inertia, I watched in dejection as an old green

Ford scraped to a stop in front of Peregrine House. The driver was a young man. He slid from under the wheel and walked around the hood to help an old woman out of the passenger side.

"Tycie," I whispered when she turned her face in my direction after kissing the young man on the cheek...a motherly gesture, perhaps grandmotherly. It was clear the man was family. I stared in surprise. I had never thought of Tycie having a life apart from Peregrine House. That was what happened to people when Miss Peregrine got hold of them. She swallowed them up and digested them like so many tea-time hor d'oeuvres. Tycie, Louisa, Jeannette, and Dr. Legare. All had succumbed to her insatiable appetite for attention. In my own way, so had I. So had anyone interested in her fortune. And as much as I hated to admit it, I was interested. Somehow, it got to it every month. I would find myself doing backflips for a fifteen-hundred-dollar paycheck. Even Cliff Stanlock had to dance to her tune. Miss Peregrine was Southern Prep's biggest donor, and Stanlock was obligated to please her. The board would expect him to run naked down Broad Street if it would make Miss Peregrine happy.

Something clicked in my brain, the self-evident simplicity of a solution. Miss Peregrine would take care of Cliffton Stanlock. All I had to do was ask her. Dr. Legare might prove more difficult to handle, but Stanlock could be squelched.

"Tycie, wait," I called out. By this time the Ford had pulled away, and Tycie was creeping along the walkway to the front door. She stopped when she heard her name called and turned stiffly.

"Lord in His Heaven. What are you doing here, Missy Arlena? Birds ain't hardly up yet."

"Happened to be in the neighborhood," I said in my hurry across South Battery. "Thought I'd stop by for a visit. Do you think Miss Peregrine will mind?"

"Won't be awake yet," Tycie said with foreboding. "She sleeps too much now-a-days. But come in anyhow. You always make her feel better. I thank sweet Jesus you don't get her riled up like that hateful Louisa. She's worse than our diamondbacks out on Edisto."

"You live on Edisto, Tycie? I didn't realize. Isn't that where the Pinckney family's old home place is, Planter's Hall? Do you know it?"

"I was born at Planter's Hall, but the Pinckneys all live in town now, here on South Battery. See that big brick house down the way. It's the Pinckney mansion."

"Yes, I went there once for two o'clock dinner. Peregrine House is more grand. Let's go inside. I need to talk to Miss Fanny. Hope she doesn't get mad at me for not calling ahead."

"She's mad all the time 'bout everything, but she don't mean nothing by it. It's her rheumatism makes her ornery."

Tycie opened the front door with a large brass key strung on a chain around her neck. I suspected it never left the safety of her bosom except to lock and unlock the front door of Peregrine House. We stepped into the foyer quietly. Neither of us wanted to alert Louisa. Tycie led me to the elevator, and we rode together to the fourth floor. I followed her to Miss Peregrine's bedroom.

"Come in," the old woman called in a drug-weakened voice. Tycie opened the door and stood to the side.

"Good morning, Miss Peregrine. It's me again," I said.

"As I live and breathe. Come sit with me while Tycie brings my pill bag and juice. Good morning to you, too, Tycie, you lazy h'ant. Did you enjoy your day off?"

"Your cousin told me to stay home yesterday, Missy Peregrine." Tycie blamed everything blamable on Louisa. Most was deserved, some convenient.

"Quiet," said Miss Peregrine. "I don't want to hear your prattle this morning. Get my pills and juice…and make my breakfast."

After Tycie left, I moved closer to Miss Peregrine to tell her my story. Her eyebrows knitted into a deep scowl as she listened to my convoluted tale. For a long time, she did not speak. At first, I thought she was angry, until she began issuing orders.

"I understand perfectly well," she said. "And you need not fret another moment. Listen carefully and do everything I say. Go to your meeting with Croomer and that wimp, Cliff Stanlock, but be there by ten thirty instead of eleven. I suspect the good headmaster will want to speak with you alone a few minutes before Croomer and his son arrive. Now run downstairs and help Tycie with my breakfast. I must make a few phone calls in private."

I blushed and smiled and hurried out of the room. I did not want her to change her mind. When I returned with her breakfast tray, she detained me another half hour before sending me away on foot. I strode the six blocks to Southern Prep at a moderate pace to keep from straining my side. It was ten twenty-five when I arrived, thirty-five minutes early. I entered the administration building and hurried toward Cliff Stanlock's office. When the secretary saw me, her eyes grew wide. Stanlock himself burst through his office door and charged across the reception area. He had a sick look on his face, ghost-white around the eyes and nose. I took a step back.

"What have you been up to?" he said. "I've had calls from three senior Board members this morning, including Grayson Pinckney. He spent ten minutes telling me how thrilled he is you're teaching here again this year. Suggested we give you a raise."

Bless Miss Peregrine's sweet alligator hide, I thought. A smile played around my lips, which made Stanlock angrier.

"What do you have to say for yourself?" he shouted.

"Why are you so upset? Didn't I just get a rash of good reports?"

"Don't be cute, you devious little..." I was certain he was speaking with more emotion than he had ever emitted all at one time in his entire impotent life. "Understand this, Miss Smart-girl-from-the-north. Croomer Legare is on his way over here, and the only thing that would satisfy him this morning is seeing you fired."

"That's not what you told me on the phone. You said you didn't know what he wanted."

"You need to get out of here. Let me handle this alone. Maybe I can smooth it over without it getting to the board."

"You mean you can't fire me without board approval?" I was grinning. "No, and I don't want it to get that far. There's enough to deal with around here without a fracas over a part-time teacher."

I laughed aloud. "Let me get this straight. You can't fire me; you don't want me to stay for the conference; you want me to leave before Dr. Legare gets here."

Stanlock blanched. "Oh, no. Look there…out the window. Here comes Legare now, thirty minutes early, and Croom Jr. is with him."

I glanced around for a place to hide. Stanlock appeared to be in danger of cardiac arrest if I did not find a hole to drop into. I scuttled into a janitor's closet and pulled the door shut behind me.

It seemed to be my lot lately to end up hiding in storage rooms. In the darkness, I smelled sour mops and musty buckets of dust-down. All that and a college prep education. I hated Southern Prep.

12

I lay in bed and watched the blades of the ceiling fan make thirty-seven revolutions before my eyes blurred and I could no longer count. All night the bed had rolled in syncopated rhythms of disturbing dreams. I was exhausted. Dreams had been my private affliction for as long as I could remember. They came to me in shapes and colors that did not exist in daylight. As I lay there entranced by the fan, I became aware of Stuart's voice thrumming in the sitting room. It irritated me. Everything irritated me. I sat up on the side of the bed, wincing at the feel of sand when my feet touched the bare floor. Where were my slippers? My robe? I gave up on any hope of comfort and padded into the sitting room shoeless. Stuart hung up the phone.

"Who was that?" I said, still in my sleep fog.

"A friend. Can't I talk to a friend without being questioned?"

I raised an eyebrow. "Depends on the friend. But don't flatter yourself, big guy. I wasn't trying to check up on you. I thought it might be Cliff Stanlock again."

I gazed at the ocean through the bank of windows separating the sitting room from the porch. They were coated with salt residue, opaque. The Atlantic appeared far away through the smudgy panes. An impressionistic watercolor, blue on blue.

"We're out of money again," Stuart said. "I didn't want to tell you. I hated to tell you." He paused and dragged a hand over his face. "I had to take steps to get us through, more borrowing."

Then big strong Stuart began to cry. Any warm feelings I had left for him disappeared in a hiss. I felt betrayed, let down. Here was the man who had spent every day of our courtship promising to take care of me. How could he stand there like that, a sniveling idiot, whining that we had no money? I thought about Roz Pinckney and Caroline Prioleau and felt jealous of their security. I gazed upon Stuart with disgust. He was a mess, crying like a child. My emotions whirled in a jumble. I hated him; I felt sorry for him. One part of me wanted to attack him, another to take him in my arms and comfort him. Why, I thought, is it always left to women to make men feel better?

"You have to stop that," I said with no feeling. My words were empty platitudes: "It isn't your fault, Stuart; something is bound to turn up, Stuart. Rest while I make your lunch, Stuart."

He moped over to the Boston rocker on the porch to rock away his sadness. I went to the kitchen to find him something to eat. When I came back with coffee and stale pasta, he looked at me adoringly, as though I had acquired wings and a halo. He thought I was playing the part of good little wife holding up bravely in a crisis. He should never have assigned me such saintliness. There are times when women have excessive dominance over men. Stuart was measuring his own self-worth in direct proportion to my approval...or disapproval if I so chose. I was bemused by his willingness to subject himself to my female temperament. Could it be he really loved me? I did not know, but in case he did, I granted him a small measure of peace.

"Let's think it through together," I said, my emotions under control. "What are the facts?"

"It boils down to this," he lisped through a mouthful of last week's linguine. "We have to survive 'til Tuesday."

"What's magic about Tuesday?"

"Jim Rhiner is sending us a check. Said he'd put it in the mail today. If it comes by Tuesday, we can puddle-jump to Friday. That's when Bill Martin is due to pay me for the work I've done on Sea Bird."

"Was that Rhiner on the phone?"

"Yes."

"But why would he send us money? We hardly know him."

"I loaned him dough all the way through college. Calling in the favor now. He's doing well these days. Married a rich babe from Philly."

"A loan, right?"

"Yes, and I don't want to hear any self-righteous lectures about the pitfalls of borrowing. We need dough."

I was quiet, thinking of the three hundred in cash in the zipper pocket of my purse, the last of Mr. Pinckney's August tip. "But what about today?" I said. "And tomorrow?"

"We'll skinny by on nothing today. Tomorrow I'll go to the grocery store and write a check for twenty bucks or so over the amount of purchase. That'll get us food and a little gas. If Jim's check comes on Tuesday like it's supposed to, we'll slide through okay."

"What if it doesn't? You know how the mail can be."

"Then the grocery check will bounce, and we'll have to let it hang out until Wednesday or Thursday, whichever day Jim's money shows up. It isn't pretty, but it's the best I can come up with. Main thing…we stick together. Things won't always be like this."

I stroked Stuart's hair and told him I loved him, but I didn't mention the hidden three hundred dollars. Something inside my chest kept me from it, something familiar, yet 'til that moment, I had not been fully aware of its presence. It had kept itself hidden, silent, waiting for the right time to emerge. It was a beast with definition and will. It told me what to say and what not to say. It drummed its evil sermon into my ears: Don't tell Stuart about the cash you're hiding. Don't tell him you've never really loved him, or that you're sick with pains in your belly and can't get through a single day without pills.

The spirit of the beast quickened within me and assumed a position of power. It pressed against my throat. I could not breathe.

I broke into a coughing spell, and Stuart became distraught. "I'm okay," I said when the coughing subsided. "Let me go to the bathroom. I'll throw some water on my face."

I did not say I was going for Percodan. I did not say the beast was crawling on the underside on my skin. My hands trembled as I twisted the cap off the prescription bottle and shook out two tablets. I shivered as they slipped down my throat. Leaning on the sink, I forced myself to look in the mirror. It was at that moment I realized the magnitude of my problem.

In a short half–hour, a synthetic serenity had put the beast at bay. I was calm and beautiful. Nothing could touch me. I settled myself on the porch swing and listened to Stuart dictating into my dictaphone. He was composing pages for Mr. Pinckney's Chapter Eight, the one I had been unable to write. I should have been grateful for his help, but since I knew he was doing it to make dead sure I would get my paycheck on time, I did not say thank you. An undisturbed hour passed before a car noise broke the peace. I moved across the sitting room to the window overlooking the street. Through my private haze, I saw Raven and Croom Jr. in the driveway, both leaning against Raven's MG. I opened the back door and called down to them. "Hi there, you two. Where have you been, Rav? Haven't heard from you in a while."

She would not look at me, just stared straight ahead as if concentrating on something down the street.

"Are you okay?" I said. "You look like you lost your best friend."

She glanced up, then cut her eyes away again. "I'm fine…mad at Mother, that's all. When Croom brought me home last night, she was waiting up. We were late, as usual. Anyway, she was drunk and got so mad she almost killed me."

"What time did you get in?"

"Four."

"Can't say as I blame her. She was probably worried sick."

Raven shrugged; I sighed. "Wish you'd phoned before you came out," I said. "Stuart and I have work to do. We can't entertain you."

"It's okay," she said, staring farther down the road. Croom remained silent. I studied Raven's perfect profile and realized with a pang something worse was wrong. I took a step down the stairway.

"What's the matter, Rav? You seem..."

She did not let me finish. She lurched forward and began shouting. "I'm losing my mind. That's what's the matter. My mother is a witch. I hate her so much I can't stand it. I want to vomit, I hate her so much."

I hurried down the remaining steps. "Don't talk like that. Your mother wouldn't want you to..."

"My mother?" she said, lifting her head so that her face caught full sunlight. I stared in disbelief. Her right jaw was swollen and bluish. An angry abrasion shone on her cheekbone. I looked into her eyes and was moved by their sorrow. Raven was an abused little animal whose spirit had folded in upon itself.

"You think I shouldn't hate my mother?" she said, her chin quivering like a child's. "Give me one good reason why not."

13

On Wednesday morning, winds from the ocean gusted cool and clean over Sullivan's. When I woke up, I decided to spend my day on the beach letting autumn-freshened breezes blow away my worries, particularly those about Raven. But Miss Peregrine had a different agenda. She called early to say she needed me at Peregrine House, though it was not our regular day. There was something she wanted me to help her take care of, something important. I hesitated, but when she told me Louisa would be away with her church cronies delivering charity goods to the poor on Daufuski Island, I became more willing to change my schedule. I looked forward to an hour or two alone with Miss Peregrine. Most of the time I enjoyed her company despite her abrasiveness. And minus the specter of Louisa Hill, Peregrine House was a lovely place to spend time.

When I told Stuart that Miss Peregrine had called, he insisted on driving me into town. At five of ten, he dropped me on the corner of King and South Battery. I carried a manila folder in one hand and a bunch of daisies in the other. I had rescued them from our Atlantic Avenue neighbor's roadside trash pile to take as an offering to the queen of Peregrine House. Too bad the joker answered the door.

"Mrs. FitzSimons...why are you here?" I said in unconcealed shock when the Raven-like frump appeared before me. My voice was an octave higher than its normal range.

Jeannette FitzSimons looked amused by my surprise. It almost helped her rotten attitude. "None of your business, Miss...Miss... what was your name again?"

"Prince...Arlena Prince."

"Yes...Mrs. Prince. Sorry to have forgotten, but your name isn't important to most folks in town. The fact is that a number of people in Charleston wish they'd never heard of you. Cliffton Stanlock is one."

Before I had a chance to collect myself, a loud crack came from the parlor. FitzSimons jumped. "It's Fanny," she said less confidently, "banging that infernal cane again." She pushed open the front door and yanked me inside. I dropped the daisies to the floor. "Leave them," she said. "Tycie will clean them up later. Hurry...get to the parlor."

I walked like a robot through the archway into the gloomy sitting room, where Miss Peregrine sat in a large antique chair next to the fireplace. She was a queen on her throne, complete with scepter and robe – her gold-knobbed walking cane and satin dressing gown. If I had not just endured a harangue from Jeannette FitzSimons, I'd have been overjoyed to see my old friend looking so well.

"You're late," said the queen. "You and Jeannette have no time to be lollygagging about on the piazza. Such ninnies, the two of you are, flapping your tongues like magpies with no thought at all about the cost of my air conditioning. Go over by the mantel and stand quietly. I'll deal with you later after I'm finished with Jeannette."

I slunk to the designated space and tried to make myself small.

"As for you, Jeannette," Miss Peregrine continued, "I've had my fill of advice on what property I should and should not sell or purchase. Do not bring rubbish like this into my house ever again.

Do you understand?" She picked up a folder from the tea table and gave it an angry toss. Several pages escaped the folder and fanned out on the hearth tiles. Fitzsimons stooped to gather them up. Miss Peregrine continued her rant.

"I will never sell my island property to developers," she said, "not one square inch. You know how I feel about that, yet every few weeks you slink in here with more of your schemes. The people submitting these bids are carpetbaggers. They'll steal your underwear if you blink once. Come to think of it, maybe that's what you want."

FitzSimons did not speak. Her face went mauve. She coughed once, buying time to compose herself. "They aren't developers," she said with a tremor. "They're part of a land-holding company, a group of businessmen interested in long term investments."

"Don't tell me that nonsense!" Miss Peregrine roared. "You don't know what these people are like. In five years, they'd have Sullivan's looking like Myrtle Beach, or Florida, or worse."

"No, Fanny."

"Get that garbage out of here. I swear, I will not let Sullivan's Island be ravished."

I watched as Jeannette FitzSimons faded from the room. Miss Peregrine's rage had burned through the despised woman's body until there was nothing left but a foul vapor.

I did not move. I did not want to be dematerialized like FitzSimons. Miss Peregrine shifted her attention toward me. "As for you, little missy," she said with scarcely an ounce less acid. "I expect you to behave today. Will I have your full attention this morning, or must I hire someone else to assist me?"

She paused a moment, waiting for me to speak, and when I couldn't, she blasted me again. "Answer me, girl," she said and cracked the cane on the floor.

"Yes," I squeaked.

"You'll follow my instructions with no back-talk?"

"Yes." I had regressed to a one-word vocabulary.

"Good. Look in the secretary where you find those early checks you need so often. My car keys are in the top drawer, back left corner."

I walked like a robot to the desk. The keys required a search, which was good. It gave me something to do with my hands. When I found them, I turned back to face Miss Peregrine again and received another shock. She had risen from her chair and was now standing straight and tall by the pink marble fireplace. Her dressing gown was in a heap on the floor. In its place, Miss Peregrine was wearing a lovely blue dress with white lace cuffs and collar. Pearls were at her neck, a diamond watch on her wrist, and an emerald on her right ring finger.

"How do I look?" she said, smiling as if she had pulled off some great trick. Somehow her face seemed less wrinkled.

"Beautiful," I said.

"Rubbish, though I love the flattery. Tycie helped me dress this morning. But that worrisome Jeannette flew in here like a bluejay and got in the way of my plans. Didn't make any difference, though. I'd already resolved not to let everyone in Charleston be privy to my business. Tycie had to move fast – what a joke that was, Tycie trying to move fast – to get my robe down here so Jeannette wouldn't know I was going out. I had trouble enough getting rid of Louisa for the day."

"But where are you going?" I asked

"No more questions. There's a conspiracy in this town to track my every move. Tycie has annoyed me to distraction all morning with her impertinent fussing about. I've been planning this outing a long time, but things kept getting in my way. Have you forgotten making that call to Grayson Pinckney's office the other morning, canceling my appointment? If you have, you've a decided lack of intellect. I called him back last afternoon and rescheduled for today, and you are going to drive me."

"Me? I can't. I don't have a car. Stuart dropped me off this morning."

"We'll take mine. Those are the keys."

"But I've never driven your car."

"Hush up. You have four things to do: drive me to Broad Street; wait for me there; drive me home; and keep your mouth shut in between. For the amount I pay you each month, it isn't too much to ask."

"I want to help you, Miss Peregrine. Really, I do." I looked down at my hands. They were trembling. "Maybe if I had a drink of water."

The old woman turned toward the parlor archway and began screeching. "Come out from wherever you're hiding, Tycie. Fetch Mrs. Prince a glass of water."

⌘ ⌘ ⌘

Carefully, very carefully, I backed the Cadillac out of the carriage house. Tycie stood to the side and smiled as if she had witnessed a miracle. She probably had. Miss Peregrine settled herself in the back seat and commanded our journey to commence. I drove to Pinckney Building on Broad Street. Parking did not present its usual problem, not when Fanny Peregrine was along. She told me to enter the back lot and pointed a crooked finger to a space marked Jonathan Prioleau. I gave her an unsure look; she pointed again; I parked. I was about to help her out of the car when Prioleau himself pulled into the lot and began tapping his horn. I pretended not to know what he wanted. Miss Peregrine ignored him. He stuck his head out of his car window and called my name.

"Mrs. Prince, is that your Caddy? You'll have to move it. You're in my reserved space."

I did not answer. Annoyed, he got out and approached the Cadillac to investigate the situation. "I said you can't park there," he began again. He stopped to stare as Miss Peregrine let down her back window. She held her head far back and looked down her nose at him.

"This is my auto," she said, "and as you can see, there's no other place to park it."

"But the lot belongs to the Pinckney firm, madam. It isn't open to the public, and the spaces in this row are for employees."

I realized he did not know Miss Peregrine. All that provocative talk over dinner at Pinckney House, and he didn't know her on sight. I grabbed the opportunity to stick him.

"Mr. Prioleau, you've arrived at the perfect moment. Miss Peregrine and I are in desperate need of a big strong man like you. I'm sure you have the keys to the back door of the building. Miss Peregrine has an appointment with Mr. Pinckney in three little baby minutes..." I looked at my watch with an exaggerated arm movement. "...and if we don't move along, I'm afraid we'll be late. You wouldn't want to make dear sweet Miss Peregrine late, would you? Not after all the nice things you were saying about her at two o'clock dinner the other day."

From the rearview mirror, I saw Miss Peregrine look at me askance. I winked at her, turned back to Prioleau, batted my eyelashes. He had not yet grasped he was being made a fool of.

"Peregrine?" he said.

Miss Peregrine spoke in a superior tone. "I am Fanny Hampton Peregrine come to call on Grayson Lockwood Pinckney, IV. And who, pray tell, are you?"

"Jonathan Prioleau, ma'am, Mr. Pinckney's son-in-law."

"Do tell," Miss Peregrine said and sniffed.

"Oh, dear," I said. "Forgive me for not introducing you, Jonathan. I thought you and Miss Peregrine were old friends the way you were going on about her the other day. Miss Peregrine, you'd be so pleased by the kind remarks Mr. Prioleau was making about you and your family over two o'clock dinner at Pinckney House, especially your dear departed father."

"Do tell," Miss Peregrine said again and looked Prioleau up and down. He suffered under her gaze. For a moment he appeared to be shrinking.

"Please, please, let me help you ladies inside," he said in a burst of southern courtesy. "You'll wilt like cut gardenias in this sun."

"Do tell," I said in a perfect mimic of Miss Peregrine. She cast me a withering look. I backed off. Prioleau stumbled all over himself helping us inside. When we stepped off the elevator on the second floor, he announced our arrival to Mr. Pinckney's secretary as if we were visiting dignitaries. Mr. Pinckney was mortified by all the folderol and took control of the situation with dispatch. Miss Peregrine was given the seat of honor across from his desk. I was told to wait in the reception area since Lillian was out for the day. Son-in-law was dismissed. But the instant Mr. Pinckney closed his office door, Prioleau reappeared in front of me angry enough to kill. I gave him a snotty look and turned away, which infuriated him more. He caught me by my arm and pulled me to his chest. I felt his breath on my face.

"You think you're so smart," he growled, "you contemptuous little tart. You're going to have to get a lot smarter if you want to survive in Charleston. This town is shark infested, or haven't you figured that out yet? By the way, the invitation to my office is still open. I like the way you smell today. Want to come down for a visit?"

I jerked away and slapped his face. A drop of blood formed at the corner of his mouth. "Tart," he said again and marched out of the reception area and down the carpeted hallway. When he was out of sight and hearing, I sank into a leather visitor's chair to wait. An hour later, I was still there, snoring in the same chair. Miss Peregrine and Mr. Pinckney had forgotten me.

14

“Wake up, Arlena,” Miss Peregrine said from an echo chamber deep in my brain. “Wake up, child. Don’t you know sloth is handmaiden to ruination.”

Miss Peregrine and Grayson Pinckney had finished their meeting and come looking for me in Lillian’s office. Mr. Pinckney laughed as I blinked and tried to focus.

“Marvelous way to earn the minimum wage,” he said. “Are you working by the hour or the day?”

My head was swimming. I had trouble understanding his words. I stood, got dizzy, had to sit again. “I’m sorry, Miss Peregrine. I waited…must have fallen asleep.”

“Stop apologizing and get yourself up. Grayson, get the girl some water. Can’t you see her brain is fogged?”

I stood again, this time more slowly. Miss Peregrine frowned. I said to her cheerily in a failed effort to redeem myself, “Are you ready to go now?”

"Yes, but not home. If you can manage to regain consciousness, I want you to drive me to Sullivan's. Haven't seen that old sand dune for a year or more. It's time I paid a visit."

"But what about two o'clock dinner? Won't Tycie be expecting you?"

"Grayson phoned and told her I'd be late. And Louisa won't be back until evening. I can gad about all afternoon. Tycie has instructions to tell callers I'm not well and have taken to my bed. For this one day, I'm going to do what I please without it being broadcast up and down South Battery."

I nodded while sipping from the paper cup Mr. Pinckney had brought from the water cooler. He took it from my hand when I finished drinking and asked if I were recovered. I said yes, and he escorted Miss Peregrine and me all the way to her Caddy, strolling along at the aging lady's side as if her snail-like pace were normal. As we made our way to the parking lot, the two old aristocrats traded memories about people who had died before I was born. It made me glad I had spent the last hour napping instead of being bored by goings-on behind closed doors of a certain office. Mr. Pinckney took his time helping Miss Peregrine into her car. I was thankful. It gave me another minute to dislodge the cobwebs from my mind before I had to begin driving. The two elderly friends said their goodbyes and promised to stay in closer touch. He thanked her for the visit and directed us out of the parking lot. The appointment was officially over.

At Miss Peregrine's insistence, I headed toward Mount Pleasant and then Sullivan's Island. As we approached the massive bridge to Mt. Pleasant, she smiled and patted my leg. I was surprised. It was a tender gesture, almost loving. I smiled back and took a cleansing breath, allowing myself a more relaxed mood. Miss Peregrine's new and pleasant attitude, uncharacteristic though it was, eased my tension.

"Miss Peregrine," I said, enjoying the tranquil feeling, "did you ever cross the harbor on *The Sappho*?"

She laughed. "About a million times. Where in the world did you hear about that creaky old ferry?"

"I specialize in memoirs, remember? Things like that come up."

"*The Sappho* was a far sight safer than this monster bridge," she said, craning her neck upward to see the steelwork above the span. Her gaze moved down to the roadway. "Great Scott, look at that multitude of automobiles. I remember the day only two or three cars could be found in all of Charleston."

I held the wheel steady as we joined the river of cars descending to Mount Pleasant. We took the main road on the right, Coleman Boulevard. It would bypass the crooked streets of Old Town and eventually become a straight shot to the Ben Sawyer Bridge that traversed the Intracoastal. Miss Peregrine continued her observations. I negotiated traffic.

"And none of these roadside businesses were here," she said. "Would you look at that? Restaurants have closed off every inch of Shem Creek all the way to the harbor. Used to be nothing but shrimp boat docks."

"Two or three are still there," I said, "just hard to see for the restaurants."

I kept my eyes on the straight-away of Coleman. Soon we saw the mile-long causeway that led to the Ben Sawyer Bridge. The marsh road along it from Mount Pleasant to Sullivan's Island had been built in the early thirties from spoil dredged from the Intracoastal. I loved the expanse of seagrass and mud flats that spread out in serene acreage along its banks. On the right, an asphalt bicycle path formed a narrow ribbon between the roadway and a row of oleanders. I reveled in their pink and white beauty. As the Caddy transported us over the causeway, I glanced across the salt marsh to check the direction of the tide. There was nothing more renewing to my spirit than ocean water flooding seagrass on the indrawn tide. Ruts and gullies would overflow until every inch of satiny pluff mud was under water.

Miss Peregrine became wistful as we turned right onto Middle Street and headed toward the lighthouse. But when she spied the walls of Fort Moultrie, her spirits lifted again. A mood to talk came upon her.

"My family has always owned island property," she said, "even when that maniac, Edgar Allan Poe, was stationed at the fort. What a pitiful excuse for a soldier he was. Can't imagine why they named the island library after him."

"But Miss Peregrine, I love Sullivan's old library. It's wonderful the way it extends back into the dungeon. It's like a cave in there."

Miss Peregrine paid me no attention. She was engrossed in her own musings. "Who'd have ever thought Fort Moultrie would become defunct," she said and clucked her tongue. "Used to be critical to defending the harbor, but that was before we had sonar and nuclear this-and-that. Those battlements up there may as well be torn down. Never did much good in the first place, not even in the big war."

Miss Peregrine was not talking about World War I or II. To her, there was only one "big war," the War Between the States. After surveying the fort, she asked me to drive north to Harbor Point. She wanted to enjoy the ocean breeze and watch ships traverse the harbor.

The view stirred her memory. She spoke of her childhood summers...swimming, marooning, playing whist (cards), sleeping outdoors in hammocks, feasting on shrimp, playing in the sand, flying kites, sailing, hiking. She laughed when she remembered her knee-length bathing suits and matching ruffled caps. Memories of old times made her think of her mother, a rare occurrence, for her mother had died when Miss Peregrine was so young. I told her what had happened to my own mother, which made her sad.

When we left the point, she insisted we drive from one end of the island to the other, up and down every street and lane, by each landmark and house, alongside every body of water. We traveled south on Ion Avenue until it converged with Middle Street, turned west on Bayonne, and headed toward the marsh. There we explored the crisscrossing back streets that had been named in honor of the mad poet, Edgar Allan Poe: Goldbug, Raven, Poe. For two hours and a tank of gas, we rode the streets and byways. Miss Peregrine would not let me stop until every palmetto had been inspected and every oleander examined. When she grew weary, she instructed me to park in the public lot overlooking Breach Inlet for one last look at the ocean. She asked if I were in a hurry. No, I was not. The afternoon had become a nostalgic trip back in time. I wished it did not have to end.

"This may be the last time I see this," she mused as we watched the roiling waters of the inlet.

"Don't say that, Miss Peregrine. You'll see it, though you may have to find another driver. You've worn this one out."

My effort to stave off her sinking mood failed, which hurt me. She had been so young and lighthearted the last few hours. I hated to see her lose the feeling.

"Arlena," she said without changing expression or taking her gaze off the water. "I've not spoken to you often about serious matters. Today, I wish to do so. Are you listening?"

I straightened in my seat and became attentive. I was a child preparing to be lectured. "Yes," I said and remained still.

She turned and looked into my eyes. "You have to understand, dear, you and yours must protect places like Sullivan's. If you don't, they'll vanish from the face of the earth forever. If your generation doesn't do its part to preserve what little we have left of natural beauty in our fair state, there will soon be nothing left. No clean beaches, no clean oceans…nothing. What a sad eventuality that would be."

I did not speak. Saving South Carolina's oceans and beaches was too big a concept for me to assimilate in one short moment. Miss Peregrine went on. "I'm merely informing you of your duty, lamb. I hope you and that citified husband of yours have developed some sense of responsibility along the way."

"What do you mean, Miss Peregrine?"

"Promise me, given the opportunity, you'll both do the right thing by Sullivan's Island, no more, no less."

"We will. We'll try. But I don't know what you're talking about."

"Trying will be quite enough," she said. "Thank you for that much. Let's not discuss it further today. I've grown tired. The time has come for a lady my age to make her way back home."

15

"How could you forget, Arlena? I've been telling you about the oyster roast for weeks. It's Southern Prep's biggest fall fundraiser."

Stuart kicked a deck chair out of the way and paced the length of the porch. But despite his scowl and show of temper, he looked better than I had seen him in weeks. White duck pants and brown leather loafers – leftovers from more affluent times – with a classic navy v-neck, sleeves pushed up to the elbows oh-so-casually to show off a Sullivan's Island tan. And under the sweater, a white knit polo, two buttons undone at the neck to reveal a section of male chest. Stuart was all golden skin, damp brown-blond curls, and straight white teeth. He had stepped out of *GQ*.

"I'll hurry," I said, contrite and bedraggled upon entering the presence of this clean and perfumed Stuart, this disarmingly stylish, good-looking Stuart. "I can be ready in twenty."

I had abandoned my shell bucket outside by the door along with any hope a simple walk on the beach would calm my jangled nerves. I now had to begin a frantic rush to shower and dress. My hands shook as I went through my routine. "Are white slacks okay for me, too?" I shouted from the bedroom. "We don't want to look like cheerleaders."

"No, wear the white cotton sleeveless that comes down to your ankles…and your black espadrilles and long black cardigan. Drape the sleeves over your shoulders and loop them in front. And clean that seashell crud from under your nails."

With the exception of my favorite hoop earrings, I dressed as Stuart had instructed. But since he forgot to mention hair, I decided to get extravagant. I brushed out all the tangles, swept my mass of heavy dark hair to one side and secured it in a large silver clamp. Several snaky tendrils escaped and wrapped themselves around my throat. I leaned over and gave my head a shake to get everything properly tousled, then stepped back from the mirror to evaluate. A thick rope of blue-black hair hung from the top of my left ear, over my breast, almost to my waist. It was bohemian, gypsy-like, not to be mistaken for the locks of a blunt-cut southern honey. I hoped Stuart would not notice. He was always afraid some prospective Southern client would be offended by my ethnic look and his Boston accent. And without clients, he reminded me daily, we would have to give up paradise and move back north.

"I'll never understand you, Arlena," he said when I joined him on the porch. "Why would you want to go to a business function looking like that. We've both worked on projects at Southern Prep, and any idiot would know that the board members could be good references. It's how we're supposed to get new work, word-of-mouth. We've been over that a thousand times, but you never seem to get it. You act like you don't care if we ever get a referral. There are times I think you do things deliberately to be offensive, or at the least out of the norm. And I can't fathom why. You took as many psych courses as I did. You know that people who take pains to be different are insecure, or have you forgotten everything you learned?"

How insulting Stuart could be, all under the guise of learn-ed discourse. I extended my claws for battle. "I know one thing I haven't forgotten," I said, chin thrust forward. "I haven't forgotten you close off everything you ever say to me with some condescending remark like have you forgotten? I haven't forgotten that, Stuart." His name came out with a hiss.

"Don't start," he said. "I want to get through the evening without an argument. This is an important event, a chance to meet people. Are you ready, or do you have to primp another hour?"

"Stop blaming everything on me." More hissing. Cold war. Stuart drove in silence the six miles to Charleston. Half-way there I wanted to tell him I was sorry for arguing back, but the words would not come out. After a while, I gave up trying and concentrated on the new pain now radiating from my forehead.

Stuart's ridiculousness and a headache to boot, I thought. Maybe they'll serve drinks at the oyster roast, something to help this head. There's always hope for a bar at a fundraising soiree. After all, the address is Old Charleston.

⌘ ⌘ ⌘

Autumn in the South Carolina Lowcountry is a carnage of roasting oysters, Southern Prep a leader in the tradition. As Stuart and I got out of the Romeo and trudged across the manicured athletic field, beach music blared from six sets of speakers. A healing surge of blood squeezed through my arteries. I sneaked a glance at Stuart and wished he weren't still angry. Surely, he wouldn't pout all evening. I tried to match his long strides, but when I couldn't, he gripped my arm and half-dragged me through the crowd. Together, we moved toward a makeshift bar at the far end of the field. I stumbled twice; he didn't notice. I wheezed every step; he didn't care. By the time we reached the bar, I was perspiring and out of breath, but when I saw how it was set up, I felt optimistic. Well, well…an open bar, we have. How nice.

Stuart ordered beer for himself and white wine for me. The bartender handed him the drinks in plastic go-cups that looked as if they might have come from a cheap motel room, which did not matter. You could get just as drunk. Stuart would not give me my cup until I looked him in the eye and pretended to listen.

"You're on your own," he said. "Try to drum up business. We'll leave around eleven. Be ready. And, Arlena, let this be your only drink."

He handed me the cup and walked away. I was left standing by myself, though I did not feel alone. I had my wine to keep me company. It took ten seconds to finish off the first small cup and five to order another. The third I asked for over ice. No more headache. The fourth in a larger cup. Euphoria. I noticed how warm the night had become. (Oh, those balmy Southern nights. Velvety, starry, intoxicating. My soul delights in mysterious moonlight…) I do believe in all my thirty years I had never gotten quite that drunk quite that quickly. I sighed, peeled off my sweater, and laid it across the end of the bar. The bartender frowned. I smiled, and the ice chip I'd been sucking fell out of my mouth. He widened his eyes and scanned the area to see who was supposed to be minding me. No one looked promising. When his gaze circled back around, I smiled again, waved to him with my fingertips, and glided away from the bar. I had decided to go exploring.

Little knots of people carried on animated conversations as I slipped and slid between them. I glided like a serpent through the landscape of the party until I'd seen everything worth seeing. This did not take long. Across the field opposite the bar, a sweating cadre of workers manned three long rows of oyster grills, those menacing contraptions specifically designed to roast defenseless animals alive. The grills were homemade devices – metal drums cut lengthwise and welded, curved sides down, to lengths of pipe that served as legs. Piles of red coals lined the bottoms of the drum halves. Gigantic metal racks lay across their tops. On the racks, dozens upon dozens of unshucked oysters steamed and cracked under wet burlap sacks. When the oysters were half-cooked, the men would shovel them into tin buckets and distribute them among groups of tables set up near the dance floor. They'd dump them on tabletops upon week-old editions of the *Charleston News and Courier*, traditional table coverings at all Lowcountry oyster roasts.

Each time new buckets of oysters appeared, barbarous shrieks arose from the crowd. Guests flew to tables, pulled on garden gloves, grabbed chisels and screwdrivers, and resumed shucking and splitting the gritty gray shells. They ate the oysters off knife blades and dripping from tips of screwdrivers. The women dipped them in hot sauce or squeezed lemon juice on them or slid them onto saltine crackers. Between orgies of devouring oysters, guests scoffed down other delicacies. Several grills supported vats of water for boiling corn on the cob, unpeeled shrimp, and hot sausages. Red peppers and jalapeños served as seasonings, and when I moved too close to the vats, spiced steam burned my eyes. In the center of every table was a large platter of sausages, boiled shrimp, and steamed corn on the cob, and beside every guest's plate a malodorous pile of shrimp peelings, corn cobs, and oyster shells. There looked to be more left over than eaten. I watched the worst of it from a distance and glided back to the bar to order myself another wine. The bartender was sorry to see me.

"What's your name?" I said.

"Isaac, ma'am."

"Well, Isaac, I used to teach school up north, but we never had parties like this, no sirree. And we dang sure never had a bar. Guess that's the South for you."

Isaac looked at me as if I were speaking a foreign language. He glanced around for rescue from a woman dumb enough to talk to hired help.

"You don't have to be nervous, Isaac. I'm not a parent. I work here same as you. I teach, part-time."

"Yes'm," he said, while making someone else a drink. His effort to remain cool was failing. He could not get away from me. When I realized I had him trapped behind the bar, the power of it went to my head.

"Isaac, Isaac, Isaac," I said. "Don't look so desperate. I'm not going to bite you. All I want is to talk. Can't you see how lonely I am?"

Isaac examined his fingernails, scratched his temple, polished a spot on the bar that did not need polishing. He appeared to have gone deaf.

"Have a heart, Isaac. Here I am alone, haven't talked to a soul all night, and you're playing hard-to-get. Let's run away together. I'm begging you."

Poor Isaac set his jaw and would not speak. I was just getting ready to torment him more when someone tapped me on the shoulder. "Let's not be too forward, Mrs. Prince," a man said. "A board member might hear."

I turned to see Jonathan Prioleau grinning a crooked grin. Isaac looked hopeful and began rearranging his liquor bottles. "Oh," I said, "if it isn't the lecher of Pinckney House. Belly up to the bar, Jonathan. Talk to Isaac and me. We're discussing the curious southern tradition of setting up open bars at school functions, or maybe it isn't southern at all. Maybe it's just Cha-ahl-ston. What do you think, Isaac?"

The bartender looked fearful. Jonathan rescued him. "It's quite Cha-ahl-ston," he said, "and exceedingly civilized. Ours is a culture rich in tradition, Mrs. Prince. We brought our customs to the New World from the royal courts of Europe."

Prioleau was drunker than I, but we were running neck and neck on obnoxious. I laughed in his face and insulted him outright. "You're an overweight, garlic-breathed fool, Jon Prioleau. You give new meaning to the term, royal ass. Now go away and leave Isaac and me alone. We have private matters to discuss. We're running away together. Isaac is thinking of going to graduate school up north to become a lawyer, maybe even a federal judge and Chief Justice of the Supreme Court, at which point all you white-breads from South Carolina will probably secede from the Union again and get your asses whipped worse than last time. Isn't that right, Isaac?"

This time Isaac backed away and disappeared into the night. Jon Prioleau laughed until his side ached. He draped his arm around my shoulders in a style that reeked of familiarity. I did not resist. "Let's dance," he said thickly. I did not say no.

He pulled me toward the temporary parquet dance floor laid out next to the dining tables. It did not surprise me he was a dance king. Smooth as silk. Cut a rug. Any observer would have known he grew up in Charleston. For an hour, we shagged and dipped and swayed and had just gotten down to some serious cheek-to-cheek when Stuart materialized at my side.

"Time to leave," he said and jerked me out of Prioleau's arms.

"Go away. I'm having fun."

"Arlena, it's late. Pull yourself together."

"Let go. You're hurting my arm."

"Hey, buddy," Prioleau said in a slur. "Leave the little gal alone. You aren't jealous, are you?" He put his hand on Stuart's shoulder and leaned on him for support. Stuart did not acknowledge him. He pulled away with a sharp jerk and focused again on me.

"We're going," he said, "now."

His fingers tightened around my wrist. I struggled to break free. He squeezed my hand until I gave in. He dragged me toward the edge of the dance floor in the direction of the parking area. But Prioleau was not finished. In drunken idiocy, he initiated a series of events that would end the night in disaster. He caught up with Stuart and me in the middle of the dance floor and stepped into our path. Stuart tried to get around him, but Prioleau was too drunk to be reasonable. He took a wild punch at Stuart's face, his fist making contact with the bone above the left eye. There was a thud. Stuart let go of my hand. He lurched sideways and fell across two couples shagging to "Sixty-Minute Man." I scrambled after him and heard myself screaming his name. The dance floor cleared except for two gallant preps who helped Stuart up.

I became hysterical. There was a cut through Stuart's eyebrow that had not yet begun to bleed. Stuart said nothing. He touched the cut in his eyebrow and gazed at the people nearby. I thought he might fall or faint. Slowly, intently, he surveyed the crowd. His eyes went past Jon Prioleau, stopped, and came back. Prioleau, who stood swaying near a tall speaker, did not realize he was in danger. It was my turn to beg to go home. Stuart would not listen. He approached Prioleau and glared into his face. Prioleau smiled and continued to sway. Stuart remained still, gathering his strength. He shoved Prioleau backward. A gentle shove, really…controlled… not intended to make a man fall. Prioleau staggered. Stuart shoved him again, harder this time. He kept at it, harder and harder, forcing Prioleau toward the tables. Prioleau asked him to stop. Stuart either did not hear or did not care. Again, Prioleau's temper got ahead of reason. He took a swipe at Stuart's face. Stuart grabbed his arm in mid-air with his left hand and swung from the right to deliver a stunning blow to Prioleau's slack mouth. He pumped two fists into his gut and finished with an upper cut to the chin. Prioleau lurched backward onto a picnic table and sprawled across a pile of new-lain garbage. Looking like a fallen street bum, he rolled to his side and spit blood on the *Charleston New and Courier.*

I ran to Stuart and tried to pull him away. I pleaded with him to take me home. He would not move. He would not listen. He would not take his eyes off Prioleau. I hoped to God that Prioleau would not get up from the table. He moaned like a child and vomited into a bucket of oyster shells. But that was not the worst. The worst was when he put his hand to his mouth and spit out three broken teeth. The men who had helped Stuart now helped Prioleau. They glanced in Stuart's direction several times to make sure he was not planning another assault. I stood at his side, crying into his sweater sleeve, begging him to get us out of there. In my desperation, I became aware of someone else close by trying to get Stuart to move. Grayson Pinckney had come to our rescue.

"Hold on, son," Mr. Pinckney said. "You meant to clobber him, not kill him. That's the thing you can't afford to forget when you find yourself in a throw-down. Jon just spit out half his front teeth. Probably cost his mama and daddy two or three thousand dollars to have those bucked things straightened. Time to quit and take your lady home. No sense hanging around 'til the last dog is hung, 'specially if it might be you."

Stuart yielded and allowed himself to be led away. The crowd opened, and we moved through unchallenged.

"Thank you, Mr. Pinckney," I mumbled between sobs. "We can handle it from here. Thank you."

Grayson Pinckney chuckled. "Don't thank me, dear. Get this brute husband of yours home before he whips up on anyone else, though I'll say it did my heart good to see Jon's rear end splattered through that pile of oyster shells."

"Stuart's sorry, sir. I know he is." Mr. Pinckney patted my back. "Done and over now. Can't undo it. Best go home to bed. Though I did learn one useful thing tonight. Next time we want to liven up one of our oyster roasts, we'll just invite a couple of damn Yankees."

16

My shoulder banged against the inside of the passenger door as the Alpha-Romeo lurched off the curb of Southern Prep's athletic field onto the asphalt of St. Philip Street. Stuart pushed the accelerator to the floor, and I realized the night's events were just beginning. I blew my nose into a tissue and wished for Darvon or Percodan, anything to deaden the pounding in my head. I had thought Stuart was going to kill Jon Prioleau with his bare fists.

"We should have left sooner," I said between snubs. "I've never seen you that mad…it was awful…you might have been hurt worse…oh."

"Stop your bawling," Stuart shouted as we swerved around the corner of Meeting Street. Again my shoulder bumped the door. Same door, same bruise, only worse.

"Stuart, what're you doing? Slow down."

"Stop yelling at me. Stop all your stupid nonsense. I'm not just leaving the party, Arlena. I'm leaving you."

"Slow down," I begged again. "We're almost to the bridge." I stared in alarm at the bleached concrete ramp. The bridge loomed before us like some magical pathway to the sky. I tried to fasten my seat belt, but the lock would not catch. We roared up the ramp at sixty miles an hour, seventy, eighty. The Romeo's engine strained.

"You're a nut case" Stuart said, forcing car after car to let him pass. "I'm through."

"Let me out," I screamed. "Stop the car." I grabbed Stuart's wrist and yanked his hand from the steering wheel. He looked at me and held up a bloody fist. For a second, I thought he might strike me. I shrank back and waited for a blow that did not come. Bridge lights shone through the windshield, and for the first time I had a clear look at Stuart's injuries. His knuckles were purple and bloody from their encounter with Jon Prioleau's teeth, and his face streaked with dried blood from the cut through his eyebrow. There was more blood on his sweater, collar, pants, and shoes. The gore added mightily to the impact of his rage. A stranger would have thought him insane. Perhaps he was temporarily, and I was the culprit who had driven him to it.

I pressed myself against the passenger door. Sea air rushed into the car as we flew over the bridge. I shivered from cold and shock, remembering mournfully my warm black sweater lying limp and forgotten on Isaac's bar. Stuart would not look at me. He stared ahead and drove as fast as the Romeo would allow. We catapulted from the Mount Pleasant incline onto Coleman Boulevard, airborne the first few feet. Not a policeman was in sight. Blurred streetlights and stoplights whizzed by. Cars veered right and left. There was a terrifying rush as the causeway to the island bridge appeared out of the night. In the tunneled glow of our headlights, the marsh road became a gray-white ribbon floating in silky darkness. It undulated above the enormous expanse of autumn marsh grass. Ben Sawyer's warning lights blinked red, yet we raced forward without caution. Stuart judged his timing to a divided half-second, then he jerked the car onto the bridge at the exact moment the guard rail started down. We slipped under, untouched. The Atlantic Ocean was now three blocks away, and Stuart had taken dead aim on it. I braced myself and closed my eyes when our tires thudded into the dunes. The Romeo lost momentum instantly. Her engine sputtered once before dying.

I opened my eyes. Somehow the car had spun around. I was now looking up the same road we had just roared down. I stared at it mute as my brain processed what had just happened, where we were, why. Bit by bit, I recognized familiar sounds – wind blowing in from the ocean, waves sliding along beach sand, a freighter's horn warning small craft of its approach. I looked at Stuart. He was leaning on the steering wheel, breathing in short gasps. I tried to get away, but my attempt was aborted when a click alerted him my fingers had pushed down the handle of the passenger door. He looked at me with fierce eyes.

"Don't move," he said. "You're going to sit here and listen while I tell you what I think of a woman who would dance with a weasel like Jon Prioleau. Trash…that's what I think, and so does everyone else. I should have decked you instead of him. I know what you did. You drank too many cups of that cheap wine and didn't eat anything, and your idiot brain went numb. Nothing new. You've been screwed up all your life."

Stuart's fury made me afraid, but not smart. I insulted him one more time. "Funny thing, you don't call me an idiot when you're depositing the checks I bring in."

"I'm sick of hearing that," he said. "I've made twice the money you have in the last six months, but you never acknowledge it. You're too busy waving your piddly little client checks under my nose. Drives me nuts. Lately, I catch myself trying to think of ways to avoid you, so I don't have to hear your complaining. That's stupid. I'm supposed to be building a business, for us together, developing a stable of clients, making new contacts, not wasting my time and energy coddling a neurotic wife."

"What am I supposed to do, Stuart? Live on the bark of trees? You want me to starve supporting your stupid dreams?"

"I'm not sure they're mine anymore. I think they're all yours. I wish your demented aunt were still alive. I'd like to ask her a few questions about that family thing you blame everything on. Maybe she could tell me why you're such a mental case. You are, you know. And it's out in the open now, or you wouldn't have put on a show with a maggot like Jon Prioleau."

"You're jealous," I screeched. "That's what this is about, 'cause I got sloshed and danced with the town lecher. I wish the town fool had been there, and the pervert and murderer and rapist. I'd have danced with all of them. There wasn't anything else to do. Who knows where you were?"

"Oh, I was mingling like a regular good old boy so maybe we could keep our jobs. Could have saved myself the trouble if I'd known you were working the other side of the athletic field to get us fired. And it's not just the jobs that'll go down with this. It's the connections, referrals, everything."

"If you think this rotten place is everything, we should have thrown in the towel a long time ago. I hope you didn't seriously think we could get a real business going in this backward little time capsule."

"You're like every other woman I've ever known. No sense of process, interrelationships, nothing. No, I never thought we could establish a business here exclusively. Most things we've done were to buy time, get experience, earn a few credentials that we could parlay into bigger projects in bigger towns down the road. But it's over now and all your fault."

"I don't have to listen to this. I'm getting out."

"No, you're not."

"You can't stop me." I dodged his grasp and opened the car door. He jumped out and ran around to my side. There was no struggle. He pushed me back into the car and told me he would twist my arm if I tried to escape.

"You're going to listen," he said. "For once, you're going to listen instead of running your own big mouth."

I tried to get around him. He dropped to his knees by the car and clamped my wrists in his hands. "Look at me," he growled, jerking me forward, forcing me to obey. Our eyes were on an even plane. "That business at the oyster roast means we'll both be thrown out of Southern Prep. Do you understand what your arrogance has caused now?"

"Stop…you're the one who started the brawl."

"No, I'm the one who finished it. You started it. Everyone was raising their eyebrows at you, rubbing yourself all over that sleazy creep."

I pulled a hand away and tried to slap him. He stopped me the same way he stopped Jon Prioleau.

"Oh, no, precious darling girl," he said. "Old Stuart's tired of being slugged. And he's more than tired of a schizoid woman dumping all her problems on him, all that junk about your long-lost mother and father, most of which I don't believe."

"You said you were leaving...go."

"And when I do, who'll be your goat then? It won't be me anymore. It won't be your aunt. You finished her off years ago. Probably wore her out and left her in a ditch somewhere. I'm worn out myself. And another thing, I can't help wondering why I have to worry myself sick about coming up with rent and grocery money every month when you've got three hundred bucks stashed in your purse. I found it yesterday. How much more do you have squirreled away? And where're you getting it? Dumbass Stuart would like to know."

I looked into his eyes. They were shining with the hard glitter of hatred. So...I was not the only one who had been visited by the beast. "Do you hear me, you little liar?" Stuart yelled. "Where did you get the money?"

I couldn't answer. He squeezed my arm. "Where?" he said again.

"Stop, please," I cried out. "Mr. Pinckney gave it to me."

"What? Pinckney pays you in checks."

"Tips, sometimes he gives me tips. I would have told you, but I wanted to surprise you. I was saving it in case we had an emergency."

"Liar. You've been hoarding it while you watched me scrounge for rent money. You let me bounce a check to the grocery store last month."

"I should have turned it over, and I would have. But you're so good at figuring things out. I knew you'd get us through."

"Maybe you were stockpiling it for a bail-out. Maybe you're planning to leave."

"No, no," I said. "I was afraid of running out of cash. We've been through that so many times before."

He looked at me in a strange way, as if not sure who I was. I thought he was going to ask about the pills, that he'd found my hiding place in the storeroom under the porch and was about to confront my habit.

"Why would Pinckney give you extra cash?" he said. "Is something going on I don't know about?"

"Nothing. I've never done anything for Mr. Pinckney except work on his project. I'm sorry about the money. If I ever get another dime, you can have it."

"You don't have to share money or anything else with me, not ever again," he said in a voice unnaturally soft. Which frightened me more than the shouting. He let go of my wrists and stood up. There was a sense of finality in his movements. So here at last was the end, the extinguishing of the flame, the death of the relationship. My emotions marshaled to save it, though instinct told me it was too late.

"It's over," he said, fumbling in his pants pocket. He pulled out a thin roll of folding money. "Here's a little more cash to go with your fat tip from Pinckney. I'll keep fifty to get by, and you'll still have Peregrine and Pinckney checks to count on for a while. Maybe you can get a real job by the time their projects run out. If you can't, I'll help until you do. The keys are in the ignition. Take it easy when you pull out of this sand."

"Please, Stuart..." I could not go on. Tears choked my vocal cords. Stuart remained unmoved. He leaned over and brushed away the sand that clung in wet clumps to his pant legs.

"I'm going to the cottage to pack a bag," he said. "Give me a few minutes. Don't come in causing more trouble. I'll be back tomorrow to pick up the rest of my stuff. And, Arlena, I want you to know, it wasn't the Pinckney thing that killed it, or the money, or that absurd business with Prioleau. It was the hatefulness, the pure and simple hatefulness you carry around in your insides. You went too far too many times. I'll be at the cottage. Don't barge in on me."

"But I want to go with you."

"It's too late for that. I'll walk home on the beach...don't want anyone to see me with all this blood on my clothes. Fifteen minutes...that's all I'm asking."

He turned and walked away. When I could no longer see his form in the darkness, I panicked and ran after him.

"Stuart, wait," I shouted, depleting the last of my strength. Once more, I tried calling out, but the words caught like thorns in my throat. My body stiffened as white hot pain tore through my insides. It stopped all conscious thought. I gagged and fell to my knees.

"Someone…help me," I sobbed to the moonless night. I raised my head one last time to look down the beach for Stuart, then I pitched forward into darkness.

17

I had never fainted before and did not know to stay prone after waking up. Twice I regained consciousness and tried to stand. Twice I passed out again. The third time there was no more getting up. Pain rolled in and out of my abdomen on waves of nausea. But somehow it did not matter. I was detached, separated from my agony by an interruption of brain function. After a time, I felt myself being pulled and lifted by hands I did not recognize. Faintly beyond a buzzing sound that roared in my ears like insects, I heard unintelligible voices, deep and low one second, high-pitched and fast the next. I could not tell if they were inside or outside my skull. Were they talking to me? Or yammering among themselves? I heard my name called distinctly. Opening my eyes for a milli-second, I saw a man's face an inch from my own.

"Don't go out again, Arlena," he said in overlapping metallic syllables. "Tell me where you hurt. I'm a doctor. I'm here to help you."

I closed my eyes to block out the spotlight shining from behind his head. Its glare pierced my eyeballs in painful, darting arcs. I could not focus.

"Hurt," I heard myself say in reverberating tones.

"Where?" the man asked, his words repeating in a hollow space in my head.

"My side," I said. He patted my hand and tried to get me to say more. Then he was gone, and I was gone, and there was nothing.

Deep in blackness I slept a dreamless sleep unencumbered by the processes of life. I existed nowhere and felt nothing. Infinity had rescued me. I wanted to float forever in that secure black vacuum. But life was not through with me. It forced its way back into my consciousness, reminding me who I was. Awareness returned in threads and wisps over hours of altered time. Millions of electrical impulses jumped back and forth across the neurons of my brain, stimulating my mind with impulses of fear. I did not want to wake up. I only wanted to drift.

Voices and visions called to me from the darkness. I fought their intrusion. For a while I was able to resist. But soon my brain betrayed me, swelling and bulging with familiar dreams that raged out of control. Then I saw it, the beast. It came at me with a jeweled axe and split open my skull, the two halves flying off into oblivion. One eye saw mile-high waterfalls, the other a wall of fire. There were two of me, eight of me, eight hundred of me, racing through space like eyeless zombies rushing to join ceremonies far more wicked than the desecration of one human soul. The sounds and colors and tastes of these visions flooded my body with pain. I'm certain if my skin were peeled back even today, its inside flaps would reveal enormous tattoos of other-world images inked into the remotest regions of my body.

For hours, days, I drifted between hallucination and reality. Nurses spoke to me in soothing tones, but I was not comforted. I forced my eyes open and realized I was bound to a white bed. I fought the restraints until the sheet under my back was wet with sweat. With strength born of fear, I pulled and tugged until my body would no longer respond. Exhausted, I lay still and prayed the beast would not return. Something touched my hand. I jerked away. Perhaps if I remained still, it would seek livelier game. Again my hand. This time I made a fist and pounded the bed. A voice called to me to keep still, a male voice, sweet and musical. Stuart had penetrated my terror.

"Can you hear me?" he said. I opened my eyes, but could not answer. Pain radiated from every pore.

"Hurt," I whispered.

"Your doctor said it would pass."

"I need medicine."

This time Stuart was silent, afraid of my rage. He was now the enemy, object of my rage. I hurled threats at him for withholding my pills. I screamed and begged to die. He stood beside me and deflected everything. Time and more time crawled by, dissipating my strength and will. But then in an unexpected moment, I awoke to a world that slid miraculously into place. I looked around a clean white room and focused on a curtainless window. Flowers and potted plants sat crowded on its sill. I continued my surveillance until my eyes met Stuart's. He did not speak, just stared. After a second, he leaned closer and whispered with apprehension, "Ready to go another round, tiger?"

"I'm hungry," I said. He looked at me another second, then laid his head on the bed and wept.

My hunger created a stir among the nurses. They examined me in turn, probed here and there, asked questions I could not answer. But Stuart did not push. He came to my bedside like a winged angel and fed me salted broth from a stone-white bowl. I was able to swallow several ounces before drowsiness overcame me, and I fell into an untroubled sleep.

When next I awoke, the wrist and ankle restraints were gone. I was overjoyed to be free, though still too weak to stand. Stuart returned with more broth which I sipped greedily through a straw. He grinned and said I looked rough. I dozed off in the middle of an effort to argue back.

Sleep and broth became my life, yet pain was a constant torment. The soreness in my abdomen and chest made me cry out at the slightest wrong move. It was worse when the dreams returned. There was nothing I could do upon rousing but lie still and concentrate on slow breaths. Gradually, after a time of sleeping and waking without the aid of pills, good times outnumbered the bad.

I knew where I was, but not why or how I got there. And Stuart, my one source of information, side-stepped every question.

"Let's walk," he said when he came to see me on the third evening I had been awake. Together, we spent five minutes figuring out how to maneuver my legs over the side of the bed without disturbing the six-inch incision below my navel. Stuart was more compassionate than the nurses. He helped me to the bathroom and back to bed without hurting me.

"I'm finished," I said, sinking back into the pillow.

"Today the bathroom, tomorrow High Battery," he quipped. "In a week, California. How's the big cut tonight?"

"A tyrant, won't let me move."

"Have you talked to the doctor yet?"

"No. He came in and checked me over earlier, but he wouldn't say a word. Guess that means you have to tell me."

"Tell you what?"

"Tell me, Stuart."

"Okay…you had a cyst on your right ovary that ruptured and bled into your abdominal cavity. There was poison and puss, and they had a heck of a time cleaning it up. You now have one ovary, one fallopian tube, and your uterus left. The infection is clearing up faster than they expected. But the worst is you lost so much blood, not to mention weight. I guess that's what cheeseburgers are for."

"Cheeseburgers? Do you have one...please?"

"Maybe," he said.

"Give it to me. I want it right now."

He disappeared into the hall and came back with a warm burger wrapped in foil. I moaned in ecstasy over the taste of broiled beef.

"I love you so much. This is the best."

"The nurses were against it," he said. "Didn't think you could handle junk food yet. Looks to me like you could handle a live steer. You should eat slower."

"I'm hungry. Dinner was hours ago. It must be eight or nine by now."

"Eight thirty to be exact, almost bedtime. Do you know what day it is?"

"I don't know what month it is."

"It's Tuesday."

"When am I going home?"

"In a week or so, maybe."

"How long have I been here?"

"Four weeks."

I stretched my eyes wide. "My aunt had a hysterectomy – I remember it – and she was in the hospital two days. What do you mean, four weeks?"

"I don't know why it was so hard on you. A ruptured cyst must be bad. And it got worse when you ripped your stitches out and had to go back to surgery."

For a moment neither of us spoke. Stuart avoided my eyes. After an awkward silence, he said, "But I guess it was the other thing that stretched it out." He was still unable to look at me.

"What other thing?"

"The drug thing, all those pills you'd been taking. It took a while to get your body cleaned out – detoxed, they called it."

Again, I was speechless. Stuart tried to explain, his nervousness apparent. "Everything went haywire after your surgery. Nothing helped. The nurses said you looked like you were going through withdrawal. They kept asking me what medications you were on. I brought some of your pill bottles from home. They sent me back to see if there were more. That's when I started finding them, everywhere, all over the cottage, upstairs, downstairs…Darvon, Valium, Percodan, twenty or thirty empty bottles. When I brought them to the hospital, everyone freaked. Some bottles were dated as far back as a year. They had doctors' names on them I didn't recognize. It took a day or two to figure it all out, and by then, you were already in la-la-land, coming off the stuff cold turkey. I've never seen anyone that sick. It was awful. There were times I thought you might…"

His voice broke on the last few words. He wiped away a tear.

"I'm sorry," I said, now groggy.

He patted my shoulder. "It's over. Get some sleep. We'll talk again in the morning."

⌘ ⌘ ⌘

Dreams continued to haunt me. Three times that night I awoke, terrified and exhausted. Three times the nurses brought in cold packs for my neck and fruit juice over ice to drink. They said not to worry, that I was doing great considering all I'd been through. I asked for something to kill the pain in my muscles, but Tylenol was the best they could offer. No one mentioned the pill bottles Stuart had found. No one mentioned addiction. I gave up trying to communicate with the nurses and concentrated on eating. Had I realized how emaciated I was, I would have understood my preoccupation with food. I would also have known my loss of strength was not from surgery, but from starving almost a month.

"I look anorexic," I said to Stuart the next morning.

"Let's just say it's a good thing I like my women skinny. Let me help you up. Dr. Merritt says you need to walk."

"Who's Dr. Merritt?" I asked as we crept along the corridor.

"The one who figured out you were hooked on Percodan, right after he figured out you were hooked on Valium and Darvon. He began to suspect something the day after your second surgery. You didn't come out of the anesthesia right. Fought everyone. The nurses couldn't do a thing with you. They panicked and called him in from his golf game. When he tried to examine you, you snatched his glasses off and gave him a black eye. And I don't mean a little one. I mean one that made his eye swell shut. It took three stitches to sew his eyebrow back together. That's when they restrained you and told me not to get close enough to get bitten."

"I have to go back to bed…can't hear anymore of this."

"Want me to carry you?"

"It'll hurt too much."

We shuffled back to 205 where my beautiful bed awaited. "I'm amazed how weak you are," he said. "Four days ago you were threatening the lives of the whole hospital staff."

"Stop," I said, eyes closed, aware again of hunger. "Could you get me some crackers from a vending machine? My stomach is growling."

"I forgot. I brought you a Butterfinger."

My sleepy eyes became alert. I grabbed the candy bar from Stuart's outstretched hand and unwrapped it tenderly. "It's gorgeous. I love you."

"Funny how you love me best when you're stuffing your face. So right after you slugged Dr. Merritt, they tied your wrists. But you were still floundering around so much, you pulled out more of your stitches, and everyone went nuts again. The nurses said you could hemorrhage if you kept tearing your incision open. They strapped you tighter. The only thing they didn't do was gag you, which would have been a good idea. You were wild, yelling and screaming like a banshee. Didn't sound like yourself, didn't look like yourself. I can't believe you went through all that and don't remember it."

"I remember the dreams."

"What dreams?"

"Bad ones."

Stuart looked disturbed. "The doctor said Percodan was dangerous…you could have nightmares for years, the rest of your life maybe. Are they getting any better?"

"When I'm eating."

"One-track mind, for sure. Why were you taking all that stuff, Arly? Dr. Merritt was amazed you could still function."

"My side hurt…I was anxious."

"Okay, your side is fixed, and you're off all the junk. Everything is great. The doctor says people who get hooked on painkillers because of physical problems aren't the same as those who use them for joyrides. He thinks you'll be all right now that the bad ovary is out."

"Stuart, you said were going to leave me. Why didn't you?"

"I don't know. Guess I forgot about it when you ended up in the hospital. Maybe I love you…can't live without you."

"I'm still sick, Stu."

"I know, but you're getting stronger every day. I can see it in your eyes."

⌘ ⌘ ⌘

The work of healing was difficult. I ate and slept like I might never get the opportunity to do either again. Nurses encouraged me to walk the drab hospital halls several times a day. Stuart came to see me morning and night. He encouraged, helped, cajoled, negotiated, and teased me into staying focused.

"I've never known anyone like you," he said the fifth morning I'd been up. "You're the Madonna herself, so frail and thin and pale, but you eat like a great white shark."

"I'm hungry," I said for the hundredth time.

Stuart feigned nervousness. "Anymore, I'm afraid to come in here without food and drink. Some days I've considered tossing in a piece of raw meat and running for my life."

"Stop harassing me. Talk about something else."

"Okay, your highness. You'll be gratified to learn the time has come for the presentation of flowers and cards. Hold your applause, please."

"Forget the cards. I've already read them. Bring on the flowers. Bring up the music."

"Certainly, madam. We have here a begonia from the granddam of Old Charleston, Miss Fanny Peregrine. And here, a sensible potted plant from my concerned parents. That about does it for tasteful remembrances. The rest of these gaudy arrangements arrived day-by-day from Grayson Lockwood Pinckney. Six gargantuan baskets all equal in ostentation. I think he's trying to express his gratitude for inciting your husband to riot. I separated Jonathan Prioleau from his front teeth, you may recall, on the night of the fateful oyster roast. If we are to believe Mr. Pinckney, he has been longing to do just that for many a frustrated year. As I speak, he's nullifying a lawsuit filed against me by Prioleau. He accused me of assault, the cad. What vindictiveness. I'm outraged."

Stuart placed a hand over his heart and bowed. I clapped. "Thespis himself," I said. "But what do you mean, lawsuit? Are we in trouble?"

"Not anymore, thanks to Mr. Pinckney. But for a while, Prioleau was threatening to wade into me in court like he waded into me on the dance floor. He isn't very graceful, I've noticed. I think he should consider ballroom lessons."

"Yeah, maybe the two of you could get in the same class. How did Mr. Pinckney stop him?"

"Don't know. He called me at home a week after our night-of-nights and told me to be careful, that his son-in-law was on the warpath. But you were so sick, I didn't care what his son-in-law did. The next day a guy brought some of those long blue papers out to the beach cottage, and it looked like old Stuart was going up the road. Mr. Pinckney called again and said he'd see to it I wouldn't be charged. He told me to keep my mouth shut and forget it ever happened. I didn't know the guy had so much pull."

"Mr. Pinckney has the pull to make Jon Prioleau kiss a cobra," I said. "Probably makes him do it every morning."

18

It soon became apparent that docility in a recently reformed addict is interpreted as great progress. I became exceedingly docile. I applied pink blush to sallow cheeks and saffron neck, massaged glycerin into peeling hands and lips, worked conditioner into brittle hair. The nurses said I was beginning to look almost normal. Stuart asked for one thing – cooperation. I gave him slavish subjugation. New to power, he became a dictator. If I would follow his every order, I'd be well in a few weeks, or so he said. I had a thought or two of my own on the subject, but I decided to keep my opinions to myself until the timing was right. Declarations of independence could wait.

Night terrors did not go away. They continued to appear without warning or identifiable cause. The beast had been forced beneath the surface. I could no longer hear him distinctly, yet he still came to me in the night. I began to realize I'd never be totally free, that my personality would have macabre overtones in harmony with the beast all the rest of my days. Stuart was my only sanity.

Dear Stuart, who lived in light and mingled with light and was part of light. The purity of his soul was my lifeline to light, my clean generative lifeline. I chose not to tell him about the beast. I did not wish to compromise the loveliness of his spirit.

The day before I was to go home, if by a stretch one could call a dilapidated beach cottage with overdue rent a proper home, I breached a solemn promise. It happened early in the afternoon, a time when doctors were absent, nurses distracted, and ordinary visitors elsewhere. It was the time chosen by Raven FitzSimons to slip into my room.

"How'd you get by the nurses?" I said, amused by her guile. I was aware Stuart had told her I was not ready to have visitors.

"Sneaked by their station in the hall…when they weren't looking," she whispered.

"It's two thirty. You're supposed to be in school."

"I'm cutting. And you can't say a thing. You're supposed to be teaching our writing class."

"I'm sick. And stop whispering. No one cares if you come in here as long as I don't get upset."

"Oh, my gosh, Mrs. Prince. You look like heck."

"Thanks…I just spent half an hour putting on makeup and brushing my hair. You and Stuart should get together, work on some new lines."

"How much do you weigh?"

"I don't know. This place isn't a health spa. We don't weigh in every day."

"I think you're anorexic."

"No wonder Stuart wouldn't let you visit me. He was afraid you night cheer me up too much. Sit here on the bed and talk to me. You look like you might sprint."

"What's maudlin?"

"I don't know…sappy, sad. Why?"

"Stuart said you couldn't have visitors yet. He said I could see you in a few days, and when I did, I shouldn't be maudlin. I didn't know what he meant. But now I think I'm going to be maudlin anyway."

"You mean you're going to cry?"

"Yes."

"Come over here and bawl your eyes out. Stuart doesn't know females are born maudlin and can't help themselves."

Raven ran to the bed and hugged me until my incision rebelled. I yelped. She jumped back, put both hands over her mouth, and dissolved into tears. I motioned her to come close again so I could hold her while she wept.

"You need tissue," I said after a moment, pointing to the medical clutter on the bedside table. "Stuart says I've been through four dozen boxes. One more won't hurt. Let me see your face. Terrific, now we both look like heck." I handed her my bedside water cup. "Take a sip. It'll make you feel better."

"I didn't mean to cry," she said after a tiny drink. "I've needed someone to talk to so badly, and you've been sick forever, and they wouldn't let me see you. I slipped into the hallway a couple times…heard you yelling. It was awful."

"So everyone tells me. I'll be glad to get out of here…forget this ever happened."

"I wish Stuart had let me talk to you sooner. It might be too late now."

"For what?"

"To keep Dr. Legare from stirring up more trouble about your job at Southern Prep. I heard Mother on the phone with him last night. She told him to call Stanlock and have you fired. She wanted Stuart gone, too, but he'd already quit. Guess he had to after the fight at the oyster roast."

"Stuart didn't start that fight."

"Mother says he did, that he was humiliated by the way you were acting with Jon Prioleau's dad."

My hands drew into small white fists. I closed my eyes and breathed slowly, trying to stave off nausea. Raven stopped talking. After a few seconds, I relaxed my fingers and asked for my water cup back. At that precise moment, Stuart opened the door.

"What are you doing?" he said to Raven. "I told you…Arlena can't have visitors yet."

Raven's eyes became saucers. She thrust the cup at me, ran across the room, and flattened herself against the wall next to the window. "I'm sorry," she said, her voice a pizzicato violin. "Don't be mad. I'll leave."

Stuart looked at me and did not like what he saw. He turned back to Raven. "What do you plan to do? Jump out the window? I think the hall would be a better exit."

He followed Raven out of the room and closed the door behind them. When he returned, the flush on his neck belied his mild manner, and the perspiration at my temples belied my own. We carried on a conversation about nothing for ten minutes, which made me feel better. I was supposed to be getting out of the hospital the next day. It was obvious Stuart was worried about the prospect. I assured him everything would be all right…I would be all right. Twice, he told me he had cleaned the cottage, washed and dried the sheets, and stocked the refrigerator. The third time, I stopped him.

"I promise not to cause trouble. I'm afraid if I do, you'll leave me to croak by myself in the cottage. Dr. Merritt says I'll be as good as new in a few weeks."

"He doesn't know, not for sure."

"I can feel myself getting stronger, Stuart."

"We'll see how it goes when you get home."

"You can't put me off any longer. We have to talk…now"

"About what?"

"Things you've been avoiding."

"I don't know what you mean."

"I hate it when you act dumb. Makes me feel like slugging you."

"Have you forgotten what happened to the last dude who tried that? The newly gap-toothed Jon Prioleau?"

"Let's start there. Did you quit Southern Prep because of the fight?"

"How did you know I quit?"

"Raven told me."

"For a woman who's been stuck in the hospital a month, you know an awful lot."

"No thanks to you. But for your information, I remember most of what you told me the night I got sick. You said we were through in Charleston, that we were both going to be fired from Southern Prep and lose all our connections."

"I was furious…could have said anything. The truth is we were finished here months ago, way before that sorry little oyster roast and sorrier little fight. I don't know where I got the idea we could establish a client base in a provincial town like this. We never got to the point of making ends meet month to month, much less a profit."

"You sound like it's over."

"Not quite, but we do need a paradigm shift. That's what they called it in those English departmental meetings I slept through at Boston U."

"Does that include quitting your job?"

"First of all, we mustn't dignify the grunt work I was doing at Southern Prep by calling it a job. It was a half-baked, part-time consulting gig. All I did was write a few lousy brochures and dream up two or three fundraising schemes. Second, I had no choice but to quit. Those people can't afford a consultant. Half the board was against hiring me in the first place. And I proved them right when I clobbered a board member…not helpful."

"I didn't know Jonathan Prioleau was on the board."

"Oh, yeah, as of this fall. Seems you don't have to be competent to serve in certain, let us say, positions around here. Being associated with the right family is enough."

"So…you quit before they got organized enough to fire you."

"Had to, but the proper word is resigned. And I must say I did it with class. My letter to Grayson Pinckney reeked. I told him I was sincerely grateful to have had the opportunity to kiss the board members' behinds. It's probably one of the reasons he saved me from Prioleau's lawsuit, that and the fact you've become – what is it he calls you – his sweet summer rose? The man is suffering from delusions about you."

"And did you write a letter of resignation for me?"

"What?"

"Did you tell Mr. Pinckney I wouldn't be back to teach my writing class?"'

"No, I talked to Cliff Stanlock. He excused you from your duties for the rest of the semester due to your illness. But believe me, it's understood you won't be invited back. It's just as well. You weren't doing it for the money so much as to please Miss Peregrine and the hope of meeting new clients."

"She'll be disappointed."

"She'll get over it. Southern Prep is history."

"You talk as if everything were history."

"Not everything, not quite yet. I've still got a pile of stuff to write for Bill Martin. He's planning a spring promotion for his condo development on Kiawah. Thank goodness he's not from Old Charleston. Grew up next to Hell Hole Swamp in Berkeley County. Doesn't give a rat's pa-toot what people South of Broad think. All he wants is to sell condos to poor schmucks who come down here from the frozen north and become enamored of springtime in the Lowcountry. He doesn't tell them they'll die of mosquitoes and heatstroke come August."

"But what will we do with no jobs?"

"Nothing yet. You're going to park your beautiful fanny on Lucretia Middleton's porch and concentrate on getting your strength back, and I'm going to forage for grubs and berries."

"What about money? Medical bills? The hospital? We haven't had health insurance for years."

"And what about the meaning of life and religion and philosophy? Why don't we settle it all right here in 205 of smelly old Roper Hospital?"

"I get the message. I'll leave it alone another day or two, 'til I get a little stronger. You'll have to spill everything soon enough. One last question for now though…does Mr. Pinckney still want me to help him with his memoirs?"

"Sure, though he did mention he thought it would be ever so much nicer if you came back on your feet instead of a stretcher. The man wants you well, Arly, all the way well, before you start trying to work again."

"What about Miss Peregrine?"

Stuart did not answer. "Tell me," I said. "I hate it when you hold things back."

"Did Raven mention Miss Peregrine to you?"

"Yes," I lied.

"I intend to break that girl's upper-class neck. I'm sure Miss Peregrine will be all right."

"Has she been ill?"

Stuart looked pained. "She was, but I think she's better now. Mr. Pinckney told me she got sick around the same time you did."

"I'll call her tomorrow."

"Not yet, Arly. It might cause more trouble. A letter is waiting for you at the cottage. Its return address is Jeannette FitzSimons' office. You were out of your head when it arrived a couple weeks ago. I thought I should go ahead and open it to see if there was some problem. It's signed by Miss Peregrine, but I'm sure FitzSimons wrote it. Miss Peregrine was too ill at the time to write anything. At any rate, it says she no longer needs your services; her health is getting worse; she can't go on with her memoirs; she's tired and ill."

"I don't believe Miss Peregrine told Jeannette FitzSimons to write anything of the kind."

"Doesn't matter. Face it, dollface. You've been canned."

19

I had forgotten autumn, its annual taming of summer's brilliant light, its graceful transition from September's shimmering whiteness to unmuted hues of October. This was the light that clarified Lowcountry air the day Stuart drove me home from the hospital. It sharpened the outline of every cloud and leaf and blade of grass. It tempered autumn's chill with solar heat. There was nothing suggestive about the light...no blurred edges, auras, insinuations of dimensions unseen, no odd movements, shadows, or flickerings. As I absorbed its beauty, my spirit began to heal in the same rhythm as my body.

Stuart arranged everything to make my homecoming easy. I looked at the harbor's blue expanse as we drove over the great bridge from downtown Charleston to Mount Pleasant and thought of the reckless crossing we had made the night of the oyster roast. Today Stuart drove slowly, taking care not to jar my incision as he maneuvered through traffic. I held a pillow against my abdomen for security. On the marsh road to the narrow bridge connecting

Mount Pleasant to Sullivan's, I picked up the odor of pluff mud. Low tide. Waves of seagrass, newly tannic, rippled in a cold sea breeze. A flock of blackbirds moved south over the marsh so low that I heard wingbeats. Their flight had special urgency, for even the semi-tropical winter of Sullivan's would not be warm enough to sustain them until spring. From the crest of the Ben Sawyer Bridge, I gazed down the alley of the Intracoastal. Sea birds and white sailboats turned the horizon into evolving artwork. My eyes filled with tears. Stuart became alarmed when he saw me weeping. I reassured him with emotional little phrases – "I'm all right; my tears are for happiness; I'm thankful to be getting well."

As he turned his attention back to driving. I talked him into a swing around Harbor Point and begged to watch the fifteen-minute approach of a Caribbean cruise vessel. It reminded me of my and Miss Peregrine's nostalgic afternoon on the island. Stuart exercised his hard-won position as Commander in Chief by denying my request to visit Breach Inlet. I did not resist. I was too tired. On arriving at the cottage, he carried me like a bride up the back stairs to the porch. The slat swing and flowerpots welcomed me. Stuart had promised I could relax on the porch as many weeks as I needed, liked a cloistered nun praying in the holy presence of ocean, beach, and dunes. That quiet time of healing will always stand apart in my mind, like a scene embroidered in vivid colors on a length of watered silk. It is a lush memory in which Stuart is always young and handsome, and I'm always blooming with the colors of renewed health. It was a time of falling in love with my husband again, of noticing and appreciating his patience, thoughtfulness, his willingness to lay bare his heart with ardent declarations of love. I rewarded him by gobbling up his attention like a hungry little caterpillar preparing for its own natural miracle. It took but a few weeks for my metamorphosis to be complete, when a lowly creature once confined to crawling on its belly suddenly attained the ability to fly.

Settling me into a cushioned porch chair, Stuart said, "That, my waif, was the first time you entered the doors of the cottage without testing the strength of the pilings." He observed my stiff posture and decided I was uncomfortable.

"I must fetch the royal footstool. The queen needs to elevate her feet." He disappeared into the living room and brought out a wobbly coffee table.

"Lucretia Middleton would die if she saw how we abuse her furniture," I said. "She told me when we moved in here this table is over fifty years old, a sacred relic."

"And looks every day of it. Here, let me put a pillow under your legs. Oh, no, it's been over an hour since you last ate. I have to prepare something quickly."

"Stop making fun of me."

"How about homemade chicken pie from Mama Chloe's and sliced tomatoes from Charley Poulnot's vegetable truck? He stopped by yesterday, said he was getting ready to close down for the winter, maybe for good. Peddling vegetables must not be as profitable as it used to be."

Stuart bustled into the kitchen while I savored the view. It had not changed. Equal parts of sky and ocean accentuated the fluffy whiteness of clouds and breakers. Foam-fringed waves flattened fresh upon tawny sand, paused, slid back again – gliding silk – into a cerulean sea. I thought about the rust stain of autumn in the marsh grass on Sullivan's back beach. Was the Atlantic taking on autumn colors as well? I had spent long days during the summer months watching it turn every shade in the spectrum, from sultry lavender to simmering vermilion, depending on the time of day, position of the sun, cloud cover, even the humidity in Lowcountry air. I dreaded the approach of the ocean's gray dress of winter.

Stuart fed me lunch and reminded me he had an appointment with Bill Martin in Mount Pleasant. I said I would be fine, that I'd nap while he was gone. He settled me in bed and opened the windows. No more canned air blown through hospital vents. I tilted my head back and inhaled as far as my incision would allow. Exhaling slowly, I fell asleep. No dreams disturbed me. Two hours later I woke up refreshed and calm to the peace of the cottage in autumn. The house was silent. Stuart had not come home yet. Disconnected thoughts formed and dissolved in my mind. They drifted one to another and did not become disturbing until I came to the remembrance of money, or lack thereof. I recalled Stuart telling me about the letter from Jeannette FitzSimons. It rekindled my old anger against her that had lain dormant the long weeks of my hospital stay. After stewing about it another five minutes, I did something stupid that would have made Stuart furious.

I picked up the phone from the night table and balanced it on a pillow. Miss Peregrine's number, I thought. I've forgotten it. I called information and remembered the number as soon as the computer voice repeated it. My nerves fluttered as I keyed it in. One ring, two, three, four, five, too many for politeness. I did not hang up. Six, seven, eight. On the ninth ring, Tycie answered.

"Peregrine residence," she said in her Edisto accent.

"Hello, Tycie. This is Arlena. How have you been?"

"Lord have mercy, Missy Arlena, you best hang up. Missy Peregrine is bad off sick, and the folks who mind her business are swarming 'round here like bees."

"May I speak with her?"

"She's too weak. One day she feels good, the next, I think she might go on to heaven. It's the way things been going around here. Never know what to expect."

I bit my lip. "Is Louisa there?"

"Yes'm, but you can't talk to her, neither. You can't talk to nobody. None of'em wants to hear from you. Been running you down something awful."

"But why? I don't understand."

"Missy FitzSimons says you're on dope; Missy Louisa calls you white trash."

"And what do you think, Tycie?"

"It don't matter what Tycie thinks. I have to go now. And don't call back. Missy Jeannette comes snooping around every day, answering the phone, plundering, ordering me about. She's worse than that ugly cousin, Louisa."

"I'll figure something out. You take care of Miss Peregrine and yourself."

"I will, and I'm gonna start by saying goodbye."

I closed my eyes in frustration when I heard Tycie's receiver click. It was final. No use calling back. I was still turning the conversation over in my mind when something bumped on the porch. Shoving the phone onto the night table, I lay back in bed like a good sick person. Another bump. I held my breath. It was difficult to see into the sitting room. Stuart had closed the blinds to darken the house, "so you can rest," he had said. Only one small corner of the room remained visible from the bed. I peered at it and saw a figure move through the darkness.

"Raven, you scared me," I breathed on realizing who it was. "Why were you sneaking around like that?"

The jittery girl darted into the bedroom and closed the door behind her. "Hiding from Stuart," she said. "He isn't here, is he? I figured he must be gone since the car isn't downstairs. I wanted to see you, but he got so mad at me at the hospital, I was almost afraid to come here."

"But not too afraid. Stop with the silliness."

She grinned like an imp, already tired of her own game. "I'm not silly," she said with a toss of her head. "I'm grown up. Croom thinks so if you know what I mean. And I never listen to adults, especially bossy ones like Stuart."

"Great...attack my husband now. Pretty soon you'll have everyone against you."

"I'll grow up to be like you. Mother says everyone in Charleston hates Arlena Prince."

A twitch took control of my cheek. I had to lie back and breathe slowly to keep from losing my temper. Raven noticed my struggle. "Wow, you still look awful. Do you think you'll ever get over this?"

My eyes popped open. I stared at her perfect face and felt old and wasted. "Yes, I will," I said evenly, "and when I do, I intend to drag you down to a pluff mud flat and rub your beautiful nose in it." I lay back again to breathe.

"You won't be able to," she said. "By the time you get strong enough, I'll be too fat."

"What?"

"I think I'm pregnant."

I rolled my eyes and wished I were back in the hospital where this sort of thing did not happen. Again, I looked at the girl before me. She was no longer smiling.

"Why do you say things like that? It isn't funny."

"My period is a week late. I'm scared...don't know what to do."

"Have you seen a doctor? Had a test?"

"I already know. I'm psychic, remember?" Her voice broke, and she began crying a disturbed little cry. I felt very much like joining her.

"You have to tell your mother," I said, voice trembling. "I'll tell her myself if you don't"

Raven's body locked in the middle of a sob. "You can't…please."

I was about to try logic again, but my words were cut short by a familiar rumble. The Romeo was coming up the drive. "It's Stuart," Raven said. "I have to go. Don't dare tell him I was here. He'd kill me."

"Call me," I said to her slender back as she ran through the sitting room toward the back porch. "Call tomorrow."

At the same moment Raven faded into the shadows of the sitting room, Stuart began his climb up the street-side stairs. I counted the seconds in my head. At thirteen, he entered the kitchen door. At seventeen, he poked his head into the bedroom.

"Hi," I said sweetly.

"Hello there. How're things in sick bay?"

"Fine," I said, smiling an artificial smile. "Things couldn't be better."

20

On Thursday at ten A.M., two days after Raven announced she might be pregnant, she returned to the cottage to confound me again.

"Guess what," she said while climbing the back steps to the porch as casually if she might have been gone on a ten-minute errand instead of two whole days. "I'm not preggie after all. Grandma Moses arrived a week and a half late. You look great today, Mrs. Prince. Stuart must be a good nurse."

I unlatched the screened door and pulled her inside. "How could you do that to me, Raven? Why didn't you stay in touch? I called your house six or seven times, scared to death your mother might pick up. I'm so mad at you I could scream."

"Isn't life stupid?" she said, flopping into a misshapen wicker chair. "You can't call me 'cause of Mother, and I can't call you 'cause of Stuart. How long is he going to be gone? I saw him leaving a minute ago?"

"You were spying?"

"Why shouldn't I? He's awful to me. You saw how he treated me the day I sneaked into your room at the hospital. Said he'd call my mother if I bothered you again."

"He didn't mean it...just trying to protect me. Now that I'm better, he'd like you to come visit me once in a while...but after school, not during. You have to stop cutting classes. Tell you what, if you promise to stop cutting, I'll help you make peace with Stuart."

"Yeah, sure, and I'll help you make peace with Mother, which we both know will never happen. If she had her way, I'd never see you again."

"Maybe she's right. No sense borrowing trouble."

"If I gave in to her on every little thing, she'd turn me over to a psychiatrist and let him pick my brain like seagulls pick blue crabs. She'd try to force me to become a proper virgin debutante, as if it weren't a bit late for that, the virgin part, I mean. She thinks my attitude toward the season stinks."

"Season?"

"Winter social season. She's getting a real bang out of my being a deb. I'm her ticket back into society. Isn't that a hoot? She bought me five new gowns last week. Won't buy a cheap pair of shoes for herself, but I can have five expensive gowns. And that's not all. She's going around apologizing to everyone because they aren't handmade. I hate it. It's like she's getting me ready for sacrifice or something. That's what they did with virgins a long time ago. Mother is trying to attract some well-off law school grad to support me. Only it won't work. I'm no virgin. Wouldn't she die if she knew I almost got myself pregnant?"

She covered her mouth to muffle her giggles. I laughed with her, though it was a sick joke that made me uncomfortable. Raven was too young to be cynical.

"You're mixed up on one point," I said. "The dangerous person in your life is Croom, Jr., not your mom. From what you've told me, I don't think he'd help you with anything, particularly not something serious like figuring out what to do about a baby. He doesn't care if you get hurt. He's too young to care."

"I'll get birth control pills. That'll fix everything."

"Call me old fashioned, Rav, but somehow I don't think you're ready. Please, talk to your mother. I know she would tell you the same thing. These are decisions that could affect the rest of your life, not simple things like what dress to wear to what party. Your mother would be frantic if she knew you were taking chances with Croom. What did he say when you thought you were in trouble? Did he try to help you?"

"I never told him."

"Yes, and I know why. You were afraid he'd run out on you."

"Yep, Croom would sprint all right. Couldn't handle a knocked-up girlfriend."

"He's a boy…too young. You can't expect him to know how to deal with something like that. There comes a time in every girl's life when she has to take responsibility for herself."

"Oh, no, not the when-are-you-going-to-grow-up lecture. I refuse to discuss this one more minute. If we can't talk about something else, I'm leaving."

"You just got here. Anyway, I'm ready to drop it. I want to ask you something else. Tell me what's going on with Miss Peregrine. Tycie says she's sick."

"I don't know much. Mother's been going over there a bunch… says Miss Peregrine is senile now…her body is wearing out."

"I've called Peregrine House every day since I got home from the hospital," I said, "and every time I call, Tycie answers and says Miss Peregrine might die any minute. She never lets me talk to her."

"You could try the other housekeeper, the nutty one, but it probably wouldn't do any good. Mother says she's wacko. Maybe you should write a private note. I could deliver it to Miss Peregrine on the sly."

"And why would I want to do that?"

"What are you, dumb? Those buzzards at Peregrine House are total snots who hate your total guts."

It was risky. I knew it even as I reached for a pen. Yet I wrote the note and handed it to Raven, who read it aloud as if auditioning for a part in a bad movie:

Dear Miss Peregrine,

Thank you for the beautiful plant you sent to me at the hospital. It made me feel much better. I plan to come see you as soon as I'm strong enough, maybe in a week or two. My surgery went well. Doctors say I'll be working again soon. Hope you're better as well. Tycie told me you've been ill. Thanks again for the plant. I miss you.

Arlena

Raven laughed and clapped her hands. She folded the note four times to make it small. This was the kind of game she loved.

"Leave Miss Peregrine alone if she's too sick" I said. "I don't want to do anything to upset her."

"I'm not stupid," she said. "I know more than you think. For instance, I know you and Stuart can't pay your hospital bill, and you won't be coming back to Southern Prep this semester, and…"

A male voice cut her off. Stuart had come in without Raven or me hearing him. "Look who's here," he said to the shocked girl. "Raven FitzSimons, mouth-of-the-south." I was surprised, Raven terrified. Her face went ashen. She rushed toward the door. Stuart took two long strides and blocked her. He stared into her eyes.

"Don't be in such a rush, gossip queen. I'm interested in where you get your information. And what's that paper you're hiding? Writing your info down now so you can remember details to blab elsewhere?"

"Stuart, don't," I said. "Raven and I were just chatting…girl talk."

He would not allow Raven to move. "She isn't supposed to be here," he said and continued to stare her down. "I told her to stay away until you had a chance to recover."

"But I am recovered. Look at me. I'm dressed and walking all over. Couldn't wait for you to get home so we could go out to the beach. Don't be hard on Raven. I told her you wouldn't mind if she came by."

"I don't like the way she talks. Dr. Merritt said you shouldn't get upset, and I come home to find the queenlet prep running off at the mouth about things none of her business."

"Let it go, Stu. It was nice to have someone to talk to. I get lonely by myself."

I touched him on the arm. He stiffened once more, then he relaxed and dropped his head. The confrontation was over. "Who cares?" he said. "I'm too beat to care."

He walked through the sitting room toward the kitchen. I motioned Raven to leave. "Come back whenever you want," I whispered. "Stuart isn't really that mad...just exhausted from stress."

Raven ran to me, gave me a hug, and left without a word. I tried to regulate my breathing before calling out to Stuart. "Hey, handsome, I'm in here all by myself. Where did you go...to the moon?"

"Kitchen," he called back. He sounded a fraction brighter. I was thankful for the improvement which got even better. "How would you like a pretend wine spritzer?" he said.

"No, the real thing."

He returned to the porch with a Budweiser for himself and club soda over ice for me. "Use your imagination," he said. "Thanks for sending brat-face home. I need your undivided a few minutes. I've been looking at the manuscript you helped Miss Peregrine write last year. How many publishers did you send it to?"

"Twenty."

"Twenty?"

"Maybe it was only ten. I've forgotten, what with being sick... the hospital..."

Stuart stared at me until I blinked. "You didn't send it to anyone, did you? Miss Peregrine gave you money for copying and postage, and you used it for pills instead, right?"

"I was in pain."

"I know. Let's not get into that again. Let's talk about the manuscript. Yesterday I took a second look at it while you were napping. It's pretty good. The problem is you never spent any time polishing it."

"So?"

"Now's the time. You're stuck here on the porch. You say you feel better. Shape it up, maybe sell it."

"I don't own but half. Miss Peregrine owns the rest."

"Half is better than nothing, and didn't you say she wants to see it in print more than anything?"

"Sure, but even if I got it in perfect shape, we don't have money for copying and postage, plus all the other hidden junk it takes to promote a writing project. *Tarnished Honor* is four hundred pages, big bucks for clean copies. And I have no idea how long editing would take."

"Don't worry about money. Just do the initial work. I've already put things in motion to get a regular job. But there's no reason both of us have to give up freelancing. You can work on something creative and let me bring in the bread and butter. I don't see that we have a choice. You're too weak to do anything else."

"You're going back to teaching?"

"Why not?"

"But you've tried so hard to build a consulting practice. It isn't fair to you to have to give up now."

"I'll get over it. Besides, self-actualization is way down on my Maslow list these days. Main priority is scrounging up money to get us out of this financial mess. Rent is the immediate concern. Mrs. Middleton told me this morning she wants us out of here by the weekend if we don't come up with a few hundred to go against our arrearage. She's been a real pain in the rear the last couple of weeks. I didn't mention it before. You were too sick to deal. But it's gotten so bad I can't keep it from you any longer. She says she doesn't want slow-paying druggies in her cottage, as if her husband wasn't the biggest drunk in Charleston. What I don't understand is how people in this town know every detail of our lives."

"I can't leave, Stuart. I'm not well enough."

"I'll take care of Lucretia. I just couldn't risk your being in the cottage alone any longer without knowing she's on the warpath. She could come out here any day demanding money."

"This is terrible," I said.

"Come on, Arly. You know you can count on me to get us through."

"I'm not trying to be difficult, Stuart, but I don't know any such thing."

⌘ ⌘ ⌘

It wasn't easy staying angry at Stuart, not after all he had done for me, but I managed for the next two hours. And just as I was about to forgive him, Raven complicated the moment by pushing open the screen door and thwacking Stuart on the back. She was so excited, she forgot she was supposed to be avoiding him.

Stuart made no effort to hide his disgust. "Don't you have anything better to do than harass the innocent?" he said when she shoved him aside to get to me.

"You can stop trying to intimidate me," she said. "I've decided it's stupid to let myself be jerked around by a loser like you. Get out of my way. I want to give this envelope to Mrs. Prince. It's full of money, lots of money. After Miss Peregrine read your note, Mrs. Prince, she asked me to deliver your back pay."

"What note?" Stuart said, red blotches spreading on his neck.

"Nothing," I broke in. "Raven ran a little errand for me. Delivered a get-well message to Miss Peregrine. I couldn't go out to buy a card so I wrote her a note instead."

"But why would you send it by a dumb teenager when I could have delivered it?" More red blotches.

"No reason. You've been so busy. Woh...look at all this cash. The envelope is stuffed."

"Fifteen hundred," Raven said. "I counted it out of a money pouch Miss Peregrine keeps under her mattress. She must have five or six thousand dollars under there. Told me not to tell anyone."

I handed the cash to Stuart and watched him finger it lovingly. He counted it hand to hand, fifteen one-hundred-dollar bills. Red blotches on his neck were still apparent, but the reason for them had changed. "And I have a letter from Miss Peregrine," Raven said. She paraphrased its contents in a series of phrases while Stuart stood by dumbstruck. "Arlena, darling...you missed your paycheck last month…here it is in cash…sorry it's late…can't wait to see you…call me soon. Love, Miss Peregrine."

"Is there anything you don't pry into?" Stuart said to the beaming Raven.

Her happy face turned angry. "You'd better be nice to me, creep," she said. "I brought the money, didn't I? And I noticed Miss Peregrine didn't put your name on the envelope. It's for Mrs. Prince."

I stopped her. I did not want to witness to Stuart strangling a young girl. "Rav, something isn't right about this note. It's not Miss Peregrine's handwriting…too steady."

"It's mine," Raven said with a self-satisfied smile. "Miss Peregrine dictated it to me. She was too tired to write it herself."

Stuart had finally had enough. "Raven, listen…Arlena and I appreciate your help, but don't you think you should be going home now? We'll try to think of something nice to do for you later, repay you for all the trouble you've gone to."

"I know when people are trying to get rid of me," she said.

"Don't take it like that. You can come back tomorrow after school. Arlena needs your help with a project. We'll try to pay you a little something to pitch in."

Raven looked pleased. For some reason, though she couldn't imagine what, Stuart had had been forced to stoop to asking for her help. She enjoyed her moment of power.

"I don't know. I might be busy. I'll try, though, since it's for Mrs. Prince."

"Thanks," Stuart said without sincerity. "Now off you go. Mother-dear will be wondering where you are."

Raven made a face and took her leave slowly. Stuart came close to losing his new-found patience. If she had hung around one more second, he would have lashed out at her again. When she was gone, he sat down next to me on the wicker sofa to go over a new plan.

"This is great," he said. "I can't believe Miss Peregrine came through. Gives us all kinds of wiggle room. We'll pay Lucretia five hundred against what we owe her – money always makes her feel better – and throw the rest at your project expenses and getting out job applications for me. Meanwhile, I'll keep plugging away on Bill Martin's condo promotion materials and finishing up my smaller projects. Even so, I'll have to beat the bushes for a loan. Those medical bills aren't going away."

"Who would lend us money?"

"My dad, maybe."

"How much do we owe?"

"Thousands. Worst screw-up of my life was letting our medical insurance go. I know it's why you didn't tell me how sick you were."

"I don't want to talk about it."

"Okay, we won't. What about *Tarnished Honor*...when can you start on it?"

"I hate this, Stuart. It isn't fair, your giving up your dream of a consulting business while I piddle around with a so-so manuscript."

"I'm not giving up anything but heartache. I'll have plenty of chances to do wonderful things in the English department of some grade B college."

"All right, but re-working a manuscript is no guarantee of selling it."

"Don't be negative. Write some letters. Find an agent. Have Raven run errands and help you proofread. Didn't you say she's a pretty good writer herself?"

"Yes."

"Then she ought to be able to help you. But right now, you need to call Miss Peregrine and thank her for sending the cash. She didn't have to. It's not as though you were on salary."

"Tycie will just answer and say she's sick. I don't want to call. I want to see Miss Peregrine in person."

"You shouldn't go back to Peregrine House. That letter from FitzSimons' office sounded final."

"Another guerilla warfare tactic to sack the Yankee ghostwriter. FitzSimons has been trying to get rid of me for months. Imagine her consternation when I survived major surgery. She must have been devastated. And it's all about money. Money, money, money. She's terrified Miss Peregrine might pay out a penny to anyone but herself. No wonder Raven hates her. Though Raven is indiscriminate. She hates everyone equally."

Stuart nodded agreement. "The girl is a boa constrictor."

21

I finished editing *Tarnished Honor* in less than three weeks. Raven made that possible by helping me afternoons. Stuart almost regretted calling her a boa. She worked for nothing, and the Friday she delivered the thrice-proofed manuscript to the beach cottage, I made a speech about appreciation and gave her my copy of *The Collected Poems of Sylvia Plath.*

"How long have you had this?" she gushed.

"Years. I thought I was Plath reincarnated."

"And you're giving it to me? And you don't want it back? It's mine to keep forever?"

"Why shouldn't I give you something personal? As sick as I've been, I may never have children of my own. But don't make me out a saint. I can always scare up other copies of Plath. People up north still read her."

"But not this copy. This is the one you had when you were a kid like me. You wrote margin notes on every page."

"A little older, maybe. I'm thirty now."

"Thanks, Mrs. Prince. I'll keep it 'til I die."

"Maybe you can give it to your own daughter if you ever have one."

Raven went silent. She dropped her head and clutched the book to her chest. At first I thought she was ill. I did not realize she was crying.

"What's the matter? Are you sick?"

"Yes, dying. I lied about starting my period. I'm pregnant. Took a home test this morning."

My skin turned to goose flesh under my clothes. "But you said..."

"Didn't you hear me? I lied."

"But that was three weeks ago. You were almost two weeks late. Three plus two, plus two more...you could be seven or eight weeks by now. Why haven't you told anyone, gotten help?"

"I thought it would go away. And now I wish I hadn't said anything to you. You'll probably call my mother. That's what you threatened last time."

"Hush, I can't think what to do." I stared at the stack of pages in my lap. I was waiting, hoping, for some sensible idea to formulate in my brain. When none came, I plowed forward without a plan. "Get the phone book," I said. "We have to look up a clinic, some sort of women's medical office. Do you have any money?"

"Seventy-three dollars. Is that enough for an abortion?"

"We're not talking abortion yet. We have to find out if you're really pregnant."

I looked in the Yellow Pages and found five clinics, all with large ads: pregnancy tests, family planning, pregnancy counseling, prevention of sexually transmitted diseases.

"Don't you have a family doctor? These ads look scary."

She laughed a humorless laugh. "Our family doctor is Croom's father. He'd have Mother on the phone before I got my clothes off for an exam."

"This is serious, Raven. It's asinine to make jokes."

"I'm not joking. I'm terrified."

"Okay, hand me the phone." I punched in the number of the first clinic – Femmes Clinique. The conversation was brief. How much for a pregnancy test? What does it involve? When can it be done? The woman said she was a nurse. She answered my questions clearly and concisely. I was satisfied. When I hung up, I tore off the top sheet of the note pad and handed it to Raven.

"This is all you need. The nurse said to bring a urine specimen in tomorrow morning. They open at seven. You won't have to miss school. She said they'd do the test immediately and you could wait for the results or call back later. And you don't have to give your name."

"What about after?"

"Maybe that will be the end of it, the test will come back negative. Let's hope your home kit was wrong."

Raven left the cottage clutching Sylvia Plath in one hand and the note with the clinic information in the other. I tried to put the situation out of my mind by busying myself with assembling mailing packages for *Tarnished Honor*. The week before, I had gone through my two-year-old copy of *Literary Market Place* and picked out names of ten literary agents. On checking them out with phone calls, I discovered one was no longer working, three nowhere to be found, and one dead of injuries from a subway mugging. (Welcome to NYC.) That left five. I knew I should have contacted them one at a time, but I ignored good form and prepared five large envelopes. After sealing and taping them up, I said two Hail Marys and three Our Fathers and slipped the envelopes into a large plastic bag to protect them from seaside dampness. My hope was that one reputable agent would see marketability in the sample chapter and ask to see more. One encouraging word and the other chapters could be mailed immediately.

When I finished with the packages, I went out to the porch to sit in the swing and worry about Raven. When Stuart came in, he mixed two cocktails and joined me.

"What's this?" I asked. "An inch? Half an inch?"

"A mini-liqueur," he said. "We don't want nightmares sneaking up on you again."

"The dreams have been gone for weeks, Stu. I haven't had one in..."

"Yeah, sure. That's why you cry out in your sleep every night." Stuart fixed a cool gaze on my face. I stared back without blinking.

"I'd like to propose a toast," I said, changing the subject. "To…" Stuart raised his glass and waited for me to finish. "…the mailing of *Tarnished Honor*."

"Salute," he responded and clinked my glass.

I sipped my small drink, savoring the taste of amaretto, wondering if I should mention Raven's latest travail, hating to spoil the moment, deciding not to.

"I got five packages ready to mail today. Will you have time to drop them off at the post office in the morning?"

"A labor of love. I'll send them off with my twenty-two job applications. You're not the only one giving the copy shop business."

I cringed when he mentioned the copy shop. I knew we didn't have money for expenditures like that.

Stuart looked worried. "Any chance Miss Peregrine might kick in a few more bucks?"

"No, Tycie is the one life-form I can get to answer the phone over there, and all she does is discourage me."

"I know, I know. I'm clutching at straws, trying to think of every angle. Let's see…five hundred due from Bill Martin, a couple hundred in cash. Who should we pay? Hospital? Rent? Doctor?"

"Shouldn't we get the car fixed?"

"Your guess is as good as mine. At this point, every decision is a judgment call."

I pulled my eyebrows together and thought hard. "Fix the car," I said. "Other things can wait."

"I'll take care of it tomorrow." He glanced outside and looked hopeful. "The breeze seems to be dying down. Let's go for a walk."

Stuart bundled me into two sweatshirts to brave the November air. As we trudged along the beach path, a cold wet wind pushed us along. It was definitely not dying down. Stuart led me toward the lighthouse. We had just found a pace when the wind shifted again and began blowing into our faces.

"We're the only people on the beach," I said.

"Only ones dumb enough," he answered. "Want to take a break…sit a few minutes in the dunes?"

"I'll freeze. Let's keep moving."

We pushed ahead. Once or twice. I jogged a step or two, which made Stuart laugh. "Come on," he said. "Let's get out of this hurricane. We can sit in the dunes and rest...contemplate the sea oats." He moved his eyebrows up and down lasciviously.

"I'm well, Stu, but not that well."

"Come on. I'll behave."

He pulled me down in the sand among the dunes and wrapped his arms around my shoulders. "Romantic," he said.

"Uncomfortable," I complained. He changed positions and patted my back. "Better now?"

"A little...but stop wiggling so much. We need to talk something over. I want you to repeat after me: Arlena is doing great."

"Arlena is doing great."

"She is totally recovered."

"She is totally recovered – except for having sex – she hasn't had sex yet."

"Stop that and listen: Arlena can go out tomorrow and visit Miss Peregrine and Mr. Pinckney."

"No way. Arlena is not that well."

"You thought I was well enough to work on that manuscript three weeks..."

"Shhh, somebody's talking over there."

Angry voices borne on the wind clacked among the dunes to our left. I listened a few seconds and jerked my head in recognition. "It's Raven and Croom," I whispered.

Stuart put a hand to his forehead. He knew the scene would be one more display of adolescent histrionics. "Be quiet...maybe they'll leave. I don't want to be bothered with nonsense today."

I nodded and sat still. The two teenagers' voices were muffled, blown about by the wind. Only a few clear sentences came through. Raven yelled out in hysterics, "I'm pregnant, Croom. Don't you understand? Pregnant!"

After that, we heard nothing but sobbing. Stuart stared at me. "Do you think she's serious?" he asked. When I did not respond, he looked deeper into my dark eyes where he picked up a signal I did not mean to send out. "Of course, she's serious," he said. "And like always you already knew."

22

I refused to talk to Stuart about Raven, and after a question or two he stopped pressing. In his own words, he "didn't care about the problems of a teenage floozy." Two more days passed before she came back to the cottage to tell me what had happened at the clinic.

"Raven," I said, holding open the screened door for the pale green girl to drag herself inside. "You promised to call me as soon as you got the test results. First, you drive me crazy telling me a bunch of junk, and then you don't call to let me know what's going on."

She sprawled the length of the porch swing and moaned like she was dying, which enraged me more.

"I had the stinking test at the stinking clinic two stinking days ago," she said. "Took some doing with Mother in my face every minute. Told her I had a seven A.M. emergency rehearsal for the drama club production and I absolutely had to go. Didn't make it to the clinic 'til seven thirty. A million girls were already there waiting at the door like criminals sentenced to the gas chamber. A nurse came out and gave us numbers and told us to line up in order in the reception area. We all got positives. Everyone came out bawling. I saw only one girl get a negative. She was bawling, too, but laughing at the same time. She had to be a negative. My own test showed up positive so fast the nurse looked at me like she thought I might start having contractions. I cried like everyone else and went straight to the drugstore and bought another home test kit to make sure the nurse wasn't wrong. She didn't look too smart to me. The home kit made a perfect little doughnut hole right in the middle of the test tube. No hope now. I'm done for."

"Are you sure?" I asked in desperation.

Raven did not answer. She looked at me as if I were a dolt.

"Only one thing left to do," I said.

"I know, an abortion. You can get them at the clinic for four hundred and seventy-five dollars. The nurse said they do them on Thursdays. Procedures, they call them. Wonder if you have to take a number?"

"That's not what I meant," I said. "You have to tell your mother. You shouldn't do anything drastic until you talk things over with her."

"I can't. She'll freak. But you don't have to worry anymore. I've decided to stop coming out here with all my problems. But there's one important thing left to say, and I mean it more than I ever meant anything in my whole horrible life. If you call my mother and tell her, I'll run away and never come back. No one will ever know what happened to me. And it'll all be your fault."

"I don't know, Raven."

"You'd better think it over before you go blabbing, Mrs. Prince. I don't have anything to lose. It won't be long before they expel me from school. And yesterday Croom told me he doesn't love me and never did, and now you might rat on me to Mother."

"I won't say a word, not unless you tell me it's okay. But don't cut yourself off from me. The last thing you need is to feel alone right now. Call me every day until you decide what to do."

"I will, promise. But I have to go now. Got a couple of afternoon classes I can't cut anymore or else. How's that for insanity?"

"Call me, Rav."

"Sure, every day."

I checked my watch as her red MG sputtered out of the cottage drive. Quarter of ten. Stuart would be back in fifteen minutes. I walked into the sitting room to call Peregrine House determined not to let Raven's never-ending troubles dominate another of my mornings. Earlier I had decided to put a small plan into action. And Stuart, though he did not know it yet, was going to be my accomplice. As soon as he came in from his appointment with Bill Martin, I intended to wheedle him into driving me to Peregrine House. That part of the plan I knew I could pull off. I wished I could get Tycie's help so easily.

She answered the phone on the third ring and tried again to get rid of me. But this time to my everlasting surprise and relief, Miss Peregrine came on the line and began shouting at Tycie to get off the phone. It was the first time I'd heard my old friend's voice since both our illnesses, and to my relief, it sounded strong.

"Hang up, Tycie," she commanded again. "I want to talk to Miss Arlena without anyone listening in."

"Miss Peregrine, is it really you?" I said.

"Of course, it's me, you ninny. Where in thunder have you been? I've not heard from you in weeks except for that pitiful little note."

"On Sullivan's recuperating, and I'm way better now. Stuart is going to drive me into town this afternoon. Is it all right if I come by for a visit?"

"Yes, they've left me to myself for a change. I told them all to get out...I needed room to breathe."

"Does it matter what time?"

"As early as possible. I want to see you. I've missed you frightfully."

"Me, too, you..." But my words died away. She had already hung up.

Stuart was back by five of ten. I met him at the end of the driveway. "How long have you been out here?" he said. "You could get chilled?"

"Stop fussing over me, Stu. You said you'd be home by ten, and since you've never been late for anything in your life, I knew you'd get here at this exact moment. Now hurry. Miss Peregrine said I could see her today."

"You're not well enough. We already discussed it."

"No, you discussed it...over a week ago. Look at me. I'm okay."

"Get in," he said. He put the Romeo into first gear and lurched down Atlantic Avenue, pouting the all the way into town. But I did not care. I was out of the cottage, off the island, zinging along in the car. It was wonderful...until we came to the formidable mansions on South Battery Street. They stood like a row of giant chess pieces poised to crush an opponent.

"Oh, help," I said, staring up. "The houses have grown taller."

"Nature of affluence, my dear. Compounds upon itself. Same principle operates with poverty, I understand, in the opposite direction."

"Are you planning to be snotty to everyone today or just me? It's time I got out and about."

"No, it isn't, but I'm tired of trying to stop you. Go...you aren't the only one with things to do. I'll pick you up on High Battery in an hour."

I watched him round the corner of King Street and wished I hadn't been unkind. I sighed and turned back toward the mansions, unnerved by having to face Peregrine House alone. A cramp of fear tightened my stomach when I thought of Louisa Hill. It took effort to make myself walk to the door and rap on its shiny knocker. Stuart's right, I thought. I'm not ready for combat.

I waited for someone to answer, Tycie being the most likely candidate. "I told you not to come here," she said, cracking the door an inch.

"Good to see you, too, Tycie, and you're going to have to let me in whether you want to or not. Miss Peregrine is expecting me."

She stared at me, lips poked out, facial lines drawn into a frown. "Stop worrying," I said. 'You can't leave me out here all day."

She harrumphed and swung open the door. "Hurry in and join the troubles. May as well. Everybody else has. But don't come crying to old Tycie when you get burned. She done told you to mind your own business. Ain't nothing going on in Peregrine House except moaning and groaning – Missy Peregrine doing the moaning, and those other two doing the groaning, flying around here like two wasps trying to sting each other in the throat."

"Who are you talking about, Tycie?"

"That 'tetched' cousin, Louisa. She's one, and Missy Jeannette… she's the other. All the time squabbling about who takes care of Missy Peregrine the most, sometimes griping about you, saying you ain't nothing but trash what's hooked on dope, then coming back around to Missy Peregrine. And me struggling up and down the stairsteps every day, thinking to myself that Tycie is the overworked mule who takes care of Missy Peregrine. Been taking care of her fifty years, same like always, same like a lifetime, not those two blowfish."

She punctuated her last remark with a snort. I hesitated a moment before responding. "I'm sorry you've had so much trouble, Tycie. I'll try to stay out of your way. Is Louisa here now?"

"Still at her church meeting, old hypocrite."

"May I go upstairs to see Miss Peregrine?"

"Do as you please. Tycie ain't gonna try to stop you, ain't gonna try to stop nobody."

Tycie turned her back on me and waddled away. I decided to go up on the elevator. No use testing my incision on four flights of stairs. I stepped off on the fourth level and started down the hall, calling out hesitantly. "Are you awake, Miss Peregrine? It's me, Arlena."

"Get yourself in here, you errant child. I'm starved for the company of a sane human being."

I ran down the hall to her room and flew to her bedside. She held out her thin arms. I sat on the edge of the bed and took her hands in mine. A rattle came from deep within her chest. "You look terrible," she said.

"Everyone tells me that. I'm used to it." I squeezed her hand. "But you don't. You look beautiful."

"Lying is a mortal sin, girl. I look dreadful, and you know it. In my dotage now, not long for this world."

"No, you're well. I'm the one who almost died."

"Yes, I understand you had a little of that female trouble folks used to hush-hush."

"I did."

"And what else was wrong?"

"Not anything."

"Arlena...you'll go to hell for lying. Now tell me about the other problem, the drug issue. I've surely heard enough from Jeannette."

"I was dependent on some medicine, having a lot of pain."

"That's an interesting way of saying you were addicted. Sounds so benign when you put it like that."

"I didn't do it on purpose, but the pain was so awful. I suppose I should have been seeing a better doctor."

"Is it over now?"

"Yes, they took out one of my ovaries."

"I wasn't talking about that part. I was talking about the dependency."

"I haven't needed medication since the pain stopped."

"I knew Jeannette was lying...there was some good reason."

"But how did she know anything about it?"

"Same way people know everything in Charleston. Raw gossip. There's a never-ending supply of if in this town."

"Are you angry, Miss Peregrine?"

"No, it makes you seem less goody-good. Nothing more boring than perfection."

"What about you?" I said. "Tycie told me you've been ill."

"I did have a little trouble getting my prescriptions regulated, but I've got them straightened out now, for a little while anyway."

"Good, we're recovering at the same time. I'm so glad you're better."

"You'll visit me often now that you're well, I trust?"

"Yes, as often as..." But my thought was interrupted by a crash. I turned to see Louisa standing in the bedroom doorway, shards of glass at her feet.

"You aren't supposed to be here," she said, her voice crackling as if electrified.

"I came to see Miss Peregrine. We're talking..."

Miss Peregrine interrupted. "How could you be so clumsy, Louisa? For heaven's sake, clean up that mess."

Louisa vanished. I moved closer to Miss Peregrine. "Sorry, dear," she said to me. "Louisa has been on a tear since I got sick, ranting and raving like a mad woman."

At that moment, Louisa came sweeping back in like a hawk diving for prey. She flew across the room and shoved a tattered folder into my hands. Then she confronted Miss Peregrine.

"Now you've done it," she said. "You've finally done it. I tried to make you listen, but you steadfastly refused…kept right on disobeying."

Miss Peregrine ignored Louisa's outburst and focused her attention on me. She spoke quietly, her tone calm and even. "We'll finish our conversation later, Arlena. As you can see, I must deal with Louisa now. Thank you for stopping by this morning. We'll plan another visit soon, tomorrow perhaps. Now go home and rest. You'll need it for when we take up my reminiscences again."

"But Miss Peregrine, I…"

"Arlena, please go. I must speak with Louisa privately."

23

I left Peregrine House angry, so angry I could not recall how I made my way to High Battery. My incision must be healed, I thought, as I stared at the harbor. That was a fast walk not to feel any pain. The yellowed folder Louisa had thrust at me was still in my hands. It felt heavy, like an albatross, a trove of dark secrets meant to expose Miss Peregrine. What was I supposed to do with the thing? Read it? Toss it? And why did Louisa think anyone would be interested in an old woman's pitiful past?

I snapped open the folder, eager to prove Louisa's stupidity. I was aware of the information on the first few pages, the part about the baby. But the name was different from the one in the family Bible. Somehow Jane Smith did not sound as refined as Constantia Elizabeth Peregrine. And a few other details were new to me. Constantia Elizabeth had grown up to marry a man from New York, Thomas Wendell Stafford. They'd had one daughter, Louisa Jane. I read the name over several times as the fact of the matter jelled in my brain. Louisa...Louisa Stafford...Miss Peregrine's granddaughter. I lifted my eyes and studied the small white triangles that were sailboats navigating the harbor.

By quirk of circumstance, Louisa Jane Stafford had also been reared at Our Lady of Grace, like her mother, Constantia Elizabeth. Jane Smith Stafford (Miss Peregrine's secret child, whose real name was Constantia), and Thomas Stafford, her husband, had both died of polio in 1946. The foundling home had taken little Louisa in, and there she had remained for all intents and purposes until Miss Peregrine invited her to live at Peregrine House forty years later.

Now I understood Miss Peregrine's peculiar interest in Louisa. She must have known about her all along, since her birth, but could do nothing to help her until old Mr. Peregrine died. I also understood her position as a spinster in Old Charleston society prevented her from acknowledging Louisa publicly. Such a thing would not have been acceptable for a lady of Miss Peregrine's generation and social position, dead father or no.

I was so engrossed in the contents of the folder that I did not see the Romeo roll up. "Pick you up, baby?" Stuart called out.

I jumped; he laughed. "I asked if I could pick you up," he said again, "the way little boys pick up little girls?"

"Sorry, Stu. I didn't hear you. I was concentrating. Louisa came after me again today. Now she's claiming to be Miss Peregrine's... Oh, never mind. It's too boring to talk about."

Still smiling, he got out of the car and joined me on the bench. In his hand was a small box gift-wrapped in silver paper. This was a different Stuart from the one who had dropped me off earlier, a more relaxed Stuart.

"What's this?" I asked.

"Something I picked up off the ground."

"Stop teasing me. What is it?" I reached for the box. He held it at arms-length, elongating the moment.

"Not so fast, my greedy pet. Promises first."

"What promises?" Another grab.

"You must love me forever."

"I promise."

"You must obey me always."

"Not a chance." I lunged for the box again. This time he let me grab it.

"Stop, don't open it yet. I want to tell you something first."

"Tell me quick. I can't wait."

"I love you more than anything in the world," he said, "the galaxy, the universe."

I looked at his face and was envious. Why couldn't I be an open book like Stuart? Why was I so splintered and layered? "And I love you," I said. It was the best I could offer in the way of sentiment.

"I'm glad," he said. "Open it. It's yours."

Inside the box was a thin bangle bracelet that matched my favorite silver hoop earrings. "It's beautiful," I said, "but where did you get money for it?"

"Worm turned today. We can breathe a little easier. "He took a pale blue check from the inside pocket of his sport coat and placed it in my hands. I felt my eyeballs swell.

"Five thousand," I read aloud from the check. "Grayson Pinckney? What does this mean? What's it for?"

"Small loan from a friend."

"What?"

"A loan, or sort of a loan. Mr. Pinckney said to think of it as fair compensation for knocking out Jon Prioleau's teeth."

"But how did he know we needed it."

"I called him after trying everyone else on the continent. Figured there was nothing to lose, maybe he'd feel sorry for us. I was in his office just now while you were playing patty-cake with Miss Peregrine. Told him my life story. Yours, too. Turned out he already knew we were in trouble. Our good friend, Dr. Legare, has been spreading the news. He must have followed your case minute-to-minute the entire time you were in the hospital."

"Jerk," I said. "He'd love to take me down."

"Seems he wasted his breath on Pinckney."

"Five thousand dollars," I said, still staring at the small blue piece of paper trembling in my hands.

"Nowhere near enough to pay everything," Stuart said, "but it'll keep us on solid footing while I interview for jobs. We'll be chipping away at that hospital bill for years. But this baby-" He tapped the check with his forefinger. "-will keep our heads up."

"We have to pay it back, though, right?"

"That's the deal loosely, though forbearance is the key word, I suspect. There's something else Mr. Pinckney wants more than money, a commitment from you that you'll help him finish his memoirs. He's worried you might give up on his pet project after all the medical problems you've been through. He wants to draw up a simple contract."

"For five thousand dollars, I'd sign a contract with Jack the Ripper."

Stuart laughed again. Had a miracle occurred? Was he somehow ten years younger? "Come on, Margaret Mitchell," he said. "Let's go home and celebrate."

"Okay," I said, finally able to smile. "But first I need to stop back by Peregrine House and return this. It won't take a minute, honest." I held up the folder and watched Stuart's smile slide off his face.

"I'm not surprised. You'll be begging St. Peter at the pearly gates for an extra minute to deal with one last piece of paperwork."

"And he'll give it to me to shut me up. On to South Battery, Julius Caesar."

⌘ ⌘ ⌘

Louisa opened the front door before I had a chance to knock. I tried not to wilt under her stare. Where are Tycie and Jeannette? I thought. How could they leave Miss Peregrine home alone with a maniac?

"Did you bring it back?" Louisa said.

"If you mean the folder, yes, not that you deserve the courtesy."

"Give it to me."

I hesitated a second too long and she snatched it from my hands. She flipped it open and began examining its contents. I watched a moment before speaking. "I didn't tamper with anything if that's what you're worried about, but I am going to tell Miss Peregrine."

"Don't come back here," she said. "I've taken care of Fanny all my life, and I'm sick of people like you and Jeannette stealing the credit for all my hard work and sacrifices. You'll probably tell everyone in town what's in this folder."

"You aren't angry, Louisa. You showed it to me on purpose, not in some little temper fit. Any excuse would have been good enough to let me know you're blood kin to Miss Peregrine. You'd like everyone to know. It's been eating at you for years. Just think, Fanny Peregrine's granddaughter and forbidden to tell it."

This time she slammed the door.

⌘ ⌘ ⌘

A five-thousand-dollar check from Grayson Pinckney and two confrontations with Louisa Hill all in one day would have been enough to exhaust anyone, particularly someone who had been ill eight weeks. I slept on the drive back to Sullivan's, through dinner, to the next morning when the phone rang at eight. So much for our celebration. Stuart jumped out of bed on the first ring and ran into the sitting room to answer it. In two seconds, he was shouting for me to come there.

"It's an agent," he said, "from New York. Get in here. She wants to talk to you."

Heart pounding, I could not get my body organized to move. "Come on," Stuart called louder, his hand muffling the receiver. I ignored the frantic thumping in my chest and made my way to the sitting room. It was a brief conversation: Sarah Goldstein introduced herself; I remembered having spoken to her when researching the agent listings; she did not recall our conversation, but had received my material; liked the synopsis; liked the first chapter; wanted to see more; yes, I'd send the complete manuscript right away; no, it had not been passed around among publishing houses; yes, she could have an exclusive contract to represent the work.

I hung up the phone and stared at the wall. Stuart shook my arm to bring me to my senses. I was too deep in shock to notice. I watched without helping as he located, sorted, stacked, and boxed the remaining chapters for mailing. When done, he raced away, package in tow, to try to make the nine o'clock mail drop in Mount Pleasant. In his hurry, he forgot to give me instructions on how to spend the rest of my morning, a huge mistake.

I considered calling Miss Peregrine to tell her an agent had contacted me. No…no use getting her hopes up without a contract in hand. I spent ten uneasy minutes wondering if I should let her know I had returned the folder and had no intention of divulging her secret. No, I decided. The situation at Peregrine House needed to cool down a while. Out of nowhere, Raven popped into my mind. Was she okay? Should I risk calling her? I could always hang up if her mother answered. But before I could decide which pot to stir, the phone rang again. Irritated, I picked up and said hello.

"Hi, Mrs. Prince. What's wrong?" Raven said. "You sound like you just took a bite out of a pickle?"

"Raven…where are you? I was about to call your house. Did you tell your mother?"

"Don't have to. Croom already helped me work things out. We scraped up enough money for an abortion. Going to the clinic tomorrow."

"Don't, Rav, not yet."

"No other way. I'm glad it's almost over." Another click with no goodbye.

I stared at the clock next to the phone and tried to think what to do next. Eight forty-five and no idea what time Stuart would be back, no idea how to help my young friend. My mind raced with nerve jangling thoughts about Raven and her mother. I wavered one more anxious moment before going to the closet to find some clothes. Informing a mother her daughter was about to have an abortion was not something one could do over the phone. I dressed quickly and dug through my purse where I found twenty-seven dollars, enough to take the bus into Charleston with enough left over for a cab ride from the bus stop to FitzSimons' office. I pulled a black pea jacket over my sweater and jeans, stuffed the twenty-seven dollars deep into my pants pocket, and walked with purpose to the kitchen door. For a second, I reconsidered. I had not gone anywhere alone since my surgery. Stuart would be livid. But there was no alternative. Someone had to Tell Raven's mother.

Slowly, timidly, I made my way down the outside stairs of the cottage and the length of the driveway to the street. From there it was a short block to the bus stop. As I walked along the roadside, a cool sea breeze blew away a little of my fear, yet I dreaded having to face Jeannette FitzSimons. Why hadn't I called to make sure she was in? What was I going to say when I got there? When the cabby pulled in front of her office, I would have told him to keep driving had the image of Raven's childlike face not been hovering before my eyes for the last hour in a surreal hologram. Seventeen-year-old, fresh-faced Raven, going to an abortion mill alone with no one to help her but Croom Legare, Jr.. With new boldness, I walked into FitzSimons' office.

The receptionist was not happy to see me. "Good morning," I said, trying to make myself official. "Is Mrs. FitzSimons in?"

"Yes, but she's tied up. Do you have an appointment?"

"No, I'm here to see her about a personal matter. It's important. I need to talk to her as soon as possible."

My urgency did not impress this woman. She put on a bored face, sighed, slid her chair back from her desk. "I didn't get your name," she said.

"Arlena Prince." She walked into FitzSimons' private office and closed the door behind her. In seconds she reappeared. "Mrs. FitzSimons will give you five minutes, no more. It's imperative you be brief."

I stepped into the inner office to a hyper Jeannette FitzSimons. She was sitting behind her disorganized desk, riffling through papers, carrying on a disjointed phone conversation.

"May I call you back in five?" she said into the receiver when I entered. "Good, certainly." She hung up with no goodbye.

Shifting her attention to me, she looked as if she got a bad taste in her mouth. "You're here," she said, "and high time. You have some explaining to do. What is the meaning of this?"

Turning to the credenza behind her, she picked up a copy-shop box and heaved it on top of her trash-pile-of-a-desk. Scrawled on the lid was the title, *Tarnished Honor.*

"Where did you get that?" I said. "No one is supposed to..."

"Never mind. What are you planning to do with it?"

"I...don't see it's any of your business."

"The material in this is derogatory. Surely, you don't intend to publish it. If you do, you're more insensitive than I thought."

"It's a story," I said, tight-lipped with anger. "And it isn't mine. It's Miss Peregrine's. Where did you get it? Miss Peregrine didn't keep a copy at her house."

"I found it in my daughter's room, which brings me to another issue. I've told Raven she isn't to associate with you, yet I find this pile of feces with your name plastered all over it hidden under her bed."

"I don't know how she got it," I said.

"You're lying."

"Why don't you ask Raven? She obviously stole it from my house."

"You mean Lucretia Middleton's house. And Raven doesn't steal. She's a child. She doesn't understand the importance of certain things. And why would she even be where you live."

My intention to stay calm evaporated. I had to work at finding my voice again. "May I have it back, please?"

"You may not. You may take nothing out of my office. And since you're here, let me inform you of something else. Miss Peregrine's family and friends have met together and decided she's too weak to continue her memoirs. Do not harass her about it one more minute."

"I agree with you on that point," I said. "Miss Peregrine isn't well enough to work, but you can't stop me from visiting her."

"I most certainly can. Louisa told me how badly you upset her yesterday. I'll stop you from seeing her by court order if I have to."

"Louisa is deranged. You know that. She's the one who caused the trouble."

"Poor Louisa suffers from an emotional disorder. She's confused at times. But I assure you, no matter her mental state, she's always protective of Fanny. I suppose a peasant like you wouldn't understand that sort of thing. Some people are so vulgar, barging in where they aren't wanted."

"I didn't come here to discuss Louisa," I said, fighting to hang onto my composure.

"What, then? My patience is running out."

I could not answer. There were no right words.

"Speak or leave. I'm too busy for cheap drama."

"Mrs. FitzSimons, I'm sorry..." I could not go on.

"What's the matter with you, woman?" FitzSimons said.

I swallowed hard before continuing. "It's Raven. She's in trouble, needs your help, but she's afraid to tell you."

"I thought I made it clear. Stay out of my daughter's affairs."

A glint appeared in her eyes. I now felt more afraid than angry. "She came to me for help," I said, "but her problem was too big for me to deal with. I couldn't do anything about it behind your back. Mrs. FitzSimons, Raven is pregnant, about eight weeks. She's planning to go to North Charleston in the morning to get an abortion. Croom Legare is going with her. It's his baby. I couldn't let them go without your knowing about it. She needs your help."

Jeannette FitzSimons' face turned red, then purple, then red again. She rose from her chair and leaned forward on her desktop. The pile of papers slipped under her weight. "Have you lost your mind," she said in a whisper. "Raven is seventeen. She's a debutante."

"I'm sorry, Mrs. FitzSimons. This is the hardest thing I've ever had to tell anyone in my life, but I couldn't let Raven go through an abortion with no family to help her. She's too young."

"Get out of my office," FitzSimons screamed, the veins in her temples bulging into pulsing ridges. She stepped from behind her desk and came at me. Fearing an actual physical assault, I backed away and fled.

24

"Have you lost your mind?" Stuart said. He was furious. He stamped the length of the porch and back again, kicking at a wicker foot-stool as he went. For once, I was not the one shaking pilings.

"I don't know. You're the second person to ask me that today."

"Yeah, and the first was probably Jeannette FitzSimons. I don't see why you had to go sticking your nose in. I knew this thing with Raven would be trouble."

"Someone had to tell her mother."

"You should have stayed out of it. Everything was going great. Mr. Pinckney's check, a call from an agent. Why couldn't you leave it alone? No telling what FitzSimons will do. I hope she'll be so busy working Raven over, she'll forget about coming after you. One thing I know for sure...Raven is going to hate your guts."

"Maybe she'll thank me later, when she grows up."

Stuart looked at me with disdain. I considered he might be right. Maybe I should have stayed out of it, let Raven get the abortion without her mother knowing. But whether he was right or wrong no longer mattered. I had already broken her confidence.

Later in the afternoon, while Stuart was in the shower, I made a secret phone call. I could have saved myself the trouble. No one was picking up at Raven's house. I gave up trying when the shower water stopped and Stuart's whistling grew louder. He makes me sick, I thought. An hour ago, he was mad enough to kill me. Now he's whistling. I stomped into the bathroom to start a fight.

"Hey," Stuart yelled from the shower stall. "You must be well. The whole house shook when you walked in here, like the bad old days."

"I don't know how you can be so insensitive," I said to the shower curtain.

"And I don't know how you can be so touchy." He pushed back the curtain and showed himself all dripping and curly-headed. I handed him a towel and re-positioned myself. One look and he knew he was in for trouble. "Raven FitzSimons is scheduled to have an abortion tomorrow," I said, "and you don't care if she lives or dies. You're doing nothing, and you don't want me to do anything, either."

"I'd say you've done enough. Thanks to you I'd bet my life there won't be an abortion. Jeannette FitzSimons will put poor Raven through far worse."

"We have to think of something…to help her."

Stuart scowled at me. "Leave it alone. It's not our problem."

Furious, I flew out of the bathroom. On the porch, I pranced up and down until Stuart appeared before me and lifted me off my feet by my bony shoulders. He held me two inches above the floor and glared into my eyes. I was frightened, but not enough to stop me from glaring back.

"Let me down."

"Not until I've said my piece. I've put up with all manner of junk from you, and my patience has run out. It's time you started behaving yourself. If you can't – or won't – you can go it alone. I need cooperation, not resistance. What's it going to be?"

He shook me a little. "Go ahead," he said. "Burn holes in me with those black eyes. I'm used to it. But don't forget, I have limits. Maybe you should think that over."

He lowered me to the floor and took his hands away to tighten the towel around his middle. He looked so vulnerable, standing there half naked, still wet from the shower. I felt a rush of remorse.

"I'm sorry," I said. "You've been more than good to me. I shouldn't…"

He looked at me with cold eyes while I stuttered over my words. He shuddered a nervous sigh and met me halfway. "Okay, I'm sorry too. I admit I behaved badly about Raven and the abortion. But you've done everything you can. It's time to let it play out however it will."

"If you say so."

"Good. Now go put on your PJs. You need rest. Tomorrow, you have to talk Miss Peregrine into signing with that New York agent – What's her name? Sarah Goldstein? – no insignificant task."

⌘ ⌘ ⌘

Miss Peregrine was happy to see me the next morning until I brought up the subject of the contract. At that, she turned up her nose in aristocratic frigidity and proceeded to wreck my life.

"I don't see why you're so excited," she said. "The woman is an agent, not a publisher."

"But there won't be a publisher without an agent. It's the first step. Don't you see?"

"No, not that it changes anything. We must decline her offer. There'll be other opportunities." She blew her nose with a honk.

I was astonished she could be so cold. Frustration overtook me. I began trembling. Tears spurted from my eyes, words from my mouth. "That's selfish," I cried. "How can you deny me a chance like this?"

"Arlena, calm yourself. Such displays are unbecoming. Ladies don't behave that way. Think how horrified you are when Louisa…"

"I'm not a lady. I'm a poor schmuck who works for a living."

"Now, now, I didn't say we would turn down every contract, just this one."

"You don't understand, Miss Peregrine. We won't get another."

I buried my face in her lace coverlet and cried. "There, there," she said. "Other agents will come along. This Goldstar person isn't the only fish in the sea."

"Goldstein," I said and burst into a new round of sobs. It was hopeless. I wanted to shoot myself.

"You must stop giving in to emotion," the old aristocrat said. "All I want is to change the ending a bit. After that we can sign the little contract with no more tears."

"Miss Peregrine," I snubbed. "I'm begging you to listen. There's no way I can say that to Sarah Goldstein. She'll tell me to drop off the planet and take the manuscript with me."

"Let her. You and I will not be led about by the likes of crass New Yorkers. Here, wipe your nose. I'm beginning to think you're still sick."

"Ha," someone said from the other side of the room. "People who do drugs are always sick."

Not Louisa. Please, not now.

"Hush, Louisa," Miss Peregrine said. "Can't you see Mrs. Prince is upset?"

"I hope you don't think I care. And what's this business about a manuscript. Surely you aren't calling your memoirs *Tarnished Honor.* Wouldn't that be too close to the truth?"

"Don't be cheeky, Louisa," Miss Peregrine said. "None of this concerns you. Dismiss it from your mind."

"Whatever you say, Fanny, though it doesn't matter any longer that you hide things from me. I can ask Jeannette what you're up to. She and I talk things over now."

"Do what you will, but you know I'm not moved by threats. I've been more than patient. Don't test me further. Now go about your work."

Louisa lifted her upper lip as if nauseated and huffed out the door. Her chill remained in the room. Miss Peregrine looked at me with sad wet eyes and spoke with a tremor. "I'm sorry you had to witness that, dear, and on top of your crying spell. Go home and rest now. We'll talk in the morning, perhaps by phone. Call when you wake up. I'll not change my decision about the contract, mind you, but I will give you an opportunity to apologize for behaving coarsely in my presence."

"All right," I said without further argument. I was her servant, her wooden puppet she had beaten into submission. I left the bedroom in dejection. On departing the house via the front piazza, I began a slow walk toward High Battery, picking up my pace when I remembered Louisa's current mood. I was certain I could feel her eyes burning into my neck from some upper story of Peregrine House. Faster and faster I walked until I found myself running. Stuart saw and called out to me to slow down.

"Are you sick again?" he said and reached out to help me as I climbed, panting, into the car. I lay my head back on the passenger seat and closed my eyes. Stuart spoke again. "Breathe, Arlena. You're gray as death. I don't want you to have some kind of seizure."

I flashed open my eyes and hit the dashboard with my fist. "I hate Louisa Hill. I hate Miss Peregrine. I hate this miserable town." Jagged breaths made my words husky. I felt dizzy. My chest ached. Odd pinpoints of light jumped about before my eyes.

"What are you talking about?" Stuart said in a panic. "What happened in there?"

"She wouldn't sign the contract. Can you believe it?"

"But why not? Makes no sense."

"She refused, plain and simple. Wants to change the ending. And you can forget trying to discuss it with her. She's adamant."

"No reason? Just mule-headedness?"

"I told you. She wants a new ending."

"But we already mailed the manuscript to Goldstein. She'll think we're crazy if we back out now."

"I know that; you know that; Goldstein will know that. But I'm telling you, Miss Peregrine doesn't care."

"She'll change her mind."

"Don't count on it."

"Then you'll have to sign without her."

"Impossible. She owns half the copyright. If I did something like that without telling Goldstein, and it came out later, I may as well blow my brains out."

"I swear, Arlena, between Raven and Miss Peregrine, I don't know who's more cracked."

"When did you see Raven? Look at me, Stuart."

"All right, all right," he said, regretting his slip. "She left a long-assed note in our mailbox this morning. I didn't give it to you. You already had too much going on."

"Where is it?"

My eyes threatened him. His own eyes glazed over. He put a hand into his jacket pocket and produced the folded note. I grabbed it and burned him with another look before turning my back on him to read:

Hi, Mrs. Prince,

At first I was mad you ratted on me, but after a while, I stopped caring. Mother went nuts. I thought she was going to kill Croom and his father. We had a couple of bad arguments. She didn't let me go for the abortion like Croom and I had planned, but after she thought it over, she decided I needed one after all, only not at the clinic in North Charleston. Yesterday she drove me to a women's clinic in Columbia. I guess she thought a two-hour drive was far enough away to keep anyone in Charleston from finding out. Croom and his father won't blab. That's for sure. And Mother said the only other person we had to worry about spreading gossip was a certain Yankee hussy. That's you. I told her you'd never tell a secret. But you did. You told mine. Nurses at the clinic said I didn't have to go through with the abortion if I didn't want to. They said it was my personal decision. I didn't know that before. I thought if you were seventeen, you had to do what your mother said. When I found out I didn't have to, I told Mother I wanted to keep the baby. She went bonkers, and the clinic people threatened to call the police. After a ga-zillion arguments, we drove back home. Now Mother is begging me every minute to let her make another appointment. I told her this morning if she didn't leave me alone, I'd slash my wrists.

Love,
Raven

P.S. I wrote this letter instead of coming to see you in person so I wouldn't have to listen to you tell me not to fight with my mother. Anyway you said not to get an abortion without her knowing about it, and now I'm not getting one at all. One thing I've found out, adults change their minds a lot.

P.P.S. I'm still going to run away as soon as I've saved up enough money. Why don't you go ahead and tell that to Mother so she'll freak out worse? Adults are all weird.

Raven

25

Next morning I woke up determined to take control of the shambles my life had become. This was determining a great deal. Though Stuart counseled against it, my first move was to call Miss Peregrine and inform her of my suspicions about Louisa.

"Dear one," my old friend said when she came on the line. "If you called to discuss that tiresome contract…"

"No, I've given up. I want to talk about Louisa. You're aware of what's in the folder she threw at me yesterday. I know you are, and the information is safe with me, but have you considered some of it might not be true?"

"You're fretting about nothing, love. Louisa isn't my granddaughter. She couldn't be. The material in that dreadful folder is false. My Constantia died when she was a baby...nine months. But Louisa has come to believe the story she made up so long ago. Still, the fact that none of the information is true doesn't mean I'll ever put her out. She's dependent on me, has no place else to go. Poor thing tried to dupe me years ago with those preposterous false documents, but she couldn't fool me then, and she's certainly not fooling me now. You must take into account she's mentally ill. Louisa can't believe anyone could care for her just for herself. That's why she pretends to be family. Are you listening…still on the line?"

"I'm here…just having a hard time understanding."

"What's so difficult? I took Louisa in because we were both lonely, not because I thought she was of Peregrine blood. I needed companionship and so did she. But she was always afraid I'd make her leave on a whim like her other employer had done. She thought she had to trick me into keeping her on. I should have straightened it out at the beginning, insisted she stop pretending. But the years slipped by, and now I've come to realize her emotional state is not only hopeless, it's deteriorating. Louisa doesn't even respond to firmness anymore. I may have to seek professional help for her soon. But I don't mind. I'm responsible for her. She has been a good and faithful friend, and now that she's in a confused state with no recovery in sight, I shall not desert her."

"But why do you let her get away with threatening you? She's trying to use that stupid folder to control you, like blackmail or extortion. And she has to know you don't believe what's in it."

"She's beyond rational thought, can no longer separate fact from fiction. Her worn-out old story about being my granddaughter is all she has to left to hold onto, in her own mind at least."

"I don't know. It all sounds…bizarre.

"It is bizarre, lamb. Louisa herself is bizarre, but aren't we all?"

"Miss Peregrine, I have something else to tell you. A few weeks ago, I found your family Bible in the Fireproof Building collection. I saw the entry you made about Constantia Elizabeth. If she died at nine months like you said, why didn't you record her death date?"

The old woman went silent. After a moment, she chuckled. "Of all the nosy…how did you ever unearth that moldy old Bible. Oh, well, I knew someone would come across it sooner or later, though I hoped it would be after I was dead and gone. I trust you didn't say anything to Grayson. He isn't aware of that particular transgression of his father's, who, by the way, would turn over in his grave if he knew I let his secret out. Death date, death date. I don't know. Must have forgotten to set it down when I made the entry. Maybe you can help me attend to it. I need your help tying up several loose ends. Can you come by to see me today? Tycie is going to the doctor around five. I'd be grateful if you'd come sit with me. I must speak with you again about the business matter you threw such a tantrum over yesterday, the contract with the literary agent. Perhaps I'll reconsider signing. I've realized I don't have the strength right now to tackle changes in the manuscript."

Shocked by her words, I stammered through an incoherent response, "But you said...you refused..."

"Now, now, dear, you mustn't pester. I may recant if you do. Come to Peregrine House at five...and don't be late."

When I hung up, Stuart questioned me with a look which I ignored. I stared past him without responding as I tried to make sense out of the nonsensical conversation. Accustomed to unreasonableness, Stuart went to the kitchen to make coffee, grumbling under his breath that if I planned on calling up anyone else to make trouble, he had no intention of hanging around to witness it, although I knew he would stop being disagreeable once he found out Miss Peregrine had changed her mind about the contract.

I promised myself not to aggravate him any further for the morning, a promise I was unable to keep. The second he disappeared from the sitting room, someone tapped on the outside porch door, someone who did not want Stuart to know she had come to pay a call.

"Raven," I said and ran to let her in. "Why are you so pale? Did you have the abortion? Did your mother go with you?"

She threw her arms around my neck and whimpered into the collar of my robe. "My life is a wreck," she said in a little-girl voice. "I can't do anything right, not even that."

"Okay, okay. Come sit down and warm up. Stuart is making coffee. You look like you could use some."

She wiped her runny nose on her jacket sleeve and walked with me into the sitting room. Stuart brought in two mugs and handed one to me, which I gave to Raven. She took it with shaking hands and pretended to take a sip.

Stuart was not happy to see her. "Getting an early start on drama this morning?" he said to the pale-cheeked girl. I frowned at him. He held up a hand in retreat. Raven did not acknowledge Stuart. She spoke only to me.

"Oh, Mrs. Prince…you still look like…"

"Don't say it. I already know. You look pretty rough yourself."

"Mother has been impossible."

"From your note, I'd say you both have. Did you let her make another appointment?"

"No, and I'm not going to. But I didn't come to talk about that. I came to warn you."

Stuart grunted and put on a bored look. I tried to keep the conversation in the realm of real. "Thanks, Rav," I said, "but you have to stop worrying. Stuart and I are grown-ups. We can handle whatever comes. You need to focus on your own problems. I'm sorry you think I tattled to your mom, but there was nothing else I could do. And I still think you should listen to her. This is no time to do things out of spite."

"I didn't come to be lectured," she said, the tremor in her voice worsening as she spoke. She set down the mug and worked her hands in her lap. Aristocratic hands, small and delicate, bluish, untouched by physical work beyond tennis matches and bicycling, fingers barely visible inside the huge cuffs of a gray wool athletic jacket that probably belonged to Croom Jr.. I watched as her white cheeks turned crimson.

"Get hold of yourself, Rav," I said in an effort to help her avoid breaking down. "Stuart and I care about you. That's why we want you to listen to your mother. You need to let her help you so you can move on."

"You're the one with the problem," she said. "People are out to get you, and you act like you're blind."

Stuart could control himself no longer. "Stop play-acting. Say whatever it is you came to say. All this build-up is a bore."

Raven moved closer to me and grabbed my hand. "See," she whispered. "I told you he doesn't like me."

I put an arm around her. "He's just trying to get to the bottom of things."

She glared at Stuart, but continued speaking only to me. "He's cold-hearted…like Mother. She hates everyone...you worst of all, Mrs. Prince."

"Not really," I said, trying to keep my voice calm despite the chill inching up my backbone. "Your mom is upset over your... condition."

She turned from Stuart to glare at me. "What...can't you say it? I'm pregnant, and everyone wants me to get an abortion. Why do those words make adults go psycho?" Raven waited, but I had no answer. "Forget it," she said. "I don't care. I came to tell you to stay away from Peregrine House. It's dangerous there."

Stuart couldn't let her last remark go by without addressing it. "Why?" he said with disgust. "Are you clairvoyant now?"

"You don't need to know, mister. It's not you they're after."

"I'm tired of your games," he said, giving in now to his temper. "You may be able to manipulate your mother and Arlena with this kind of drama. But it stops with me. Did you hear that, poor little rich girl? If you know anything, spill it and get out."

Raven jumped to her feet and clamped her hands over her ears. She squeezed her eyes shut and screamed a long, piercing scream. Then she pushed up the sleeves of her sweater. Two stark white bandages encircled her wrists. With jerky movements she ripped them off to expose several gashes stitched with black surgical thread.

"Are these drama too?" she screeched. "Look at them. You think my mother is listening to me now? Oh, yeah...she is, you cruel dog, like you'd better start listening."

⌘ ⌘ ⌘

I felt sick. The scene with Raven had taken the last of my strength. Stuart paced. I lay on the sofa and wept. Though she had been gone over an hour, her presence hung in the air like fog. The cottage, which on most days exuded airiness and light, now emitted gloom.

"They're alike," Stuart said as he paced. "Nutty mother, nuttier daughter. I...you...are done with them. No more visits. No more calls, notes, nothing."

"I'm sorry you've had to put up with all this," I said with a little hiccup. "It's too much. I know it is. And now you're going to have to drive me back into town for more punishment. Miss Peregrine said she might reconsider signing Sarah Goldstein's contract. I didn't get a chance to tell you before Raven came in."

"What?" he said. "Nope, I'm not falling for it. I'm going for a run. Raven got to me with those wrists. What a waste that girl is. And Miss Peregrine isn't far off it."

"But I have to go, Stu. The contract..."

"That old woman would say anything to get attention. I'd lay down a hundred dollars she has no intention of signing. And you don't have to go running over there to blow sunshine up her butt. You can't. Look at yourself. You can barely sit up. And aren't you just a little concerned about what Raven said? According to her, everyone close to Miss Peregrine is out to get you. Doesn't anything scare you off?"

"Raven is an alarmist. I admit it. And she went too far this time, needs professional help, worse than Louisa."

"I'm gone," Stuart said, zipping his jacket. "Try to take a nap. We'll both feel better in a couple of hours."

I looked at my watch. Eleven A.M.. Maybe, I thought, if I rest my eyes five minutes... I woke up three hours later at two and spent another hour trying to clear my head. Coffee and aspirin helped. A shower helped more. I dressed in black jeans and a black sweater and plaited my hair into one long black braid. It hung rope-like down my back. I went out to the porch and stood self-consciously as Stuart looked me up and down. He suggested I write noir poetry to round out the effect. He also asked if I had stopped wearing makeup to support my literary image or out of laziness. I sighed and went into the bedroom to smear on lip gloss and blush. Which changed nothing. I still looked somber and dark. I went back to the porch to be evaluated again, whereupon Stuart pronounced me hopeless and disappeared into the kitchen. When he came back, he had a huge bottle of wine in one hand and two of Lucretia's tenant-grade wine glasses in the other. "For our nerves," he said. "We need it."

"But I've only had a few drops since..."

"Yeah, since your surgery. It's time you loosened up."

I went along with him, knowing half an hour into the wine bottle, he would do anything I wanted. And what I wanted was to go to Peregrine House. I had to drink far too much to accomplish my goal, but by five minutes to four, Stuart had put up a white flag and agreed to chauffeur me into town. Gratitude made me behave myself most of the way, but by the time we reached the row of storefronts along King Street, the wine had dissolved the last of my good judgment. I demanded to be taken to Meeting where the flower ladies set up shop every day to peddle their wares to tourists. I wanted to take Miss Peregrine an evergreen wreath. Stuart, who was drunker and more unreasonable than I, responded by giving me a stink eye. We argued for a block and a half. He swore under his breath, scraped to a stop at the intersection of King and Broad, and told me to get out of the car, that I'd have to walk wherever else I wanted to go. Which I did, not realizing the trek to Meeting Street to buy the wreath, and the longer trek to Peregrine House on South Battery, would be too much.

And it was. Moving at a much slower pace than everyone else on the sidewalk, I crept along, trying not to draw attention, resting at every corner. Twice, I had to stop and take fifteen-minute breaks on park benches that were chained to wrought iron fences outside private residences. The journey, from the time Stuart put me out on the corner, until I reached Miss Peregrine's front door, took an hour and a half.

By the time I reached her walkway, I was exhausted and feeling the worst effects of the cheap wine. I sat down on the front piazza steps to rest before entering a different brand of chaos. Despite not wanting to, I found myself scanning High Battery across White Point Garden to see if I could spot the Romeo. As mad as I was at Stuart, and as mad as he was at me, I knew he would not leave me stranded. I covered the area twice with visual sweeps, but spotted nothing of the car or Stuart. He had better show up, I thought. When I come back out on this porch, he'd better be here to pick me up if he knows what's good for him.

I rose and knocked on the door with dumb bravery. No one answered. "Open up, Louisa," I said aloud, "or I'll punch you just for being slow." False courage, this, another bad effect of the wine. I rapped harder. Still nothing. When my temper got the best of me, I forsook the lovely doorknocker and began banging on bare wood with my fist. As a last resort, I kicked a dent in the brass plate covering the bottom of the door. I was on the verge of another display of poor judgment when something peculiar happened. The lock clicked and the door swung open with a horror-movie creak. I waited for a monster to appear.

"Is that you, Louisa?" I said, my anger now uneasiness. "Answer me or I'll tell Miss Peregrine you've been acting out again." Tiny muscles twitched around my eyes. My scalp tingled with nerves.

"Louisa…" I was shouting now. "…I'm not afraid of you."

Still no response. Muttering, I pushed the door open wider, but the dusky outdoor light of late afternoon could not penetrate the darkness of the foyer. I was used to non-threatening daylight on my other visits to Peregrine House. But now, the long shadows of early evening waxed forbidding. My uneasiness progressed to fear.

"I'm coming in," I said and stepped into the foyer without giving myself time for second thoughts. I propped the wreath against the grandfather clock and walked up the first flight of stairs, stopping on the stairwell to catch my breath. "I know you're around here somewhere, Louisa," I said to the empty staircase. "Miss Peregrine is going to be furious when she finds out you've been causing more trouble."

From somewhere below, someone cackled out a message. "I doubt that, Mrs. Prince."

"You're impossible," I said, though not fully convinced the voice belonged to the deranged housekeeper. "I don't know why Miss Peregrine puts up with you."

Whoever it was spoke again. "Miss Peregrine puts up with all manner of stray dogs and cats." I still wasn't certain this was Louisa. The voice, though female, sounded alien.

"Go…see the old lady," it said next. "She's waiting for you. Pity you didn't come sooner."

"You'll be sorry, Louisa. I'm going to tell her what you've been up to."

"She won't care. She'll protect me. I'm blood of her blood."

So then, it was Louisa. My own voice rose to a shout. "You're an imposter, and Miss Peregrine knows it. All you want is to take advantage. She'll listen to me this time. I'll make her see reason."

I ignored the tenderness in my still-testy incision and ran up the last three flights of stairs. Laughing obscenely, Louisa followed me upward, flight after flight. The pain in my abdomen almost doubled me over, but fear forced me to keep going. On the last step of the last flight, I heard another peculiar sound. A wail, muffled and sorrowful, rose and fell behind the door to Miss Peregrine's bedroom. When I stopped to listen, Louisa plowed into my back, almost making me fall.

"What is that?" she said, her voice a knife-edge. I did not respond. I was too shocked by her sudden presence. She ignored me and concentrated on the sound. It stopped a second and began again. She walked past me toward the bedroom door. I could have been another piece of antique furniture for all the attention she paid me.

"Who's there?" she shouted as she moved down the hall. Though still lightheaded from my dash up the stairs, I forced myself to follow her. What if Miss Peregrine needed help?

Louisa spoke louder. "Is that you, Tycie?"

The moaning ceased. I heard a scuffling sound, but Louisa had gotten ahead of me in the dark hallway, and I could not tell what had caused the commotion. Another scuffle and a bump.

"Tycie, you liar," Louisa shrieked. "You said you were going to the doctor. Why did you come back?"

I heard a slap and a yelp. "Tycie," I called out. "Is that you?"

"Yes, in here." Another slap.

"Take your hands off her, Louisa," I shouted and ran into the room. Surprised by my appearance, Louisa released Tycie and let her drop to the floor.

"Tycie…are you all right?" I said.

I tried in vain to help her up, but Tycie was not concerned about herself. "See about Miss Peregrine," she said. "I'm afraid she's dying."

I let go of Tycie and pushed past Louisa. The bedroom was dark. I fumbled for the switch on the bedside lamp, turning over a drinking glass in the process. At last, I touched the switch and winced with eye pain as the light came on in blinding brilliance. Through throbbing eyeballs, I found myself looking into the blue, immobile face of my employer.

"Miss Peregrine," I cried out and shook her shoulders. Her head fell backward, revealing unseeing eyes. I let go of her and put both hands over my mouth. My body jerked in a nervous chill. Louisa came to my side and stood in silence. I heard myself moaning into my own cupped hands.

"Now you've done it," Louisa said, her voice strangely calm. "You've killed her."

I looked at Louisa in astonishment, rendered speechless by the racking chill that had taken over my body. She turned and walked into the hallway. I had never seen her so composed. In less than a second, she reappeared in the doorway half-carrying the sobbing Tycie. She dragged her to me and dropped her to the floor. Weeping as the chill worsened, I crumpled next to Tycie. She wrapped her arms around my neck and clung to me as she cried for the soul of her dead friend.

26

Confusion swept through Peregrine House. One moment I was weeping with Tycie, the next surrounded by unfamiliar people. Police officers swarmed through rooms and hallways, and though I knew Louisa had summoned them, I did not understand why. Stuart was there and Jeannette FitzSimons, Dr. Legare and other medical people, also neighbors and curiosity hounds off the street. Tycie's grandson rushed in at the height of the confusion, his eyes enormous at the sight of his distraught grandmother. Without a word he picked her up bodily and carried her out of the house. Stuart and I followed as far as the foyer where Dr. Legare stopped us.

"What's all this business Louisa is talking about?" he said.

Stuart tried to dodge him. "I don't know," he said. "Would you mind stepping aside? I'm trying to get my wife out of here."

"Not 'til she has talked with the police. Louisa claims she had something to do with Miss Peregrine's death."

"Louisa Hill is a lunatic. You know that. Now get out of my way. My wife is ill." He gave the haughty aristocrat a beefy left shoulder. I gasped as Legare fell across the bottom three steps of the staircase. At the same moment, a brawny policeman stepped through the parlor archway.

"What's going on out here, boys?" he said.

Stuart answered the question before Legare could get to his feet. "Nothing, officer. I'm trying to get my wife home. She's sick. I'm afraid she's going to faint."

Stuart kept his eyes riveted on Legare. I started to cry again, whimpering. After watching Legare flounder about on the floor a few seconds, the officer adjusted his holstered firearm, walked to where the doctor lay struggling, and hauled him up.

"And I suppose the good doctor here happened to trip over his own shoelaces. Is that right, sir?"

Said the flustered Croomer Legare, "This goon struck me. I shall press charges."

Stuart spoke calmly, but with disdain. "He was harassing my wife, accusing her of God-knows-what. Look at her. She's ill...had surgery recently. I have to take her home."

"Ill?" Legare said, red-faced. "In Charleston we call it drug addiction, an expensive habit from what I understand."

Stuart lunged for Legare again, but this time the burly officer blocked him almost without effort. Stuart looked surprised. He gave in to the man's strength, but the officer took no chances. He kept one huge hand firmly gripped around Stuart's upper arm.

"You're not from around here are you, boy?" he said. "I can tell by that Yankee accent." Stuart tried to pull away, but the officer held him fast. Legare took advantage of the moment to jump in with more accusations.

"That's right. He isn't. Nor is his wife." He gestured toward me. "They're troublemakers. Ought to be tarred and feathered, run out of..."

"...town on a rail," the policeman intoned and winked at Stuart and me. "I'm assuming you're Mrs. Prince, young lady, and this here brawler your husband?"

"Yes," said Legare. "You will arrest them both this instant."

The officer was not pleased to be ordered about by the effeminate aristocrat from South of Broad. "Dr. Legare," he said, "several hysterical ladies are carrying on something awful in the parlor. One looks like she might pass out any minute. Do you suppose you could amble on back, see if there's anything you can do to help out? I need to ask Mr. and Mrs. Prince a few questions."

Legare narrowed his eyes and lifted his chin. He fixed a cool gaze on the policeman. "You'd do well to be cautious about whom you insult in this part of town," he said. "You may have regrets later."

"Yes, sir," the officer answered, though his eyes met Legare's in an unwavering stare. "I try to be cautious about everything. Thank you just the same for reminding me."

Legare took a spotless white handkerchief from the inside pocket of his coat jacket and blotted his perspiring forehead. His poise had suffered. He did not speak to Stuart or me again. He dipped his chin an inch and walked away. The policeman waited until the doctor was out of earshot before speaking again.

"Okay, folks," he said when he thought it safe. "Let's sit a spell in these fancy chairs and talk things over. By the way, I'm Sergeant Ray Bob Hanahan."

"Stuart Prince," Stuart said, nodding, though he could not shake hands. He was having too much trouble getting me to a chair. I had gotten dizzy and could not walk without help.

"I'll try not to keep you, Mrs. Prince," Hanahan said to me despite the fact my eyes were closed. "I know all this has been tough on you. Are you aware Louisa Hill is saying you killed Miss Peregrine? She claims you were mad at her about some paper you wanted her to sign, a contract or copyright…something like that."

I opened my eyes and started to speak, but Stuart cut in. "Louisa Hill is a certified nut case, man. Didn't you catch that when you talked to her?"

"Matter of fact, I did notice something was a hair off. Didn't think much about it. Everybody's got a tendency to get upset when the grim reaper comes knocking, 'specially if they think foul play was involved."

"Fanny Peregrine was pushing ninety, Sergeant. She died, that's all. She's been dying for months."

"Mind telling me what a copyright is, Mr. Prince?"

"Not now. My wife is sick. We need to get home before she falls on her face. Come on, Arlena. We're going."

Stuart pulled me out of the chair and across the foyer toward the door. I stumbled, knocking over the wreath that was still leaning against the grandfather clock. The officer reached out to catch me. "Whoa, boy," he said to Stuart. "This little gal is wobbly. Take it easier on the git-go."

Stuart turned to steady me. I mumbled that I had to sit down. "No, Arlena. We have to get you to the car," he said. "Louisa is trying to make trouble."

"I can't walk any farther."

Stuart gave up. He leaned over, picked me up, and carried me outside. The policeman followed and watched with interest as I threw up a half-pint of liquid the color of red wine on Miss Peregrine's prized azaleas.

"Whew-ee," he said. "Smells like this little lady's been hitting the bottle this evening. I'm not surprised she's a mite staggery."

"That's not the problem," Stuart said. "She's sick."

I coughed and gagged. "I'll get her a wet towel," Hanahan said. "Must be towels around here someplace."

"She's all right now. I'll make her spit. Do it, Arlena. Spit it out."

I spat and begged for the towel the policeman had offered. He handed me his neatly folded handkerchief. I thought through my tears that every man in Charleston must carry the things, every man except Stuart.

"I'm okay now," I said, sniffling, "but I need to go home."

Stuart put his face close to mine and spoke as if trying to communicate with a mental patient. "Arly, listen. Pull yourself together. The car is parked on High Battery. Can you make it?"

"Why is it way over there? I can't walk that far."

"It's the same place I always wait for you. But I got scared when police cars started showing up, and I ran over here to find you. I don't know how Louisa rounded up all these cops so fast. She must have told 911 an axe murderer was on the loose."

"Yes," said the sergeant. "Miss Hill is the one who called all right. Reported Miss Peregrine dead – murdered – and her killer was about to get away. But when the first two officers got here, she changed her story. Said she was confused, didn't remember what happened. Another woman was with her trying to keep her from falling apart, name of FitzSimons, I think. Miss Hill must have called her first, then the police. Anyhow, by the time I got here, she was going around and around on her story. First said Miss Peregrine died in her sleep...but later she started throwing your name around, Mrs. Prince, saying you as good as killed the old lady, getting her upset over that copyright business. Yes, sir, she was powerful wound-up, in shock from the look of her. It wouldn't be smart putting too much stock in any of her ramblings tonight."

I began weeping again. "We have to go," Stuart said one more desperate time. "Can't you see my wife is on the verge of collapse?"

"Where do you stay?" the sergeant asked as Stuart led me along Miss Peregrine's front walk.

"Sullivan's. We rent the Middleton cottage."

"Thank you, Mr. Prince. I'll try to get out there tomorrow morning, talk things over. Y'all be careful going home now, you hear? Those bridges can be the pure devil after dark."

⌘ ⌘ ⌘

The rest of the night was difficult after Stuart and I got back to the cottage. Familiar frightening dreams jarred me awake again and again. Every time I opened my eyes, I was sick to my stomach and perspiring with fear. And every time, Stuart had left the bed. Twice, I found him pacing the porch in the dark; once, dozing on the sofa in the sitting room; and last, standing in the bedroom doorway staring at me. As dawn broke over the ocean, I pleaded with him to try to get one more hour of sleep. He refused. At eight thirty, I stopped begging, took a shower, and dressed for warmth in sweats and wool socks. When I emerged from the bedroom, smells of toast and brewed coffee drifted into the living room from the kitchen. In a little while, Stuart brought out a tray bearing a plate of buttered English muffins and two steaming coffee mugs. He set the tray on the rickety coffee table and relocated his brooding spot to an easy chair. The moment I sank down opposite him on the sofa, a car engine coughed outside. He got up and looked out the window.

"A cop," he said, squinting, "the guy from last night."

My stomach fluttered as I watched him walk toward the door and open it to the uninvited visitor. "Morning, Mr. Prince," Hanahan drawled. "Is it all right if I come in and talk with you and the missus a few minutes? Nothing serious, mind you…just wanted to let you know what's going on in town."

"Sure," Stuart said.

Hanahan stepped inside and took off his hat. He was a hulk of a man, filling the narrow doorway as he passed through. "Morning ma'am," he said in my direction. "Hope you're feeling better this morning."

I nodded and lowered my eyes.

"Sit here," Stuart said to him and pulled up a chair. "Would you like coffee? It's fresh."

"No, thanks. Don't want to put you out. I know you're both exhausted…I'll get right to the point. I came to tell you about Miss Hill. She's been doing a heap of talking these last few hours, wants me to arrest you, Mrs. Prince."

I looked at Stuart. His face went red. My own face stiffened with fear. The sergeant held up both hands to reassure us. "Now don't go getting yourselves all worked up," he said. "Ain't nobody paying her no mind. Mrs. FitzSimons is doing the best she can to keep her under control. Dr. Legare – you remember him – said Miss Peregrine just up and died, that's all, same as you told me last night, Mr. Prince. I have to say, sounds reasonable, a woman her age."

"Can't you stop Hill from making false accusations?" Stuart said. "It's got to be against the law, going around calling someone a murderer."

"Best to ignore her. I mean, you could go to the trouble of getting a restraining order and all, but frankly, I think you were right when you said she's a bit off."

"Anyone there last night could've told you," Stuart said.

Hanahan nodded. "With that in mind, I think the two of you ought to keep your heads down a while, lay low. Miss Hill will get tired of running off at the mouth soon enough when she finds out ain't nobody listening."

"What exactly is she saying?" I asked. The sergeant looked at me in surprise. It was the first time I had been coherent in his presence.

"I reckon the gist of it is she thinks you've been tormenting Miss Peregrine about a business paper, a contract or copyright, the thing I was asking you about last night. But worse, she said you've been squeezing money out of the old lady to support some kind of drug habit. And a couple times she went slam out of her mind and started ranting you killed poor Miss Peregrine outright. Not that it matters what she says. Nobody else seems to think you've done anything out of the way, including Tycie Roosevelt."

"When did you see Tycie?" I said.

"Drove all way to Edisto last night. She was one scared little woman. Told me she didn't want anything to do with dead folk. Edisto people – the older ones, anyway – are scared of h'ants, you know."

I slid to the edge of the sofa to get closer to Hanahan. "What else? Did she tell you anything helpful?"

"Said she ain't talking to no whitebread policeman. But when I told her about Louisa Hill badmouthing you, old Tycie came to your defense. Decided to talk to whitebread, after all. She thinks highly of you, Mrs. Prince. Don't get me wrong, though. She didn't make the mistake of going off on Miss Hill. Island people got horse sense. They know who and who not to rile."

27

Hanahan had just driven away when the phone rang. Stuart picked up to an overwrought Grayson Pinckney demanding in his best courtroom style that we come to his office at once. Stuart agreed. I balked...until he reminded me Mr. Pinckney was quite probably the only friend I had left in Charleston. We walked into Pinckney Building at five of ten. Mr. Pinckney was in a state.

"Ah…you're here early," he said, his face flushed from activity. "Good, good. I need to speak with you before the others arrive."

"Others?" Stuart said as Lillian hustled us to a row of chairs set up in Mr. Pinckney's private office.

"Don't waste time with idle questions, boy. We can talk at length later. Right now I need brief you on a few details. We've got ourselves a crisis here."

I looked at Stuart. His eyes had grown dark with anxiety. Alarmed, I turned back to Mr. Pinckney in hope he would offer reassurance. He persisted in his uncharacteristic jumpiness, hardly noticing when I asked him a simple question.

"What crisis?" I said. "Stuart and I have had enough for one week."

Mr. Pinckney busied himself adding an extra chair to the row. "And the week isn't over," he said. "The reason I was so willing to make you that substantial loan the other day is about to be made clear. I'm going to have to break some news this morning in regard to the demise of Fanny Peregrine…God rest her soul…news that's bound to upset a few people. The two of you could become the target of a host of ill feelings."

"Briefly, the situation is this," he went on. "Fanny changed her will a few weeks ago, in secret. You accompanied her here the day she started the process, Arlena. Do you recall?"

I searched my brain and nodded. "…the day I fell asleep in Lillian's office."

"Yes, and after our meeting, you drove her out to Sullivan's. Poor thing had become nostalgic, too much talk about the past, I suppose. Dwelling on memories has a way of making one want to visit the old places. She was having a difficult time with her personal life, suffering from common pettiness of certain loved ones. I think that's how she put it. She told me she still cared about them, always would, but no longer had confidence in their judgment, particularly when it came to managing her estate, her considerable estate.

"It isn't an unusual phenomenon, you know, people becoming disenchanted with their heirs. Fanny felt she needed to adjust her will. She wanted to make sure the bulk of her father's fortune would go to philanthropic interests instead of a few individuals. Before she became dissatisfied with her first will, Fanny had been comfortable with quite simple instructions, everything divided among her closest friends, her family as she was fond of calling them. She did not include me in this elite group at the time, though attitudes have a way of changing. We all know the members of her so-called kin: Jeannette FitzSimons, Croomer Legare, Louisa, Tycie.

"Originally, Fanny expected Jeannette and Croomer to provide for Louisa and Tycie out of their own portions of her estate and also to assume responsibilities associated with her various causes. But she had begun to fear this wouldn't happen in the manner she wanted, which was the crux of the problem, her basic loss of faith. For a number of reasons, she had become convinced her heirs didn't care about things charitable, cultural, environmental, or any other of Fanny's lofty interests.

"Thus, we have a new will to read this morning, one that's going to cause an uproar. Arlena, don't be shocked, but you and I are included in this revised document. Fanny has made some interesting provisions for the two of us. We are to be employed by her estate, if we so choose, to serve as co-directors of a foundation that will exist for the sole purpose of lending support to Fanny's favorite philanthropies. One of these is the sponsorship of several environmental protection projects to be implemented on Sullivan's Island. Her wish was for you, guided by me, to manage those efforts. In return, you'll be paid handsomely in addition to having the option of living rent-free in one of the island cottages owned by the estate.

"For our efforts managing the foundation, we'll be paid per annum, though I'll do the bulk of the work as I pray to God my health holds out long enough for my grandson to grow up and take over my duties. We...you and I...will also manage a large block of the estate's investments – stocks, securities, and such – from which we will receive a percentage of annual profits. That's where the real money will come from. It's important for you to know I've already signed on contractually to fulfill my part of the bargain. You, however, still have a few days to think things over before committing... seven, to be exact. In short, your choices are these: buy into the plan I've just outlined...the whole kit and caboodle...or take a one-time, one-hundred-thousand-dollar payment from the estate and be on your way. Fanny wanted you to have a say in the matter. It was not her purpose to imprison you, not at your tender age. On the contrary, she wanted to help you actualize your talents. She meant for you to have control of your own future, something she never had. You're looking at the difference between a lifelong commitment and a once-in-a-lifetime windfall of cash. The choice is yours."

I stared at Grayson Pinckney through unblinking eyes. His words had not penetrated my understanding. They banged around inside my head like steel balls in a tilt machine. "My one regret," he continued, oblivious to my dazed condition, "is that Fanny didn't explain all this to you herself. She meant to, planned to. But the grim reaper came around too soon. Perhaps that's the way it always happens. At any rate, the morning you drove her here, she retained me to work out the details of this rather complicated new document. We started the process at that time. And, no, she didn't cut her other friends out entirely. She simply changed things around. The new will still provides for the continued care and sustenance of Tycie and Louisa, plus lump sums for Jeannette and Croomer and trust funds for each of their children's educations. Fanny even took care of Tycie's grandson in that way. But the millions are now earmarked for specific philanthropies, which isn't going to sit well with her family."

"But why, Mr. Pinckney?" I said. "Why me?"

"Why, indeed? No one answer, my dear, but I think the trifle that turned her decision was your attitude toward Sullivan's. Fanny told me you and she participated in many spirited discussions about that old sand pile, you defending its virtues faithfully, she playing devil's advocate. She said Jeannette and Croomer wanted to sell Peregrine coastal properties to investors whose plan it was to develop them commercially. This offended Fanny's sensibilities more than anything else. Her concern was for the environment, not the bottom line. She had a deep and abiding love for the coastline of South Carolina, gave millions every year to help protect it. And now she wants the two of us to continue her noble effort. Southerners are always carrying some banner or another. This one happened to be Fanny's. She hoped you'd be proud to be a part of her vision, you and your husband."

My vocal cords went rigid again. Stuart had to speak for me. "If it's all so wonderful, sir, why does it feel like we've been handed a hot coal? What about it, Arly? Does any of this make sense to you?"

I stared down at my hands. "I can't fathom it," I said, "but you know how Miss Peregrine was. It's the kind of thing she was capable of doing. Only there must be a catch somewhere? What is it, Mr. Pinckney? What's the catch?"

Grayson Pinckney frowned and stroked his chin. "To be honest, I've been wondering the same thing. Then, when I heard through the grapevine how Louisa Hill was behaving last night, the things she was saying about your involvement in Fanny's death,

I realized I had my answer. Hill herself is most probably the catch we both fear. Not to mention Ray Bob Hanahan, a known pot stirrer. I admit, I wouldn't be nearly as nervous if that mongrel hadn't emerged from the swamp and started sniffing around."

"What do you mean?" Stuart said, the skip in his voice matching the one in my heart.

"Think, boy. The ravings of a mad woman can generally be discounted if they don't fit in with the other facts. After all, Louisa's accusations toward Arlena, even if true, aren't bad enough to implicate her in murder. Ray Bob would have to figure against it. The only motive he might come up with would be the copyright Louisa was yammering about. But he must not think it's important, or else he'd already have done something about it."

My heart began to quiver when I realized what Mr. Pinckney was getting at. "But when he finds out I'm included in her will, I'll have an instant motive."

Observing I was on the verge of panic, Mr. Pinckney spoke to me more quietly. "He may not jump to that conclusion, Arlena, though we need to be prepared in case. Ray Bob Hanahan is an ignorant man who considers himself cunning…a dangerous combination."

"But Miss Peregrine didn't tell me she was going to do this. How could anyone say it was a motive when I didn't know."

"There's no way you can prove that. It could get to the point where it would be your word against Louisa's."

"But Louisa is out of her mind…literally." I said too loudly.

"Stop," Stuart said. "None of this is Mr. Pinckney's fault. He's doing the best he can to help you."

I spoke no more. I couldn't. The iron band of pressure closing off my throat was now crushing my skull. My eyes felt too large for their sockets. I grabbed Stuart's hand and held onto it when Lillian's voice rattled through the intercom that the others had arrived.

"Thank you, Lil," Mr. Pinckney said into the speaker. "Send them in and get my son-in-law up here. I need him as a witness."

Mr. Pinckney looked hard at Stuart and me and warned us a last time. "You must present an unflappable front," he said. "It's imperative."

Lillian led Jeannette FitzSimons and Croomer Legare into the office. "Jeannette…Croomer, good morning," Mr. Pinckney said. "You've already met Mr. and Mrs. Prince, I presume. Please, have a seat. Make yourselves comfortable."

Stuart rose, nodded, sat again. We both remained silent. Mr. Pinckney sat down behind his desk and did battle alone, his usual aplomb suffering no discernible strain. Stuart and I were grateful for his presence, especially upon observing the furtive glances between FitzSimons and Legare.

"Where is Miss Hill?" Mr. Pinckney said. "I asked that everyone be on time."

"Still at Peregrine House," FitzSimons answered. "Last night took a toll. Croomer had to give her a sedative to help her sleep. She'll be down a few hours yet."

"And Tycie?"

Jeannette answered again. "She won't be coming either. We couldn't get in touch with her. What's this all about, Grayson? Croomer and I are both exhausted. We've endured hell."

"I'm sure you have, Jeannette. Forgive me for having to infringe upon your time of grief. Truly I had no alternative."

"Get to the point, man," said Legare. "I have to make rounds at the hospital. Life goes on."

As Mr. Pinckney was about to respond, Jonathan Prioleau entered the room and took a seat next to Stuart. The memory of their fight at the oyster roast sprang into my head. I felt as if the oxygen supply in the crowded office had dwindled to a perilous proportion. Mr. Pinckney picked up a blank legal pad from his massive desk, tossed it to his son-in-law with a tad too much force, and instructed him to take notes. Without speaking, Prioleau took a pen from his breast pocket and readied the pad. He allowed himself one visual survey of the room to identify who was present. It was clear he had no knowledge of the meeting's purpose.

Mr. Pinckney let it be known he was ready to begin. Everyone waited for his next move. First, he handed out copies of the will to everyone except Stuart and Jon Prioleau, both of whom stretched their necks to see mine. "You don't have to read this now," he said, "but as you can see, it is Fanny Lockwood Peregrine's last will and testament. You three individuals – not you Jonathan, nor you, Mr. Prince…I'm talking about the others now, plus Louisa and Tycie – are remembered by the kind departed lady. Jeannette and Croomer, you will receive lump sums of one hundred thousand dollars each. You may collect your checks within the week. In addition, Raven, her brother Mills, and Croom, Jr. have been provided trust funds to cover the entirety of their educational expenses. Abraham Roosevelt, Tycie's grandson, will enjoy the same consideration. Personally, I think helping these young people finance their educations was an exceptionally thoughtful and generous gesture on Fanny's part. I wish she had done the same for Jon, Jr., my own grandson. But that's for me to do, of course."

He coughed once and plunged ahead before anyone could interrupt him with questions. "Louisa is to live in the South Battery house as long as she wishes, though she will not own it. The house will remain part of the estate. Nevertheless, she may occupy it for her lifetime. The same arrangement has been made for Tycie, although Fanny understood Tycie would probably elect to stay on at Edisto rather than move in with Louisa.

"As for you, Mrs. Prince, yours is a different situation. In a sense, you'll remain an employee, but of the estate rather than any one person, if you feel so inclined, that is. I've been given the same opportunity. Fanny…Miss Peregrine…made special provisions to this effect detailed in our own personal copies of the will. They have to do with what we discussed in our private meeting earlier this morning. The balance of the estate will remain intact. Proceeds from investments are to be dispersed in a systematic manner to help organizations and institutions Fanny has supported over the years, which makes for a long list, I must say. Well, ladies and gentlemen, that about covers it. We can hammer out details later. Croomer, my man, you still have time to make rounds."

I looked at Legare and FitzSimons. They were both pale with shock. FitzSimons' gaze roamed the room, stopping first on Stuart's face and second on mine. I lowered my eyes to avoid her stare. She lost interest in me and confronted Mr. Pinckney.

"You know this isn't a legitimate will, Grayson," she said. "It can't be. I have Fanny's will. I helped her write it years ago."

Legare kept quiet, his eyes trained on Mr. Pinckney, who said, "It isn't difficult to understand, Jeannette. Fanny decided to make out a new will a few weeks ago. Had a change of heart, so to speak, about what she wanted to do with her holdings. You're a lawyer. You've seen this sort of thing happen countless times, and I sincerely hope, out of respect for Fanny, you'll be gracious about honoring her last wishes."

Croomer Legare stood up with a flourish. "This," he said, shaking the blue folder in Mr. Pinckney's face, "is not what Fanny wanted. It's outrageous. I won't allow you to give credence to such an obvious pack of lies."

Legare's entire body trembled with fury. Stuart and I stopped breathing. There was a moment of silence before FitzSimons got to her feet and leaned far across Mr. Pinckney's desk. Her nostrils flared like two small red wings.

"Grayson," she said with peculiar hoarseness. "I have had to endure every kind of abuse imaginable at the hands of this woman..." She pointed her forefinger at me. "...and now I'm called here to be insulted with a bogus will I'm certain she has somehow orchestrated. I assure you, I won't let her get away with it. I'll see her rot in hell first."

28

Stuart led me out of Mr. Pinckney's office while the arguing was at a pitch. We moved in silence down the carpeted hallway, agreeing with head nods to pass up the elevator and take the stairs. I gave no thought to where we were going. I only wanted to escape. But even descending stairs are cruel to recent surgical patients. I was winded by the second-story landing, in pain by the first. Stuart saw I was in trouble, but he did not seem to care. He was intent on getting us out of the building. Holding me fast by my hand, he pulled me through the hallway of the street floor, through the ornate reception area, and out its walnut doors to freedom.

There I thought we would rest, but Stuart thought to go faster. Ignoring my pleadings to stop, he rushed me across Broad Street, traffic bearing down on us from both directions.

"Why…are we…running?" I said, my words coming in spurts and starts as he hurried me toward the Romeo. "I have to stop, please."

"Get in the car," he said. 'We're going to look for Tycie." He shoved me into the passenger seat, ran around the hood, and climbed in on the driver's side. "Didn't Mr. Pinckney say she lives on Edisto?" he asked, coaxing the engine to life. "That's where Hanahan said he went to talk to her?"

"Yes, but I don't know where on the island. What's the point? What can she do?"

"We have to find her. Jeannette FitzSimons was dead serious back there. Tycie is the only person alive who can say for certain you didn't do anything out of the way to Miss Peregrine. Louisa is hardcore insane. No one will listen to her. But FitzSimons and Legare are professional people, both of whom hate your guts. That leaves Tycie, no one else. We have to find her, tell her what's going on. Let's just hope she'll back you if it comes to it. She has to know those other three are dangerous."

On Highway 17, as we raced toward the Edisto turn-off, I braced my hands on the dashboard. Stuart had pushed the Romeo to eighty. "You've gone mad," I said, tears flowing. "Everyone has gone mad. Please, Stuart, let's leave here. I'm afraid of these people."

"You think the police won't come after us? Things look bad for you, Arly. FitzSimons and Legare could have you thrown in jail any minute. You saw how nervous Mr. Pinckney was. He's more afraid of them than we are."

I put my face in my hands and sobbed. Stuart made no effort to console me. At the turn-off, he took a hard left and focused on driving. At eleven thirty-five precisely, we crossed the Dawhoo River Bridge and rolled onto Edisto. Stuart pulled to a stop in front of a dilapidated gas station and killed the engine. He asked me a question I could not answer right away. "That guy Hanahan told us Tycie's last name. Can you remember it?"

I stopped snubbing and tried to think. Somehow, from a cloudy abyss, the name floated forward in my mind. "Roosevelt...Tycie Roosevelt," I said.

Stuart's eyes flashed recognition. He got out of the car and strode toward the store. Two untidy men sat on either side of the door. They remained motionless as Stuart approached and began speaking. I strained to hear the conversation, but the distance was too great. Stuart gestured toward the road a few times. There was much head-nodding and finger-pointing in the same direction we had just come from. The men appeared to be speaking knowledgeably as Stuart frowned and peered up the road. When he came back to the car and got in, I forced myself not to quiz him. For several minutes we proceeded slowly, looking for some landmark, I assumed. A sand road appeared on the right and Stuart turned into it. The white sand looked smooth on the surface, but the Romeo began jouncing and lurching on contact. I could keep quiet no longer.

"Where are we going?" I said.

"Freedmen's Village, whatever that is."

"Look, there," I said, pointing toward a cluster of box houses in the clearing ahead.

"A little remote, for my taste," Stuart said. "Wonder how long it's been since anyone from above the Mason-Dixon line came back here? Is that marsh grass behind the houses?"

I squinted. "Yes, and a tidal creek. Are you sure this is the right place?"

"I think so. Those old codgers said Tycie's house was natural wood with blue painted shutters. They didn't mention there were five more. Do you see anyone outside?"

As we approached the cluster of houses, the sand road diminished to a trail. Stuart scoped the area and decided if we ever wanted to get the car out, we would have to park and walk the rest of the way. I was afraid to go any closer, but more afraid to stay alone in the car. When we stepped into the clearing, a slender young man appeared in the doorway of the first house.

"Hello," Stuart said, smiling, nodding, reaching too hard for friendliness. "Excuse me, do you know Tycie Roosevelt? We're looking for her."

The man did not speak. He picked up a shaved stick propped next to the doorway and pointed it toward the house opposite his.

"Thanks," Stuart said. More smiling. More nodding. The man remained silent. He faded back into his blue-trimmed dwelling, a shadow melting into darkness.

Stuart and I adjusted our course and moved toward the house across the way. As we walked, I observed the arrangement of structures in the clearing. Nothing could happen in the common area without every person in every house knowing about it. Another man stepped into view, this time from Tycie's front entrance. He was old and hoary headed.

"Do you think he's her husband?" I whispered. "I've never heard her say a word about being married."

"Maybe," Stuart said. He called out to the old man, "Excuse us, sir. We're looking for Tycie Roosevelt. Is this where she lives?"

The old man dipped his chin. "She's at the praise house," he said, "funeralizing Sister Washington. That makes two women folk she'll bury this week. The other one is Missy Peregrine."

"Where's the…praise house?" Stuart said. "Maybe we can speak to her after the service."

"Up the road. You'll hear the singing before you get there."

"Hardtop road?" Stuart said. "The one we turned off to get here?"

"That's right. Go along a spell and turn left. Can't miss it. It's the only church."

Stuart kept talking as we backed away. "Thank you for your help. We want talk to Tycie about Miss Peregrine. My wife worked for her too."

The old man's eyes grew wide. His thin body stiffened. "What's your name, man?" he said.

"Stuart Prince, and this is my wife, Arlena. She and Tycie are friends."

"Best you leave my wife alone. Missy Peregrine is dead and gone. Tycie can't do nothing about that now."

"She doesn't have to. We just want to talk with her a few minutes."

"Git on back to Charleston, boy. People like you don't belong in Freedmen's Village. Ain't you paid no mind to the blue markings on our houses? People here are protected by the voodoo."

"We're going. Sorry to have disturbed you. Thanks again for your help."

Stuart clamped a hand on my arm and guided me toward the path. I did not comprehend what had just taken place. "Don't talk," he said. "The last thing we need is to antagonize a crowd of locals who practice voodoo. Walk faster."

"Now what?" I asked after we were back in the car and Stuart was forcing the gears into reverse.

"We intercept Tycie at the praise house and try to get some sense out of her. Then we git on back to Charleston like we've been told."

The abused little Romeo bumped onto the highway with a shudder. Stuart shifted into second and began watching for the church. It turned out to be a picturesque white building set neatly in the center of a leaf-strewn lot close beside the road. A giant live oak dominated its sloping lawn. The somber old tree appeared to have escaped the dark woods that edged the church grounds all around. Stuart eased the Romeo onto the sand driveway and parked close to the tree.

"Want to walk around and stretch your legs?" he said. "Looks safe enough, and there's no telling how long it takes to funeralize somebody."

"I don't know. Maybe we ought to leave."

"No. I'm talking to Tycie if I have to kidnap her. You saw the old man's reaction when I mentioned Miss Peregrine's name. He knows something…something Tycie told him. People don't try to spook you with voodoo unless they're scared themselves. Let's walk. I'm jumpy."

We got out of the car and picked our way through the maze of twigs and limbs that had fallen from the huge oak. Another acre of lawn, also littered with debris, spread out behind the church. Its autumn-brown grass was wiry and thick. We stood looking at the building a few minutes in full sunlight before stepping back into the shade of the tree.

The music beating inside the church was rich with complicated rhythms and counter melodies, African in origin, yet with English lyrics. I had heard spirituals before, even sung them, but this syncopated melody made imitations seem lifeless. It was loud and pulsing, like the spirit choirs in my dreams. I inched closer to Stuart for comfort, though he seemed to have forgotten I was there. The woods bordering the churchyard had captured his attention.

Silent shadows floated in and out among the black-green tangles of vines. At first, I thought I was imagining things. Soon though, I realized this was no illusion. A human form stepped from among the trees. It was wholly a part of the forest, a wild thing belonging to nature. Surely if Stuart and I kept quiet and still, it would return to its murky home. We waited, but the shadow did not retreat. It remained at the edge of the lawn, stalwart and still. I could not see its eyes, though I could feel their focus on Stuart and me.

In a haze of time, the figure was joined by another and another, until thirty or more men formed a half-circle at the edge of the clearing. One by one, men emerged from the woods and formed an arc of strength. There was no escape. We were blocked all around. Stuart stepped forward to shield me from view. I held my breath and waited for the unfolding.

A strident male voice rang out. It sounded like Tycie's husband. "I told you to leave the island, man," the voice called to Stuart. "Why did you come here to scare old Tycie, as if she ain't scared enough? Now you're in sorry shape. The conjure woman has spoken. She means to put a hex on you…keep you from harming my Tycie. You're going through the rite to rid you of your poison so Tycie can be free of you and that witch woman in town."

"We're not here to cause trouble," Stuart said. "We need to talk to Tycie for one minute, that's all. You're right, there's a woman in town who's no good. She hurts people. Her name is Louisa Hill. We think Tycie can help us stop her from injuring anyone else."

"She's the one threatened to cast a spell on my Tycie. Touched in the head, she is. Bad to the bone. But the brass-ankle conjure woman who lives on Snake Island has promised to take away her power. She's the Queen Mammaloi. I won't let my wife die of a witch spell, not if I can help it. If you come to Edisto Island and meddle in our business, we make you pay the price. It'll be dark soon. That's when the conjure woman takes out the poison."

More shakily, Stuart said, "You're right. We'll leave, and we won't come back." He gripped my hand and pulled me along the back wall of the church building. We headed in the direction of the car, but the men closed ranks and stopped us at the corner of the building. Stuart panicked. His body went rigid. He slid his grip upward from my hand to my wrist and plowed headlong into the line of men. We crashed into a wall of muscle, bounced back, and landed on the grass like two ragdolls. I lay stunned. Stuart scrambled to his feet and attacked the first man in his path. He struck one ineffective blow before the man knocked him out cold. I clamored to his side and screamed his name, but he did not respond.

I became aware of the men closing in. I glanced up in terror, but I could not defend myself. Rough hands overpowered me. One man dropped to his knees. I looked into his face and knew I had seen him before. He was Tycie's grandson, the one who had taken her from Peregrine House the night Miss Peregrine died. I opened my mouth to speak, to beg mercy, but he held my temples in both his hands and forced me to tilt back my head. At the same moment, another man held a bottle to my lips and poured a bitter liquid into my mouth. I gagged as the thick syrup slid down my throat in oily strings. It dripped over my chin and cheeks, one stream defying gravity and running upward into my eyes. I closed them against the burning. After a moment of struggle against the mental fog caused by the drug, the dream beast sprang forth in my head, incarnate, grotesque, hammering out his rhythms upon other-worldly drums. His barbarous moans mingled with the funeral choir still keening within the church. My last thought was of Tycie's heartbreaking cries on the night of Miss Peregrine's death. In my hallucination Tycie was still on her knees crying for the soul of her dead friend. Then I choked on the last drops of the vile liquid and went limp in the arms of the grandson.

29

When I regained consciousness, my perceptions were still clouded by the drug, yet I sensed it was nighttime. Strange rhythms beaten out on hollow drums pounded inside my skull. Rattles vibrated all around me. From some lightless, airless, metaphysical dimension, a choir of male voices hummed a funeral dirge in sorrowful dissonance. I opened my eyes to a whir of motion. Slowly, I focused on a great pit alive with leaping flames. Firelight danced in the air.

I was too frightened to move. I scanned the scene with my eyes, too afraid to turn my head. Stuart lay on his back beside me, still as death, eyes closed. I watched his chest rise and fall in jagged breaths. At least, he was alive. We were strapped down beside each other on a wooden incline slanted upward at our heads. I whispered Stuart's name, but he remained immobile. Before I could say anything else, a solo animal scream went up answered by an explosion of drums. An obsidian hand shook a rattle two inches from my face.

"She sees," a female voice croaked from somewhere behind. I strained my neck, but could not make out who had spoken. A rough hand covered my face with a gauzy cloth. I could barely see through the filminess. Then I felt another hand adjust the incline. One quick jerk raised my and Stuart's heads a foot higher. At the same moment, there appeared before us a roundish woman with a face a wash of blue. As if afraid of her presence, the music died away. A hush settled over the proceedings. The woman snatched the gauze from my face, and I saw her clearly for the first time. She was obese, with wild orange hair and loose flesh that hung from her throat and arms. I could discern nothing about her face. It was painted all blue except for her eyelids, which were red and outlined in white.

"I am the Mammaloi," she said and thrust a human skull inches from my eyes. I opened my mouth to scream, but a whimper was all that came out.

"Come, Damballah," the woman cried and raised the skull high above her head. Her hands and arms jerked in spasms. A clamor of music went up, but it stopped abruptly when she lowered the skull. The woman stared at me with glowing eyes.

"I am the Mammaloi of Snake Island, the conjure woman who casts out evil spirits. Tonight, I will take out your poison as you go through the rite. You bring evil-evil to our islands. I beg Damballah to protect us from you. I beg him to bring the white fire. Come, Damballah, come."

Again, she held the skull aloft. Her swag-bellied body shook as the drums and voices roared. I looked beyond her to the center of the room and saw more dancers, men and women dressed in yellow. They took turns cavorting around the pit. The woman who called herself the Mammaloi danced separately and closest to the fire. After a time, her legs folded beneath her, and she sank into a heap on the ground. Two young men picked her up and carried her to a throne-like chair a few feet from the incline on which Stuart and I were strapped. There she drank from a tin dipper and leaned back to rest.

Drums and rattles grew louder and more frantic. Voices that at first had been low and mournful now rose to a roar. Blue-faced dancers in white robes took the floor spontaneously, writhing and shaking, working themselves into a frenzy. They formed a circle around the pit and clapped out complicated rhythms, their bodies swaying in perfect time. The orange-haired woman rose from her throne and waddled to the edge of the pit. She tossed in a handful of gray powder. Flames shot to the rafters. Black smoke poured through a hole in the ceiling. The dancers leaned backward in unison, widening their circle around the fire. Something was about to happen. A young man stepped into the circle and bowed low before the Mammaloi. He handed her a gleaming machete. She smiled wickedly as the drums speeded up, lifted the great knife, and shook it at the dancers. They cowered before her as she leaped about on bare feet, brandishing the cruel weapon. With every sweep of the blade, the dancers fell away, fear on their faces. I was terrified to think what she might do next.

I looked at Stuart. He was still unconscious. Slowly he rolled his head to the side. I prayed our captors would not notice. Stuart's eyelids fluttered open. He blinked in confusion. I called out his name, but he could not hear. He tried to get up before realizing he was restrained. He looked down at himself and at me. His eyes stretched to abnormal proportions as I mouthed his name again. The machete sliced the air above our heads. We forgot each other and stared at the Mammaloi. She swung the machete over our bodies lower and lower, closer and closer. The dancers' bodies vibrated out of control. "Damballah, Damballah," they screamed. I was certain we were about to be murdered and dismembered, our bodies never to be found. I prayed with all my might I would go first. I did not want to watch Stuart die.

But with perfect timing the oddly graceful Mammaloi glided back to the fire. The man who had produced the machete now handed her a live rooster. She shook the writhing bird and threatened it with the knife. Her eyes glistened. Her mouth dropped open in triumph. The twitching dancers leaned forward in one motion, screaming for the kill. But the Mammaloi tossed the rooster aside and slowly approached Stuart and me. She leaned over and breathed into my face. Her stench was nauseating. She held the machete an inch from my eyes and growled, "If you ever come back to our island, you'll feel the edge of my blade." Stuart struggled in his restraints. He was in anguish at not being able to help me. The Mammaloi shook the machete at him and shouted, "You, too, hostile man." She slapped him with her other hand. I closed my eyes, and when I opened them again, the terrifying woman had gone. Someone was pushing back a pair of tall plank doors at the far end of the enclosure. A section of purple sky glimmering with stars appeared beyond the doorway.

Someone else, male from the feel of the hands, cut mine and Stuart's bindings and forced us to our feet. Stuart called my name and reached out to help me. The man struck him and told him to keep still. He shoved us toward the door and out into the night. Grateful, I filled my lungs with fresh air. In the distance across a broad stretch of seagrass, the pale light of a gibbous moon outlined a row of palmettos. They stood at the edge of a vast marsh, their long fronds rattling in the wind. To their left as far as we could see, pearl-lucent water shimmered in the Canaan of southern moonlight.

"People like you ain't to know Snake Island's whereabouts," our guard said. "I have to bind up your eyes."

"Aren't we still on Edisto?" Stuart said. I wished he had kept quiet.

"Shut your mouth," the man answered as he tied strips of burlap around both our heads and pushed us forward into darkness. I fell to my knees in the sand. He jerked me up by a handful of my hair which caused me to cry out. Stuart tried to help me again. Together we took a few more unsuccessful steps, after which the man swore and ripped off our blindfolds.

"Get in the boat," he said. I looked around once more and concluded the location of Snake Island was forever secure, blindfolds or no.

"Are we going to Edisto now?" Stuart said.

"I told you to shut your mouth, man. Yes, we're going to Edisto, but I'll have to row with the tide. Ain't got no motor."

After an interminable time of pitching and rolling, the boat struck bottom. Our rower clattered his oars together and dropped them to the bottom of the boat. Stuart helped me over the side into knee-deep water and dragged me to a muddy bank. The water was cold. A steely sheen reflected off its dawn-pinkened surface. I looked at Stuart and gasped, before realizing he could look no worse than I. We dipped our hands into the brackish water and tried in vain to wash smoky ash from our faces. I shivered from humiliation and cold. Stuart moved closer and put his arm around my shoulders. He scanned the area, trying to get his bearings. The man in the boat had already pushed off and was floating away on the tide. Stuart took my hand in his and helped me along the only path he could find that led away from the wooded bank. We had gone but a few yards when we came to the clearing of familiar, blue-trimmed houses.

Shutters and doors were shut tight. I caught a faint odor of wood smoke. We avoided the open space in the middle of the clearing, slinking in and out among the narrow-trunked pines, until we reached the sand road where we had parked the Romeo so many hours before. We made a short and futile search for the car before remembering we had moved it to the churchyard. Stuart cursed under his breath as we crept up the road toward the highway. Once on the hardtop, we broke into a jog. No one got in our way. No one pursued us. Several times, I had to stop and rest despite Stuart's angry protests. Somehow, we made it to the church without being seen. At least we hoped we had not. At times, the trees along the road seemed to burn with pairs of eyes. When we turned into the driveway, Stuart sprinted forward, overjoyed to have spotted the car.

"It's here," he breathed, on reaching our little Romeo. "Thank goodness, it's still here."

He jerked open the door. "No key," he said, striking his thigh with his palm. "They must have taken it."

"Maybe we lost it in all the chaos," I said.

In a flash of memory, it came to Stuart he had put the key in his shirt pocket. Within a minute, we were racing for the Dawhoo River. As we neared the bridge, a faded green Ford came speeding toward us head on. It was Tycie's grandson. I looked over my shoulder as the car whizzed by. Tycie was in the passenger seat. "Stuart… it's Tycie, and the boy is driving. Look, he's turning around, coming back our way. Shouldn't we wait?"

"You can't be serious. No way we're waiting for that mad man."

"But you said we had to talk to Tycie…life or death."

"He's her grandson, the one who helped kidnap us. We have to get off this island."

I recalled the evil syrup sliding down my throat. "Yes…he was in the churchyard. I remember now."

"He's bad news, Arly. We'll find another way to talk to Tycie. Hold on, we're coming to the bridge."

I watched the Ford fall farther behind. It stopped, turned around, and headed back toward the island's interior. At the same moment, the Alfa Romeo rolled across Dawhoo River Bridge. The little car lurched forward upon reaching the other side of the river as if loosed from an invisible bond. The spell of Snake Island was broken, or so Stuart and I prayed.

30

It was four in the afternoon by the time we got back to Sullivan's. We had been gone seven hours, though it felt like seven days. Stuart informed me I looked like death and would end up back in the hospital if I did not get cleaned up and rest. Exhausted, we showered and fell into a comatose sleep on our unmade bed. I opened my eyes at half past six, instantly alert, instantly fearful. Stuart had left me alone in the bedroom.

I got up and checked the house. From the porch, I peered with binoculars through the screen to see if I could spot him on the beach. Maybe he had gone jogging to clear his head. Slow waves flashing with phosphorous rolled toward the shoreline. I stared, entranced.

"Hypnotized?" Stuart said from somewhere at my back. I jerked my body around. He was standing in the doorway to the porch.

"Don't startle me like that," I said, "My nerves are shot. I didn't know where you were."

"Hope you're rested," he said. "It's time to take another stab at finding Tycie."

"Not if it means going back to Edisto."

Stuart didn't have a chance to rebut. From the shadows of the sitting room, a female voice stopped him. "You won't have to," Raven said, not caring that her presence had the power to send Stuart into orbit.

He whirled around to face the invisible girl. She stepped forward into the half-light. "Are you insane?" he shouted at her. "One of these days you're going to sneak up on somebody like that and get your head bashed in. I don't know who's worse, you or your mother."

The pale girl moved past him to the porch, acknowledging me with her eyes. I started to speak, but she held up a hand to stop me. She turned back toward Stuart and stared at him with contempt. Without flinching, he stared back, though what he saw was terrible. Her face was chalky, eyes bloodshot, lips bluish. She tightened her mouth into a thin blue line and brushed back a lock of hair.

"You're a jerk, Stuart," she said. "If it weren't for you, Mrs. Prince wouldn't be in this fix. You've never taken care of her, not the way a real man would."

"Don't, Rav," I said. "You shouldn't..."

"Shouldn't what?" she said, turning on me like a hostile cat. "I guess you don't want to face the truth about your husband. He's a bigger waste than Croom. At least Croom admits he doesn't love me. But Stuart here goes around pretending. If he cared a dip about you, he'd never have made you sell your soul to creeps like Grayson Pinckney and Fanny Peregrine. Men are all jerks."

Stuart was seething. I moved to his side and took a firm hold on his arm. I feared what he might do next.

"Raven," I said, mom-like. "I don't want you talking to Stuart in that tone of voice. It isn't fair to take it out on others because you're mad at Croom. Behave yourself or you'll have to leave."

"Don't worry, I don't plan to stay long. I came to tell you Mother has been beside herself since she heard about Miss Peregrine's new will. If I were you, I'd leave Charleston. It's bad for you here. But if you're serious about seeing Tycie – I heard you talking about her just now – I may know where she'll be tonight."

Stuart attacked her with words. "If you have something to say, lose the drama and say it!"

Raven cut her eyes at him again. They were enormous blue crystals set deep in her porcelain face. "I won't tell you anything, scumbag. I wouldn't give you a drink of water if you were dying."

"Rav, please," I said. "Stuart only wants…"

"You be quiet, too," she cried out. "You can't tell me what to do. You're not my mother. I drove out here to try to help you, and now I don't know why. It was a stupid idea. You never helped me. All you did was rat on me. You didn't even pay me when I worked on your stinking manuscript."

"Raven, I…"

"Raven, Raven, Raven," she repeated in staccato. "All I ever hear is 'Raven, do this; Raven, do that; Raven…drop dead!'"

When certain her tirade had played itself out, I went to her and pulled her close. She wept in my arms like a child while I stroked her tousled hair.

"Don't cry," I said. "No one is mad at you. Stuart and I appreciate your trying to help us." I cast Stuart a withering glance to make sure he kept his mouth shut. He looked as if might throw up.

"No one loves me," she said, a vibrato on every syllable. "I might as well run away. I wanted to tell you about Mother, but if I'd known you were going to be mean…oh, who cares? All anyone ever wants is to use me. Even you, Mrs. Prince. You're not thinking about anything right now except how much information you can squeeze out of me about Tycie. She's supposed to be at Peregrine House tonight. That's all I know."

Stuart's expression went from hateful to hopeful. I pressed Raven for details. "But why would she come back. Louisa was awful to her the night Miss Peregrine died."

"I was eavesdropping on Mother…heard her talking to Louisa about the memorial service they're planning for Miss Peregrine. Then they started arguing about her belongings. Mother thought they should give a few things to Tycie. Later, she called Tycie's grandson…at his dormitory, I think. He's a student at the College of Charleston. Told him to bring Tycie to Peregrine House this afternoon. He said he couldn't leave town to go pick her up until after his last class, five-thirty or so. Which means he and Tycie won't make it back to Peregrine House until late, seven or seven thirty."

"Are you sure, Raven? It'll be dark by seven. Wouldn't Tycie rather come in daylight?"

"She doesn't have a choice, not if she wants anything of Miss Peregrine's. Mother and Louisa are greedy. Tycie has to do what they say, or they won't give her a scrap. She's lucky they called her at all. Mother has already moved a ton of silver and china and crystal to our house. She packed it up and hauled it away while Louisa was sleeping off those pills Dr. Legare gave her."

"But Louisa is supposed to have those things. She's supposed to have use of Peregrine House and everything in it as long as she lives. It says so in the will."

"Mother claims she's clearing things out to keep certain people – namely, you and Mr. Pinckney – from getting their hands on them. I know that was a lie, though. She's bringing it all home for me. She told me this morning that everything she's ever done was for me. I felt like a worm. I'm going to stop being such a brat."

"But it's true…your mother is difficult, Raven. I can't think of one kind word to say about her. And from what you just told us, she's taking criminal advantage of Louisa and Tycie."

"Don't talk about my mother." It was clear from Raven's tone she was on the fringe of hysteria. "You're the one who said to let her help me. You went to her office and broke her heart, telling her…you know…and now you're saying more bad things. I want you to stop. I feel so guilty when I think about how I've treated her. She's had such a hard life. From now on I'm going to do everything she says."

"I understand, Rav. Really, I do."

"Leave me alone. You never liked my mother."

"But you've criticized her more than I ever have."

"I didn't mean it. I love my mother."

I turned to Stuart for help. His face was stony. He stared at Raven with unfeeling eyes while I continued trying to reason with her. She refused to listen and began lurching toward the porch door before I finished talking. The last we saw of her, she was running down the beach, blond hair streaming in the wind.

"Good riddance," Stuart said. "Talk about unhinged...maybe she'll go finish what she started on her wrists, do the world a favor."

"Don't, Stuart...please. Everything...everybody...so messed up. I have to call Mr. Pinckney, let him know I don't want any part of Miss Peregrine's will. He can tear it up for all I care."

"No, it's the only card we have left to play. And let's say you did throw it in. FitzSimons and Legare may not be satisfied with just that. They may want a piece of your hide. You have to choose a path and stick to it."

"But I'm scared. Those Edisto freaks...Louisa...Raven. And I already know you're going to try to drag me to Peregrine House again tonight to look for Tycie, who probably won't even be there. You can't depend on anything Raven says."

"Maybe not, but going to Charleston beats the heck out of driving back to Edisto. Go find your black pullover and black jeans. The last thing we need is for some blue-blood to spot us prowling around South Battery after dark."

31

We talked little on the trip to town and less after we arrived South of Broad. Six blocks above the battery, we turned off East Bay onto a narrow side-street and parked among the lesser homes of Tradd and Church. From there we walked to White Point Garden along tree-darkened sidewalks to avoid being seen. No one was in view as we stationed ourselves in the gazebo.

"A car..." Stuart said after fifteen minutes of waiting. "...stopping in front of the house. Is it a Ford...green?"

I studied the vehicle and decided it was a Chevy, not a Ford... black, instead of green.

"Look," Stuart said more urgently half a minute later.

I peered into the darkness. "I can't see a thing," I said. "What? Where?"

"The house...front door," he said, a catch in his voice. "Someone is coming out."

I focused on the entrance to Peregrine House and strained my ears to pick up sounds, though it was impossible to hear anything above the wind. I squinted, looking for movement. "It's Tycie," I said. "I can see her headcloth. Is that Jeannette behind her with two grocery bags? If that's all they're giving her, they're greedier than I thought."

"Where do you suppose grandson is?" Stuart said. "He should have been here by now. And what if Grandpa Voodoo comes with him? I wish we had hidden closer. If we try to make a move from way over here, someone from another house might see us and call the cops. Where the devil is he?"

"Watch the direction Tycie walks," I said. "She'll head straight for his car."

Tycie finished her goodbyes and doddered across the piazza to the steps. She pulled her coat tighter around her shoulders, descended the steps, and started down the walkway toward the street.

I bristled in anger. "Do you suppose Jeannette FitzSimons would be mean enough to make her wait out in the cold?"

Stuart didn't answer. His eyes darted here and there, searching for the grandson's car. My own gaze zeroed in on Tycie. At the end of the walkway, she turned right and shuffled toward King Street. "Maybe she's supposed to meet him on the corner," I said, "or a block or two down."

"And maybe if we follow her, the boy will see us and blow our brains out. Come on. Let's sneak up to King. Try to avoid the streetlamps."

We walked along the left side of South Battery. Tycie continued on the right. When she reached the corner, Stuart lost patience and urged me to call to her.

"Tycie," I said weakly. "It's Arlena." No response. "Tycie," I called louder.

This time she heard, and after a brief visual search for the location of my voice, she walked straight toward us. Then she was no longer walking, but running. The grocery bags dropped to the pavement as she jogged across the street. My mind could not make sense of it, feeble old Tycie moving so fast. But when she snatched off her blue headcloth, the mystery evaporated. The woman before us was not Tycie. It was Louisa, hair slicked back, eyes wild. In her hand was a silver revolver, its slender barrel pointed toward Stuart and me.

She held the gun higher. Stuart and I stood still, the sense of the situation exploding in our heads. This woman was not of the same ilk as superstitious residents of Edisto. She was a full-blown psychotic who would kill us with no conscience. Puffed up by the power of the gun, Louisa's usual rudeness became outright aggression.

She spoke to us in a sneer. "If it isn't Sullivan's resident junky and her poverty-stricken husband. Turn around, both of you. Move toward the house at a normal speed and don't give me reason to shoot you. I suppose you've noticed this gun has a silencer."

We walked several paces in front of her, eyes straight ahead. "Explains the missing car," Stuart whispered.

"Stop talking, man" Louisa said. "Keep quiet 'til we get inside. I'm sick of you causing me trouble."

We followed her instructions. We had no choice. Stuart used the excuse of my faltering gait to move closer. "Do everything she says," he breathed. "Don't cross her. And watch out for Jeannette FitzSimons. She's around here somewhere. I saw her in the doorway earlier."

Louisa pushed us through the front door and shouted at Stuart to be quiet. I begged him with a desperate look to obey. She kicked the door shut and turned the lock. The floorboards creaked as she stepped closer to Stuart and me. She prodded him with the gun. I shrank back. "To the parlor," she said, "for a little chat."

We moved quickly to the left. The parlor was dark except for a wood fire hissing in the ancient grate. An impressive fire, it was, though it gave off little warmth and no comfort. Louisa went over and inspected it. Without a sound, she retreated into shadows on the far side of the room. We heard a fumbling sound and a click. I squinted against the sudden glare of an antique table lamp complete with chimney globe. Harsh light shone from beneath Louisa's chin, distorting her features.

"Sit," she said, "on the sofa. And don't do anything stupid. Jeannette told me to be careful about tricks. She had a feeling you might be sneaking around here tonight, especially after Raven paid you that 'spontaneous' visit earlier. She helped us set this little trap. Maybe I should call Ray Bob Hanahan and tell him where you are. He'd be curious about why you're roaming our neighborhood at night."

Stuart and I lowered ourselves onto the sofa, trying not to antagonize our captor. Louisa switched the gun to her left hand to accommodate a poker with her right. She leaned forward to stir the fire. Stuart tensed as he watched her, a tiger ready to pounce.

"First fire of the season," she said. "Fanny didn't like fires. Wouldn't let me have them. Said the chimney was too old, might have cracks. A spark could escape and start a fire between the walls. She was a stubborn old woman, Fanny. Sometimes I had to punish her, like I'm about to punish you."

I watched in terror as she drew circles in the air with the end of the gun barrel. Had she forgotten, somehow, we were there? Had she slipped so deeply into her own private hell she was fading in and out of reality? Stuart sat on the edge of the sofa, sizing up every opportunity to grab for the gun.

"I've been thinking it over," she said. "There're other people who need punishing...Jeannette and Croomer. I don't trust them. First they told me not to say you killed Fanny. But later, after they found out you cheated us out of millions, they said I could accuse you of anything I wanted. Croomer is going to do an autopsy on Fanny. He's determined to prove foul play was involved in her death. Funny, he wasn't interested in an autopsy until the new will popped up. But I don't care if he slices her up. I never touched those pill bottles without gloves. You did, though, Arlena Prince. Croomer thinks he can prove Fanny died of an overdose of her own medications, and you're the one who administered them."

"Louisa, please," I said.

"Good. I like to be spoken to politely. Fanny never did that. She treated me like a servant, not her own granddaughter. What a big secret that was, almost as big as the one about my mother, who, believe it or not, was your high-and-mighty Miss Peregrine's illegitimate daughter. The pretentious old battle-axe never cared whether either one of us lived or died, not that it matters now. Fanny left me use of the house and barrels of money. Jeannette showed me the will this morning, the real will, not the fake one you and Grayson Pinckney cooked up. She said the two of you have been trying to cut me out."

"No, Louisa," I said. "She's lying. The new will says you can live in Peregrine House the rest of your life and have all the money you'll ever need. Ask Mr. Pinckney if you don't believe it."

"Pinckney wouldn't tell the truth. He's a liar like the rest of you. Look at this bare room. Jeannette has taken everything of value, even the paintings...stripped the ground floor almost clean and the upper levels worse. She's the biggest liar of all and a coward. She wanted me to scare you tonight so you'd destroy the new will and leave town. Said she'd go after you herself, but couldn't handle more problems, not with Raven in trouble. Innocent little Raven needs her mama, and her mama can't risk going to jail. Have you ever heard anything more ridiculous? Jeannette thinks I'm the biggest idiot in Charleston. What she wants is for me to do her dirty work. The only reason I believe what she says about the original will is I read it with my own eyes. But she went too far when she started stealing Fanny's things. It's up to me to stop her."

"You're right," I said. "You can't trust her."

Louisa snorted. "You're one to talk. You convinced Fanny to turn her back on me. You're jealous. That's why you talked her into leaving me out of her will. But now I'm going to make you fix it back like it was. And Jeannette and Croomer won't stop me. They've found evidence you're a criminal."

Stuart held his hands out in submission. "We apologize for everything, Miss Hill," he said. "We never meant to hurt you. Arlena and I promise to destroy the new will and leave town…tonight if you want. You'll never hear from us again. I give you my word."

"Oh…hubby dear has seen the light. But I don't trust hubby dear either. I accept your promise, Mr. Prince. Now let me show you how I'm going to make sure you keep it."

With that she jerked Miss Peregrine's afghan off two cardboard boxes near the fire. "Look," she said, lifting a five-gallon gas can out of the closest box. A gun in her right hand, a gas can in her left. Stuart was having difficulty restraining himself. Louisa, pleased by his reaction, grew bolder. "If you don't leave me alone," she said, "I'll soak Peregrine House in gasoline and burn it to the ground with the two of you inside. I might do it tonight."

"But why?" the frantic Stuart said. "You're right. You've been right all along. Miss Peregrine should have left everything to you. We'll explain that to Mr. Pinckney. Let us call him…right now."

Louisa scoffed at his words and brandished the gun until an unseen someone in the foyer shouted a command to Stuart. "You'll do nothing of the kind, Mr. Prince." There was no mistaking Jeannette FitzSimons' nasal twang. She strode to the middle of the parlor and addressed Louisa. "For pity's sake, woman, move those cans away from the fire."

"Don't come any closer," Louisa said, now pointing the gun at FitzSimons. "I'm not going to let you waltz in here and start telling me what to do. I'm giving the orders tonight."

A surprised FitzSimons sidled closer to Stuart and me. It was clear she did not expect to be the third recipient of Louisa's hostility. Across the room, Louisa sucked in a long breath and exhaled in irregular puffs. "You've got nerve," she said to FitzSimons. "You're the one who gave me the gun, helped me with the disguise, told me what to say to these two interlopers. Why are you changing your tune now?"

FitzSimons was having trouble hanging onto her composure. "You've done well, Louisa," she said, "but enough is enough. Everything is good now thanks to you. You don't have to carry this any further. The gas cans are unnecessary."

"Oh, I see. A gun, yes…but a couple of gas cans, no. Big surprise, huh. Tell me again, why was it so important for me to have a gun?"

Jeannette tried to speak with confidence, but she failed. "Protection...in case these two tried to harm you."

"Ha, what you wanted was for me to use it on them so you wouldn't have to. But all your worries are over now. Hubby here says they're leaving town. No more new will, Jeannette. Your plan worked. They're running for their lives...literally."

"As they should. They aren't a part of us. Fanny would have realized that if she'd lived a little longer. Now give me the gun without a fuss. I'll make sure no one ever knows you had it. If the Princes say anything, I'll swear they're lying, trying to make you look unstable so they can cheat you out of Peregrine House like they tried to cheat you out of money."

Louisa shifted her weight, but she did not lower the gun. "You haven't been listening, Jeannette," she said. "I'm no longer kowtowing to you. Besides, you should be concerned about the gas cans, not the gun. You see, my backstabbing friend, the gun is for the Princes, but the cans are for you. Take a good look. Common old gas cans, much easier to come by than guns. You can buy them at any hardware store. What I'm saying is this: I'll burn Peregrine House to cinders if you don't stop walking off with Fanny's things. Do you hear me, Jeannette? I'll burn it to the ground."

"How can you talk like that, Louisa? Fanny would spin in her grave. She wanted you to enjoy living here. It's what we all want."

"I don't believe you. Next thing, you'll try to commit me to some asylum. I know you and that fast daughter of yours are already planning to slide in here and take over."

FitzSimons shook her head. "You're wrong. There's nothing Raven and I want more than for you to have the security of this house. Croomer feels the same way. It's your home. You've lived here forty years…longer."

"But can I sell it?" she said, thrusting the gun forward.

"Fanny didn't want that, but you can stay the rest of your life. Isn't that enough?"

FitzSimons' tone was slippery. Stuart and I glanced at each other. It was clear the old will gave control of Peregrine House to someone other than Louisa, the most likely candidate being FitzSimons herself.

"There you are," Louisa said. "I can live here, but I own nothing. Fanny didn't trust my judgment. I accept that. But what I don't have to accept is you and Croomer and Raven conspiring to take away even my privilege of living here. Why can't the three of you leave me alone?"

She waved the gas can about with no regard for the fire. Gasoline splashed onto the rug. "All right, all right," FitzSimons said. "We will. The house is yours. That's final. Now put down the can and help me get rid of these two troublemakers."

FitzSimons took one foolish step forward, whereupon Louisa panicked and threw the gas can onto the fire. Stuart grabbed FitzSimons and me by our forearms and flung us backward over the sofa. He tumbled over on top of us the moment the gasoline ignited. An explosion blasted the room. After the initial shock, Stuart roused FitzSimons and pushed her through a nearby doorway. He and I followed and found ourselves in a cold hallway. Stuart yelled at FitzSimons to get me out of the house. Then he ran back for Louisa.

"No," I screamed. "The other can hasn't blown yet."

He pulled away and ran back into the smoke-filled parlor, returning in seconds with Louisa draped over his shoulder. Jeannette FitzSimons led us through a maze of corridors that meandered through the heart of the mansion. After traversing the complicated warren of halls and rooms, we escaped to the cool of the garden. And there beneath the branches of Miss Peregrine's moss-draped grand oaks, we heard the other gas can explode.

32

Stuart knelt on the grass and let Louisa slide from his shoulder. "Is she dead?" FitzSimons asked, dropping to her knees beside Louisa.

"Unconscious, but still breathing," Stuart answered. "We'll watch after her. You go next door. Call an ambulance and the fire department. Hurry, the house could go up."

"Shouldn't I go with her?" I said.

"She'll do better alone. Everyone knows her."

"But someone's already coming…sirens."

Stuart ignored me and concentrated on FitzSimons. "You can't wait any longer," he said to her. "If they get here soon enough, they'll be able to contain the fire."

Jeannette FitzSimons nodded, got up, and disappeared into the night. Stuart straightened out Louisa's arms and legs and made sure she was still breathing. Though nothing of the fire was visible from the garden, acrid smoke wafted through the trees like ghosts of ancient aristocrats.

"Let's go," he said when he had finished caring for Louisa.

"We can't," I said, surprised he would leave anyone who was incapacitated on the lawn of a burning building. "It's spreading too fast."

"She'll be okay until FitzSimons gets back? Are you hurt?"

"I don't think so."

"Then stop arguing and move. We can't be anywhere near here when cops start showing up."

Stuart took my hand and led me to the side of the house. People were already gathering in the street out front. We turned back and stole to the rear of the garden, slinking behind the carriage house like two burglars. I followed close behind while Stuart looked for an opening in the high brick wall. There was none. After a quick search, he motioned we would have to climb over. He showed me how to use inset bricks as footholds. Climbing up first, he dropped to the ground on the other side. I followed. We found ourselves in the garden of the mansion behind Peregrine House.

"But why are we hiding?" I whispered in puffs. "We didn't do anything."

"You want to spend the rest of the night talking to Ray Bob Hanahan or explaining all this to Mr. Pinckney?"

Nothing was left to say, running the only alternative. We hunched low and moved through several un-walled gardens, though we could have marched through with a drum and bugle corps for all the attention anyone paid us. Everything important was happening on South Battery. Squadrons of fire trucks and police cars had already gathered, blue and red lights flashing.

We came to another wall. Stuart found a tiny gate and we slipped through to a side street. People were milling about as if enjoying broad day. A shout arose…a male voice called out, "It's the Peregrine mansion on South Battery…an explosion."

We hurried north on King Street against the crowd hurrying south, and except for being jostled by a few fire voyeurs, we made it to the car without incident, though the sight of the Romeo shocked us. Every window was smashed. Stuart swore as he brushed away glass and hustled me into the car. He climbed in himself and drove slowly across the peninsula, working his way along one-way streets and alleyways toward East Bay and the giant bridge. He had a single destination in mind, the Middleton cottage on Sullivan's.

"The windows," I said in a whine as he drove in silence. "What do you think happened?"

"How should I know? This place is one big nut farm. Nothing surprises me."

"Go faster."

"I don't want to risk getting pulled over for something stupid like speeding. Jeannette FitzSimons is blaring our names up and down South Battery by now. We need to get through Mount Pleasant without tangling with the police."

"What are we going to do?"

"One thing I'm sure of…we can't admit to being at Peregrine House tonight. If we make it home without getting stopped, it's FitzSimons' word against ours."

"But the car windows…"

"I wish I could believe it was simple vandalism, a kid with a tire iron and nothing to do, but I'm afraid it's more."

"These people are accusing me of murder, Stuart. We have to call Mr. Pinckney and tell him to destroy the new will."

"Good, and after that, we can place an ad in the *News and Courier* announcing you've turned the Peregrine estate over to its rightful heirs and should now and forevermore be considered innocent of any wrongdoing. It's not going to be that simple."

"I want out. They might try to kill me next."

"FitzSimons knows better. If you were to die, your part of the estate would go to your heirs, not anyone in Charleston. They're trying to scare you off. It's turned into a game of nerve."

"Stop it. Are you concerned about my life or the will?"

"Come on, Arly. You can't keep getting hysterical."

I began crying again and did not stop 'til we reached the cottage. Stuart parked the car between the pilings under the house.

"Let's get you in bed," he said. "You're going to end up in the emergency room again. We were lucky to make it back without being spotted. I was afraid one of those cops at Peregrine House would radio ahead to the Mount Pleasant Police. Guess the fire got in the way of everything."

When we reached the top step, Stuart uttered a frightened oath and jerked me behind him. The kitchen door was wet with bright blue paint. I put my face in my hands and begged him not to go inside. He wouldn't listen. He left me crying at the top of the stairs and went through the house alone. Nothing else was out of order, though the paint itself was enough to strike terror.

"It had to be those Edisto freaks," Stuart said when he came back to the door to get me. "Probably broke the car windows too, as if last night wasn't enough. Though I'd rather take my chances with twenty Mammalois than one Louisa Hill. Let's get out of these clothes. If Hanahan comes snooping around, we don't want him smelling smoke on us."

A police car rolled up before my hair had dried from the shower. Darkness in the cottage greeted it. Our plan was to claim we had been home all evening and knew nothing of a fire. Stuart lifted a blind slat an inch to see what new demon had come to visit.

"Hanahan," he said, "with the biggest flashlight I've ever seen. He's going under the house, probably to check the car."

"What if he sees the windows?" I said.

"Broken car windows don't connect us with house fires, but it still looks bad. Maybe he won't pull the tarp back far enough to see. He's coming up the stairs now. Go in the bedroom. Let me handle him alone. I'll pretend we were asleep."

I tiptoed into the bedroom and hid in a dark corner. In a second, Hanahan was pounding on the outside door. Stuart let him bang away a good long time before switching on a light in the kitchen. "Who is it?" he called out. "People are trying to sleep."

"Sorry, Mr. Prince. It's Ray Bob Hanahan again. We had more problems in town tonight. I hate to tell you, but your wife's name came up again."

Stuart muttered and unlocked the door. The two men's voices grew louder. I crept to the far side of the bedroom.

"There was a fire at Peregrine House," Hanahan said. "Whole left front got burnt out. Part of the old staircase went, a real shame. It was one of them rare kinds, spiraled and curved-like. Gonna take a pretty penny to fix it...woh, I didn't see this here paint on the door. What in tarnation? All kinds of peculiar things going on tonight."

"Vandals," Stuart said. "How did the fire start?"

"Don't know for sure. Louisa Hill was alone in the house until Mrs. FitzSimons showed up. Good thing. She had to pull Miss

Hill out. Unconscious, she was. Ambulance took her to the hospital. Last I heard, she hadn't come around enough to say much. But Mrs. FitzSimons is a different story. She's been saying a heap. Claims you and your wife started the fire with gasoline of all things. Sounded to me like she was talking out of her head, about like Miss Hill was the night old Miss Peregrine got murdered. Excuse me. I meant to say died, not murdered. Nobody's saying anything else yet. Frankly, I wouldn't worry. What she's claiming don't make sense, seeing as how you're probably about to tell me you've been home all evening."

"We have," Stuart said. "And we're tired of people from town accusing us of crimes. Do we need a lawyer?"

"I don't think that's necessary. Miss Hill and Mrs. FitzSimons seem like the kind of women who like to tell tales, same as I like to sit on mine. Still, all anybody wants to talk about is the fortune Miss Peregrine left your wife."

"Is the house still standing?" Stuart said, ignoring Hanahan's leading remark.

"Yep, but looks mighty pitiful. I knew you and Mrs. Prince would want to know, the house being part of the estate and all. Shoot, you two might find yourselves living in that castle someday if they can fix it up from the fire."

Stuart could not keep himself from responding to this last jab. "Sergeant Hanahan," he said. "The way things were explained to us, Peregrine House belongs to Louisa Hill for all intents and purposes, and since Jeannette FitzSimons appears to have taken charge of Miss Hill's affairs, I'm sure she'll manage the house. Now if you don't mind, I'd like to go back to bed."

"Sorry, Mr. Prince, but you can't blame a fellow for wondering why she's over there telling everybody you and Mrs. Prince torched the place. You folks have had more bad luck the last few days than anybody I've ever come across. And now your car windows. Saw'em when I drove up. Wind must have blown the tarp off. I tried to put it back on for you. What happened anyway?"

"Vandals," Stuart said again, "same ones who threw the paint on the door, we think. Did you get the tarp back on securely? We're trying to keep dampness out."

"I think so. Good idea, that tarp. It'll keep your interior from ruining. Look here, Mr. Prince, I'd like to ride back out here tomorrow if it's all right with you…to talk with your wife. Those ladies over at Peregrine House are working overtime stirring up trouble. It's getting harder and harder to keep the facts straight. Oh yeah, and I saw Dr. Legare again. He loves to talk fancy, don't he? Seems to be the only male animal around here trying to help clear this thing up, except for you and me, of course."

"If that's all, Sergeant…" Stuart said.

"Yes, sir, for now, but you didn't say if I could come back."

"Call first. We may go out."

"I'll do that, and thanks for speaking with me tonight. Some folks might not have come to the door. See you tomorrow."

The outside door opened and closed. I heard Hanahan clomping down the outside steps. Stuart came into the bedroom and flopped down on the bed.

"It keeps getting worse," he said. "Tycie is the only chance we have left."

"Forget Tycie. She's terrified of Louisa and Jeannette. Even if she knew anything, she wouldn't tell us. Our only real chance is doing away with the will. I'm going to Mr. Pinckney's office in the morning and tear it up myself."

"For an intelligent woman, you're a real rock head sometimes. I get so sick of trying to reason with…"

Another car noise. "What?" Stuart said. He jumped up and hurried to the window again. "It's a Cadillac. Someone's getting out… looks like Grayson Pinckney." He adjusted the blinds and moved to the same door he had just closed on Hanahan. Now he opened it to Mr. Pinckney.

"Evening, boy," Mr. Pinckney said. "Kind of dark in here, don't you think? How about turning on some lights for an old man. Don't see as well as I used to, though I did spot that snake, Ray Bob Hanahan, crawling down Atlantic Avenue a minute ago. Hope you didn't tell him anything."

"No, sir," Stuart said, switching on a table lamp, "but he's coming back tomorrow."

I brushed Stuart's shoulder as I flew past him to Mr. Pinckney and threw myself into his arms. "Oh, Mr. Pinckney," I cried. "I'm so glad to see you. I was planning to come to your office in the morning to tell you to get rid of Miss Peregrine's new will. Stuart and I want you to destroy it."

Grayson Pinckney looked me straight in the face, though he did not respond. He turned and addressed Stuart as if I hadn't spoken. "Get your car keys, boy. We going to hide that clunker of yours under my cottage down the way. Then no one can tell if you're here or not. I want you two to lay low a few days, especially while Ray Bob is sniffing under every bush. Looks like we're under siege. Someone threw blue paint on Pinckney House tonight, same as on Lucretia's door out there. We've got ourselves a bona fide voodoo warning. Wouldn't want to know from whom, although I'm certain it's linked to the fire."

"Arlena and I didn't have anything to do with that, Mr. Pinckney. We haven't been to town since…"

"Stop lying, boy. Get your keys and be quick about it." Stuart picked up the keys from the coffee table and held them out to the old gentleman. "No," Mr. Pinckney said. "Go downstairs and give them to Julius Caesar. He'll drive your car to my cottage. I'll follow in the Caddy. That way he won't have to walk back. Caesar ain't no young buck anymore."

As Stuart was doing what he was told, Mr. Pinckney turned to me. "There's something you need to understand," he said. "You're going to be charged with murder whether you destroy the will or not. I will represent you gratis. I would do it for any one of my employees. For now, we're stalling for time. I'd let you stay at my cottage a few days, but the water and electricity have been turned off for the winter. And I don't think it would do you any good for your lawyer to be discovered harboring a suspect. Only thing you have to do at the moment is remain calm. Don't get emotional like some other women I could name. In the morning early, I'll send Caesar out to fetch you and Stuart to my office. We'll all be more rested then…able to map out a strategy. I promise to do everything I can to help you, but you have to face reality, Arlena. The lid on this thing is about to blow."

33

Stuart and I huddled together in the bedroom for the rest of the night, sleeping off and on, imagining noises, expecting worse than fires and voodoo. When dawn broke over the ocean, we dressed and waited for Caesar. He arrived at five of seven, and since there was little traffic on the bridges at that hour, we made it to Pinckney Building by seven twenty. We found Mr. Pinckney staring out his corner window at the Queen Street intersection below. He did not turn around when we entered.

"Will wonders never cease," he said and checked his watch. "It's not seven thirty yet, and Jonathan is coming in. The man hasn't shown up for work before nine in a decade. Something must be up."

At the mention of Prioleau's name, Stuart shot out of the office and ran down the hall. I stared after him in stunned silence. Mr. Pinckney turned to see what the commotion was. "Must be a fire under that boy's rear end. Where's he off to?"

"Prioleau," I breathed.

Mr. Pinckney and I tripped over each other getting to the stairs. On the street floor we found Stuart holding Jonathan Prioleau in a headlock. Mr. Pinckney bellowed at him to let go. Stuart would not listen. He was too angry. He forced Prioleau to his knees, grabbed a handful of his hair, and whipped back his head.

"Talk, dirt bag," he growled through clenched teeth, "or you might find yourself making another trip to the dentist."

"I don't know anything," Prioleau squeaked.

Stuart gave him a knee to the back and yanked his hair again. "You knew we were going to be here this morning. Who told you?" he shouted. Another knee, another yank.

"No," Prioleau said. "All I did was take the money."

At that, Mr. Pinckney stepped forward. He leaned over until the tip of his Roman nose came within inches of Prioleau's pug. "What money, you low-down scoundrel?" he said.

"From Dr. Legare. He's been paying me for information. Said he'd give me thousands if I'd help him get rid of Miss Peregrine's new will."

"Turn him loose, Stuart," Mr. Pinckney said. "He's in a talking mood now." Stuart released the panting Prioleau and propped him against the wall. Mr. Pinckney breathed into his son-in-law's face. "Spill it, weasel, or I'll inform Caroline you're after every secretary in this office."

"I don't know anything else. I swear it."

"Why are you here so early? I'm no fool, man. Talk."

"Legare called me at Pinckney House last night while you were outside looking at the fire. He said if I wanted bigger cash, I should get over here this morning and find out what's going on."

"And how did you know the Princes would be here?"

"I didn't…a coincidence. I couldn't believe it when I saw Prince coming after me."

Mr. Pinckney frowned and turned toward Stuart. "Croomer Legare is more involved than I thought," he said. "I assumed it was mostly Jeannette and the Hill woman. But now I'm sure the good doctor is also interested in Fanny's fortune. He sent a message to me by courier yesterday. Said there's evidence Miss Peregrine was murdered, an overdose of pills. He threatened to tell the police unless something fair was done about the will."

"He's right about her being murdered," Stuart said. "Louisa Hill said the same thing…last night."

Mr. Pinckney looked pained. "I won't embarrass you, Prince, by asking what in the name of heaven you were doing in her company or why you felt the need to visit Peregrine House. Suffice it to say I already knew you'd been there. Jeannette was broadcasting news of it even as the old mansion burned."

"We'll deny it," Stuart said.

"Don't be an ass, man. The fire is the least of your worries. Arlena is about to be arrested for murder. Everything else pales next to that."

I let out a cry at the word murder. "Mr. Pinckney, please. Tear up the will."

"No," he said and turned away. His coldness infuriated me. I grabbed his arm and pulled him back around.

"Listen to me," I said. "You, too, Stuart. And you, Jonathan. As of this minute, the new will is null and void. I reject it out of hand."

"You're the one who needs to listen," Stuart said. "Didn't you hear Mr. Pinckney? Things have gone too far. Louisa can't let herself be implicated any further. Jeannette FitzSimons is desperate. So is Legare. And you're the convenient scapegoat."

"I won't have it," I said louder. "Jonathan, call Croomer Legare. Tell him he can have the money, all of it. Stuart and I are leaving town."

I looked into the faces of the men standing before me and realized they thought I had snapped. "Stop staring at me," I demanded. I ran back up the stairs to Mr. Pinckney's office and began shuffling through papers on his desk. Just as I found what I was looking for, all three men – Stuart, Jonathan, and Mr. Pinckney – stepped into the room.

"Look," I said and shook the blue folder. "It's the thing that's caused all the trouble." Two and three pages at a time, I ripped the will into shreds. The men watched as strips of blue and white paper fluttered to the carpet.

"Stop," Mr. Pinckney said.

"Too late. I've destroyed it. Jonathan, make the call."

"It's a mistake," Mr. Pinckney said.

He and Stuart reached out to take hold of me at the same moment. I eluded them both and rushed down the hallway, my heart beating in over time. Fear fed my strength as I raced down the stairs, all three men charging after me. I ran faster…out the front door, across the street, down a narrow alleyway. I ran until my lungs felt like bursting. At the end of the alley, an opening appeared. I found myself on the other side of the block where cars were whizzing up and down the street as if nothing were more important than beating the next red light. I stopped to catch my breath and wait for my heart to slow. The bus, I thought in panic. I'll ride the bus back to Sullivan's and hide in Lucretia's cottage. No, that's the first place they'll look. Where, then…where? Mr. Pinckney's cottage...yes, they won't think of looking there for hours.

I brushed off my clothes, smoothed my hair, and stepped into open sunlight. The bus stop was a four-block walk. Several times I ducked into doorways and alleys in case Stuart and Mr. Pinckney, maybe even Jon Prioleau, were still hunting me. From one hiding place, I saw a taxi cruise by with a man in back who looked like Stuart. I waited until it turned the corner before scurrying the rest of the way to the bus stop. But not until I had already boarded the bus did I remember I had no money. The driver recognized me from other trips and said I could pay later. I was on my way toward a seat at the back when Stuart and Mr. Pinckney began shouting my name from down the street. The driver twisted his body around and stared at me. His eyes were all questions. "Drive," I shouted, "they're after me." He shut the door and sped away.

I fell onto the bench seat at the back of the coach and stared out the rear window. Stuart and Mr. Pinckney were chasing the bus on foot. The driver turned left on Meeting Street and headed for the bridge to Mount Pleasant. As my pursuers receded in the distance and disappeared, possibilities whirled in my mind. If I could stay out of sight a few hours...maybe the whole night...everyone would have time to get word I tore up the will with my own hands... all my problems solved.

The driver let me off at the Middle Street stop on Sullivan's. As I ran up the block and dashed between houses, I hoped against hope he would not tell anyone where he last saw me. I scuttled in and out of backyards, around green garbage bins, behind fences, and up and down sand dunes, somehow managing to reach the Pinckney cottage before exhaustion overtook me. The Romeo was still parked under the house and hidden from view by the palings of a tall wooden gate. I forced the gate open enough to squeeze through and collapse in the sand next to the Romeo. It took only and minute or two to cry myself to sleep. I did not wake up until I heard Stuart calling my name. His voice intermingled with my dreams.

"Sweetheart," he said. When I realized he was kneeling beside me, I opened my eyes and smiled at him before realizing where I was. But in an instant, the morning's developments came roaring back to my mind. I began struggling with Stuart like an injured animal trying to escape. I did not give in until I saw Mr. Pinckney standing over us, his feet planted wide apart.

"I'm sorry, dear," he said. "You've been through hellfire these last few days at the hands of Charleston arses, and I'm afraid I've been the biggest arse of all. Can you forgive me?"

"I'm tired," I said. "What's happening now? Did Jonathan call Croomer Legare like I asked?"

"We don't know," Stuart said. "Mr. Pinckney and I have been searching for you. Prioleau stayed behind in the office. You need to see a doctor, Arly. People break down under stress."

"Leave me alone. I'm hiding here until everyone gets word I destroyed the new will."

"Come on, baby. Let's get some coffee at Mama Chloe's. Mr. Pinckney has a taxi waiting."

"Go without me. Take the taxi with you. I don't want to chance being seen."

Stuart tried to pull me up against my will. "I'm not leaving you here," he said. I resisted. Stuart looked over his shoulder at Mr. Pinckney. "Go without us, sir. She's set on hiding out a few more hours. I'll stay with her."

"Neither of you is staying. This little lady is going to get up off her backside and go with us to Mama Chloe's if I have to haul her there like a sack of grits. I'm starving. Haven't raced around this much in twenty years. I think my sacroiliac has slipped."

Stuart turned back toward me. "What do you say, Arlena. We could all use something to eat. I'll tell the driver to park the cab behind the building."

"Look outside," I said. "If no one is there, I'll go. But I'm not talking to anybody."

"People don't come this far down on the beach in November," Mr. Pinckney said, peering through a space between the gate palings. "Not even a stray dog out there. Let's get ourselves over to Chloe's. I'm famished. Old men have to eat to keep their strength up."

34

“I’ve made a decision,” Stuart said to Mr. Pinckney and me after we were seated at the back of the restaurant,” and I don’t want either of you trying to talk me out of it. I’m going back to Edisto. Arlena, you’ll have to stay with Mr. Pinckney.”

“You can’t,” I said, close to bolting again. “Mr. Pinckney, please. Tell him it’s too dangerous.”

But Grayson Pinckney did not hear a word I was saying. His attention was arrested by something at the front of the restaurant. I turned to see what he was staring at and recoiled at the sight of Ray Bob Hanahan. He stood motionless in the doorway, his snake eyes trained on me.

I stood up on reflex. Mr. Pinckney and Stuart each grabbed an arm and pulled me back into my chair. “Stay calm,” Stuart said. “Don’t say a word. Let Mr. Pinckney handle this.”

The dignified Grayson Pinckney rose from the table. “Morning, Ray Bob,” he said as the officer approached. The two men shook hands. Neither had a choice about it. Mr. Pinckney continued playing the gentleman. "Have you had the pleasure of meeting Mr. and Mrs. Prince?"

"Yes, Mr. Pinckney. The Princes and I met at the Peregrine mansion a few days ago…somehow I thought you would have known that, sir. Anyhow, I'm sorry to have to come out here and ruin a nice day."

"And how might you do that?"

"By delivering bad news. Dr. Croomer Legare found out this morning Miss Peregrine died of an overdose of pills. He thinks it wasn't accidental. Fact is, we have an eyewitness who'll swear Mrs. Prince is the one who gave them to her."

"That's not possible," I blurted out and stood again despite Stuart's efforts to stop me. I would no longer be silenced. "If anyone killed Miss Peregrine, it was Louisa Hill," I said, all the while tussling with Stuart. "She as good as confessed last night. Tell him, Stuart."

Stuart looked unsure. "Let Mr. Pinckney do this his way, Arly."

Hanahan scratched his head. "Strangest thing, Mrs. Prince. Louisa Hill is saying the same thing about you. Seems like the two of you keep going 'round and 'round. Weren't for some of them other things, I wouldn't know who to arrest."

"What other things?" Mr. Pinckney said with aristocratic coldness.

"Fires, copyrights, fingerprints on pill bottles, bits and pieces of evidence like that. We lifted a perfect set of Mrs. Prince's prints off a barbiturate bottle found in Miss Peregrine's bedroom."

"And how did you know they were hers? You had nothing with which to compare them."

"Sure, I did, Mr. Pinckney. You talk like I'm ignorant or something. I got a clean set of your lady's prints the same night Miss Peregrine died. Louisa Hill gave me a coffee cup Mrs. Prince had been drinking out of earlier. "Still had the smell of peach brandy in it. Guess you could say I was already a little suspicious or else I wouldn't have been nosing out fingerprints. Ain't no never mind. It's the kind of thing easy enough to check."

"But I'd never hurt Miss Peregrine," I said tearfully. "She was my friend."

"I don't know, Mrs. Prince. Hard to imagine a pretty lady like you involved in a thing like this. Guess drugs do funny things to people. Miss Hill says you're a straight-up addict."

"You can't listen to her. She's mentally ill," I said.

"Arlena, stop," Stuart pleaded.

But I didn't stop. "Someone has to tell him," I said, "and you aren't doing a thing."

Mr. Pinckney pulled me back into my seat and forced me into silence with a stinging look. He spoke curtly to Hanahan. "Who's been filling your head with that nonsense, Ray Bob? Mrs. Prince doesn't have a drug problem."

"Maybe not now, sir, but she did a few weeks ago. Dr. Legare and Mrs. FitzSimons both talked to her doctor. You know how this town is. Ain't nobody got no secrets."

"Indeed," Mr. Pinckney said and paused before adding, "Ray Bob, the time has come to inform you that Mrs. Prince is my client. I intend to do the best I can to help her with this matter, and you, sir, will cease your threatening remarks unless you can produce a paper with teeth in it."

"If you mean a warrant for her arrest, I wouldn't have come without that." He reached into his breast pocket and pulled out a folded document. Grayson Pinckney jerked it out of his hand and flipped it open. "Are you daft, man? This is a murder charge, first degree."

"Yes...and now I have to read Mrs. Prince her rights."

I was stricken dumb. Hanahan rattled off the Miranda rights and motioned me toward his car. From the corner of my eye, I saw Mama Chloe wringing her hands and weeping. Stuart lost control and grabbed for Hanahan. Only through the efforts of Mr. Pinckney and two bystanders did he avoid being arrested along with me. I was informed by Hanahan I would have to ride to Charleston in the back of his prowler. "Rules," he said. Again, Stuart made advances.

"I'm all right," I told Stuart with no emotion, though I was clearly in an unnatural state. "It'll all be over soon. Croomer Legare and Jeannette FitzSimons will straighten everything out once they know I've torn up the will. I wish I'd done it sooner."

"The will," Hanahan said. "I meant to mention that earlier. Dr. Legare says it ain't no good no way, that Mrs. FitzSimons could prove Miss Peregrine wasn't of sound mind and body when she wrote it. I reckon she could get something like that done, her being a lawyer and all."

"You don't know anything about it," I said to my captor in a newly steady voice. I stared into his eyes. He felt my contempt, faltered, discovered a speck of lint on his sleeve.

"Let's go, Mrs. Prince," he said on regaining his poise. "I got no choice but to take you in. Please don't give me no trouble. I don't want to hurt you none."

Mr. Pinckney held Stuart back as Hanahan guided me to the squad car. The zealous officer helped me into the vehicle and was about to close the door when someone called out my name. I turned to see Raven running across the street. She had left her MG parked on the curb opposite the restaurant, engine still running, driver side door hanging open.

"Mrs. Prince, Mrs. Prince, wait," she shouted. "What's happening? Where is he taking you?"

She ran past Stuart and Mr. Pinckney, eyes darting from Hanahan to Stuart to me.

"Aren't you Mrs. FitzSimons' daughter?" Hanahan said.

"Yes, now back off or I'll scratch your eyes out."

"Hold on there, missy. Ain't no call talking smack. Mrs. Prince is going downtown to answer a few questions…no concern of yours. Now run along and stay out of trouble. Aren't you supposed to be in school this time of day?"

Raven raised her hand and slapped him full across the face. "I'll kill you…you arrogant…" Stuart and Mr. Pinckney grabbed her to stop her from doing worse. Hanahan's composure was destroyed. His face went crimson. He trembled as he spoke. "This woman has been charged with murder, young lady, and if you lay a hand on me again, you'll be charged with assault on a police officer...a felony."

"She didn't murder anyone," Raven screamed, thrashing about between Stuart and Mr. Pinckney.

"Stop, Raven," I said. "You can't help me."

But my words went unheeded. Raven leaned over almost double and bit Mr. Pinckney's hand. He gasped as she jerked away and ran back to her car. No one tried to stop her. She whipped the MG around in the middle of the street and sped toward the Ben Sawyer Bridge.

"God Bless America," Mr. Pinckney said as he wrapped his bleeding hand in his handkerchief. "I'll spit to Georgia if females aren't the most vicious devils on the planet."

Hanahan closed me into the police car and prepared to leave. As he pulled away from the restaurant, Mr. Pinckney and Stuart rushed to find the parked cab. The cabby succeeded in catching up with the squad car at the base of the swivel bridge and trailed it through Mount Pleasant. It wasn't until I saw the steelwork of the great bridge that I realized traffic had come to a stop along its massive left span. Hanahan braked the squad car and cursed, "Hell's bells, if it ain't one thing, it's another."

Traffic had come to a stand-still at the bottom of the ramp. People were getting out of their cars and running up the incline like wolves to a fresh kill. For a moment, I thought a section of the bridge had collapsed. Hanahan clicked on his blue light and inched the cruiser forward. He forced his way between several stopped cars, but soon could go no farther. I stared ahead, trying to determine the problem. People on the bridge pointed upward. I lifted my eyes to the high suspension work, and what I saw chilled my blood. A girl stood balanced on a connecting length of steel that towered above the left span. She was far away, but her long blond hair whipping in the wind made her identity unmistakable. It was Raven.

"Unbelievable," Hanahan said. "A jumper is up there."

I banged my fists on the back of Hanahan's seat and begged him to let me out of the car. For security, the back seat had no inside door handle. Otherwise, I would have already been outside and running to help Raven.

"What's the matter with you?" Hanahan said. "No way you're going anywhere."

"But I know her," I said. "It's Raven FitzSimons, the girl from back at the restaurant. Don't you recognize her?"

"Danged if it ain't," Hanahan said, staring up.

"Please…let me try to get her to come down."

Hanahan looked at me and made a quick decision. He exited the vehicle and opened the door that held me captive. "Get her talking if you can," he shouted as I dashed away. "Sometimes if they talk, they don't jump."

I raced up the ramp, shoving people aside as I went. Raven remained motionless on the beam except for her hair, which blew wildly about her face and shoulders as if anxious to be set free. She had climbed to the highest reachable point from which to jump. Her back was to the roadway, eyes on the water.

"Raven," I called out, but she did not hear me. I shouted louder, "It's Arlena, Raven. Look down."

She startled and turned her face to an angle that would allow her to scan the roadway. When she spotted me waving my arms like a mad woman, she leaned farther over the water and covered her face with her free hand.

"Keep your eyes open, Raven. You'll get dizzy."

"Go away," she cried out. "My life is garbage. I'm pregnant; my boyfriend hates me; my mother hates me. And now I'm hearing voices. They're screaming inside my head. 'Everything will be all right if you can work up the courage to kill yourself.'"

"What voices?"

"Scary ones. I'm afraid of them, but I know they're telling the truth."

"No, they're lying. I know about them. I hear them too."

"But they won't stop talking about the bad things I've done, things I can't live with. Mother said you cheated us out of Miss Peregrine's estate. She wanted me to help her frighten you into getting rid of the new will. I'm the one who set you up the night of the fire. I lied when I said Tycie was coming to Peregrine House. Mother told me to trick you. But she didn't say she was going to accuse you of murder. She hates you, Mrs. Prince, but she hates me worse…for getting pregnant and ruining all her plans."

"Everything is going to be okay, Rav. I don't want Miss Peregrine's money, never did. I destroyed the will this morning. It's gone. When Mr. Pinckney tells your mother, she'll leave me alone. And she'll leave you alone, too. Come down. We can talk this out."

For a second, she looked as if she might give in, but then she stiffened and leaned even farther out. I looked around to see what had frightened her. Croom was running up the ramp. The look on his face was sheer terror. I knew the second I saw him he was going to do something stupid. I called to him to stop. He ignored me and ran to the base of the steelwork. He pulled himself up to the first set of connectors and began a swift climb. Raven shrieked at him to stay back. He would not listen. He reached out for her in the middle of a scream, his fingertips brushing her hair. That was the moment she vaulted over the edge and fell straight down. She looked like a white-throated sparrow shot out of the sky on the wing. I did not see her hit the water. All I saw was Stuart standing over me, trying to get me to move.

"Come on, we have to run," he said.

"Did you see?" I cried. "Raven jumped. I'm going to the riverbank. I have to help her."

"It's too late. We're getting out of here."

"But what about Raven? She could drown."

"No hope. Now come with me without an argument for once."

"Back off. I'm going to find Raven."

He gave up arguing and forced me in the opposite direction of the swiftly moving crowd. "No…no," I cried out. "She's hurt, and Hanahan and Mr. Pinckney will be looking for me."

"Hang them all," Stuart said, slowing down not at all. "I'm taking you somewhere safe." He clasped my hand tighter in his and plowed headlong through the throng. We did not stop until Mr. Pinckney and the cab driver appeared in our path.

"Don't get in our way," Stuart said to them, his free hand clenched in a fist. "Arlena is right about one thing. We have to hide out 'til this thing blows over. Let us go before Hanahan shows up."

"You shouldn't," Mr. Pinckney said. "It'll make things worse."

Stuart would not listen. "Step aside, sir," he said.

Mr. Pinckney complied. "All right, I won't try to stop you. God be with you, son. I'll tell Hanahan I saw you going the other way. Take the taxi. I already gave the driver a hundred dollars. There'll be more for him at my office if he gets you out of here safely." The cabby nodded. "Go," Mr. Pinckney said.

The three of us – Stuart, the cabby, and myself - hurried down the Mount Pleasant ramp. The crowd moving against us retarded our progress. Without giving me a reason, Stuart dropped my hand and rushed back to Mr. Pinckney. I watched as he leaned close and said something into his ear. Mr. Pinckney frowned and gesticulated. Stuart shrugged and shook Mr. Pinckney's reluctant hand. He returned to the cabby and me. We picked up our pace when we caught sight of the yellow taxi parked on the shoulder. I was grateful traffic was moving toward the bridge instead of away from it. All lanes to Mount Pleasant were clear. The cabby made a U-turn and screeched his tires as we fled.

"Where to?" he said to Stuart, his voice as excited as fearful.

"Isle of Palms," Stuart answered without hesitation. "We have to find a boat."

"I'm not going back to Edisto," I said. "I already told you."

"If I can do what I just did, you can go with me to talk to Tycie."

"What…what did you do?"

"I told Mr. Pinckney to send word to everyone you've rescinded any claim to Miss Peregrine's estate and have decided to move back north. You're no longer a part of this fiasco."

"I haven't been since early this morning. I was serious when I tore up those papers."

"Fine…now he's convinced. But we still need to find Tycie to make sure she'll take your part if you need her. Throwing in the will may not be enough to satisfy FitzSimons and Legare. They may want blood."

35

"Did you hear? Some society girl jumped off the bridge," a clerk said when we rushed into Two Brothers Marina on Isle of Palms. "Name of FitzSimons. It's all over the radio. Broke right in to tell it. They're trying to find the body now, probably using them grappling hooks."

I closed my eyes against a wave of nausea and leaned against the wall. The cabby stood by while Stuart took care of business.

"Where's the manager?" he said to the clerk. "We want to rent a boat."

"On the dock, gassing up his dinghy. He's going over to the harbor...wants to see what he can see when they pull her up."

I winced again and wrapped my arms around my body. Stuart raced outside and down the back stairs to the dock. The driver searched the store and found a crate for me to use as a seat. He took his hat off and stood next to me like a bodyguard. The clerk prattled on about the drowning of Raven FitzSimons, debutante of Old Charleston.

In a few minutes, Stuart came blowing back in and began giving orders. The taxi was to be kept on Isle of Palms overnight. Stuart had given one of the marina owner's cronies twenty dollars to hide it. Another crony had agreed to drive the cabby back to Charleston after dark to avoid the police. Bubber Hampton, marina owner, would take us to Edisto by boat. No time to lose. Hanahan had probably already radioed an all-points bulletin about the disappearance of a dangerous murderess. The clerk produced jackets, toboggans, and mittens for the boat trip. We never thought once about anyone from the marina calling in our location. Patrons and staff of Two Brothers were experienced at circumventing the law.

"Did you tell Mr. Pinckney where we were going?" I said to Stuart. He waited a moment to reply. His attention was on helping Bubber shove off from the dock.

"No," he said, "only that I wanted to keep you out sight…just long enough for everyone to find out what we've done about the will. I'm sure he knows where we'll be. He wouldn't forget what I said in the restaurant about talking to Tycie again. But he won't have to come right out and lie about it to Hanahan."

The trip was slow. I buried my face in Stuart's shoulder to block the wind. We were too cold and miserable to talk. After an hour of suffering, we tied off at a rotting dock on Edisto's Intracoastal bank. Bubber stayed in the boat. Stuart and I climbed the rickety ladder to the dock. Stuart asked Bubber how long he could wait for us. The old man studied the sky full of yellow clouds and said we would have to leave two hours before nightfall to make it back in daylight. Otherwise, we'd be caught in the dark with no lights or radio on the boat. It was already four P.M.. Stuart thought a moment while Bubber fidgeted. Then, oddly decisive, he told Bubber to go back alone, that we'd call him later if we needed him. I felt a terrible sense of desolation as the boat motored away from the dock. Stuart and I watched it round the curve along the shoreline and disappear from sight.

"No marina here," Stuart said, "but Bubber told me an old fishing store is up the way. Maybe we can get directions."

We trudged along a path perpendicular to the Intracoastal to a shack of a store fronting a dirt road. Stuart tried the door which swung open with a jingling of bells. We stepped inside. Half a dozen men turned to look at us from a circle of straight chairs around a free-standing stove. They stared without expression from indolent eyes. I shrank back. The memory of Snake Island made their faces seem evil, though no particular one was familiar. The men did not appear to recognize us, though I was certain they all knew we were the same ignorant townies who had visited their island earlier.

"We're lost," Stuart said to the gathering. "Looking for a church on the road to Dawhoo Bridge."

"What for?" one of the men asked.

"Supposed to…tune the piano."

"Ain't got no piano. Somebody told you wrong. How did you get on this side of the island? Dawhoo Bridge is on the other side."

"By boat…we live near Ashepoo Cut."

The men exchanged looks. Stuart had said something stupid. He tried to recover. "We won't stay long…a few minutes to look the piano over. We'll bring our tools back later."

"Told you, man. Ain't got no piano. Who asked you to tune a piano everybody knows we ain't got?"

Stuart hesitated. "Preacher called us yesterday. I can't remember his name."

A murmur of laughter rippled over the group. One man resumed whittling, bored by Stuart's lies.

"Preacher be dead," said the spokesman, "of the gravel."

"Gravel?" Stuart said.

"Kidney gravel."

Stuart refused to give up. "Any coffee in that pot? We could use some."

This time his question was answered by a basso somewhere in back. "No coffee," he said. "Ain't open to the public today."

Stuart was suddenly brave. "I don't know who you are, mister, but I'd recognize your voice anywhere. You're part of the Snake Island posse. But you can back off today. We're not afraid of that nonsense anymore."

I stared at Stuart. He may not be afraid. I was terrified.

"Stuart, don't," I said.

Basso stepped into the light. "Ain't no such place as Snake Island unless you've been clear to Haiti."

"Right," Stuart said, adjusting his attitude. He held up his hands in surrender. "We shouldn't have bothered you."

"True," Basso said. "And you shouldn't have bothered Tycie's husband, neither. I got a notion to throw you in a gator nest for scaring that old man."

"But we didn't scare him," Stuart said, his tenor unattractive compared to his adversary's bass. "We've been looking for Tycie everywhere…haven't been able to find her. My wife has been accused of killing someone, which she didn't do. Tycie could help her by telling the police what really happened. What's it to you?"

But his question was cut short by a sudden jingling of the doorknob bells. Everyone looked toward the door. Tycie's grandson stepped inside, the same boy who had strong-armed me in the churchyard while someone poured the evil syrup down my throat. He turned to leave when he saw Stuart and me, but Basso's voice stopped him.

"Stay where you are, boy. These town folks are looking for trouble today. We need your help."

"Mama Tycie said leave'em alone," the boy said.

"Your grandmama is an old woman. Don't know good from bad no more. We gotta protect our own. Now get some rope out of the storeroom."

"Mama told me not to be taking part in any more voodoo rites. The devil is in that brass ankle, Mammaloi."

"I told you. Tycie is old. Lost her reasoning. Anyhow...no voodoo nowhere is strong enough to hex these liars. We ain't gonna do nothing but go up the crick a ways and dump'em on the bank. Now get some rope, or I'm gonna stretch your neck like a chicken's. It ain't nothing for me to whip a man."

"Got no rope…don't plan to look for any. And you aren't my boss, William. I'm a law-abiding citizen of Edisto Island and no criminal."

With that, Tycie's grandson backed out the door and forced it shut. The bells fell to the floor. Stuart and I made moves to follow him, but the circle of men sprang into action. I struggled and cried as they overpowered us. Stuart's face went scarlet. Veins stood out on his neck as the men pinned his arms back and forced him to bend over at the waist. Basso tied his hands, gagged him, and pressed him against a wall. Two other men were in the process of binding me when grandson came back in, which would have made no difference, except this time Tycie was with him.

"I heard about your tripas talk, Big William," she said. "And I mean for you to listen to your elder. Ain't gonna be no trouble with these folks. Cut them lines off their hands. A big man like you ought to be ashamed, trussing up a slip of a gal."

"Stay back, old woman. This is menfolk's business. We gotta protect our own."

"Tripas," Tycie muttered again and brushed by him to get a better look at his captives. She gasped when she saw my face. "Great goodness, Missy Arlena," she said. "You're gray as death, looking like a h'ant from the graveyard. William, I ought to beat you with a hickory stick. Untie this child's hands."

Basso grumbled under his breath and took his time taking off the rope. I ran to Tycie when it fell from my wrists. Stuart was not far behind. Grandson wasted no time hustling us outside and into his car, which raised a cloud of dust as we sped away.

"Tycie, we've been looking for you everywhere," I babbled as we bounced down a road scarred with potholes. "Everything is dreadful in Charleston. People are saying someone murdered Miss Peregrine. They think it was me. We came to Edisto earlier to try to find you, but someone..." (the grandson stiffened) "...took us to a voodoo island and scared us out of our minds. That was before I was accused of murder. The police are after me now. Louisa and Jeannette have told them so many lies. And Raven FitzSimons jumped off the big bridge this morning. She's dead...dead."

Tycie stared back at me from the front passenger seat. "Not Missy Raven," she said. "Charleston's got a mantle of evil hanging low over her crumbling walls. Wickedness is choking that city."

Stuart leaned closer to the driver, Tycie's grandson. "Where are you taking us?" he said to the back of the boy's neck. Then to Tycie, "Arlena needs to talk to you calmly a few minutes, Mrs. Roosevelt. It doesn't matter where as long as it isn't Snake Island." Again, the grandson stiffened.

"We're going to my house," Tycie said. "And don't you worry, police can't trick no old woman like me into saying what she don't want to say. Ray Bob Hanahan already tried to fool me. So did those devil-angels from South Battery Street, two blackbirds from hell."

"Louisa?" I said. "And Jeannette?"

"And Dr. Legare. Greedy vultures, all three. Like Beezlebub and his hoards, whisperers of evil lies."

36

Stuart leaned nearer Tycie. "Maybe we should go somewhere other than your house," he said. "William might call some of his friends and tell them we may be heading there. Arlena isn't exaggerating about the trouble we're in. Half the Charleston police force is probably after us by now."

"William's more scared of the police than you are," Tycie said. "He won't call nobody."

"What about the others? They could have heard something on the radio. Isn't there somewhere else to hide, somewhere safer?"

Tycie touched her grandson's arm. "Turn around, Abe. Take us to the praise house. We'll do our talking in the church."

Grandson effected a one-eighty in the middle of the road and headed in the opposite direction. He didn't stop 'til we got to the church. Tycie spoke to him sternly. "Hide your automobile behind the building and walk back to the store. Tell those trouble hounds they'll answer to me if they call the law on Missy Arlena. Liquor will be flowing before the moon comes up. That's when the false witch,

Mammaloi, does her evil. But she don't fool me, not like she fools other folks. Go on, child. Hurry."

I glanced at the young man's face and remembered his hands at my throat. Would Tycie believe me if I told her he had taken part in the rite? I decided against trying to find out.

Grandson gave Stuart and me a sharp last look from the car window before pulling his car behind the building. Stuart said to me out of Tycie's earshot, "He could be more trouble. I can't tell who he hates worse, us or Big William."

"Be grateful he loves his grandmother," I said. "It's the one thing that might save us."

Inside the praise house, Tycie seated herself on the back pew and folded her hands in prayer. Stuart and I sat on either side.

"Amen," she said aloud and opened her eyes. "I was praying for the souls of the dead, Missy Peregrine and Missy Raven. The Lord takes the young and the old." She bowed her head again and wiped her eyes. "I wish he'd take me."

I drew in a breath and began my strange story. "We came to ask you about Miss Peregrine," I said and paused for a response that did not come. Stuart urged me on. "I know you're afraid," I continued. "So are we. A police officer, Ray Bob Hanahan, arrested me earlier today. He thinks I killed Miss Peregrine. Louisa and Jeannette have been lying to him. Dr. Legare, too. I don't know what to do."

"I'm afraid," Tycie said. "Missy Louisa threatened to hurt me if I opened my mouth. I spat in her face and told her she had no hold on me. The good Lord watches over old women. But she squinted up her wicked eyes and said she'd come after my grandchild if I didn't do what I was told. Daddy Abraham and me…we're the only family young Abe's got. But Daddy Abe is a no-account drinker, all the time studying about voodoo. My grandson depends on me. I can't do nothing that might harm him."

Stuart could restrain himself no longer. "Did you see Louisa kill Miss Peregrine, Tycie?"

She did not answer, just kept staring at her own clasped hands in her lap. "Please, if you know anything, tell us," Stuart said. "They're blaming Arlena. You can't stand by and let them get away with this. You saw something. I know you did."

Tycie glared at him with angry eyes. "You make me sick," she said. "You aren't old, living in fear."

"What do you think we're living in now? Someone has to stop Louisa," Stuart said.

"It isn't only Missy Louisa," Tycie said, her wide eyes looking far to one side. "It's all of them. They killed Missy Peregrine together."

"What do you mean?" Stuart said.

Tycie rose from the pew and lifted her arms. She rocked back on her heels and looked toward the ceiling. Her body trembled. "Dear Lord," she cried out, tears streaming. "I saw them drug Missy Peregrine. And now they want to hurt my grandson."

Stuart reached out to steady Tycie. "Tell us what you saw," he said.

Tycie grabbed his hands and stared at him with fearful eyes. "I was hiding in Missy Peregrine's bathroom. They didn't know. Missy Louisa thought Abe had already come to take me to the doctor. But Abe was late. He'd forgotten me. He admitted it later. I went up to Missy Peregrine's room to sit with her while I waited. She was sleeping like always 'cause of the pills they made her take. I was afraid she might die, afraid of Missy Louisa, afraid of all the evil doers in Peregrine House.

"I heard them coming up the stairs – Missy Louisa, Missy Jeannette, and Dr. Legare. Oh, Lord, save me, I prayed. I ran into the bathroom out of sight and watched from the dark when they sneaked into Missy Peregrine's room. Louisa shook her to see if she'd wake up, but she didn't. She was too dead asleep. Dr. Legare got nervous and wanted to leave. He said what they were doing was bad business and she'd die soon enough. That made Missy Jeannette angry. She said if he wanted to take part in the will, he had to take part in the killing. I saw when they gave her the pills, too many pills. Missy Louisa and Missy Jeannette held her head, and Dr. Legare made her swallow them. I cried, too scared to get in their way.

"I was still crying when they rushed out of the room, like fallen angels fleeing God. They left Missy Peregrine to die alone. But she wasn't as alone as they thought. I was there, only I stayed hidden, waiting and praying and crying. And then you came into the bedroom, Mr. Prince…big as life, an answer to prayer. I didn't know what you'd come for and didn't care. I just thanked the Lord for sending somebody to save me.

"But the sight of you shocked me so bad, I couldn't speak. And it scared me worse when I knocked over a jar on the vanity table. It frightened you too, Mr. Prince. Must have, you ran back into the hallway before I could tell you it was me. Everything started happening fast after that, and for a moment, I thought you hadn't been there at all, that my mind was playing tricks. Though I did know I heard something fall to the floor when you ran out of the room, something smaller than the jar I'd turned over. From the bathroom, I could see a brown prescription bottle lying on the rug near the bed. It must have popped open when it struck the pine floor and bounced onto the rug. Pills were scattered all over. At first, I thought they were Missy Peregrine's pills, until I saw they were the wrong color. I knew I should pick them up, but I couldn't bring myself to leave my hiding place, not until Missy Peregrine called out my name.

"Tycie," I heard her say, "help me."

"I forgot about being scared and ran to her side. I held her while she took her last breath. That was when Missy Louisa came barging back in and you right behind her, Missy Arlena. When I heard the two of you outside the door, I leaned down and grabbed up the pills and bottle and hid them in my pocket. I didn't want anything belonging to Mr. Prince left in the room. Three evil angels killed Missy Peregrine, not Mr. Prince, and I didn't want him blamed.

"It wasn't a second before Louisa came flying in like the demon crow she is. She slapped me to the floor and would have done worse if you hadn't stopped her, Missy Arlena. Oh, how I hate that evil woman. Lord, forgive me for despising her so. But how can I not when I saw her and those other two devils kill my Missy Peregrine?"

Her testimony over, Tycie threw back her head and let out a piercing scream. She lurched forward into Stuart's arms. He helped her lie down on a wooden pew.

"She fainted," he said. "Hand me a stack of those books. We have to elevate her feet."

"But they're Bibles."

"It's a good use."

Stuart propped Tycie's feet up and patted her hands and cheeks. "Can you hear me, Tycie?" he said. Her eyes opened slowly. She looked old and wasted. Stuart spoke again. "Lie still, Mrs. Roosevelt. You need to rest."

"I was right," he said to me when he looked up from Tycie. "I knew she'd seen something."

"But I don't understand. She said you were in Miss Peregrine's room before the police and everyone else got there, before I got there. How can that be?"

He put a finger to his lips and led me to the front of the church where we could talk without disturbing Tycie. "No..." he said, a peculiar intensity in his voice. "No way I was in that room. She must have been hallucinating from stress. But you can bet money those other three were there. That's the important thing. I'll talk to her when she wakes up. I'll tell her to be careful what she says to people. The last thing we need is for both of us to be implicated in murder."

"But the pills. She said you dropped a bottle of pills."

"Listen to yourself, Arlena. You're talking out of your head. Tycie's mixed up, that's all. Who wouldn't be, after everything she's been through? Why would I have pills? You were the one into that. Give Tycie a break. She got a couple of details wrong after the trauma of witnessing a murder?"

I looked at Stuart with fierce bright eyes at the mention of the word murder. "These people are monsters," I said. "No wonder Raven jumped."

Stuart kneaded his temples with his fingertips. "Tycie's gotta talk to Ray Bob Hanahan, give him a statement."

"She will," I said. "I'll make her."

"I don't know if you can. She's terrified."

"And rightly so," a voice cut in from the shadows behind Tycie's pew. "She should fear for her very life."

Stuart and I turned to see Dr. Croomer Legare standing behind the pew where Tycie lay in her faint. "You know everything now," he said with a sneer. "Tycie must have done some talking. It has always been my opinion if women would keep their mouths shut, the world would be a better place. Louisa woke up from her concussion this morning, more out of touch than ever, raving about Tycie, raving about you Mrs. Prince. Said she thought Tycie may have seen us in Fanny's bedroom. Jeannette and I were surprised to hear that. Louisa, you see, had neglected to tell us Tycie was in the house that evening. We thought she'd left with her grandson. Poor Louisa has her lapses. I had no choice this morning but to give her another sedative, make her sleep, along the same line I kept making you sleep when you were in the hospital, Miss Prince…excuse me, Mrs. Prince. If I hadn't spiked your IV every night, you'd have been over withdrawal in days instead of weeks. My mistake was in letting you come around at all. But I was soft. I thought discrediting you would be enough, that you'd get the message and leave town. I didn't realize you had designs on Fanny's estate. Jeannette and I were naive not to pick up on that. No matter…I'm getting rid of you and Tycie both now, perhaps even Jeannette. She's distraught over Raven...could be the next suicide, as early as tonight."

"It's too much," Stuart said. "People are already on to you."

"People are stupid. It took an intellect as sharp as mine to figure out where the two of you went after Raven did herself in. Hanahan never thought of Edisto. Hadn't been for me, he'd still be looking for you in Georgetown. I'm somebody. A medical doctor. My heritage is South of Broad, superior to lower classes…"

That was all he had time to say. Abe, who had sneaked into the front entrance of the church, cracked him over the head with a board.

"You got him!" Stuart said. "He's out cold!" He rushed toward the grandson who had no intention of letting Stuart get near him.

"Stop," he yelled. He grabbed Legare's gun and pointed it straight at Stuart. "Where's Mama Tycie? What have you done with my grandmama?"

I looked at the pew where Tycie lay. Abe's eyes doubled in size as his grandmother's head rose into view. "Hush, Abe," she said. "We're in the house of the Lord. Nothing bad will happen to us here. Now give the gun to Mr. Prince and come help your grandmama up. Night air has made her arthritis worse."

"But Dr, Legare looks like he might be dead, Mama. I don't want to go to jail."

"He'll be all right," Tycie said. "Stop fretting and help me to your automobile."

"Things were bad back at the store?" he said. "By the time I got there, Dr. Legare and Hanahan had already cornered Big William and made him tell everything he knew. I hadn't been there a minute when Legare lit out for the church in his car. I couldn't catch him on foot. He made it here ahead of me."

"Hanahan and Legare," Tycie said, "asking Big William questions?"

"Yes, ma'am. William told them you'd be at home or at the church. That's how Dr. Legare knew where to find you."

"Help me up, son. We're going home. Missy Peregrine left something for me to give Missy Arlena."

I moved closer to Stuart. Abe continued clutching the gun. "Didn't you hear me, Abe?" she said to her grandson when he was slow to obey. "Give the gun to Mr. Prince. You're too young to be toting a firearm."

Grandson held the butt end of the pistol toward Stuart, who wasted no time racing up the aisle to grab it. I went to Tycie and helped Abe get the old woman to her feet. We all walked in a wide half-circle around Dr. Legare and out the front door of the church. I sneaked a look back.

"Do you think he's dead?" I said to Stuart. "Shouldn't we check?"

"No, but even if he is, we're never going to admit we saw the boy hit him."

Stuart picked up the board Abe had used on Legare and hurled it into the woods. "Tycie," he said, "is there someplace we can hide 'til Hanahan leaves the island?"

"We won't need to if we can get to my house quick enough. Drive faster, Abe. I have something important to give Missy Arlena. Then we're all going to Charleston in Daddy Abraham's boat."

"Something for me?" I said.

"Two things," Tycie answered. "One is a promise from me to you I'm gonna tell the police how Missy Peregrine died."

"Thank you, Tycie. I'll be grateful for the rest of my life."

"That's not all," she said. "Missy Peregrine wrote you a letter, only I've been too scared to give it to you. Been hiding it all this time."

"What does it say?"

"Don't know. It's sealed."

"Is my name on it?"

"Yes'm. Mine, too, but I didn't open it. No use. Can't read no way."

"How long have you had it?"

"Mailman brought it to Edisto the day after Missy Peregrine died. She knew her end was near…wrote the letter a few hours before she went to sleep that last time…told me to give the letter to the mailman in Charleston. It came to me here on the island the next day."

"You mailed it to yourself?" Stuart asked.

"Missy Peregrine told me to, said it was important to make sure Missy Arlena got it directly after Mr. Pinckney read her will. But no one has mentioned the will yet, and I've been too afraid to ask about it."

"There's a new will, Tycie, and you're in it." Then, forgetting momentarily I'd destroyed the original, I added, "Mr. Pinckney has the paperwork safe in his office."

"Praise God," Tycie said. "Maybe Missy Peregrine left me enough money to pay for Abe's schooling."

Everyone grew quiet as Abe drove into the settlement of blue-trimmed houses. He parked behind two pine trees at the edge of the clearing, and the four of us walked to the same house where Stuart and I had talked to Daddy Abraham the evening of Snake Island. I expected the old man to meet us at the door. He did not, and Tycie didn't comment on his absence. We went into the house and stood by as she unlocked a wooden trunk. Deep inside under a stack of ancient quilts was the unopened letter. It was addressed to Tycie in Miss Peregrine's wobbly script and postmarked the day of her death. My name was also on the envelope in small print at the bottom left corner.

Tycie handed the envelope to me and began rummaging around in the trunk again until she found a small prescription bottle. "It's the one Mr. Prince dropped in Missy Peregrine's bedroom," she said, "the night she died."

I took the bottle and stared at its label, shocked to see my own name typed neatly around the curve. It was one of my old Darvon prescriptions, still nearly full. I looked at Stuart. He offered no explanation. I was about to press him when grandson silenced me.

"Someone's outside," he said. "We have to run…hide."

Tycie sighed. "We run. We hide. But no more after tonight. God is going to protect us for telling the truth."

37

Smelling of alcohol and the great salt marsh, Daddy Abraham staggered into the house just as Tycie was re-locking the trunk. We were grateful he was the source of the noise. Stuart took the opportunity to seize the letter and prescription bottle and pocket them. There was no time to deal with either now. And I, owner of both, was too stressed to be trusted to keep up with anything on a nighttime boat ride from Edisto to Charleston.

"Are you liquored up, old man?" Tycie said to her husband.

"Stop complaining," he answered, "and listen. Big William is drunker than ten of me and meaner than a swamp snake. He and a policeman from town are packing guns and looking for these two." He gestured toward Stuart and me. "They're on their way here."

"Missy Peregrine left me some money when she died, old man, and Abe is going with me to get it. But if you tell William we took your boat, Tycie ain't gonna give you a dime. You hear me, old man?"

"Left you money?" he said.

"It's a fact, she did. And if you want a new truck, you'd best keep your lip tight."

Daddy Abraham went quiet. I could smell his whiskey from across the room.

"Git…the back way," he said when automobile engines and men's voices disturbed the silence outdoors. "Big William and the policeman are in the clearing."

Grandson turned to Stuart and spoke earnestly. "You'll have to carry Mama Tycie," he said. "I'll take you to the boat…but watch your step. Vines will catch your legs."

We followed the young man in silence. He led us out the back door and across his grandmother's dark yard. We crept into the same desolate stand of trees that Stuart and I had encountered on the last leg of our terrifying journey back from Snake Island.

"It's got a motor," Stuart breathed in elation when he saw Daddy Abraham's johnboat with its Evinrude four-stroke.

"Yeah," grandson said, "but we can't crank her yet. Take this oar. We have to paddle up the creek. Motor would make too much noise."

"Does William know where you keep your boat?"

"Doesn't matter. Daddy Abe will put him on the wrong trail. By the time William figures it out, we'll be half-way to Charleston."

Stuart and Abe rowed in tandem. The boat made whooshing sounds as it sliced through black water. I handed Tycie the knit cap the clerk from Two Brothers had given me. She pulled it on over her headcloth and hunched against my shoulder. Stuart and grandson rowed fifteen minutes before we sighted green and red channel lights. Grandson cranked the motor with one jerk of the rope. We had reached the Intracoastal.

"We'll dock at Adgers Wharf," the boy said when harbor lights appeared an hour later. "Nobody prowls around Adgers at night asking nosy questions."

To my eye, no familiar landmark was visible, but Abe knew every dock and piling. He tied up to the side of a creosote wharf and began the delicate business of getting his grandmother disembarked. Stuart and I helped as best we could before climbing out of the boat ourselves.

"Are we going to Pinckney House?" I said to grandson after we'd gotten Tycie up the metal ladder to the dock.

"Yes," he said, "on foot. Mr. Prince and I will have to make a basket seat for Mama Tycie."

"You can't march along East Bay Street in the middle of the night, carrying a little woman on your forearms," I said. "Someone is bound to notice."

"We'll cross East Bay and go the rest of the way on side streets," Stuart said. "Isn't Tradd up the way?"

I tried to get oriented to our location. "I think so, but we can't waste time looking for particular streets. Hanahan might be around somewhere. He may have made it back to Charleston faster by car than we did by boat."

Stuart said with force, "Hanahan isn't important anymore. He's out of the picture now that Tycie wants to make a statement. We'll be home free after that."

"So why did we have to freeze our rear ends off sneaking away from Edisto?" I said.

"Running from Big William and Legare, assuming the boy didn't kill him."

"I hope I never see Legare again. All I want is to get to Pinckney House. Do you still have the letter? Shouldn't we read it now?"

"Too dark, no time. You can read it at Mr. Pinckney's."

Stuart and grandson faced each other and locked arms. Tycie sat across their forearms and held on around their necks. I acted as lookout as we walked up the dock and stepped onto the cobblestones of Adgers. We scuttled across East Bay Street and hurried along its sidewalk a few feet before fading into the shadows of Tradd. At Pinckney House, I led the group through a wrought iron gate in the back wall of Miss Roz' garden. Once we were inside the gate, Tycie demanded to walk on her own. This made for slow going across the Pinckneys' mossy flagstones. Stuart took the lead toward a shrubby corner he hoped would shield us from light. He left us there hidden in shadows while he sneaked up to one of the three back doors of Pinckney House and rapped with bare knuckles. A male voice rumbled from within.

"Who's there?" said the voice. "I'll call the police if you splash this house with paint again." Though not positive, I thought the voice belonged to Peter, Mr. Pinckney's butler.

"I'm Arlena Prince's husband," Stuart called out. "Tell Mr. Pinckney we're here. He knows us."

After a short wait, outdoor lights flashed on. "Is that you, Prince?" Mr. Pinckney said, flinging open the back door. "Where have you been, man? Everybody in town is looking for you and your wife."

Stuart stepped into the light and raised an arm. The rest of us converged on the door. Mr. Pinckney held it open as we paraded inside.

"My stars," he said. "You brought half of Edisto with you. Is there a Wadmalaw contingent?"

Miss Roz led us to the front parlor, where I sank gratefully onto a sofa near the fire. I thought my mind was playing tricks when I heard the voice of Croom Legare, Jr. "Are these the cigars you wanted, Mr. Pinckney? I found them upstairs in your study."

I looked toward the archway that separated the parlor and foyer. When Croom saw me, he stopped dead still, the cigar box open in his hands. I tensed and rose to face him. It was clear he had not heard us come in and that our presence was an unwanted surprise.

"Yes, son," Mr. Pinckney said. "Put the box on the table there. Arlena, sit down and relax. You're making me nervous. Croom, Jr. has unburdened his soul to me this evening. The death of dear Raven shook some sense into his head. Stuart, you sit too. You look like a wildcat ready to pounce. Great ghost, man. You're a worse mess every time I see you."

We sat, though Stuart remained tense, ready to spring at any provocation. Tycie and Abe took twin chairs opposite Stuart and me. Croom, Jr. balanced his own large frame on a footstool at the end of the sofa. Mr. Pinckney stood before the fire.

"Good evening, Mrs. Roosevelt," Mr. Pinckney said to Tycie in a tone all respect. "To what do I owe this unexpected nocturnal visit?"

Tycie would not look at him. She cast a glance in my direction and quickly stared down at the floor. I assumed she wanted me to speak for her.

"Tycie..." I stopped and looked at her again to make sure I was doing the right thing. She nodded. "Tycie wants to tell you and the police what she saw the night Miss Peregrine died."

"Indeed," Mr. Pinckney said. "And what might that be, Mrs. Roosevelt?"

With facial expression alone, Tycie begged me to speak in her place again. "She saw," I said. "She was a witness to..." I could not get the words out. In the middle of my pause, Miss Roz fluttered back into the room and told Mr. Pinckney that Sergeant Hanahan was at the door. Stuart stood...again. Mr. Pinckney ordered him to sit...again.

"Hellfire," he said to Stuart. "You're more skittish than a marsh tacky pony."

Stuart poised himself on the edge of the sofa. Mr. Pinckney left the room with Miss Roz. No one spoke while he was gone. I looked at Croom, Jr.. His face was red and swollen as though he had been crying. Mr. Pinckney returned with Hanahan who stopped under the archway and swept the parlor with his eyes. His gaze halted on me before moving around the rest of the room in silent observation. Mr. Pinckney pointed to a chair well away from the inner circle. Hanahan sat down and placed his hat on his knees. Mr. Pinckney crossed the room and reclaimed his stance by the fireplace.

"All right," he said, "with Mr. Hanahan present, we have an excellent witness to whatever might be said here this evening. We'll have a few others soon. Miss Roz is rousing my daughter and her husband, Honor and Jonathan Prioleau. Now, to bring you up to date, Ray Bob. Mrs. Prince was just telling me..." He stopped in mid-sentence to wave Miss Roz, Honor, and Jonathan to an out-of-the-way corner. "Where was I? Oh, yes, Mrs. Prince was telling me that Mrs. Roosevelt – Tycie – witnessed a crime. She was about to share the details. Go ahead, Mrs. Prince."

"It was the murder of Miss Fanny Peregrine," I said. A murmur went up from the corner where Miss Roz' party stood.

"Is that correct, Mrs. Roosevelt?" Mr. Pinckney said. Tycie nodded. "And who did you see kill Miss Peregrine? Can you name the name?"

"Not just one," she answered. "Three…Missy Jeannette, Missy Louisa, and Dr. Croomer Legare."

Mr. Pinckney turned toward Hanahan and spoke to him curtly. "Did you hear that, Ray Bob? This woman is an eyewitness. I'm certain she'll give you a detailed statement before the evening is out."

"Yes," Tycie said, newly bold.

Mr. Pinckney leaned forward and patted her shoulder. "Fine, Mrs. Roosevelt. That's fine. We all thank you. To move on, there's a young man among us who has told me a heartbreaking tale this evening. Croom, my boy, I know you've been through pure misery these last few days, but can you find the strength to tell your story one more time?"

"I think so, sir, only it's hard."

"I know. Make it as brief as you can."

"My father," Croom began, stopping a second to take a breath and starting over. "I heard my father on the phone with Mrs. FitzSimons, Raven's mother, talking about doing away with Miss Peregrine. They were in it together along with the housekeeper, Louisa Hill. Dad said he needed money right away. He was in financial straits."

Croom could not go on. He dropped his gaze to the floor and wiped away a tear. "You'll be okay, son," Mr. Pinckney said. "Did your father realize you heard?"

"Yes, sir, and it upset him. He said he needed my help."

"What kind of help?"

Croom looked at Stuart and me and winced. "He wanted me to scare Mr. and Mrs. Prince into leaving Charleston. I was the one who smashed their windshield and threw paint on Mrs. Middleton's cottage door. I was downstairs hiding in the storeroom when they came home from Edisto one morning. A bunch of voodoo nuts had kept them out all night, scared them half to death. Father had told me to trash their stuff. He was hoping it would scare them into giving up their part of the estate and leaving town. I went out to the beach cottage to see what I could do. They weren't home when I first got there, but just as I was about to break into the screened porch, I heard their car in the driveway around front. I barely had time to run down the back porch steps and slip into the storage room. It was a miracle they didn't see me. Guess the voodoo thing had gotten to them. I could hear everything they said after they went upstairs. Their bedroom is right over the storeroom. They talked over an hour about voodoo rites and secret islands and people with blue faces and houses with blue trim. That's when I thought of throwing paint on the cottage.

"I sneaked away after they got quiet. Figured they'd gone to sleep. Later, sometime in the afternoon, Raven told me she and her mother were planning to set a trap for the Princes. I don't know everything except they lured them into town after dark... told them Tycie was going to be at Peregrine House. I decided to go back to Sullivan's to keep an eye on them. It was late, almost dark when they left the cottage. I followed them back to Charleston, and when they parked their car on a side street off East Bay and started toward Peregrine House, I waited for them to get far enough away so they couldn't hear. Then I broke their car's windshield and windows with my baseball bat. They made it easy for me, parking out of the way on a street with dim lighting. Afterward, I doubled back to Sullivan's and threw blue paint on the cottage. I did a lot of driving that night."

"And did you vandalize my house?" Mr. Pinckney said.

"Yes, sir. I knew my father was angry at you because you helped Miss Peregrine write the new will. I decided on the spur of the moment to hit your house. I've done a lot of dumb things the past few weeks."

"How old are you, Croom?"

"Seventeen."

"And what made you come forward today?"

At that, Croom put his head in his hands and wept. "There, there, boy," Mr. Pinckney said. "It's almost over. Why did you decide to tell the truth?"

"I saw Raven die. She jumped off the bridge and killed herself. I still can't believe it."

Again, he broke down with emotion. Tears glittered in his eyes. "She's gone, and it's all my fault," he said. "From the beginning she wanted to tell the police the truth, what her mother and my father had done. I talked her out if it more than once. It wasn't long before everything came crashing down, especially when her mother wanted her to get an abortion. Her life was falling apart.

And the worst was she thought I didn't love her. But I did. I loved her more than anything. I just didn't know what to do about her being pregnant. I'm seventeen. I don't know a lot of things. And now she's dead. I hate my father. I hate Mrs. FitzSimons. I want to die like Raven. I never wanted any of Miss Peregrine's money. I was trying to help my father."

"It's over now, son," Mr. Pinckney said. "You've done the right thing by speaking out." He indicated with his eyes that Miss Roz should come over and comfort the grieving boy. Stuart and I looked at each other. I bit my lip in an effort to stay in control of my emotions.

"Ray Bob," Mr. Pinckney said. "Would I be correct in assuming you will now destroy that dog-eared warrant for the arrest of one Arlena Prince?"

"Correct, sir."

"Good. There's nothing further to discuss."

"Mr. Pinckney," I said. "Stuart and I have something to show you. It's a letter from Miss Peregrine." I looked at Stuart, who had a stricken expression on his face.

"Are you sure you want to do this now?" he said. "Maybe we should wait."

"Yes, now. Give the envelope to Mr. Pinckney."

Though he didn't want to, Stuart pulled the rumpled letter from his shirt pocket and handed it over. Its seal was still unbroken.

"Miss Peregrine had Tycie put it in the mail right before she was killed," I said to Mr. Pinckney. "Check the postmark. It should have the same date."

"Why have you not produced it before?"

"Tycie has been hiding it. It came to her on Edisto the day after Miss Peregrine died. She was afraid to give it to me. Louisa had threatened to kill her grandson if she talked to anyone."

Mr. Pinckney walked across the room in long strides and presented the letter to Hanahan. "Examine the envelope," he said. "Make sure you can say in a court of law it was sealed when I showed it to you. Look there on the back. It's the Peregrine family crest."

Hanahan turned the letter over in his hands and gave it back to Mr. Pinckney. "Yes, it's sealed."

Mr. Pinckney handed the letter to Jonathan Prioleau and issued the same instructions. When satisfied the envelope had been thoroughly inspected by more than one witness, he directed his gaze toward me. "Do you wish to share your letter with the group?" he said.

"Yes, sir," I said, my voice raspy from exhaustion. "Will you read it for me? I don't think I can."

Grayson Pinckney picked up a silver letter opener from the writing table next to the archway and slit open the envelope. He put on his spectacles and read aloud:

Dearest Arlena,

I awakened early this morning and have spent some time gazing out my window at the harbor. It will not be long before my old Peregrine eyes will be closed to these sights forever. Even now, I'm unable to very see far, though my memory still tells me what is there. In my mind, I can picture blue water stretching toward Fort Sumter and Morris Island. Sullivan's is somewhere beyond. I see gulls flying into the wind. They hang suspended in the heavens. Oh, look, sailboats are running before the wind, and stacks of beautiful white clouds are changing shapes in the sky. Now I see the smudge that is Sullivan's. It makes me think of my childhood, those carefree days when no monstrous bridge connected the island to Mount Pleasant. Lately, I've pined for those innocent times before my life stopped at age sixteen. To have a child out of wedlock in my day was a moral outrage in Charleston. Father never forgave me. He said I was a whore and a sinner, no matter being born to an elegant family. But I was neither, just a frightened girl who had nowhere to turn. And isn't it ironic the child I bore lived only nine short months? Please, forgive me, dear. I know it is not logical that you should make me long for a daughter I never knew. All my life I've searched for her, though I know she lies dead in a northern grave. The search has been my life's heartache, especially considering Louisa's derangement. I wanted so much to care for her, like a mother would care for a daughter, but she lives in a dark world of confusion. I no longer know how to reach her. Then there was Jeannette. She could have been the one, but over the years, greed crippled her into something unlovely. Perhaps, I expected too much, assumed too much. You see, Arlena, I always thought Louisa and Jeannette loved me. I thought they cared enough to use my father's fortune to help preserve the natural treasures that belong to us all: the beauty of Charleston, rarity of Sullivan's, marshlands, beaches, islands, swamps, tidal creeks, rivers, and inlets, even the grand old Atlantic. But I was wrong. They never loved me. It was my father's money they were after. Filthy lucre as he would say. And now I must face something terrible enough to break an old woman's heart. For months I've lived with the knowledge the people I care about most deeply are trying to shorten my life. With the exception of Tycie, I've lost faith in everyone around me. Louisa, Jeannette, and Croomer have been tampering with my medication. I'm ill most of the time. For a while, I was able to monitor the medicine myself. But they've caught on to that now and have become more clever at deceiving me. Maybe I should save them the trouble and end my own life. Unfortunately, I was born a coward. By now you must know about the new will I drew up with the help of my old friend, Grayson Pinckney, and why I had to change things. Grayson is my last chance at trusting someone like family. I hope you and he are satisfied with the provisions I made for each of you. Now about this long epistle. I hope it has not put you off. My intention was to discuss all this with you face to face, but I fear I'll not have the opportunity. Things have been tense at Peregrine House of late as you have observed. I'm writing this letter in case anything happens to me. They think I don't hear when they whisper, but I do. Arlena, please be kind to my good and faithful Tycie. She is to give you this letter should anything unexpected befall me. You, in turn, are to deliver it to Grayson. He will know what to do legally. One last thing, you must not fret over the general sorriness of one old woman's misfortunes. Life in its fullness was never meant to be soft. Not from the first. I believe this from the bottom of my heart. And if it is true, life in Old Charleston has always had a glorious expression. It is the reason I am not more shocked by the ruthlessness of my loved ones. Give my love to that Lancelot of yours. I cannot recall his name. Allow him to heal the wounds of your childhood. He is the balm I never had. Let him make you whole before you turn into a wizened old woman like me. I suppose you have realized this letter, sadly, is my new ending to *Tarnished Honor.* Makes for a real stinger, don't you agree? Too bad it will never be published. Now I must close quickly, for Louisa is on the stairs. Take care of yourself, precious darling girl. I continue to think the best of you and everyone.

Forever yours,
Fanny Peregrine

A tear ran down Grayson Pinckney's face as he refolded the letter. With great dignity he took off his glasses and dabbed at his eyes. He walked to where I was sitting and handed me the letter. I stood to face him. "There's one last thing I have to tell you, sweet rose," he said, his aristocratic eyes, delphinium blue, locking with my own jet blacks. His voice quavered as he spoke. "After experiencing the heartfelt sincerity of Miss Peregrine's epistle, I'm relieved to have ignored your and Stuart's requests to destroy the original new will. The copy you shredded was just that, a copy. Thanks to my good judgment, you are still an heiress."

38

You are still an heiress. My story should have ended with those words of Mr. Pinckney's if there can ever be a final ending to a human story. Something in us longs for a satisfying conclusion – villains found out, questions answered, loose ends tied up. We dream of being rescued from the messiness of life by some gloriously happy Act IV.

Still an heiress, indeed. In real life, there is always another road to go down, another treacherous journey to make. Still an heiress…such lovely, comforting words that ended one disturbing story and promptly began another. But the unfolding of the latter was quite different from what anyone expected.

After our late-night at Mr. Pinckney's home – the night he read Miss Peregrine's letter to the group, and Tycie gave her statement to the police – Stuart took me back to the cottage where I slept two days straight, dreaming of my father and his pretty lies. When I awoke, groggy and stiff from too many hours in bed, I walked out to the sun-warmed porch and found Stuart in jeans and a flannel shirt. He sat reared back in a new lounge chair, sipping from a bottle of beer, poring over one of those elaborate advertisement booklets of the sort you find in automobile showrooms.

"Hello, hello, hello," he said when I stepped into the sunlight. His face was open and relaxed. "Glad you woke up. How would you like a cold brewski to celebrate the beginning of our new life?"

I glanced at the plastic ice bucket, also new, resting on the floor by the chair. Three sweating long-neck Budweisers stood at jaunty angles in the ice. Two empties sat to the side.

I re-fixed my gaze on Stuart's face, but I did not return his smile or respond to his banter. He plunged forward, undaunted, accustomed to having to salvage any meager goodness left over from my frequent bitter episodes.

"I thought you might sleep forever," he said. "Two days is a long time. Tell me when you feel hungry. I'll feed you. There's bacon in the fridge, and eggs. I'll fry some up for you. But come sit with me a minute first and see what money can buy." He held the slick booklet next to his face and grinned like a little boy. "We're going to give the Romeo a decent burial."

I remained unresponsive. His chatter struck me as banal. He dragged a hand down over his face. My silence had chilled the encounter enough to destroy all pleasantness.

"What's wrong now?" he said. "I thought you'd feel better once you got some rest. Guess that was too much to expect."

I narrowed my eyes and continued staring. He slapped the booklet shut and tossed it to the floor next to the bucket.

"What?" he said, louder. His deck shoes scraped the gritty floor as he struggled out of the chair. "What do you have to complain about now? Nothing is ever good enough for you. Here we are, problems solved, money forthcoming..."

"Why were you in Miss Peregrine's room the night she died?" I said without a trace of emotion. "And why did you have one of my prescription bottles with you?"

He glared at me. Angry now, he turned away and panned the spectacular seascape that was our backyard. Seagulls crisscrossed each other's flight paths high above the surf. Indifferent waves glinted silver.

"For the last time," he said, enunciating each word carefully, yet not turning to look me in the eye, "I was not in that room. I wasn't even in the house until I came to rescue you. And I don't know anything about a prescription bottle. Tycie said it had your name on it, not mine. You could have dropped it yourself. Did you ever think of that?"

My skin went clammy. After a moment I said, "Tycie can't read, Stuart. She never said whose name was on the bottle. Not once did she say."

"Then you did," he said. "Somebody did. No, I remember now. I saw it on the bottle when you handed it to me at Tycie's house, right before I put it in my coat pocket."

"Where is it now?"

"I don't know. Must have fallen out of my pocket in all the confusion…Daddy Abraham, the boat, getting Tycie back to Charleston."

"It did not fall out of your pocket."

Stuart breathed before restating his response. "I don't know where it is, and I'm not going to worry about it. It's lost, gone, which suits one or two players in this soap opera just fine. Tycie, for one. She didn't want to leave anything lying around that might confuse the police about who murdered Miss Peregrine. She knows Jeannette, Louisa, and Croomer killed her. She saw them do it with her own eyes. And now she wants them locked up so they can't come after her for speaking out."

He turned and faced me, meeting my gaze for the first time. "I'm not the enemy," he said with fake calm. "You're making a mistake attacking me like this. I'm going for a run. Be back in a couple of hours. If I were you, I'd do some hard thinking before you carry this any further. Some things are best left alone."

I watched him cross the dunes in graceful strides like I'd watched him a hundred times before. He was distancing himself from me as swiftly as my parents had done on the day they sailed out of Boston Harbor on Beautiful Ghost Dream with the same ocean horizon as a backdrop. The difference, I understood all too well, was Stuart would come back. Not because he wanted to, not after I had practically accused him of attempted murder. He'd come back because of the money, though I understood I could expect little more from him than his physical presence. Emotionally and spiritually, he had departed forever, for trust within our relationship died the moment I asked him why he was in Peregrine House the night of the murder and why he had my prescription bottle with him. Stuart had made it plain he would never tell me his true story. Our two hearts were now separated as cleanly as if some wicked knight had galloped up and hacked them apart with his sword... all because of two, essential, unanswered questions.When Stuart was no longer visible on the beach, I went to the telephone in the sitting room and called Grayson Pinckney's office. Heretofore, I had been put on hold for long periods while secretaries discussed in whispers whether or not I was worthy of being put through to their boss. But today the waters parted. I was thankful there was no change in Mr. Pinckney's attitude. He was his same old polite self. I made an appointment with him for eleven the next day, then I went back to bed and slept through another night.

I awoke at nine the following morning, eyelids no longer able to filter out the bright sunlight streaming over my face. Headachy and sweating from sleeping too much, I got up and trudged to the bathroom. There I found a note from Stuart taped to the mirror of the medicine cabinet. He had gone for another run and would see me later. I did not care to see him at all, not until I'd had a chance to talk to Mr. Pinckney alone. This was the day I intended to set in motion plans for my own liberation, and I did not want Stuart interfering.

My purpose in scheduling an appointment with Mr. Pinckney was to ask for...no, beg for help. I realized I had been under too much strain to make sound decisions, particularly ones involving Miss Peregrine's new will. Of the two options she had provided me, working for the estate would be much more lucrative...that is, if I could settle my nerves from the harrowing experiences of the last few weeks and give a real job my full attention. But I knew I couldn't, not for a long while. I needed time to rest, think, plan. And time was what I was hoping Mr. Pinckney would give me.

I dressed quickly to make it out of the house before Stuart returned. It was an odd drive into town. Every few miles I had to remind myself to slow down. The murderers were all in custody, and I was no longer being hunted like a wild animal, yet I felt so panicky at one point that I had to stop at a convenience store and drink a few ounces of sparkling water to settle my sick stomach.

Mr. Pinckney was glad to see me when I walked into his office. He listened attentively as I tried to explain, stuttering over my consonants from nervousness, that I needed at least a year to decide what I wanted to do about Miss Peregrine's new will. She had stipulated I was to have seven days from the time of the first reading to make a firm decision about which option I wanted to choose. But I was already into the fifth day and still had no idea which one. How Mr. Pinckney would react to my request for extra time, I did not know, nor if he had the legal power to manipulate the terms to the extent I was asking. He surprised me by expressing no surprise at my request and agreeing with everything I needed, though a puzzled look crossed his face when I told him I wanted to keep our conversation confidential, especially from Stuart. Yet puzzled or not, he refrained from quizzing me, and for this I was grateful.

The one thing I had not worked out in my mind was how to explain to Stuart the missing lump sum. If I wanted him to believe I was permanently forfeiting the option of a paid job with the estate, the cornerstone of my plan, he would expect me to receive the one-hundred-thousand-dollar check immediately. Mr. Pinckney helped me solve the problem by advancing me this amount out of his own funds, of which he had plenty, thanks to the largesse of Miss Peregrine. He said if I decided to come back in a year to help run the foundation, he would consider it money well invested. He assured me he would collect twice that much in his first year's percentage bonus from the estate's investment returns.

I stressed to him no one was to know anything of the details surrounding our conversation. He did not press for reasons. I sat quietly as he wrote out our agreement in longhand and made a copy for himself. When he tried to give me the original, I asked him to put it in his own safe. He hugged me instead of shaking my hand. I left his office relieved. The first phase of my plan had been put into action, that is, the new agreement between Mr. Pinckney and me signed and sealed. I was to collect the lump-sum check the next morning. Now I could go back to the cottage and initiate the second phase of my plan.

When I arrived, Stuart was back from his run, showered, shaved, and enjoying a salad on the porch. He didn't ask where I had been, just said hello, testing the waters as to whether I was going to continue where I had left off the day before. When I did not – I'd resolved in my mind never again to ask him why he was in Miss Peregrine's room at an inappropriate time or why he had one of my prescription bottles with him, for I now knew I would never get a truthful answer – Stuart relaxed and resumed eating, pausing at intervals to comment on the weather or offer me a bite of spinach or a sip of tea.

"No, thank you. I ate something earlier," I said.

I sat down beside him and made all the correct responses while waiting for him to finish his lunch. When he did, I asked if he'd like to walk out to the dunes to sit and enjoy the sun. He said, yes, and would be ready as soon as he had put the dishes away. I went to the bedroom to get a heavier jacket and find Miss Peregrine' letter. I stuffed it into my jacket pocket, wound a woolen scarf around my neck, and went to meet Stuart on the porch. He insisted on holding hands on our trek along the beach path, which made me feel guilty considering what I was about to tell him. He laughed when the breeze put my hair in disarray. Now it was my turn to avert my eyes.

Still weak and wobbly – the truth was I had not eaten lunch – I was grateful to alight on a driftwood log and allow the sun to warm me. After a few minutes, I told Stuart I wanted to hear Miss Peregrine's letter again and would he mind reading it to me. I shed a few tears while he read aloud. When he finished, I took the letter from him, tore it into tiny pieces, and stuffed them into my jacket pocket. That act was the artful prelude to the biggest lie I would ever tell him.

Stuart gaped at me, incredulous, as I spun my tale: I was through with Charleston and everything associated with it. I wanted to take the lump sum option Miss Peregrine had provided me in her will, buy a car (that idea had sprung from having observed Stuart studying the fancy car sales brochure), and move back to Boston.

Stuart disagreed with everything I said, except my wish to buy a car. I had prepared myself for an onslaught of sharp words and was not disappointed. There on the hard driftwood log – jittery, breathless, trembling like a captured bird – I sat for half an hour and endured the first of a dozen of Stuart's impassioned speeches on the folly of making hasty decisions. This proved more difficult to withstand than I first expected. For though I knew what I was doing and why, there were times I wanted to forego the protective façade of my lie and shout to Stuart he was right and I was wrong so that I could know the bless-ed relief of giving in. "Oh, Stuart. The better choice is to stay in Charleston and cash in indefinitely on poor dead Miss Peregrine's estate."

But I did not fold, not once, not ever. In weak moments over the next few hours, I would close my eyes and go over in my mind the agreement between me and Mr. Pinckney. It was the only thing that got me through Stuart's elongated tantrum.

Somehow I managed to stand firm to the end, forcing him to acquiesce if he wanted to realize for himself even a portion of the hundred thousand. The next morning we went to Mr. Pinckney's office together to pick up the check, the sheer amount of which salved a little of the pain Stuart was experiencing from watching me make what he believed was a dead-wrong decision.

We were free to go back north then – Massachusetts, odd consulting jobs here and there, ordinary lives, even an ordinary and inevitable separation a few months down the road when the money ran out. Stuart, I discovered, had expensive tastes when cash was in the bank.

It was strange way to spend six months, living together in the same apartment, but sharing nothing of our hearts. I never regained confidence in Stuart, nor he in me. We both tried for a while, and I did manage to grow a little less fearful of the myriad dark motives I had assigned him due to the pill bottle incident. But when the fear departed, it left in its wake a revulsion I soon realized would be permanent. Tycie had described a scene in Miss Peregrine's bedroom that included Stuart as a participant. And after months, I realized I would never be able to get the sinister possibilities of this reality out of my highly calibrated mind. And though neither of us ever mentioned the incident again – the day I confronted him at the beach cottage was the one and only time we discussed it – my unanswered questions festered like puncture wounds. Each time they forced their way into my thoughts, I added more grisly details to the skeleton of a plot suggested by the few facts I knew.

What did I think Stuart had done? The answer to that question was not the important thing, for I was certain Stuart had done nothing. It was what I thought he had intended to do that had me on the run. Tycie had described a scene in Miss Peregrine's bedroom that told its own story, one I made a study of reconstructing in my head fifty different ways, fifty different times a day for weeks on end, until I came to know there was only one version I would ever be able to believe. Stuart had gone into Miss Peregrine's room to give her extra pills in the hope of hastening her death, though before he could do the actual deed, he was interrupted by three others more deadly than he. But why did he risk taking along a prescription bottle with my name on it? Did he have some nightmare of a plan to implicate me in Miss Peregrine's death? Did he already know I was included in her will? Had Mr. Pinckney let it slip somehow the day he made Stuart that first loan? Did he think if I were convicted of murder, I'd be out of the way, and he could do whatever he wanted with any money Miss Peregrine might leave me?

Perhaps if Stuart had talked to me, had told me some version of the truth no matter how ghastly and not left me to my own hysterical imaginings, I could have become desensitized over time to whatever madness had overtaken him and eventually let it go. Maybe this would have worked for me the way it works for phobics whenever psychiatrists force them to confront their fears to effect a cure. But Stuart chose avoidance over confrontation, a course of action that proved disastrous for our marriage.

I gave myself a year to put the horror of possibilities out of my mind, but six months had not gone by before I came to the conclusion I would need a hundred years to achieve such a goal. Once or twice, I thought I had made progress, but the suspicions always came slithering back, the serpentine poisonous suspicions. As weeks turned into months, I came to understand my dark fears would never dissipate, in fact, were growing worse. I soon became aware I could not live with my fears, not indefinitely. On coming to this realization, a great burden fell away and left me with a sad truth: if I could not live with my fears, I could not live with Stuart.

When I told him I wanted to begin the process for a divorce, he seemed relieved. For he had not been able to get past the idiocy of my decision concerning Miss Peregrine's will. His disappointment at losing the chance at what he referred to as a real future morphed after a time into disappointment in me. Thus, six months after moving into the first decent apartment we had ever had, I packed selectively, taking nothing that would not fit into two oversized suitcases, and called a cab to drive me to Logan Airport. I was going back to Charleston.

On arriving at Logan, I made a call to the Boston Gynecological Group, which turned out to be the most important call of my life. Its subject was pregnancy. Not whether I was or wasn't – I already knew the answer to that – but the gender of my baby. My secret baby. For Stuart knew nothing of this development. According to the doctor's calculations, I was four months along, the earliest possible time in those days to get an accurate reading from an amniocentesis test. Which was the reason for the call, to hear results from the amnio procedure I'd had the week before. But my interest in the test was not the same as my doctor's, which was to check my baby for Down Syndrome. I felt certain in my heart I had a normal baby. What I wanted to know was whether it was a boy or girl, a secondary piece of information that can be garnered from the test.

Thus, I made the call and was told by a nurse whose voice was all honey and warm fruit that I was going to have a little girl. A daughter. An angel. My heart sang a melody not of this world right there in Logan Airport. For the first time my sorry life had meaning. I beamed at everyone for hours – at the clerk in the fast-food restaurant who sold me a bagel and a bottle of orange juice, at the man in line behind me who picked up my purse when I dropped it, at the clerk who took my boarding pass at Gate 9, at the stewards and stewardesses who welcomed me aboard the plane, at my seatmate, at the couple across the aisle, at everyone. Life was good. God was in his heaven. And I had found my natural song.

I held my arms across my abdomen as the plane banked right and headed south. It nosed its way upward until it broke through the gray mist of a New England day, discovering in a burst of light the sun-drenched sky above the clouds. My heart thumped with joy. My stomach fluttered with anticipation. I was on my way to claim what was rightfully mine, a gift from the universe that had passed to me through the hands of Miss Fanny Peregrine, a chance to build a good and wholesome life. Mr. Pinckney was thrilled to find out I had decided to do the right thing. On the day of my arrival to Charleston, he went to the trouble of sending Caesar out to Sullivan's to fix up one of the old Peregrine cottages for me to occupy. I smiled as I considered the pleasure of touching down at Charleston Airport, renting a sensible car, and driving out to the beach. Meetings with Mr. Pinckney about my new job responsibilities could wait a day or two. My baby and I needed time to commune with the ocean.

My baby, my baby, my baby. I could not get enough of knowing she existed and was all mine. I did not want to share her with anyone just yet, especially not Stuart. He would have to wait, years perhaps, though I had matured enough to know it would be right in the future to allow him to be a part of her life. Not as my husband, never again that, but as a parent helping to care for the child he and I had conceived. I could not permanently deny my baby her father. I knew too much of that pain.

My plan was to name her Raven. This I had promised God each time I had prayed my baby would be a girl, twenty or thirty times a day since I had found out I was pregnant. There were so many injured daughters I wanted to make things right for, so many broken relationships between parents and daughters – my own parents and myself, Miss Peregrine and baby Constantia, Jeannette FitzSimons and Raven. So many. Over time, my prayer re-shaped itself into another more fervent plea, that God in his wisdom, for the sake of all those who had gone before us and failed, would help little Raven and me get life right. On the plane that morning, on my way back to Charleston and the beginning of a new beginning, I closed my eyes and imagined we could. I have always liked to imagine.

The End

ABOUT THE AUTHOR

TERRY WARD TUCKER, PhD, is a graduate of the University of North Carolina at Chapel Hill. *Charleston's Elegant Sinners* her edgiest Lowcountry novel yet. Tucker's earlier novel, *Moonlight and Mill Whistles,* received *ForeWord Magazine*'s Silver Book of the Year Award. Winston Groom, author of *Forrest Gump* wrote, "Terry Ward Tucker tells a lovely and captivating story in *Moonlight and Mill Whistles.* Her writing is a joy to read." Pat Conroy praised Tucker's lowcountry novel, *Moonbow Over Charleston.* "Terry Ward Tucker paints a moonbow upon Charleston's night sky and gifts us all with its loveliness. Thank you, Terry!" Tucker also writes faith-based novels, screenplays, devotional books, and Bible discovery guides. Linda Flannery, Executive Producer, Inspire You Entertainment, wrote about Tucker's faith-based novel, *Moon River,* "Be inspired as Terry Ward Tucker draws you into the story of Anne York's battle with infertility. You'll find yourself, along with Anne, praying God-centered rather than self-centered prayers. Get a blessing! Read this book!" Terry served as screenplay co-writer for *Only God Can,* faith-based feature film produced by Inspire You Entertainment, and sole screenplay writer for *Hate Won't Win,* a new movie in development based on the shooting massacre at Mother Emanuel Church in Charleston.

www.ingramcontent.com/pod-product-compliance
Lightning Source LLC
Chambersburg PA
CBHW070836020826
48982CB00020B/1365/J
9781734112283